IMPOSSIBLE STORIES II

Zoran Živković

Impossible Stories II

FG-RS0021L2
ISBN: 978-4-908793-05-9

Cover: Youchan Ito, Togoru Art Works

Neoclassic Fleurons font used with permission of
Paulo W–Intellecta Design

Cadmus Press
cadmusmedia.org

IMPOSSIBLE STORIES II

Zoran Živković

Translated from the Serbian
by

Alice Copple-Tošić

Cadmus Press
2016

Contents

Four Stories Till the End

Contents

1. The Cell

A KNOCK WAS HEARD on the door of the cell.

I stopped playing the violin and laid it on the dresser next to the couch.

"Come in."

The door opened without a sound and the guard appeared.

"You have a visitor," he said, smiling at me.

I nodded and he moved aside to let the visitor in. I didn't immediately recognize the large figure in a dark suit that almost filled the doorway. Gloom permeated the cell, while neon lighting brightly illuminated the corridor in front of it. The contours of the man were drawn like an eclipse of the sun edged by the corona, making it impossible to see what they surrounded. It wasn't until the visitor spoke that I realized who it was.

"Good evening," said my lawyer as he walked inside. The guard closed the door after him. Once again the cell was lighted solely by the lamp with a large green shade on the desk.

"Good evening," I replied, stepping forward to greet him with outstretched hand. We shook hands warmly and then I indicated one of the two armchairs facing us.

"Please sit down. I hope you find this one more comfortable than the other, which wobbles a bit."

"Oh, it will be fine, don't you worry," said the lawyer, settling himself in the armchair as it groaned under his weight. He placed the large black briefcase he always carried with him in his lap and laid his hands on top of it.

"Would you care for a drink?" I asked. "I'm afraid the choice is rather limited. All I have is orange juice."

"I'd prefer something a bit stronger, but it can't be helped. Is it chilled at least?"

"Yes, it is." I opened the little refrigerator at the other end of the cell, took out a container and poured thick orange liquid into one of the four glasses. They were sitting on a tray on top of the refrigerator, covered with coasters. I put a coaster on the coffee table between the armchairs, and placed the glass on it.

"Thank you," said the lawyer with a brief nod.

I went back to the couch and sat down.

"I'm sure you're not aware, of course," said the visitor after drinking half the glass of orange juice. "You're a young man, it's ancient history to you. But when I started my law practice, many years ago, the conditions in jail weren't anything like this pleasant. All right, I agree, the choice of drinks might not be very discriminating, and the furniture could be of better quality or at least better maintained, but those are merely details that are easy to fix. You would be horrified if I were to describe the first visits to my incarcerated clients. I myself was shocked. It almost made me change my profession. But now I'm glad I didn't. I'm not fishing for compliments, but if it weren't for people like me we'd still be in that barbaric period."

He stopped for a moment and took another sip of juice.

"It was particularly difficult," he continued, "for inmates on death row, such as yourself. It was tacitly understood that prisoners' surroundings during their last hours were more or less unimportant. Considering what they had in store for them, it allegedly made no difference. The trauma caused by the inhuman conditions would not be of long duration. Pure cynicism.

Shouldn't the same criteria be used for those of us who, after carrying out your sentence, retire to the warmth of our homes, convinced that we are lucky not to be in your shoes? But who among us can be certain that they won't be joining you shortly? No one knows what the day may bring, or the night. And the statistics are inexorable: there are far more casualties outside of prison than inside."

I nodded. "That's true."

The lawyer's face expanded into a smile. "There, you see. I must admit, though, just between you and me, there's one thing I miss from the old days. I know it's a little selfish, but it can't be helped. I'm no saint, I have vices too. Can you guess what it is?"

"No, I can't."

"Smoking," replied the lawyer diffidently, opening his arms with a shrug. "Before, no one would hold it against you if you lighted a cigarette in a cell. Actually, no one paid any attention. You'd offer one to your client, of course. Now if I even flicked a lighter or struck a match, the alarm would start wailing the very same instant. I'd be debarred in no time flat. It's not just visitors who are forbidden to smoke, though, the condemned can't either. Not even one last cigarette. And that's going too far, I think you'll agree. Even hypocritical if you ask me. All right, tobacco kills, that's beyond all doubt, but in the given circumstances that one cigarette couldn't possibly do much harm. The anti-smoking lobby, however, is completely deaf to the voice of reason. They stick blindly to their principles and are powerful enough to put them into effect. Do you smoke?"

"No."

"Smart man. If you did you'd be in a terrible fix right now. I don't know how I'd make it through such torture. Even this short time in here with you without a cigarette is hard for me. But there's a good and bad side to every profession. Is there something else you miss?"

I thought it over briefly. "The limited number of channels on the cable television bothers me. It's almost entirely sports, action films and quiz shows. There are practically no programs on art or culture."

"Why, that's unacceptable!" The lawyer opened his briefcase, took out a notepad and pencil and wrote something hurriedly. "This is a violation of basic human rights. You have my word that we'll put an end to such mental tyranny. It won't be easy, not in the least, the members of the board who make the regulations in this place are as unbending and conservative as the church fathers. But we know how to get around them. We've been locking horns with them for decades. I promise you that the very next man on death row will have complete freedom to choose whatever cable TV channels he wants."

"Thank you."

We spent a few moments looking at each other in silence, both of us smiling.

"You don't hold it against me, I hope?" he said at length.

"What?"

"For losing the case."

"Oh, no. Certainly not."

"You are very kind. Such understanding is rare among people who share your fate, unfortunately. They expect lawyers to be miracle workers, and when there is no miracle they shift the entire blame onto us."

"You did everything you could."

"I really did. I'm glad you realize that. It's critically important in my line of work to part with my client as friends, regardless of the outcome. Nothing distresses me more than a dissatisfied client. No matter how unfounded his dissatisfaction may be, it's always a heavy burden on my conscience. And believe me, it isn't at all easy to live with a troubled conscience."

"I believe you."

The lawyer's face lit up again. He nodded, then picked up the glass from the coaster and finished the juice.

"A little more, perhaps?" I offered.

"No, thank you. I'm actually quite fond of orange juice, but I have to watch it. Stomach acid, you know."

"I have problems with it too."

"Not much fun, is it. But it can't be helped. You have to live in spite of adversity. All right, then. Let's get down to business. I'm sure you wonder why I've come."

"To say goodbye, I suppose."

"Yes, of course. But not only for that reason. I'm here to tell you a story."

"A story?"

"Yes. Don't worry, it's very short. I won't take up much of your time. That would be thoughtless of me considering your circumstances. I hope you want to hear it. You'll see, it's quite edifying and entertaining."

"I love edifying and entertaining stories."

"Excellent. I heard the story early in my childhood from a distant relative on my mother's side, the widow of a retired colonel in the medical corps. She visited us from time to time in our family's summer cottage, when the city was overcome by unbearable heat. She told it to me behind my parents' back, before I went to sleep one particularly sultry evening, full of noisy crickets and a looming storm that bypassed us in the end. Under the thrall of the story I couldn't sleep for a long time that night. It became etched in my memory forever. As an adult, it has often come to mind in the most unexpected circumstances, but I have yet to tell it to someone else."

"I'm flattered to be the first."

"Think nothing of it. You certainly deserve it. My elderly relative heard the story from her husband, but not until he was on his deathbed, and he'd heard it many years before from a superior officer he'd treated for a particularly serious form of tropical fever. The man had related it in a state of delirium caused by his high temperature. Later, when he recovered, he firmly denied any knowledge of it. Nevertheless, I never doubted the authenticity of the story, even though it's quite strange, as you will soon see for yourself."

"I can hardly wait."

"A missionary lived with his wife and five daughters on the edge of the jungle. In his leisure time he liked to paint. He was inspired by the lush plant and animal world that surrounded him. He would take his painting equipment and head into the jungle, returning with exquisite canvases. He produced eleven paintings, but the twelfth turned out to be fatal, unfortunately. He'd almost finished it when a bird such as he had never seen landed on a nearby tree.

"The beauty of the bird was enchanting. Its feathers changed color with the slightest shift in the angle from which it was viewed and it seemed to glow with some sort of inner radiance. And when the bird started to sing, the missionary was filled with a pleasure he had never felt before. Although such a thought was blasphemous for a member of the clergy, he felt he was beholding an epiphany. He was barely able to pull himself out of this spellbound state, then fell vigorously to work to paint the bird. Just enough space remained on the canvas.

"The moment he finished, the bird spread its wings and flew off, resembling a fireball rising in the air, leaving a brief trail of glittering dust. The missionary felt a sharp pang of sadness, as though suffering a great loss. He was consoled, though, by the fact that he had put the bird on canvas. He hastened out of the jungle to show the wondrous creature to his wife and daughters.

"When he finally removed the lightweight material covering the painting on the veranda of his house by the sandy seashore, having first told the household briefly and excitedly about his unusual experience, a terrible surprise awaited him. On the spot where he had painted the bird gaped white canvas, as though he had never put his brush to it. He stared at it in disbelief, paying no attention to the bewildered faces of his womenfolk. And then something seemed to break inside him. Without a word of explanation, he grabbed the canvas and rushed back into the jungle.

"They waited for him to return, but there was no sign of him anywhere. When the sun began to set on the watery horizon, his wife and daughters became seriously worried. Never before had he stayed in the jungle so late. The approaching night would bring great danger when predators set out to hunt. Something urgent had to be done. As dusk was falling, a group of natives with lighted torches headed out in search of the missionary.

"They came back one hour and fifteen minutes later, empty-handed. They'd searched intensively for the missionary and called out to him tirelessly, but there was no trace. All they found was the painting leaning against a tree. When his wife and daughters looked at it, they had a surprise in store for them. The white spot where the bird had first been painted was filled once again. In its place was the missionary, gazing at something beyond the edge of the picture, his face filled with an expression of infinite bliss.

"A wide swathe of the surrounding jungle was thoroughly combed in the following days, but the earth seemed to have engulfed the painter. They did not even find remains that would indicate he'd been the victim of a large predator. Finally, they gave up the search. A new missionary disembarked with his family two and a half months later, and the wife and daughters of the previous one took the same boat back to civilization. On the fourth day at sea there was a terrible storm. The boat crashed into the rocks and many passengers drowned. All six members of the vanished painter's family somehow managed to reach the shore, but they lost all their luggage. The missionary's twelve paintings ended up at the bottom of the sea, along with everything else."

After he had finished, the lawyer looked at me for several moments without speaking, then reached for the empty glass on the coffee table. He picked it up, then put it back down on the coaster, gesturing dismissively with his other hand.

"So, what do you say?" he asked me.

I responded with a short, silent look before I answered. "Edifying and entertaining, as you said yourself."

"Yes, quite so, isn't it? I hope it will be of use to you."

"I'm sure it will."

He got up from the armchair and it squeaked again.

"Well, there's nothing more to be said. The time has come to say farewell."

He held out his hand. We shook hands firmly once again.

"It was an honor and a privilege to defend you."

"And mine to be your client."

He bowed, and I did the same. Then he went up to the door and knocked. It opened the same moment and he went out without turning around. The lawyer's large figure was replaced by the smiling guard.

"There's another visitor. Would you like to receive him right away?"

"Let him in."

The guard nodded to someone who was hidden by the door. This time the visitor didn't have to speak in order for me to recognize him. The bright light from the corridor created an aureole around a body so tall and thin that it could only be the prosecutor.

"Good evening," he said in a high-pitched voice that got terribly on my nerves.

"Good evening," I replied without much warmth in my voice.

The door closed behind him, but he didn't move from the threshold. We stood there for a while in tense silence, which I finally broke.

"Have a seat," I said, indicating the wobbly armchair.

"Thank you," replied the prosecutor. When he sat down, the chair rocked gently under him. He grabbed hold of the arms disconcertedly but didn't get up. He was carrying a briefcase similar to the lawyer's, but he didn't put it in his lap. Instead he placed it on the coffee table, pushing aside the lawyer's empty juice glass.

I had no recourse. "Would you like something to drink?" I asked.

The grimace that appeared on his face was probably a smile. "Orange juice, please."

"I'm sorry, there isn't any orange juice," I lied without the slightest stab of guilt. "All the drinks I have are alcoholic."

The new grimace was probably meant to express repugnance. "I don't drink alcohol. Not while I'm on duty, or otherwise. I had no idea that those on death row were allowed to drink."

He shook his head reprovingly.

"Oh, yes," I said as I sat on the couch. "The bar is quite well stocked. I could even make you an exotic cocktail." I indicated the empty glass on the coffee table. "My lawyer was very pleased with what I fixed him."

The prosecutor picked up the glass, brought it to his nose, then put it back on the coaster.

"Your displeasure with me," he said after a brief pause, "is somewhat understandable. I would probably feel the same if I were in your shoes. But please believe that I have nothing against you personally."

"Your behavior in court didn't exactly lead to that conclusion."

"My behavior was professional. A prosecutor is never expected to show any sympathy for the accused. That would be quite unseemly."

"I didn't expect any sympathy, but nor did I expect such fiery antagonism. It was almost vehement."

"That wasn't very spectacular. I can be far more brutal. You should have seen me at some of the other trials."

"So that means I was lucky?"

He took off his thick glasses, retrieved a handkerchief from the inside pocket of his jacket and wiped them thoroughly.

"You shouldn't take things so much to heart," he said after putting his glasses back on. "A trial is actually a stage play with strictly defined roles. The fact that we have to play-act has nothing to do with our true selves. Do you really think that prosecutors are insensitive sadists by nature who enjoy raging at another human being, even if they've committed a capital crime?"

"That's the impression I got," I admitted.

"Why, that's terrible. Being a prosecutor is one of the most thankless professions. It's no wonder that such a small number of us reach retirement age in that position. And we do all sorts of things to make amends for merely doing our duty conscientiously. Take your cell, for instance. Do you think you'd have all this comfort if it weren't for our decades of persistent lobbying and self-sacrifice?"

"I thought lawyers got the credit for that."

"Lawyers?" He seemed truly astounded. "He didn't tell you that, did he?" He nodded toward the door.

"Yes, he did."

"Really, now! Just when I thought their high-handed insolence had reached the limit, they manage to outdo themselves. Give lawyers credit for this?" His gesture swept around the cell.

"That's what I was told."

"Is that so? Well, let me tell you how things really stand. The lawyer chaps haven't moved a finger to ease their clients' lives, particularly those on death row. They don't give a fig about the conditions in which you spend your last hours. The moment the trial ends and they pocket their fat fee, you cease to exist for them. Only we, the prosecutors, who are strictly speaking your opponents, are concerned for your welfare, so we can appease our guilty consciences. Fair enough, I can understand the lawyers' apathy, they're notorious for that, but not their propensity for posturing. Truly outrageous!"

"Well, he did come to visit me."

"Don't fool yourself. He certainly didn't do it from altruistic motives. He must have gotten something out of the visit. Fellows like that never do anything unless they can turn it to their advantage." He stopped for a moment. "What did he want, if I might ask?"

We looked at each other briefly, without speaking.

"To say goodbye," I replied at last.

"That's all?"

"And to tell me a story."

"Tell you a story!" The prosecutor jumped up out of the armchair, causing it to rock wildly.

"Why don't you move over here?" I proposed, indicating the other armchair.

"Forget it," he snapped. "This really beats all! There's got to be a limit! I'm going to send a sharp complaint to the bar association!"

With a nervous movement he snatched his briefcase off the coffee table, knocking over the lawyer's juice glass in the process. With complete disregard, he took out a notebook and started writing something rapidly in it. I bent down and picked up the glass, thinking how lucky it was that it was empty. Otherwise it would have left an ugly stain on the carpet. Orange juice stains are hard to get out.

When he had finished, he closed the notebook energetically and put it back in his briefcase.

"There! That will teach him a thing or two. I hope he gets disbarred."

"Excuse me," I said hesitantly, "but I'm afraid I don't understand. What's wrong with telling me a story?"

"What's wrong?" repeated the prosecutor in a voice whose intensified shrillness tore at my nerves. "How can you ask! What's wrong is that everyone knows we alone do that! Only prosecutors tell stories to the condemned! That's how it's always been!"

"So you're going to tell me a story too?"

"I was going to, that's why I came, but how can I now in such a rattled state?"

"How about if I double check to see if there's a bit of orange juice left? It has a therapeutic effect on the nerves, it might help calm you down."

The prosecutor slowly nodded his head. I took a new glass off the refrigerator and filled it halfway. Before I put it on the coffee table, I removed his briefcase and put it on the floor. The prosecutor drained his juice before I even got back to the couch.

"The story I'm about to tell you," he began, "I heard in confidence from a fellow prosecutor who finally, on the seventh attempt, managed to kill himself, no longer able to bear the burden of the work we do. He took his life by closing himself hermetically in a large freezer. The autopsy established that he suffocated before he froze. I don't think his intention was to end his life in such a terrible way. He counted on a gentle death from the cold, but had overlooked the fact that he would first run out of air. Isn't it terrible how all the prosecutors are dropping like flies?"

"Awful," I agreed.

"After his fourth failed suicide attempt they put him in a mental hospital where he spent two months and seventeen days. There he became friends with an orderly. Just before they let him out the orderly told him the strange story of a veterinarian who had been driven mad by a manuscript that later caused his death."

The prosecutor paused, and I repeated in bewilderment, "A manuscript?"

"Yes. Believe it or not, manuscripts can be fatal. One of the veterinarian's girlfriends secretly wrote a novel over more than three and a half years, and when she finally finished it, she took the sole copy of the manuscript to her friend for him to evaluate. He sat down immediately to read and spent the whole night at it. At dawn when he finished reading, he phoned her at once to tell her how delighted he was.

"Although the telephone rang a long time, she didn't answer. At first he thought she was a sound sleeper and didn't hear the phone ringing. He waited for morning to come and then called her again, but still there was no answer. When his call later in the afternoon was still without success, he became worried. He drove to her apartment, hoping that her phone was just on the blink, and that was why she didn't answer. He rang the front doorbell for a very long time, to no avail. Not even inquiries at the neighbors' led anywhere. No one had seen her since the morning of the previous day.

"Not knowing what else to do, the veterinarian went home. He continued calling his friend all that day, but had less and less hope of reaching her. Filled with foreboding, he finally went to bed, but sleep simply refused to close his eyes. Instead of tossing and turning restlessly in bed, he picked up the manuscript and started to read it again.

"Towards the end of the second chapter he had a surprise in store that made him shudder. He came across a part that he was certain hadn't been there the night before. In disbelief he read the episode about a woman whose description was very reminiscent of the novel's author. She was carrying a large cage containing a sweetly singing bird with magnificent plumage.

"Wide awake, the veterinarian read on impatiently.

He expected the woman with the bird to appear once again, but there was no further mention of her for the rest of the novel. Once again he finished reading the manuscript at daybreak. Now he wasted no time telephoning. Equipped with an axe, he went straight to his friend's apartment. The neighbors were wakened by the din coming from her front door and called the police.

"When they arrived, the police patrol found the door broken down and the frantic veterinarian sitting on the living room floor, his head buried in his hands. He did not resist when they took him away, even though the deadly axe lay next to him. The statement he gave to the inspectors at the station was so muddled and unbelievable that instead of putting him in jail they took him straight to the mental hospital.

"The doctor whose care he was under finally agreed to grant his plea and bring the manuscript that he'd talked about incessantly and was supposedly the cause of all his troubles. Although the doctor combed the apartment thoroughly, he found no manuscript.

"When the doctor returned to his patient empty-handed, the man's first reaction was to explode in anger, so they had to put him in a straitjacket, and then he fell into a deep depression. All attempts to get him out of this state were unsuccessful. He faded steadily and then finally, on the morning of his ninety-sixth day in the clinic, he was found dead. The report on the veterinarian's death made no mention, as though it was unimportant, of the colorful feather found inexplicably on his pillow, or of the unusual serenity adorning the deceased's face.

"The police sealed the apartment of the veterinarian's girlfriend, expecting her to appear, but she never did."

The prosecutor picked up the empty glass, then looked at me.

"Sorry, there's isn't any left," I lied again, opening my arms with a shrug.

He eyed me suspiciously. I thought he was going to object, but instead all he did was ask, "What do you think of the story?"

"Edifying and entertaining."

This time his suspicious look lasted somewhat longer, but once again he refrained from comment. "It's better than the lawyer's, isn't it?"

He paused a moment, waiting for me to reply, but since I didn't take sides, he continued. "It must be. Chaps like that are infamous for letting their imaginations run wild. If you haven't had any experience with them, the blarney they rely on can carry you away. We, however, stick strictly to the facts. Prosecutors' stories might be somewhat drier, with less embellishments, but as a result you can rely on their authenticity."

"To be sure," I agreed.

His third suspicious look didn't pass without remark. "Unfortunately, I see that my visit has done nothing to change your attitude towards us, the prosecutors. Frankly, my hopes weren't very high. Only on rare occasions do we part with the condemned on at least good, if not friendly terms. It seems this is inevitable."

I shrugged my shoulders. "So it seems."

The prosecutor rose from the armchair carefully, making it rock again. "It can't be helped. I did everything in my power. My conscience is clear at least in that respect."

He extended his hand in a rather awkward movement. I hesitated a bit before I accepted it. Our handshake was weak and fleeting.

He stopped at the door and turned around. "Think about the story I told you. It's more edifying than entertaining."

I nodded. "I will."

He knocked, the door opened and his slight figure quickly slipped out, as though slinking away. Just as the guard appeared in the lighted rectangle left by the prosecutor, a droning voice was heard in the corridor.

"Out of the way! Let me through!"

Having no time for words, the guard stepped aside obediently, and a short, stocky man rushed inside, his black robe fluttering around him.

"Good evening!" said the judge gaily, opening his arms. I hastened to his embrace.

"How are you?" he asked cordially, once we had moved apart, our hands resting lightly on each other's shoulders. Before I could reply, the judge continued, "What a stupid question. Who could be fine after a visit from that guy? You'd feel more cheerful if the undertaker had come to take your measurements." He laughed merrily at his witticism.

I waved my hand dismissively and indicated the armchair in good repair. "Please sit down."

He ignored my recommendation and headed for the couch. He ran his fingers over it, as though checking the springs, then settled down at one end, raised his feet, and straightened the hem of his robe.

"There!" he said. "Comfort above all things. I didn't work so hard for all these years in vain."

"You, too?" I asked, sitting in the armchair.

"What do you mean—'you too'? Why, who else?"

"The lawyer and the prosecutor . . ."

"The lawyer and the prosecutor?" he thundered. He stared at me in disbelief, as though I'd uttered some inconceivable stupidity, then started to laugh. It was an uproarious laugh that I remembered well from the trial. The entire courtroom echoed from his peals of laughter. He would shake all over, holding onto his robust stomach. I knew from experience that this could last for minutes.

I waited patiently for his attack of hilarity to pass. When he finally got hold of himself, tears started to roll down his round, ruddy cheeks. He searched around inside his robe and took out a large, white handkerchief with an embroidered monogram. First he wiped his eyes, then blew his nose.

"I have to write this one down. You've really made my day." He put his handkerchief away and took a large notebook with a pen attached to it out of another inside pocket.

"What did you say? The lawyer and the prosecutor?" He stopped writing because he was overcome by another seizure of laughter. It was shorter than the first one.

"That's what they claim," I said, trying to defend myself after he'd put away his notebook.

He waved his hands dismissively, then said through his giggles, "Please stop. That's enough. I'll die of laughter. Besides, my doctor has forbidden it. Because of my blood pressure. He says a capillary might burst, and then there will be hell to pay."

He cracked his knuckles, and then laughed at that too.

I brought my index fingers to my lips and nodded.

"The lawyer and the prosecutor?" he repeated once again, but this time managed to get hold of himself. He nodded in return and put his index finger on his lips too. "All right, if laughter is forbidden, other pleasures aren't. What will we use to toast with?"

"I'm afraid all I have is orange juice," I replied, but even as I said it I realized I'd made another mistake. I couldn't take back my words, however.

"Orange juice?" said the judge, not hiding his amazement. A moment later the cell resounded with his merry laughter once again.

After using his handkerchief to remove the traces of laughter from his face, the judge waggled his finger at me threateningly. "You're really determined to do me in!"

"Forgive me," I said contritely. "I'll be careful what I say."

"Orange juice, indeed! Not even blockheads like the lawyer and prosecutor would drink that!"

He gazed at me fixedly, expecting me to substantiate this. Even though I failed to do so, the expression on my face seemed to be explicit enough.

Now his laughter was accompanied by clapping hands and banging on the back of the couch. The judge even raised both feet briefly and kicked them in the air. When he got hold of himself, he reached for his notebook once again.

"I have to write this one down too. Orange juice, was it? Divine."

"Just one glass each," I said, trying to soften the effect. "The prosecutor actually drank barely half a glass."

This was also a mistake. "Barely half?" repeated the judge, losing his breath once again. I concluded that the best thing would be to keep my mouth shut.

He took out another handkerchief, gray in color, with the same large monogram. He was clearly well prepared for the calamities that struck him.

"All right, give me the glasses," he said after returning the handkerchief to his robe.

I looked at him in bewilderment.

"You don't think I came unprepared, do you?" He patted the bottom part of his robe. "Glasses, if you please!"

Even though I had no idea what was on his mind, I headed obediently for the refrigerator and picked up the two glasses that were left. When I returned to the couch, the judge was holding a bottle filled with something strong.

I handed him a glass. "I really shouldn't," I said.

He frowned at me as he took the glass. "Why?"

"It's against regulations."

"Regulations?" repeated the judge, his face immediately flushing. As he shook with laughter again, I seriously worried that the doctor's warning about bursting capillaries might come true.

"Please don't make me laugh," he said after using

his handkerchief once more. "Have you forgotten who you're dealing with? Judges make the regulations here, don't they? As far as I can recall, I'm still a judge. Your glass!"

I had no recourse. I held out the glass and he filled it almost to the brim with the reddish liquid in the bottle. He poured himself the same amount, then raised his glass. We clinked a bit too strongly, spilling some of the drink on his robe, bringing a chuckle from the judge.

"Don't hold back," he said, seeing me hesitate. "You'll be in need of a strong drink, considering the story I'm about to tell you. It'll be easier for you to take."

"You too," almost slipped out. Luckily, I bit my lip at the last moment. I sat down in the armchair in good repair and took a cautious sip. My care was well taken. The drink was fiery. This didn't stop the judge from swallowing half his glass in one gulp.

"I heard the story from a stuntman I sentenced to life in prison because he killed forty-three animals in a zoo. Not at random but with cold-blooded calculation: he attacked only the poor females. His victims included a beautiful white elephant, three penguins, a very rare species of koala, and a pregnant two-humped camel. Can you imagine—killing a pregnant two-humped camel! That criminal would have got even worse if it hadn't been for the extenuating circumstance that he'd committed the crime in a state of shattered nerves owing to unrequited love.

"I used to visit him in his cell until he was done in by a poisonous snake that slithered unnoticed into the prison yard and bit only him, among all the prisoners, as he lay unsuspecting on the grass. Who says that culprits don't get the justice they deserve? Even though they didn't catch the snake, I'm sure it was a female.

"During one of my visits he told me a bizarre story from one of his jobs. He'd been working on a film directed by a young and talented man. It had been a real pleasure to work with him, even though great demands were made of the stuntmen. The director knew exactly what he wanted, he was effective and dealt with his associates skillfully. The shooting ran smoothly. Problems arose, however, when they watched the rushes.

"An interloper appeared in some of the key scenes. No one could explain how a bird had gotten into the footage that no one had seen at the shoot. Its large size and brightly colored, glistening feathers made it impossible to ignore, as did its rapturous song. Although disturbing, this mystery was less important for the director than the matter of what to do about the interloper.

"The bird, of course, couldn't be left in the film because there was no reason for it to be there. It was like a foreign body. The simplest, but by no means most inexpensive, way to remove it was to re-shoot the scenes that it had spoiled. The director somehow managed to persuade the producers to increase the film's budget so this could be done, but when the new rushes arrived from the laboratory, the hefty sum was proven to be wasted. By some mysterious means, the bird had remained in the footage.

"The director flew into a rage. The once even-tempered, good-natured man became hysterical and hot-headed. He fired almost one-third of the crew, including the excellent cameraman, but this didn't solve the problem. He then tried to wangle more money out of the producers to get rid of the fiendish bird by computer processing, but they refused. It would be more expensive than re-shooting the scenes and the outcome was uncertain. The word had already gotten out that the film was cursed. It was wiser to abandon the project than continue throwing money into a bottomless pit.

"This decision was a heavy blow for the director. He tried everything he could to prevent work on the film from stopping, but the producers were inexorable.

They didn't turn their backs on him, though. In spite of the failure, they offered him another film to direct. He refused. His desire to get the better of the pesky bird had already become an obsession.

"He gave almost all his savings to buy the film footage that could not be used anymore. Then he took out a loan to rent a computer imaging studio where he fanatically endeavored to get rid of the interloper. He worked alone, convinced that everyone had plotted against him. One night the studio caught fire. It burned to the ground.

"They combed through the ashes, but found no trace of the director. By some miracle, all that was spared from the fire was the piece of film that the poor man was working on. The police looked at it, but could see nothing unusual in the sight of a young cineaste running after a bird, as costumed stuntmen did their reckless jumps all around them. People in the film world, after all, are well known for their strange behavior."

The judge seemed barely able to wait for the story to finish so he could do the same thing to his drink. The second half of the glass disappeared like the first, in one gulp.

"So?" he asked after wiping his mouth with a finger, still holding the glass.

"Edifying and entertaining," popped out, even though I was aware of the reaction it would cause.

He laughed uproariously, trembling all over with his guffaws. If his glass hadn't been empty he would certainly have spilled it. Liquid almost poured out of the bottle he was holding in his other hand, even though it was barely half full. Since his hands were occupied, he couldn't wipe the tears that streamed down his newly flushed cheeks. At last, still giggling, he put his feet on the floor and got up from the couch.

"Edifying and entertaining, eh?" It looked like he would burst out laughing again, but he restrained himself, putting a finger to his lips. "You're quite the scalawag. That's why I like to visit the cells on death row. It's never as cheerful anywhere else as it is here. If the doctor hadn't prohibited me from excessive laughter, I would stay here longer. But it wouldn't really do for a judge to meet his maker in this place."

He turned this way and that, not knowing what to do with the bottle and glass. I thought he'd put them down on the coffee table, but he handed them to me instead. I took them both in one hand because I was still holding a full glass in the other.

"Keep it," he said, nodding at the bottle. "I can see you're not much of a drinker, but you never know when you might need it."

I thought about protesting, but kept silent, not wanting to give him a reason for convulsive laughter.

"Thank you," I replied.

"Well, then, that's about it." He came up and gave me a hug. The bottle and glasses rattled between us.

He stepped back, keeping his hands on my biceps. "Take some advice from a man of experience. Always look at the bright side of things. Laughter can surmount any obstacle."

I nodded. He patted me lightly on the cheek, then headed for the door.

He'd already raised a hand to knock on it, when he turned around. "Edifying and entertaining, you say? Excellent! I can't remember the last time someone made me laugh so much."

The door didn't close behind the judge. The guard appeared in the rectangle of light. He just looked at me without saying a word.

"Another visitor?" I asked, setting the bottle and glasses on the coffee table.

"No," replied the guard, sounding ill at ease. "I was just thinking. . . . If you have a little time, perhaps . . . I won't bore you for very long. . . ."

"Come in, come in," I said, indicating the armchair that wasn't broken.

The guard came in, took off his cap and closed the door behind him. He sat in the armchair, his eyes downcast. I waited for him to start, but all he did was twist his cap in his lap.

"Would you like something to drink?" I said, breaking the silence. "I don't have any more clean glasses, unfortunately, but I barely touched that one." I indicated the full glass on the coffee table.

"Oh, that's all right, thanks a lot. It's an honor to drink from your glass."

He picked it up and drank a little. This seemed to give him a bit of confidence.

"I have to tell you. . . . You might not know it, although you might easily take it for granted. . . . This is a prison, after all. . . . Such things are to be expected. . . ."

He stopped, lowering his eyes to his cap once more. I waited a little for him to continue, but since he didn't, I asked, "What do you mean?"

"The room is bugged. I've been eavesdropping," he said in a soft, apologetic voice.

"Oh, that," I said. "I didn't know, but as you said, I should have taken it for granted."

"I'm only carrying out orders. I'm sure you understand."

"Of course."

"Right now the microphones are turned off, naturally. I took care of it personally. This conversation is not being taped. No one actually knows I'm here. I hope that this visit remains our little secret."

"Of course, of course," I hastened to set his mind at rest.

The guard sighed audibly, then took another drink from the glass.

"You see, eavesdropping has its good sides too."

"Is that so?"

"Yes. If the microphones hadn't been turned on during your last three visits, I wouldn't know what you talked about with the lawyer, the prosecutor and the judge, and thus wouldn't be able to warn you about the kind of people you're dealing with."

"What kind?"

The guard didn't continue right away. He looked around the cell, as though someone else might be there listening in, then bent forward in the armchair, drawing close to me.

"This is for your ears only," he said in a whisper. "I'd lose my job instantly if anyone found out I was talking like this about court officials. But I have to. In the name of truth and honor."

He fell silent, waiting to see what impression his words had had on me.

I nodded. "Truth and honor above all."

"They lied to you. Every single one."

"How can that be?"

"Yes, they did. Shamelessly. I listened to them and couldn't believe my own ears. Men in such high positions, twisting the truth so blatantly. To the detriment of us, ordinary guards."

"I'm not sure I quite understand you."

"Did you really believe," said the guard, his voice returning to normal, "that any of them deserves the slightest credit for the fact that this cell looks like a hotel room?"

"That's what they claimed. Indeed, they took issue with each other, so in the end I wasn't exactly sure who deserves my gratitude."

"I'll tell you who. Only us. The guards' union."

"Really?"

"Why, of course. It's not at all difficult to guess why. In the best of cases those gentlemen drop by death row just once to pay a visit. If they're moved at all by what they see here, they quickly forget it. They don't really care about human suffering, regardless of how much they try to convince you otherwise. We're in the best position to know. You should just hear what they say when they come out of this cell. Such two-faced insensitivity is truly rare."

"Who would have thought?"

"Yes. Unlike them, however, the nature of our work puts us in constant contact with the condemned. Do you think it's easy to watch them spend their last days in inhuman conditions?"

"I thought guards had to be hardened to that."

"That's a typical prejudice," he said, spreading his arms as he shrugged. "The most god-awful stories are told about guards, we're supposed to be hardhearted, brutal, even sadistic, but please believe me that isn't at all true. Well, fair enough, I won't say there aren't some psychos among us, that's inevitable, but what profession doesn't have its share? You'll even find them working in a nursery school. Among us guards, however, their number is inconsequential. In any case, they can't become members of the union. We make real sure of that. We only let family men into our membership, who are compassionate, with a gentle disposition. If they like animals or enjoy gardening that's all in their favor. In spite of these strict criteria for joining the union, the great majority of the guards are members."

"I didn't know that."

"Few people do, unfortunately. That's why there are so many misconceptions about us. The best way to fight such stereotypes is through actions, not words. What do you think, where did the money come from for all this comfort surrounding you?"

He made a sweeping gesture about the cell. I shrugged in ignorance.

"Donations from union members."

"I never would have thought."

"Our generosity will seem even greater if you bear our modest salaries in mind. You might well say that we take the food out of our own mouths in order to make things as comfortable as possible for death row inmates. And we intend to keep on doing it. For example, plans already exist to remodel the bathroom completely. We'll put in a big Jacuzzi. Nothing can soothe the understandable anxiety of the condemned like a whirlpool massage."

"Excellent. I love whirlpool massages in a Jacuzzi."

"Unfortunately, you won't live to see it, but those who come here after you will truly enjoy themselves."

"How lucky they are. I envy them."

We sank into silence. The guard looked at the glass in his hand. When he finally spoke, his voice had softened again almost to a whisper.

"There is one more thing, . . ." he started, then stopped.

"Yes?"

"Those stories they told you . . ."

"What about them?"

"I'd like to tell you a story myself. If you don't object, of course."

"On the contrary. Please go ahead."

"I might not be as adept as they were with words. . . ."

"It makes no difference. What's important is that the story is edifying and entertaining."

The guard's face brightened. "Oh, I believe it is. It's quite out of the ordinary in any case." He raised the glass and this time took a good swig.

"We had a colleague who suddenly decided to become a stone-carver. It shouldn't come as a surprise. The life of a guard is not at all easy. Many men can't put up with the hardship it brings and so they change professions. Former prison guards have ended up in all sorts of places. They can be found among circus clowns, whale hunters, wigmakers, herbalists, stuntmen, and polar explorers.

"The members of the stone-carvers' guild always met the last Saturday of the month at a tavern in the suburbs. There they would let themselves go, enjoying the good food and drink, singing, making music, playing cards and dominos. Fascinating stories were told to general amusement. I stayed in touch with my former colleague even after he changed jobs and he would tell me these stories from time to time. One of them made a particularly strong impression on me.

"An old sculptor received an unusual commission. He was to carve the bust of a young boy. There were two special circumstances, however. He had to finish the job in just five days and the boy, who suffered from some mysterious disease, could only be seen once, very briefly. The sculptor refused at first to work under these conditions, but the fee he was offered made him think twice. The sum would provide him with a trouble-free retirement.

"He visited the boy, who was lying in the darkened room of a castle. During the several minutes he was allowed to spend at the sickbed, the young boy did not open his eyes. Although visibility was poor, the sculptor was dazzled by the beauty of the pale young face. He seemed in the presence of a sleeping angel. He could barely tear his eyes away from the boy. As he was leaving the room, the gentle song of a bird came from one of the dark corners.

"Returning to his studio, he first made several charcoal sketches while his memory was still fresh, then set to work. He took his hammer and chisel and began to carve the best piece of marble he had. He made surprisingly rapid progress and felt almost no fatigue. The hours stretched out, one after the other, and he watched with rapture as his hands slowly transformed shapeless stone into the boy's enchanting likeness.

"During the five days he had available he slept very little and ate even less. Strangely enough, he had no trouble coping with the tremendous effort in spite of his advanced age. An eagerness suffused him that he hadn't felt since his youth. Everything whirled around him as the stubborn material yielded submissively. The money he was to receive ceased to be of any importance. This was no longer a commission he was fulfilling for the money. He was creating the work of his lifetime.

"At the close of the fifth day, he raised the hammer and chisel for the last time, and then stepped back a bit from the finished bust. It was perfect. The angelic face seemed to come to life in the stone, radiating diaphanously. He stared at it fixedly for a long time, making up for the short-lived pleasure in the boy's room. Before he finally went to bed, he covered the bust with a flannel cloth so that its beauty would not be squandered with no one to look at it.

"Those who had placed the commission arrived at the appointed hour the next morning. As the sculptor removed the cloth, he looked not at the boy's bust, but at his visitors' faces, expecting to see their admiration. Instead he saw expressions of disbelief. Not understanding, he slowly turned towards his masterpiece. Then his eyes grew as big as saucers. On the pedestal was something that had no cause to be there. The boy's head had been replaced with a large bird.

"The sculptor screamed in horror. Quickly veiling the sculpture again, he hurried the visitors out of his atelier and locked himself inside. No one knows what happened there. As they stood in front of the door, strange sounds reached the bewildered visitors' ears: the sculptor's angry shouts and curses, the blows of metal on stone, the noises of smashing and crashing. The oddest sound of all was the birdcalls, shrill and delightful by turns.

"This noise and commotion lasted a good two hours

and then suddenly everything quieted down. The visitors exchanged worried glances, not knowing how to interpret the unexpected silence or what to do. Finally they knocked on the door of the atelier. There was no answer. They consulted with each other briefly, and then decided to break down the door.

"When the heavy door finally yielded to their blows and they rushed into the atelier, there was no trace of the sculptor. They looked around the large room in disbelief. There was no other exit and the three large windows were shut. They even searched the only two places that were not immediately visible: in a small closet and under the bed, but just as they suspected, there was no one there either.

"Finally, shrugging their shoulders in resignation, they turned their attention to the pedestal holding the sculptor's veiled work. They hesitated slightly before one of them finally mustered the courage to take off the flannel cloth. What they saw under it made them draw back. Instead of the bird they'd expected was the stone head of the sculptor. There was no sign of the distress from two hours before when he'd escorted them out of the atelier. Now his face radiated serenity."

Finishing his story, the guard brought to his lips the glass he'd been holding as he talked, then changed his mind at the last moment and placed it on the coaster on the coffee table.

"I mustn't have any more. I'm on duty. It's a lovely drink, though."

I took the bottle that the judge had left and handed it to him. "Keep it. I won't be needing it."

He shook his head. "That's very kind of you, but it is strictly against regulations."

"No one will know. Didn't you turn off the microphone?"

"Yes, I did, but . . ."

"Take it as a gift in return for the story you told me."

"Did you like it?"

"Edifying and entertaining, just as I hoped."

A smile spread over the guard's face. He took the bottle, looked left and right, then quickly shoved it under the jacket of his uniform. He nodded briefly and stood up.

"I won't take up any more of your time. It was a real pleasure talking to you. I will always have fond memories of this conversation."

I got up and put out my hand. "I will too."

We shook hands and he held onto mine a moment longer. He stopped at the door and turned around. It seemed he wanted to say something else, but instead he just shrugged his shoulders as though apologizing for something. He hastened out and the door closed behind him without a sound.

I went to the dresser and picked up the violin. I placed it on my left shoulder, and then raised the bow. I was unable to continue playing, however, because everything around me was suddenly plunged into darkness. In the pitch black enveloping me I felt as though I were floating, that nothing supported me from underneath. Or that I had become disembodied.

Then the light on the desk once again filled the cell with a subdued green glow. I turned around slowly. Everything looked exactly the same as before. I raised the bow, but it did not reach the strings this time either. A knock was heard at the door.

"Come in," I said.

No one entered.

Placing the bow under my arm, I got up, went to the door and opened it.

Standing in front of me on the white floor was a large bird akin to a bright, blazing fire.

"Hi," I said.

The bird fluttered up and landed on my right shoulder. I went out of the cell, turned around, closed the door after me, and then headed down the corridor.

2. The Hospital Room

SOMEONE KNOCKED ON THE door of my hospital room.

I raised my eyes from the book I was reading as I lay in bed.

"Come in!"

The door opened a crack and the duty nurse stuck her head inside. Red locks fell from beneath her white cap. She looked at me through the thick lenses of her outsized glasses and smiled.

"How are you?"

I smiled in return. "Fine, thank you."

"Wonderful!"

Her head slipped out and the door closed.

I went back to my reading. I'd just become engrossed when another knock was heard.

"Enter!" I said with a hint of irritation.

This time the door opened wide and an unknown man appeared. He was well advanced in middle age, short, with thinning hair, wearing a brown hospital robe over his striped pajamas. In his left hand were three goose quills.

"Excuse me," he said hesitantly. "I know it's late already, but perhaps you will receive me anyway. I believe you would be very interested in what I have to tell you."

As I vacillated, he hastened to add, "I'm from room 217 down the hall," as though it were some kind of recommendation.

"Come in," I said at last. I marked the place where

I'd stopped reading with a ribbon and put the book on the bedside table next to the only lighted lamp in the room. Its oval shade made a small, bright cone around the head of my bed.

The visitor entered, closed the door behind him and stayed where he was. I indicated two armchairs to the left of the bed.

"Please take a seat."

"Thank you." When he settled in the chair he seemed to blend into the shadow of that part of the room. He placed the goose quills on the coffee table between the armchairs.

"Please let me introduce myself. I am a retired circus ticket-collector."

"Nice to meet you."

"You might not be aware, but circus ticket-collectors are the victims of grievous prejudice. All kinds of things are said to belittle our work, in particular that it is run-of-the-mill. Supposedly anyone could do it. But I assure you that isn't so. Can you imagine the qualities circus ticket-collectors have to have if they want to be successful?"

"No, I can't."

"They must be very clever and constantly on their guard. I'm sure you have no idea what manner of tricks are used to try to see a show for free?"

"I don't," I conceded.

"A book could be written about it. The choice of tactics depends on the season. In winter they mostly use long coats so they can sneak in children underneath them. It's truly amazing how many of them can fit into specially made inside pockets. The record is held by a tall tram driver who hid no fewer than eleven kids under his raincoat. The only thing that gave him away was when one of them sneezed after they'd passed through the gate. A real shame, one might say."

"A shame indeed."

"The preferred method in autumn is using an umbrella. If it's kept open while entering the circus that usually means there is someone in the upper part. We've found not only children there but adults as well, although they weren't very big. But a closed umbrella is suspicious too, even when it's inside a cover. You wouldn't think that someone could fit inside, but never underestimate the human body. We in the circus are in the best position to know everything it can do. We've found some of our best artists by hiring those we've discovered in umbrellas instead of turning them over to the police. Sometimes a cloud has a silver lining."

"Sometimes, yes."

"You might think there's no way to enter the circus without a ticket during the summer when no one has long coats or umbrellas. That's not so, unfortunately. For years we had an awful time every summer with an amateur magician. We did everything under the sun to outwit him, to no avail. He smuggled at least three people into every show. Once he even brought in seven. Imagine that! Just like he'd slapped us seven times."

"Quite unpleasant."

"But the worst thing was that we never discovered how he pulled off the trick. All he would wear was a t-shirt, shorts and clogs. He wasn't even wearing socks. Even so, we searched him thoroughly every time. Down to his bare skin. And we never found anything. At the end of the show, however, he would inform us triumphantly of how many spectators had slipped in with him. He even introduced them to us. You can imagine how we felt."

"I can."

"Our hands were tied. We couldn't press charges because we had no proof. There was also no basis on which to ban him from the circus. The irate owner spared no expense to beat him at his game. He put an infrared detector at the entrance, bought dogs trained to find avalanche victims, installed TV cameras everywhere, but nothing worked. The amateur magician continued to mock us with utter disdain. Finally, the owner swallowed his pride and made the same offer he had to the artists from the umbrellas: to work with us. But the offer was scornfully rejected, in spite of the quite handsome fee."

"Strange."

The ticket-collector sighed.

"Perverse, if you ask me. In the end we had to accept our fate. We could do nothing to stop him. Our sole consolation was the fact that he only bothered us in the summer. If he'd come in the other seasons the owner would have shut down the circus. And who could blame him for that?"

"No one."

"No one, of course. Compared to that, what happened to us in the spring was pure child's play, although it too was unusual. Did you know that spring is the best time for hypnotizing?"

"No, I didn't."

"Little is known about it. There is still no full explanation as to why this is so. According to some, it has to do with the increased amount of pollen in the air. Others consider strong geomagnetic activity the root of the cause. There are other hypotheses as well. In any event, as soon as the spring months arrived we had almost daily attempts to hypnotize the ticket-collector. You could never guess how fast it can be done."

"I couldn't."

"The record is just six seconds! And that happened even though the ticket-collector was experienced, prepared for the danger that threatened him, and even wearing very dark glasses. None of that helped. He suddenly stiffened and started waving spectators into the circus without checking their tickets. If we hadn't intervened at once, who knows how many people could have slipped in. Maybe even half the tent."

"That many?"

"Yes. Here again, unfortunately, there's not much we can do in the legal sense. How can you prove hypnosis where it leaves no trace? As soon as the spectators entered without tickets, the ticket-collector snapped out of it, but couldn't remember a thing. Luckily, we heard about a simple way to put an end to this nuisance. With the help of hamsters."

"Hamsters?"

"That's right. You might not have noticed, but white hamsters always turn the wheel in their cage counterclockwise. No one knows the reason why, but it makes no difference. In any case, if we put a cage with a white hamster next to the ticket-collector, at the slightest attempt to hypnotize him the hamster immediately changes the direction of the spin. It's enough to have someone keep an eye on the hamster and the problem is solved. It's a highly reliable warning system."

The visitor sank into silence. I waited several moments for him to continue, but when he didn't I asked, "Is that what you wanted to tell me about?"

"Oh, no. That was just in passing, to introduce myself properly. Anyone who's done my job fears they won't be taken seriously. I trust it wasn't too boastful."

"It wasn't."

"Very good. Then I'll get to the point."

He didn't start right away. He paused briefly, as though collecting his thoughts.

"I dreamed about you."

"Me?"

"Yes, you. Don't be surprised. From time to time I dream about people I don't know. I can't explain why this happens. Surely there must be a reason."

"Surely."

"It was a very mysterious dream, as you will see for yourself. Do you mind if I tell it to you?"

"No, I don't."

"You were in a cabin on a ship. It was the dead of night and you were asleep. You were suddenly awakened by alarm bells. You jumped out of bed. In your initial confusion you couldn't remember where to turn on the light. The siren kept on wailing. Finally you turned on the light on the bedside table and put on your glasses."

"I don't wear glasses."

"You wore them in my dream. You quickly took off your pajamas and got dressed. As you were putting on your shoes, the alarm stopped ringing. You didn't know what this meant or what was the best thing to do. You even thought of going back to bed, but then you felt the ship start to rock. You decided to go out of your cabin and see what was going on."

"Why didn't I call the ship's officers on the phone?"

"I don't know. You expected to find lots of agitated passengers in the hallway, but no one was there. You headed for the deck. You had to hold onto the handrail on the wall because the ship was rocking more and more. You passed through a series of empty hallways and finally came out onto the deck. What you saw there confused you. Above you was the clear night sky sprinkled with a multitude of stars, without a breath of wind. The sea was stormy nonetheless. Huge waves were rolling all around."

"How is that possible?"

"It's possible in a dream. A wave poured over the deck and drenched you. The water was very cold. Soaked through and through, you went back into the hallway and closed the door behind you. You had to rush back to your cabin and change clothes. You headed back, but after the third turn you realized that you were lost."

"On top of everything else."

"That's nothing. Your real troubles have yet to come. Just a moment later the lights went out in the hallway, and somewhere from the direction of the deck came the crash of a door breaking and the roar of water gushing inside. You stood there in the darkness frightened, not knowing what to do."

"It wasn't easy for me."

"Not at all. Your situation seemed hopeless. But then a glimmer of hope appeared. You could already hear the water not far behind when a thin strip of light appeared under one of the doors in front of you. You headed in that direction, holding your hands stretched out in front of you so you wouldn't run into someone in the pitch black."

"But the hallways were empty."

"They were, that's right, but someone might have appeared. You couldn't be sure they wouldn't. In any case, you didn't come across any obstacles on the way to the door with the light under it. You stopped in front of it. Good manners required that you knock at least, even though the wall of gushing water was already at your heels."

"I wouldn't think twice in such a situation."

"Well, in my dream you hesitated. Albeit briefly. And then you put out your hand, felt for the knob and quickly opened the door. But you didn't go inside right away. You stopped at the threshold because you were assaulted by a blinding light. You couldn't see anything. You squinted, feeling your eyes burn from the terrible glare. You had the sudden urge to capitulate, but then you felt cold water splashing about your feet. In an instant, you chose what seemed to be the lesser evil. You went into the cabin and feverishly closed the door behind you."

"And then?" I asked, since the visitor had sunk into silence.

"Then nothing. That's the end of the dream. I remember that I woke up covered in sweat. As though it had happened to me, not you. You really gave me a hard time."

"I apologize."

"You have no reason to apologize. No one's to blame for the fact that I dream other people's tight spots."

He opened his arms with a helpless shrug, then got up from the armchair.

"There, I told you my dream. I hope you found it interesting."

"I did."

"I'm glad. Now I have to go. I didn't intend to stay so long. But a man gets long-winded and the time just flies. Good night."

"Good night."

He had already reached the door when something crossed my mind.

"You forgot the goose quills." I pointed to the coffee table between the armchairs.

"No, I didn't," he said tersely, as though this was explanation enough. He nodded and went out before I had a chance to say anything else.

I looked at the feathers again. Then I picked up the book from the bedside table and opened it to the place I'd marked. I didn't have a chance to continue reading, however, because I was interrupted by a fresh knock at the door.

"Enter!"

The cheerful face of the nurse appeared once again.

"Is everything all right?"

"Yes."

"Great!"

A smile quickly spread across her face as she pulled her head back into the corridor.

I turned my eyes back to the book and started to read, but I didn't get very far. I'd barely finished the first paragraph when another knock was heard. This time it was subdued, more like scratching.

"Come in!" I replied in a low voice.

A woman entered the room and quickly closed the door behind her. She was tall and thin with graying hair. The brown hospital robe reached almost to her feet, drawing her out even more. There was a brass inkpot in her left hand.

She turned around the room, as though fearful she might see someone. After making certain there was no one else but me, she let out a sigh.

"Good evening." Her voice was high-pitched.

"Good evening."

"Please forgive me for disturbing you at this late hour. In addition, I shouldn't even be in the men's ward. I'm from the floor up above, room 419. I was lucky that no one saw me coming. I hope my luck holds out when I go back. It would be quite awkward if they caught me, arousing all sorts of suspicions. You know what people are like. Who knows what all might cross their minds."

"I know."

The smile faded from her thin face. "Who would believe that the only reason I came here was to tell you something?"

"Is there something you want to tell me?"

"Yes. Nothing else. Will you let me? I promise it won't take long. You'll go back to your reading in no time at all."

She nodded at the book I was holding. I closed it and put it back on the bedside table.

"I'm all ears." I indicated the armchair where the previous visitor had sat.

"Thank you."

The woman settled into the chair and placed the inkpot next to the goose quills.

"Please forgive me," she began at once. "Since the circumstances do not allow me to present myself properly, I will have to withhold my name. What I will say, however, is that until I retired I was an animal keeper in a circus."

"A circus?"

"Yes. I won't hold it against you if you have little regard for that profession."

"Certainly not. . . ."

"Most people find the job I had unremarkable. And do you know who did the most to demean such a highly responsible job in the public eye?"

"No, I don't."

"The trainers."

"The trainers?"

"Yes. They shamelessly grabbed all the glory for themselves. The audience gives them thunderous applause in the circus ring, full of admiration, and no one ever thinks of the animal keepers. The trainers, however, spend at most two hours a day with the animals, putting them through their paces, and that's only on working days, not weekends. Then there is the fifteen minutes of the show, and that's all. And let me ask you, who is with the animals all the rest of the time, practically from dawn to dusk?"

"The keepers?"

"That's right. Perhaps you think the animal keepers' job is undemanding? What's there to philosophize about, anyway? You feed the animals and clean them, just about anyone could do that. But if that's what you think then you are terribly mistaken."

"That's not what I think."

"I could spend hours telling you about the complexity and intricacy of the keepers' work. Now, of course there is no time, but please let me illustrate just one aspect of our daily life. Quite briefly. May I?"

I nodded my head.

"This, I hope, will provide convincing testimony of the ordeals that circus animal keepers go through. Have you ever wondered, perhaps, how our charges go to sleep?"

"I haven't."

"It's a very delicate procedure, particularly when the animals are nervous or even stressed out after a performance. Considerable patience and skill is needed to get them to go to sleep. Each of them requires a different approach and it's not at all easy to figure out what each animal likes the best. Take elephants, for example. Can you imagine what relaxes and lulls them to sleep the best?"

"I can't."

"Music."

"Music?"

"Yes, music. But not just any. Heaven forbid! If you put on something modern you get the opposite effect from what you want. The elephants become agitated. Do you know what they find particularly irritating?"

"No."

"Atonal music. They run amuck and are capable of breaking through the bars of their cage. Perhaps you read in the newspaper not long ago about an elephant that escaped from a circus and was only caught on the third day?"

"I didn't."

"Well, inexperienced keepers recklessly played atonal music to that poor beast, although they must have known that only late Baroque music is appropriate for elephants. And not every piece. They mustn't be given compositions with cellos. As soon as they hear a cello they raise their trunks and start to sound off gaily, and then sleeping is out of the question. Piano concerts are the most suitable. It's enough for them to listen for just a few minutes and they immediately fall sound asleep. Does the piano have a soothing effect on you too?"

"It does."

"That's nice. Lions, however, are quite another thing. You can put on whatever music you want, they won't take the slightest notice. As though they're deaf. But they are quite responsive to reading."

"Reading?"

"Yes. Everyone is surprised to hear that. And they are even more amazed when they learn that lions are finicky about what you offer them. They don't like prose at all. They start roaring as soon as they hear it. Science fiction infuriates them. They raise such a fuss that the whole circus reverberates. That doesn't surprise me much. I give science fiction a wide berth too. What about you?"

"I have nothing against it."

"Fine, there's no accounting for taste. In any case, the lions are poetry lovers. But not just any kind. If you read them an elegy that causes them to mate. Who knows why? And who can sleep while there's mating?"

"No one."

"No one, of course. Heroic epics are the best way to put lions to sleep. It's enough to read just a few verses, in the original if possible, and they fall asleep as blissfully as a newborn babe."

"Well, I never."

"Yes. But that certainly isn't the most unusual way to put circus animals to sleep. Just wait until you hear about the giraffes."

"Are there giraffes in the circus?"

"Only in the best. We tried just about everything until we discovered that they are art lovers. We can't bring original paintings into their cages, of course, but luckily the giraffes don't insist. It's enough to put a small white screen in front of their cage and show slides. And that, you will agree, is far and away the easiest and least expensive way."

"I agree."

"We do have to be careful about what we show them, however. Abstract works bring about a very adverse reaction. They just turn their backs and stay awake all night in protest. And that's not what we want at all, is it?"

"By no means."

"Works by the early Impressionists have the most beneficial effect. They provide the giraffes with a long and invigorating sleep, which is extremely important given these animals' highly sensitive nerves. You might not be aware, but in spite of their size, giraffes are quite volatile creatures."

"I wasn't aware."

"They are, unfortunately. Unlike the monkeys, for example, who are much calmer, although it isn't exactly easy to put them to sleep, either. We need technical assistance with them too. They're mad about the movies."

"What's that you say?"

"That's right, but not just any movies. Someone unfamiliar with the monkeys' taste might assume they prefer cartoons or maybe comedies. But none of that is right. What would you say, what kind of movies do monkeys prefer?"

I thought for a moment. "Cowboy movies?"

"Certainly not! They bristle at the very sight of the Wild West and in such a state it's impossible to put them to sleep. But if we show them a neorealistic film, particularly if it's in black and white, first they applaud and then they become totally engrossed in watching it. Soon, however, they start to yawn. Within ten minutes the cage resounds with collective snoring."

"Unbelievable!"

"That's nothing. There are even more unusual ways to put circus animals to sleep. If you only knew what we have to do for the seals and eagles. But I won't bother you anymore with that. I hope that what I told you has helped you get a better picture of our job."

"Certainly."

"That's good. And now let me get down to the main reason for my late visit. I'm here to tell you about a dream I had not long ago."

"So, that's it."

"I don't usually dream and when I do it's always about people I know very well, but this was an exception. I dreamed about you."

"Me?"

"You. Strange, don't you think?"

"Well, in a manner of speaking."

"But the dream itself was really strange. You were traveling in an airplane. The flight was very long. You dozed off. The shaking of the aircraft woke you suddenly, as though you'd entered an area of turbulence. You opened your eyes and were first surprised by the fact that the seats to your left and right were empty. You remembered quite well that a plump woman and a young man with a butch haircut had been sitting there. Do you know anyone who fits those descriptions?"

"No."

"Fine. You looked towards the other side of the aisle. The three seats there were also empty. This worried you. Although the 'fasten seatbelt' sign was on, you opened your seatbelt and slowly stood up. You were in the front part of the airplane so there were only a few rows of seats in front of you. They were also empty. This seriously disturbed you. All that was left was to look behind you, but you were reluctant to do so. It's not hard to imagine, is it, what you found there?"

"It isn't."

"Your suspicions came true. You were the only passenger in economy class. A shudder went down your spine. Confusion and fear turned you to stone for some time, as you stared at the rows of empty seats."

"That's not acting very bravely."

"No, but who could blame you? I was panic-stricken too, even though all this was happening to you, not me. Finally, you came to your senses. You decided to look for one of the crew members. Maybe there was a stewardess behind the curtain that divided off the first class area. You didn't put much hope in it, but what else could you do?"

"Nothing."

"Unfortunately, as you feared, there was neither a stewardess nor any passengers in first class. Everything was eerily empty, and the relentless shaking of the plane only increased your unease. Without much hope you made your way towards the pilots' cabin. There had to be someone there."

"Aren't passengers strictly forbidden there?"

"Yes, but this was a crisis situation. You weren't going to go back to your seat and wait for things to sort themselves out, were you?"

"No."

"When you peeked hesitantly into the pilots' cabin, however, after no one responded to your knocking, you were sorry you hadn't gone back to your seat and waited. Sometimes ignorant bliss is better than terrifying knowledge."

"The pilots were gone as well?"

"Without a trace. But it wasn't just their empty seats that terrified you. What you saw out the front window forced you to run from the cabin as fast as your legs could carry you. The plane was headed for an enormous, craggy mountain. My blood ran cold when I saw it. I was filled with relief when you closed the door firmly behind you. Thank you."

"You're welcome."

"But the relief didn't last long. As soon as you turned from the door, the lights went out. You were in total darkness. You'd been standing there uncertainly for a few moments, thinking of what to do next, when you heard an ominous sound coming from behind the curtain that partitioned off economy class. Do you know what it was?"

"The crash of wings falling off?"

"Even worse. The roar of a blazing fire. You stuck

your head through the curtain against your will and what a sight you beheld. There was a raging fire in the rear half of the plane, advancing out of control. It would soon reach you."

"I have a phobia about fire."

"I hate it too. You closed the curtain hurriedly and went back to the middle of first class. You realized you were in a trap. You couldn't go forward or backward. Panic had already started to get the upper hand when you noticed a thin strip of light under the door to the toilet on the left. You didn't hesitate a moment and reached the door in two steps."

"In spite of the darkness?"

"In spite of the darkness. You couldn't find the handle right away, though. As you searched for it in fear, fire reached the curtain and it went up in flames. At the same time, a terrible racket could be heard behind the door to the pilots' cabin as though everything was breaking to pieces in there."

"How stressful."

"Just imagine what it was like to dream it. Finally, in the somewhat better light, you found the round knob and turned it feverishly. But nothing happened. The door stayed closed, as though there was someone in the toilet. Even though you could feel the intense heat of the fire, you were covered in cold sweat. You tried again, more forcefully, and the lock finally released. You opened the door, but didn't go inside. In fact, you jerked back a little and raised your hands above your head."

"Why?"

"Because of the radiance. There was such a glare in the toilet that you couldn't look inside. What you really wanted to do was close the door again, but the rapid development of events wouldn't let you. Fire had already engulfed two rows of first class seats and something was just about to break violently out of the pilots' cabin. You had no choice. You walked into the light and quickly closed the door behind you."

"That's the end, isn't it?"

"Yes. How did you know?"

"Intuition."

"I hope you found it interesting, in spite of being unfinished. I took quite a risk coming here to tell it to you. And that's only half the trip. I only hope I manage to return to my room without being seen. Wish me luck."

"Good luck."

The woman stood up and headed for the door. I had to remind her too.

"You forgot the inkpot."

The reply was brief once again. "No, I didn't."

She opened the door just enough to slip through and quickly stole down the hall.

I picked up the book again, but this time didn't have a chance to read one single line. I'd just opened it to the place that was marked when there was a knock on the door. Before I could say anything, the nurse stuck her head inside.

"Still not sleeping?"

"No."

"Very good!"

She smiled at me again before she withdrew her head.

I sighed and closed the book, sensing what was to come. And indeed, just a few moments later another knock was heard, sharp but slow. Again, I was not required to give permission. The door opened before I had said a word and a tall, heavyset man entered the room. He had thick gray hair and a mustache to match. The collar of his short, tight hospital robe was raised. A large, curved unlighted pipe was clenched in his teeth. There was a sizable blotter in his left hand.

I was just about to say it was too late for a visit, but

he pre-empted me, putting his right index finger to his lips. Although I didn't understand the meaning of this warning, I consented with a curt nod.

Standing by the door, the visitor first examined the room carefully. This clearly didn't satisfy him because, without removing his finger from his lips, he made an additional inspection. He went into the bathroom and stayed there briefly. I heard the sound of the plastic curtains on the bathtub being moved and the toilet being flushed. Coming out, he went up to the small closet. He opened it quickly, coming face to face with several items of my clothing. Finally, he approached my bed, knelt down and looked under it.

When he got up, his finger was no longer at his lips. He didn't address me, however, until he had settled into the armchair where the previous two visitors had sat. He put the blotter next to the goose quills and ink-pot.

"Good evening," he said at last.

"Good evening," I replied rather coolly, returning the book to the bedside table.

"I'm from the floor below you, room 223."

"Nice to meet you," I said in the same cool tone.

"Are you alone?"

"Isn't that what one would expect, given that this is a hospital and it's rather late?"

"Expect, yes, but if you were in my line of work you'd know you should never take things for granted."

"Your line of work?"

"Yes. Until retirement I was a circus detective."

"I had no idea that circuses have detectives."

"Of course they do. You might well say that there would be no circus without us."

"Really?"

"Yes. You can't imagine what a dangerous place it is. Not a single show goes by, almost, without some serious threat."

"I never would have thought."

"Of course you wouldn't. Great care is taken that news about the security risks isn't leaked to the public. It would frighten away the spectators, and we simply couldn't allow that to happen. Tell me yourself—would you go to the circus if you knew your life was at risk as you innocently enjoyed the show?"

"No, I wouldn't."

"There, you see. The danger, though, is considerably less than it appears thanks to the vigilance of circus detectives. I don't want to sound boastful, but we are proud of our skill and cunning. Nothing escapes us regardless of how cleverly and deviously it is planned. Have you ever heard of an accident in a circus?"

"No."

"That is the best confirmation of our success. But we certainly don't have an easy time of it. If you only knew what vicious types we have to deal with. The circus seems to attract the most deranged minds. There must be some reason for that."

"In all probability."

"Here, you be the judge. I'll give you a few truly strange cases. In just a few words, of course, because as you yourself said, it's late. I hope you'll find them interesting."

I was cornered. "I hope so too."

"Let's first take the case of the checkroom attendant poisoner who only had three fingers on each hand, owing to an accident. What a devious plan he tried to carry out, crushed by this loss! He was prevented in the nick of time, thereby averting casualties of great proportions. Do you know how many lives were endangered?"

"No."

"One hundred sixty-eight."

"One hundred sixty-eight!"

"That's right. He managed to sprinkle one of the

most poisonous powders that exists into that many pairs of gloves before he was exposed. Had his plan succeeded, the spectators would have put on their gloves as they left the circus, never suspecting the danger. No one would have noticed anything wrong because he'd placed barely a few specks of powder. By the time they reached home, nothing could have saved them. It was enough for just one grain to come into contact with their skin, so very tiny it easily entered the body through the pores and reached the bloodstream. This would soon lead to cardiac arrest, seemingly without any reason. Not even the most exhaustive autopsy would have revealed any trace."

"Terrible!"

"Terrible, you bet. But wait until you hear the case of the female fire fighter with arsonist inclinations. But she wasn't an ordinary firebug, the kind we have no trouble dealing with. Here it required utmost ingenuity for us to connect her to the unusual incidents that started to accompany every show when she was on duty. The day could have been perfectly clear, but as soon as the spectators entered, heavy storm clouds would appear out of nowhere."

"Out of the blue?"

"That's what it seemed like. Soon there would be torrential rain, thunder and lightning. As the show moved along, the storm would become more and more violent. The circus, of course, has regulation lightning rods, but there's a limit to everything. When it reached ninety-seven thunderbolts a minute, we became seriously worried."

"Ninety-seven a minute!"

"Yes. A real cannonade. One more strike and the system would have collapsed with the circus tent blazing like a gigantic pyre. Everything would have burned."

"Dreadful! What did you do?"

"It became clear to us that such frequency could not

be natural, so we set out to look for whoever was causing it. And we certainly had something to find. One of the arsonist's distant ancestors on her father's side had been burned at the stake because of his diabolical gift for calling up a hurricane. It wasn't clear whether she was his reincarnation or had only inherited his destructive powers. Either way, as soon as we removed the female fire fighter, the storms came to an end."

"You must have been relieved."

"You bet. There's no letup in our work, however. We'd just solved this case when we came up against the serial killer usher. He would put an insect surreptitiously on the lower part of the ticket he returned to the spectators after taking them to their seats. Although minuscule and seemingly harmless, it is one of nature's deadliest creatures. Its sting causes instantaneous suffocation."

"How awful!"

"Yes. Luckily, we stopped him before a single victim fell, but if we hadn't, it would have been a true massacre. He intended to kill every circus spectator whose name had at least two vowels."

"What did he have against those poor people?"

"Nothing, of course. The deranged state of his mind had its roots in a childhood trauma. The usher's mother was a member of a fanatical sect and she forced him to learn how to read, although he was barely three years old. Whenever he misread a letter, she punished him with an electric shock. When he couldn't read a consonant he got one shock, and for a vowel it was two shocks."

"It must have been very painful."

"Indubitably. But does that justify his intention to take revenge on the innocent, and at such a harmless place as a circus?"

"No, of course."

"In any case, there are worse fates for children. When

one of the circus cleaning ladies was a little girl, her lustful stepfather had had his sadistic way with her for years. This left such deep scars in her that she decided to hurt as many similar short, bald, overweight, middle-aged men as possible. And boy did she hurt them! As she was cleaning the stands before the show, when no one was looking she painted the seat backs with a colorless, odorless liquid. She'd stolen it from some military laboratory where she'd previously worked. The person sitting there wouldn't suspect that they'd been condemned to death accompanied with unimaginable suffering."

"That's not possible!"

"Yes it is. Not right away but about three months later. The agony would start with exhaustion, a high temperature and bloody diarrhea, and in the final phases it resembled the worst forms of leprosy. The sick would be covered with scabs and open wounds, and in the end pieces of flesh would fall off."

"Gruesome."

"Most certainly. Luckily, no one died that way. As with all the other help in the circus, the cleaning lady was kept under constant observation, and she was thus prevented at the last moment. We never did find out, though, how she knew where the spectators that physically resembled her stepfather would sit. She refused to tell us, although she was offered a greatly reduced prison sentence in return."

"What a wonderful bedtime story," I said, after the visitor had finished.

"How do you think I feel? My sleep became disturbed as soon as I got a job in the circus. I thought the situation would improve after retirement, but it didn't. You can't imagine what I still dream. I wake up in a cold sweat almost every night. For example, I dreamed about you not long ago. Believe it or not."

I sighed. "I believe you."

He looked at me suspiciously, seemed about to ask me something, but refrained.

"I presumed you would be interested in hearing the dream. That is actually why I came. It won't last long."

I almost sighed again. "I'm listening."

"You were on a train. You were in the corridor trying to find your compartment, but without success. You were certain it was somewhere close by, but you just couldn't find it. It crossed your mind to look at your ticket to see where your seat was located. You checked through all your pockets, but there was no ticket."

"How awkward."

"You wondered if the conductor could help you so you went to look for him. You stopped in front of his compartment at the end of the corridor. You knocked but no one answered. You pressed the handle, but the door was locked. You stood there for a moment, uncertain what to do."

"I should have kept looking for him."

"That's just what you did. You went into the next car. The corridor stretching before you was completely empty. You hesitated a moment, then headed down it. What else could you do?"

"Nothing."

"You reached another conductor's compartment, but the same thing happened once again. No one answered your knock and the door was locked. This filled you with apprehension."

"Small wonder."

"You thought things over, then concluded that you actually had no choice. There was no sense in going back. You knew what awaited you. All you could do was keep going forward. Someone was bound to appear—anyone, not just the conductor—to help you out."

"But no one appeared?"

"No one. When you entered the corridor of the next

car it echoed emptily. Then you decided to go into the first compartment there. If nothing else, you might find a free seat until you cleared things up about your place. But that door turned out to be locked too."

"That one too?"

"Yes. Filled with foreboding, you rushed to the next compartment, but the same thing happened. You practically ran from compartment to compartment, briskly trying every handle, although it was already clear to you that none of the doors would be open."

"Quite unpleasant."

"The apprehension inside you quickly grew into panic. You headed for the next car, but a surprise awaited you. There was no next car."

"I reached the locomotive?"

"There was no locomotive."

"Well, what was there?"

"Nothing. That was the end of the train. But the lack of a locomotive didn't stop the train from rushing ahead pell-mell. Not far away yawned the opening to a tunnel. You quickly returned to the corridor, frightened by the black pit ready to swallow you up."

"I really don't like tunnels."

"Now you were completely panic-stricken. You ran back down the corridor, as though this could save you from entering the tunnel."

"People act irrationally when overcome by panic."

"When you reached the other end of the car, you stopped dead in your tracks. There was nothing there anymore. The rest of the train had disappeared without a trace. But that's not all. A tunnel just like the one in front was quickly approaching the back of the car."

"A tunnel was rushing at the train?"

"At the only remaining car. You went back to the corridor again. You ran down it, but stopped in the middle, realizing that you were trapped. Totally disoriented, you watched as the darkness of two tunnels drew nearer and nearer to both ends of the car. In just a few minutes they would meet."

"And the lights in the corridor?"

"They weren't on. When the two darknesses touched, you were in the pitch black. Then you noticed something you would have overlooked if you could see. A strip of light was shining under the door of the compartment facing you."

"At least there was some benefit from the darkness."

"But what good was it since the door was locked? You'd tried to open it not long before when you tried them all. You probably wouldn't have tried again if you hadn't been compelled by what now reached your ears. A crashing sound could be heard from both ends of the corridor, as though the car had collided with something simultaneously at both ends."

"As though one collision wouldn't be enough."

"Yes, everything is exaggerated in dreams. For better or for worse you pressed down on the handle and pulled it towards you. The relief that overcame you when the door opened without resistance was only briefly confounded by the tremendous radiance shining out of the compartment, blinding you. You hesitated a moment, but the noise was now very close and left you no time for second thoughts. You entered the light and quickly closed the door behind you."

"So I saved myself, then?"

"Well, that's not clear. That's when I woke up."

"Too bad."

"Yes, but that's how it is with dreams. They often stop at the most exciting moment. Well, now, I won't bore you any longer. It really is late. Good night."

"Good night," I replied.

He got up and headed for the door. He had already grabbed hold of the knob when he turned around.

"Listen to my advice," he said in a low voice. "Be

constantly on the alert. You never know where danger might lurk. Things are often not what they seem."

He placed his finger to his lips again. I pointed to the blotter on the table without saying a word. He just waved his hand dismissively and opened the door. He peered outside briefly, then went into the hall without looking back.

I wavered for a moment about whether to pick up the book again. I had intended to spend the evening reading, but things had turned out otherwise, unfortunately. It seems there isn't any peace even in a hospital room. I decided to go to sleep, not only because it was late but because my head was full of everything that had been told to me, making it difficult to focus on the book.

I reached for the switch on the bedside table lamp, but my hand stopped halfway. The door opened without any knock and the nurse stepped inside, carrying a bunch of paper under her left arm. It was yellow, like parchment.

"Finally," she said with a loud sigh. "You can't believe how much work I had. But that's how it is in a hospital. Nothing happens for nights on end, and then you're needed everywhere at the same time."

She came up to the bed, removed a case from the breast pocket of her coat and took a thermometer out of it.

"Open wide!" she said in a tone that allowed no objection.

I opened my mouth obediently. When my lips closed around the glass tube, the nurse headed for the armchairs, settling in the one the visitors hadn't occupied. She put the paper next to the other objects on the coffee table.

"Working in a hospital isn't easy. On nights like this I'm sorry I left my previous job. Take a guess, where do you think it was?"

I shrugged my shoulders.

"If you guessed all night you'd never hit it. In a circus."

I tried to say something, but it came out completely unintelligible.

"I know it seems strange to you. Many people close to me regarded it with suspicion, even scorn. In the end they convinced me to change jobs, even though I knew I would regret it. There were lots of good things about being a nurse in a circus, and only a few bad. But there was one thing I liked best. Do you know what it was?"

I shook my head silently.

"No one died. I didn't lose a single patient in the circus. There is no place in the world as harmless and benign as the circus."

If my mouth hadn't been full I might have mentioned something of what the retired detective had told me. As it was, I continued to listen.

"Actually, not only did no one die but there weren't any medical problems at all, with the exception of a minor injury from time to time that could have been taken care of without my assistance. In that regard I had almost no obligations. But if you assume the reason I liked the time I spent in the circus is because I was idle, then you are wrong."

She looked at me reproachfully. I tried to indicate that I thought nothing of the kind, but I'm not sure I succeeded.

"I was up to my ears in work, but of another kind. I helped the performers get physically in shape for their acts. You might think that no expertise is needed, but that's far from the truth. An entire branch of sports medicine is devoted to warming up. It's a real science."

I had to nod before she would continue.

"It was actually beneficial to both parties. I warmed them up for the strenuous acts awaiting them, and in return I came to know those wonderful people in exceptional moments."

She noted my bewilderment and smiled again.

"The preparation was not only physical but mental, the latter no less important. They had to enter a special state of mind. Without that nothing could be accomplished in the circus ring. And each performer had a special way of reaching full concentration. Do you know, for example, what the women trapeze artists did?"

I shook my head.

"Mathematics."

She waited for a fitting expression of disbelief to appear on my face.

"Yes, mathematics, not ordinary but higher math. As they practiced under my supervision, they solved problems that would do credit to a professional mathematician. Without any assistance, not even pencil and paper. They did it all in their heads. And really fast. They were even better than a computer. All you could do was stand there and watch them in amazement."

I reached for the thermometer to take it out for a moment and say something to this, but she gestured with her finger not to do it.

"And they loved to compete with each other," she continued. "Which one of them, for example, could find as many numbers as possible belonging to a particularly complex series, in a very short time. Did you ever try something like that?"

The thermometer made an arched movement from left to right.

"Better not if math isn't your strong point. It can give you a terrible headache. I know from personal experience. It was even harder to follow the discussions among the jugglers. During their warm-ups they dealt exclusively with theological problems. You never would have thought that, would you?"

The thermometer went back and forth again.

"It's all the more unusual given the fact that jugglers

are atheists down to the last one. You might even say fundamentalist atheists. This, however, did not stop them from being superbly knowledgeable about matters of faith. If you'd only heard their scholarly discussions, citing leading church figures, as though each and every one of them had graduated from the seminary. What subtleties were involved! I had no idea that religion could be so intricate. Have you ever wrestled with the quandaries that crop up there?"

The thermometer replied negatively for the third time.

"You're lucky. I certainly don't advise you to try it. Believe me, you could easily lose yourself forever. But there are even more difficult things than theology. Listening to the women illusionists as they warmed up, gaily chatting about time, sometimes I was overcome by a genuine dizzy spell. I barely held onto my sanity. Have you ever wondered about time?"

I mumbled something, hoping that it was unintelligible enough.

"If you want to keep your wits about you, stay away from it. Chasms gape behind this seemingly simple question that will swallow you up forever. It's enough just to start thinking about what would happen if you were to go back into the past, and you're done for. I still don't understand how the illusionists managed to debate the paradoxes that spring up everywhere as though they were ordinary concerns, while I needed tremendous willpower to hold onto my reason. But not even that was the worst."

She stopped for a moment and sighed.

"I had the worst time with the clowns. They were interested in nothing less than the ultimate questions. They even had virulent arguments about them. Once they almost came to blows. If I hadn't been there to separate them, anything might have happened. What led to the quarrel was their complete disagreement over a fundamental philosophical quandary. One of the clowns claimed that everything that happened in the universe was the product of chance, while the other considered that everything was the result of some purpose. What do you feel about that?"

I opened my arms with a helpless shrug, indicating the thermometer.

"Yes. The smartest thing is actually not to feel anything. If only I'd been able to resist the temptation to go into the details of that problem. But I didn't, unfortunately. The clowns had a nice time shouting at each other, getting it out of their system, then headed for the ring to do their number, perfectly prepared, and I was left to deal with that fiendish question. They planted a seed in my brain that I couldn't get rid of by any means. It became an obsession that threatened to destroy everything: my sleep, appetite, natural optimism, enthusiasm for my work. Even my complexion. I had to take two weeks of unpaid leave, at the peak of the season, to get back to normal."

I shook my head in sympathy.

"But, as I said, in spite of these minor difficulties, I have very nice memories of the circus. I like to remember it, and sometimes even dream about it. Why, I dreamed about it not long ago, which is nothing unusual, but it was certainly strange to find you in the dream."

I pointed at myself with both hands, trying to act shocked.

"Yes, you. And not in some minor part but as the main character. It was as if you were dreaming my dream, not me. Shall I tell it to you?"

I nodded my head.

"You stepped into a radiant room. Blinded by the bright light, you couldn't see a thing. You were completely confused. You didn't know where you'd come from, although you were vaguely aware that you had entered there seeking refuge from some great misfortune, so you couldn't retreat. You turned around, squinting. At that moment there was a round of applause. This only increased your bewilderment. But your eyes gradually adjusted to the brightness. You made out a line of people in pairs beginning a few steps away from you. You hesitated briefly, then headed towards it. When you reached the first clapping and smiling pair you saw a tall tram driver in a raincoat with a child's head peering out of it, and an amateur magician in a t-shirt, shorts and clogs. You bowed to them, then continued to the next pair. The man on the left was holding two umbrellas, one open and one in a cover, while the man on the right was wearing dark glasses and holding a cage with a hamster tirelessly turning the wheel. You returned their smiles, then stopped briefly. The next two pairs were not only animals but they were asleep. First there was an elephant and a lion, and then a giraffe and a snoring monkey. You passed by them on tiptoe so as not to wake them. Then you came to a checkroom attendant clapping grotesquely with three-fingered hands and a female fire fighter who seemed to have sparks of electricity coming out of her, and after them was an usher repeating vowels over and over and a cleaning lady with a pockmarked face. For some reason all four appeared contrite and repentant. The line ended with circus performers. The first pair was a trapeze artiste and a juggler. She was tall and slim, dressed in a turquoise tricot. She stroked your cheek as you passed by her. The juggler stopped throwing rings for a moment to pat you on the back. At the end were an illusionist and a clown. She was wearing a long black gown and a large silver ball floated in front of her. The ball rose a bit so she could bend down and kiss you lightly on the forehead. The clown opened his arms wide when you turned towards him and gave you a big bear hug, then pointed to something up ahead.

You looked in that direction and saw a small table covered to the floor with dark-red felt. On it were three goose quills, a bronze inkpot, a blotter and paper. Suddenly the applause became deafening, as though you were surrounded by an invisible audience greeting you with delight before your act."

She fell silent, looked at me carefully, then added in an apologetic voice, "There's nothing else. That is the end of the dream."

She sat there a moment longer, then got up, came over to the bed and took the thermometer out of my mouth. She turned it a bit to see the line of mercury. When she had read the temperature, she sighed deeply, then put the thermometer back in its case and in her pocket.

"Its time to go to sleep."

She took hold of the edge of the sheet and blanket, pulled them a little and covered my head with them. I heard the click of the switch on the bedside lamp, her footsteps walking away, then the opening and closing of the door.

I waited for a while, lying still, and then lifted the covers off me and got up. I didn't turn on the light. I felt with my feet for the slippers by the side of the bed and put them on. The way to the door was marked by a bright strip of light under it. I took hold of the handle, but didn't press down right away. I turned around. There was nothing behind me but darkness and silence. Nothing that made me want to stay there any longer.

I squinted when I began opening the door, ready for the light that would flood over me.

3. The Hotel Room

THERE WAS A KNOCK on my hotel room door.

I picked up the video player remote control from the coffee table in front of me and pressed the "stop" button. The television screen turned a dark blue and the sound went off.

"Come in," I said, looking towards the door.

A woman appeared wearing a dark-red uniform, carrying a basket full of apricots. She was as tiny as a munchkin. The oversized cylindrical cap she wore descended to her ears, covering more than half her forehead.

"Please excuse me for bothering you. I am your maid. I just wanted to leave this."

She raised the basket a bit, smiling.

"Thank you."

She went over to the left side of the room, where a long cabinet extended almost the whole length of the lateral wall. She placed the basket next to the one I'd found when I entered the room. It contained peaches.

Returning to the door, the maid stopped.

"Should you need anything, just ring once right here." She indicated a white button on the wall underneath the light switch. "I am at your service."

I returned her smile and repeated, "Thank you."

The maid bowed and her cap slid forward, dropping down to her eyes. She pushed it back with a look of discomfort. Holding it with both hands, she bowed again. Then she quickly left the room.

I pressed the "play" button on the remote control. The movie returned to the screen, but it was not destined to stay there very long. After barely a few scenes, there came another knock.

I frowned. I don't like to be interrupted in the middle of a movie. Perhaps I should have put a Do Not Disturb sign on the door. I looked around but didn't see any sign to hook on the outside doorknob. I sighed, then stopped the player once again.

"Enter," I said with an edge of reproof.

A woman entered, also wearing a hotel uniform. She was in her early fifties and had a fair amount of excess weight that emphasized her matronly curves. She was wearing a conical cap that seemed one size too small, so it only covered the crown of her head. She stood at the door, her hands folded.

"Please excuse me for bothering you," she said in a voice that was somewhat deeper than one would expect given her appearance. "I am the hotel mine guide. I just wanted to see whether you might need our services."

"Hotel mine?"

"Yes. It's absolutely natural, you can be sure of that. We don't stoop to trickery like our competition. Nothing is artificial here."

"I didn't know the hotel had a mine."

"Why of course, what are you thinking of? This is a five-star hotel, after all. It was actually the mine that helped us receive such a high ranking. And we could have had at least one star more if the mine produced silver or gold instead of just zinc. But what's to be done? We are satisfied with what we have. The vein is very rich."

"Where is the mine?"

She pointed down with her index finger. "Right below us, just as prescribed by the regulations. Would you like to visit it?"

I shook my head. "No, thank you."

"It isn't at all tiring. An elevator takes you all the way down the deepest shaft. It moves so fast you're down there in no time."

I shook my head again.

"Is it perhaps the safety factor that worries you? If that's what's wrong, rest assured. Not a single visitor has yet had an unpleasant experience in the mine. In addition, should anything happen, even something terrible, as a hotel guest you are insured."

"It's not about that. What would I do in a mine?"

"Isn't it obvious?" replied the guide with a question. "You would mine zinc."

"Why would I mine zinc?"

She smiled. "You might not be aware, but the price of zinc is steadily rising on the world market. And hotel guests are allowed to take all the ore they dig. It hasn't always been like that, there used to be limits, but they were lifted not long ago. Naturally, you aren't expected literally to dig. That would not be in line with a hotel of this category. You can use state of the art mining equipment, and there are experts to show you how it works. If you are hardworking, your efforts will certainly be repaid. Zinc has made some of our guests quite wealthy."

"I don't intend to become wealthy."

She eyed me reprovingly. "Quite so. But that makes no difference. The mine offers other features besides extracting zinc."

"What features?"

"That depends on the guest's affinities. If you have an adventurous spirit, you can investigate the undeveloped parts of the mine. There are plenty of abandoned corridors that are guaranteed to be unsafe, without lighting or ventilation. Some of them have poisonous gases, others are flooded with ground water, some are on the verge of collapse, and one is linked to stories about the ghosts of dead miners. I must warn you, however, that your basic insurance is not sufficient for this. You would have to pay a supplemental premium."

"Why would anyone expose themselves to dangers in such places, and pay for it to boot?"

"You would be surprised at how many people stay in the hotel just for the sake of having exciting experiences in the wilds of the mine. Some spend their whole stay with us down there. We've even lost all trace of several, but the hotel bears no responsibility. Guests go there at their own risk."

"I don't want to go there."

"Quite so. Perhaps you would like to visit our mine's summer resort. There you would be completely safe, surrounded by absolute comfort."

"Summer resort?"

"Yes. Our hotel is particularly proud of this amenity. In this respect we are far ahead of the competition. Guests can spend summer vacations the whole year round. There is nothing to indicate that you're deep underground. You have the impression of being on a seashore with the sun high in a blue sky, translucent turquoise water, fine sand and palms swaying in the breeze. We have water skiing of course, and surfing was recently introduced. Guests leave there as tanned as if they'd been in the tropics. If you want to get the rest you truly deserve, then our summer resort is the right choice for you."

"I'm not here to rest."

"Quite so. Would you be interested in trying some form of creative activity? The hotel mine has not overlooked guests with such inclinations. The mine has a special department for those who want to devote themselves to art."

"How is it possible to devote oneself to art in a mine?"

"Oh, it's quite possible, yes indeed. You can't imagine how many works of art have been created here. It would be excellent publicity for the hotel, but unfortunately we must be discreet. For some reason those who've created something here don't want word to get out that they found inspiration for their work underground."

"What sort of artistic inspiration is there underground?"

"I'm not an artist so I'm unable to give you an answer, but something clearly exists. If that weren't true, would there be waiting lists for our artists' cave?"

"Artists' cave?"

"Yes. It was discovered by accident. Located at the very bottom of the mine, it is spacious, full of stalactites and stalagmites, and an underground river runs through it. A narrow, twisting opening leads to the cave, so the only way to get in and out is to crawl. But this disadvantage has not deterred artists of all kind—musicians, writers, sculptors, painters—who can barely wait to seclude themselves inside. Not a single one has yet returned from the cave without a new work of art."

"Really?"

"It seems impossible, but believe me it works, even if you're a beginner or have no talent. I highly recommend you give it a try. The first time is free, so you have nothing to lose. There might be a way to cut you in at the front of the line, but I can't promise anything. The word has spread about the artists' cave. It's in great demand."

"Thank you, but I don't think that will be necessary."

"Quite so. If you change your mind, however, be sure to let me know. We are at your service."

"I won't change my mind. This will suit me just fine."

It seemed as if there was nothing left to say, but she continued to stand by the door.

"I shouldn't tell you this," she said at last, hanging

back. "The management is very strict with regard to hotel secrets. But you won't give me away, I hope."

"I won't."

"Although you feel that you are just fine, I don't advise you to stay in this room."

"Why?"

"Because it brings bad luck."

"You don't say. How's that?"

"Four suicides were committed here."

"Four?"

"Yes. And they certainly weren't ordinary, unimaginative hotel suicides of the kind that no one blinks an eye at anymore. These four were quite exceptional, each in its own way. The first one in particular made quite an impression on me. Would you like me to tell you about it?"

My eyes dropped to the remote control in my hand.

"I won't take up much of your time," the mine guide hastened to add. "You'll see, the story is truly remarkable."

I sighed. "All right. But please be brief."

"Of course. The suicide was a young man who had registered under a false name. His real identity was never discovered, nor were the motives behind his suicide. He left no farewell letter. He had brought a CD player and very powerful amplifier to the hotel with him, enough to wire an entire auditorium for sound. We, of course, are equipped with the latest sound equipment, so this aroused a bit of suspicion, but who could have suspected what this equipment would be used for? The young man was found lying in the bathroom, in an empty bathtub. He was wearing headphones hooked up to the amplifier, which was laid across his chest along with the CD player. Blood poured out of all the openings in his head: nose, mouth, eyes, ears. The unbearably loud sound was what killed him. It was so strong that those who first entered the bathroom had to put their hands over their ears, even though the music was only coming out of the headphones. The police making the onsite investigation did not report what the poor young man was listening to, so we never found out what piece of music led to his death."

She stopped talking and stared at me fixedly. "A very strange suicide, wouldn't you say?"

"Very," I agreed.

"If you want, I'll make arrangements for reception to give you another room."

"No, thank you. I'll stay in this one."

"Quite so. If I can be of any assistance, please ring twice."

She indicated the same white button as the maid. Then she bowed, turned around and left the room.

I glanced at the door to the bathroom, and then raised the remote control towards the player. I didn't have time to start the film, however, because another knock was heard at the door. Before I had a chance to respond, the pint-sized maid entered the room. The new basket she carried was full of strawberries.

"Pay no attention to me," she said with a smile and a bow, holding onto her cap. She went up to the cabinet, put the basket next to the other two, and hastened back to the door. She bowed once again and quickly left the room.

I looked at the three baskets for a moment, and then pressed the "play" button. The film ran even less time than before. The knock that came was thunderous, as though someone was banging their fists on the door. I stopped the movie with an angry motion.

"Come in!" I said sharply.

The woman who entered corresponded perfectly to the style of the knocking. She was wearing a hotel uniform and a four-sided pyramid-shaped cap that was firmly pulled onto her head, but a worker's outfit such as those worn in a heavy industrial plant would have suited her much better. She was in her forties, of medium height, with a broad neck, large muscular arms, almost no waist and legs that resembled sturdy pillars. When she spoke, however, her thin, squeaky voice clashed utterly with her appearance.

"I'm sorry to disturb you. I'm the hotel packing plant guide. If you will allow me, I'd like to briefly acquaint you with what we offer."

I stared at her. "Packing plant?"

"Yes. It covers the whole second floor. It is an entire complex that focuses on raising animals, something that makes us especially proud. Here you can rest assured that we know the pedigree of literally every bite you eat, not like in lower class hotels, and even some of our own rank, where you have to hold your breath whenever you put something in your mouth. Have you tried our food yet?"

"No, I haven't."

"You'll appreciate its exceptional quality the moment you taste it. Our guests even have the privilege of personally choosing the animal they will eat. Of course, sometimes during a short stay they can't eat a whole animal, particularly if it's big. A large steer, for example. But whatever is left of the chosen animal that the guest is not able to eat in the hotel can be purchased at a large discount when he leaves. Some people check into our hotel solely for the chance to purchase top-quality meat at a giveaway price. You shouldn't pass it up either."

"I don't need meat."

"Very well. Would you perhaps be interested in watching an animal being butchered?"

I shook my head. "How could that possibly interest me?"

"You would be no exception by any means. If you only knew what an increase there's been in the number of overnights in our hotel since we've made it possible to watch the butchering either in person or on a closed circuit television. We were amazed to find out how many people are curious to know how it's done and how much they are ready to pay to satisfy their curiosity. Have you ever seen an animal butchered?"

"No, I haven't."

"Of course, we don't do it in a primitive way, the process has been rendered utterly humane, but it's still a shocking experience. If you think that the butchering attracts only sadistic types and psychopaths then you are highly mistaken. The most frequent spectators are family people, there are even more women than men. If we were to allow children to attend, they'd certainly be the most numerous. Although the law is not strictly against it, allowing children would nonetheless give us a bad reputation. You no doubt wonder why ordinary people flock to see animals butchered."

"I do."

"Contrary to all expectations, watching a butchering has been shown to have a beneficial effect on neuroses, psychoses and phobias, and who in today's world full of stress and tension does not suffer from those? Ordinary people actually the most, isn't that so? It also provides relief from depression, apathy and low spirits, insomnia and a poor appetite. In such cases you might seek the help of a psychotherapist, to be sure, but why waste your money when it's considerably less expensive here? In addition, we give a three-month guarantee. Do you have any of the ailments I mentioned, perhaps?"

"No, I don't."

"Very well. This, however, is not where it ends. We were quite surprised when it turned out that watching an animal being butchered has a beneficial effect on purely physical ailments. Water on the knee, for example, disappears like magic after two or three sessions. Hemorrhoids quickly shrink and athlete's foot clears up in a flash. Serious cases of crossed eyes and stuttering require a few more treatments. The most difficult is restoring tooth growth, but if the patient is persistent enough there is no lack of success. Are you troubled by any of these maladies?"

"No."

"Please don't be reticent. Everything you tell me will remain strictly between us, just like talking to a doctor. Hotel ethics strictly forbid me from revealing what you tell me to anyone, even the police."

"I have nothing to tell you."

"Very well. Then perhaps you'd like to visit our packing plant spa."

"Packing plant spa?"

"Yes. The great demand for our medical services has led us to expand our activities. The thermal spring under the hotel was also a contributing factor. Although enclosed, the spa is by no means inferior to those that are outside. Quite the contrary. Can you count on perfectly nice weather every day in an open-air spa? Or immaculately clean air that isn't polluted by traffic? Or the complete absence of mosquitoes all summer long?"

I shook my head. "I can't."

"And wait until you see our parks. They are without equal! An ideal place for long, invigorating walks through the lush growth. The tree-lined paths are a particular favorite. Even though the trees are deciduous, their leaves stay green all year round, even the hundred-year-old oak that is under state protection. There is also a lake inhabited by swans. The most popular gathering spot for visitors, however, is the geyser that shoots up all of forty-six meters. Have you ever been near a geyser?"

"No, I haven't."

"Here's a chance to make up for the loss. The main purpose of the spa, of course, is the treatment we offer. We are simply besieged by people suffering from arthritis. Daubing on the spa's mud has a truly healing effect and patients leave us rejuvenated. Infertile women are also quite numerous. Bathing in the spring several times is enough for them to become pregnant. And of late we have been experiencing a genuine invasion of people with a short left leg. The word has spread that our spa works wonders. Allegedly, whoever drinks one hundred twenty-seven and a half liters of mineral water will have their short leg grow to its full length. We immediately issued a disclaimer so we wouldn't be accused of exaggerating the whole thing, but nothing worked. The onslaught of the lame has not subsided, although there is no proof that any of them left here with both legs the same length. But those who believe in miracles don't need proof. You don't have a short left leg, do you?"

"No, I don't."

"You're not bothered by arthritis?"

"No, and I'm not infertile."

"To be sure. Would you like to visit our spa anyway? It's a pleasant experience even if you are perfectly healthy."

"No, I wouldn't, thank you."

"Very well. This is not all the hotel packing plant offers, however. Perhaps you'd be interested in the artists' swimming pool?"

"Artists' swimming pool?"

"Yes. It's an Olympic-sized swimming pool filled with the blood of the butchered animals. The blood is constantly refreshed so it's always clean. The pool is frequented exclusively by artists who carry on erudite discussions about different aspects of creativity while they're in it. This was not the original intention of the pool, but ever since it was accidentally discovered that swimming in blood has a stimulating and inspirational effect on reflections about art, an exclusive club has been founded that has taken a permanent lease on the pool. Entrance is restricted to members only, but I might be able to pull some strings and get you in just once, to try it out. You might like it."

"I won't. Blood disgusts me."

"I understand. One really needs to have a stomach for artistic extravagances. If you are the sensitive type, though, maybe you should change rooms."

"Why?"

"What I have to say is highly confidential. The hotel management has covered it up, but guests come first as far as I'm concerned. I believe that no one has the right to hide the truth from them. Four suicides took place in this room."

"Oh, that."

She looked at me darkly. "You've heard about them?"

"A bit."

"Do you know about the suicide with books?"

"No."

"It's a truly bizarre case. I'd like to tell it to you."

"I don't have a lot of time," I said, raising the remote control.

"I'll make it very short. Just a few sentences. May I?"

I sighed and nodded my head.

"An elderly lady came to the hotel with no fewer than nineteen large suitcases. The bellboys were bewildered at their weight. When the woman was served tea and cookies somewhat later, she was found taking books out of the suitcases. That wasn't too unusual—our guests sometimes bring in much stranger things—but the girl from room service noticed that the books were all identical, as though copies of the same book. Unfortunately, she couldn't make out the title of the work. I'm afraid that will remain a secret forever—along with the woman's identity, by the way—because all the copies were burned. They were used for the poor woman's funeral pyre. Her completely carbonized body was found in the bathroom, and subsequent investigations established what happened after she was left alone. For hours she had patiently torn the pages of each book into tiny pieces and filled the bathtub with them. After she'd destroyed the last copy and the bathtub was overflowing, the woman first disabled the fire alarm on the ceiling with adhesive tape, then sprinkled the bits of paper with gasoline from a bottle she'd brought with her, and finally she sank into the bathtub. When she was on the bottom, all she had to do was strike a match and everything around her burst into flame. An autopsy established that she died of suffocation and not from the flames, but that is little consolation. It was a terrible way to leave this world, wasn't it?"

"Terrible," I agreed.

"If you think that you won't be able to use the bathroom after this, feel free to ask for another room. You won't have to give any reason."

"It's not necessary. I'll keep this one."

"Very well. Should you nevertheless find an opportunity to visit the hotel packing plant, we would be honored. All you have to do is give three rings here and I'll come at once."

She pointed her thumb at the wall behind her.

"Thank you, but I don't think I'll have time."

The packing plant guide's face suddenly dropped in dejection, but she said nothing more. She bowed and left the room.

Yet another knock prevented me from watching the cassette. This time the maid did not wait for me to invite her to enter. She opened the door just enough to squeeze through, then quickly closed it behind her. This time the basket was filled with plums. Her smile and bow were not accompanied by any words. She hastened to the cabinet, added the new basket to the others, and then went back to the door. Before she stole away, she briefly lifted her left index finger to her lips, giving me a sign to keep mum. I nodded my head.

I enjoyed the sight of the colorful fruit for a moment,

and then returned to the film. When a knock was heard in the very first scene, I was annoyed but not surprised. I actually would have been more astonished if there had been no knock. I angrily pressed the "stop" button.

"Enter!" I said, almost shouting.

The woman who marched in couldn't have been more than thirty. She was tall and slender. The hotel uniform seemed a little tight on her, while the cube-shaped cap matched the sharp features of her face. She was holding a short stick under her arm. She stood at attention in front of the door and bowed briefly.

"Allow me to introduce myself," she said brusquely, as though reporting. "I am the hotel weapons factory guide."

I looked at her in silence for a few moments. "Do you have one of those too?"

"Of course we do! It's impossible to imagine a hotel of this category without such a factory. Furthermore, ours is located in a prominent place. It covers the entire top floor and roof, not like our competition where everything is quite low-key. In addition, many different types of weapons are produced here, not just light arms as in most other hotels. We can make almost anything the guests want."

"You arm the guests?"

"They arm themselves with tailor-made weapons. Our only role is to provide the needed parts and offer technical assistance. Sometimes it isn't easy to satisfy the guests' desires. They can be very demanding. But we never shrink from a challenge. We are proud of some of the weapons that were created in our factory. You might not be aware, but the first sniper slingshot appeared here. The stealth crossbow too, and so did the electronically guided javelin, the neutron trident, the atomic sword and the laser catapult. But we are proudest of the plasma mace. It has entered all the military encyclopedias. If you need a weapon, regardless of how complex or unusual, you are in the right place. Indulge your fantasies."

"I don't need any weapons."

"Of course. Have you ever thought of becoming a commando? We have an excellent training camp as part of the weapons factory. Not many can match the quality of our equipment and experts. We achieve considerably better results than in other hotels, even those with more stars."

I smiled. "It would be hard to make a commando out of me."

"You're mistaken. We are able to turn a guest in the worst physical and mental shape into a top-notch commando in only twenty-three days. Naturally there are no shortcuts, you have to expect blood, sweat and tears, but in spite of the tremendous exertion no one has yet complained. On the contrary, many return on a regular basis to refresh their skills and keep in shape. And the diploma we offer when you finish commando training opens many doors, even to special units. Quite a few guests started brilliant military careers right here. Would this interest you at all?"

"No, it wouldn't."

"Of course. Perhaps you would like to take one of our higher education courses? The one for hit men is quite popular."

"Hit men?"

"Yes. It does last forty-seven days and the fee is quite high, but the investment certainly pays off. There is always work for a properly trained hit man and his services are richly rewarded. For a modest commission we are happy to help you find customers. In addition, we will provide you with all the necessary weapons and tools. That's included in the price."

"No, thank you."

"Of course. Perhaps you would like to earn the diploma of a certified terrorist?"

There was no need for me to repeat her words in question form. The expression on my face spoke volumes.

She nodded her head. "This is the latest addition to our program. Unfortunately, we are not able to advertise it publicly, even though it would result in great demand. The course instructors are renowned terrorists who are on the wanted lists of all international police. In sixty-three days they will transfer all their hard-won knowledge to you, making you entirely qualified to carry out terrorist acts of the greatest proportions. The cost of this course is necessarily very high, but the income of a hit man is usually small compared to the fees you would receive from terrorist organizations with our diploma. One act would be enough to set you up for life."

"No, thank you," I repeated.

"Of course. If none of this interests you, then you might like to visit our weapons factory ski center. It's located on the roof of the hotel, on a mountain that is not very high, indeed, but is celebrated for its gentle slopes and wonderful conifer forests. We have three first-class ski slopes, for downhill, slalom and cross-country skiing, and they're open at night too. There are two high-speed ski lifts and we recently opened an Olympic ski jump. You can also try the snowmobiles or simply enjoy long walks in the fresh mountain air. The correct low temperature and snow cover are provided all year round."

"I don't like spending time in the mountains."

"Of course. In that case we have one more thing to offer you: the artists' firing range."

"Firing range?"

"That's right. It is frequented by artists, most often writers who, for a variety of reasons, have become afflicted with writer's block. Nothing removes writer's block as successfully as shooting at live targets."

"What live targets?"

"People."

"Writers shoot at people?"

"Yes, but with air guns."

"But air guns can be lethal too."

"They can, that's true. That's why the targets' heads are protected. The writers can only shoot at bare torsos."

"But hitting a bare torso must surely be very painful."

"Yes, it is. The targets, however, do not gripe about it. They stoically bear the pain for the sake of their fat fee. Everyone is happy with this arrangement. The targets get away with some bruises and swellings. It only rarely happens that an air gun pellet breaks a rib. And after only a few direct hits into flesh the writers resume writing as though they'd never had any block. It's even happened that they get down to work right there in the shooting gallery, overcome by a sudden wave of inspiration. If you try it yourself you'll see how beneficial this therapy can be."

"I don't suffer from writer's block."

The weapons factory guide looked at me briefly in silence.

"I wouldn't like to give you the impression that our department is extremely brutal and savage. There are worse places in this hotel. We don't have to go any farther than your room."

"My room?"

"Yes. You certainly aren't aware that it was the scene of no fewer than four suicides."

"I am aware."

"You are?" She looked at me in amazement.

"Yes."

She seemed about to ask me something but changed her mind.

"Of course. One of them was particularly unpleasant, even for me, in spite of the fact that as a soldier I am hardened to various forms of death and dying. I must tell it to you."

"If you really must . . ." I said, nodding my head towards the remote control in my hand.

"In a nutshell. The girl, whose real name was never discovered, brought into the hotel a marble bust, a cement drill, a hook and some rope. She used the drill to make a hole in the bathroom ceiling, above the bathtub. She fixed the heavy-duty hook into it and then attached one end of the rope around the bust and threw the other end over the hook. She lay down in the tub and began to pull on the rope, lifting the bust straight above her head. When it reached the hook, the girl let go of the rope. The bust plummeted like a guillotine and smashed her head. Eyewitnesses say the sight was gruesome. The bathtub was spotted with blood and brains. The police did not report which piece of sculpture was involved or whether it was damaged."

She paused to see what kind of impression this had made on me.

"Gruesome," I said.

"Gruesome, yes. After that no one can expect you to bathe in the same bathtub. You are perfectly within your rights to ask for another room."

"I think I'll stay here."

There was another pause.

"Of course. In any case, should you decide that our services might be needed, just ring four times on this buzzer."

She took the stick from under her arm and touched the button over her shoulder.

I nodded my head.

She bowed curtly once again, and then marched out of the room.

I put my thumb on the "play" button on the remote control, but didn't push it. I raised my eyes to the door expectantly.

But there was no knock. The maid just entered without even turning towards me and headed straight for the cabinet. A fifth basket full of apples joined the others there. The pint-sized woman returned to the door but did not go out. She stopped in front of it.

"I would like to tell you something in confidence."

"Go ahead."

"I'm not just a maid in the hotel."

"Really?"

"Yes. It's actually just a front. My main job is as the hotel cemetery guide."

"Does the hotel have its own cemetery?"

"Any hotel that cares a fig about itself has one. Even the lowest categories are not without a few graves."

"I had no idea."

"Of course not. We keep this a secret because it's against the law. You won't find a word about it in our official brochure. The hotel would lose its license instantly if word got out that it has a cemetery. We have to take every precaution so no one finds us out. Only hand-picked guests are given this honor—those who pass the fruit test."

"Fruit?"

"That's right." She gestured to the left, towards the five baskets on the long cabinet. "Guests have different reactions to the fruit I bring them. The first kind pounce on it right away, without even washing it before they eat it. The second kind change the order of the baskets. The third kind mix the fruit in them and the fourth kind ask me to take out some or all of the baskets. The fifth kind place them around the room. Some immediately empty the baskets into the garbage can, toilet bowl or even throw them out the window. Believe me, there are highly different reactions to the fruit. We evaluate whether or not we can confide in a guest based on their reaction. It is a highly reliable test and has not failed us once. I am happy to be able to tell you that you passed the test."

"Seriously?"

"With flying colors. Would I have mentioned the

hotel cemetery to you otherwise? Even so, if you decide to visit it we'll have to follow a special procedure. We would take you there in a wheelchair, blindfolded and with plugs in your ears, so you don't find out where in the hotel the cemetery is located. This is for your protection as well as ours. The less you know, the better. No one will be able to get you to reveal something you don't know, regardless of the force that is used."

"But why would I want to visit the hotel cemetery?"

"There are lots of valid reasons. First of all, it's not an ordinary cemetery, it's quite special."

"How so?"

"As in all better hotels, our cemetery has a theme. While you might find the graves of prominent scientists, politicians, military leaders, athletes or entertainers in other places, our specialty is artists. We are very proud of our collection of graves of famous musicians, writers, sculptors and painters. Some of them date back not only centuries but even thousands of years."

"But how did you get their graves?"

The former maid did not reply at once. She looked at me inquisitively and then sighed.

"We handle it in various ways. Mostly we get them on the black market."

"Is there a black market for that too?"

"Sure there is. And it is quite extensive. There's no grave that can't be bought if you're willing to pay enough."

"But how can you hide the disappearance of a grave? That would be hard even for the ordinary deceased let alone famous people."

"The whole grave isn't stolen, only the coffin. Outwardly everything stays just as it was. Those who visit the grave don't suspect that there is nothing under the gravestone."

"But that isn't . . . right."

"It isn't, I agree, but when you're pressed by the

competition, you're not very picky when it comes to means. In any case, if we'd been concerned about moral rectitude, someone with fewer scruples would have taken over in a flash. Unlike many other hotels that make do with false graves of the great, everything here is guaranteed authentic. When buying corpses we go to great pains not to be deceived. A DNA analysis is mandatory."

"Even so . . ."

"Recently we started acquiring graves in a very legal way."

"How?"

"We draw up contracts with artists while they're still alive. Not a single one will refuse to bequeath you their earthly remains if you offer the right price. It's a real pleasure doing business with them. They are practical people who don't beat around the bush and hesitate. This way, with a bit of patience, we'll enhance our collection considerably. But it is already exceptional right now. I recommend you visit it without fail. As you know, this opportunity is not open to everyone."

"I'd rather not."

"As a visitor you have the right to take something small from one of the graves—a handful of earth, a sprig of flowers, a piece of the tombstone. If you don't want to keep it for yourself you'll have no trouble selling it to a collector. With our certificate of origin, it will be well worth the trouble."

"No, thank you."

"As you wish. What would you say to the possibility of personally burying an artist?"

"Me bury someone? I'm not a gravedigger."

"It makes no difference. Our professional gravediggers will instruct you in how to do the job. You'll see, even though it is physically demanding, it gives great satisfaction."

"Burying someone gives satisfaction?"

"That's what everyone who's tried it claims. Some come back for that reason alone, even though the supplementary fee for this enjoyment is rather stiff. They say it's an experience beyond compare, and is all the more exceptional the greater the artist you bury. If you are interested, I might be able to get you one of the greats, even with a bit of a discount."

"I'm not interested."

"Perhaps you would like to be buried yourself? Temporarily, of course."

"Temporarily?"

"Yes. You decide how long you want to stay in the grave. Guests can stay underground as long as they like. Some ask us to take them out after just a few minutes, but the average is around two and a half hours. The record is held by a guest who stayed in the grave forty-three hours and six minutes."

"How could someone stay in a grave that long?"

"It's not hard at all. The burial places are very comfortable: they have air conditioning, relaxing music and even a little refrigerator. There is absolutely no light, but the absence of light makes the temporary grave an ideal place for introspective seclusion. All those who come out of them say they truly feel resurrected. Unfortunately, this service is the most expensive we offer, but if you feel you need to come face to face with yourself and make a reckoning of your life, don't complain about the money. A grave is the best place to do it."

"I don't think I need that."

"As you wish. Perhaps you would enjoy a bit of recreation in the cemetery's sports center?"

"The cemetery has a sports center?"

"Yes, quite modern. We have courts and fields for almost every sport, even some exotic ones. For example, you can do underwater archery, swim in quicksand, play antigravity table tennis or mentally lift weights in a hyperbaric chamber."

"Mentally?"

"That's right. Just with the power of thought. The record is seven hundred sixty-four kilograms and believe it or not, it's held by a woman about my height. Physical proportions make absolutely no difference and neither does experience. Beginners are known to achieve exceptional results. Would you like to give it a try? You might have a real knack for it without even being aware."

"I wouldn't, thank you."

"If you prefer classical disciplines, our coaches are exclusively Olympic medal winners. And our training fields are state of the art. Our marathon track is a real thorn in the side of our competition. We are also famous for our training ground for group parachute jumping. And wait until you see our main stadium with sixty-seven thousand two hundred fifty seats, completely covered and with Astroturf! Everyone openly envies us that. You will certainly make no mistake if you decide to use one of our sports amenities."

"I'm afraid I'm not much of a jock."

"As you wish. All I have left to offer you is a visit to the artists' crypt."

I didn't say anything. I just kept my eyes on her.

"It's an original, very old crypt. Artists visit it like they're on a pilgrimage. Apparently the crypt contains works that for one reason or another were never finished: uncompleted novels, half-painted pictures, sculptures just appearing out of the stone, fragmentary compositions. Unfortunately, none of it can be taken out or copied in any way. Even so, it seems to do the artists a lot of good to see what the creators failed to accomplish, so there is quite a line to enter the crypt. Do you perhaps have some unfinished work of art?"

"No, I don't."

"It's unfortunate that none of what we offer attracts you. However, you would find even the hotel cemetery a more pleasant place than staying in this room."

"Do you mean because of the bathroom?" I nodded towards the bathroom door.

"Yes," she said after a moment's hesitation. "Quite an unpleasant thing. Particularly the last suicide."

"I assume that you want to tell me about it?"

"Unless you have something against it."

"I hope you won't be long-winded." I lowered my eyes to the remote control.

"I won't. Just the main points. An elderly gentleman who did not register under his real name came to the hotel with a small suitcase. Later it turned out that he had a small canvas, several tubes of paint and a bottle of paint thinner inside the suitcase. He was found dead in the bathtub. At first glance the cause of his death could not be ascertained; an autopsy revealed that he'd poisoned himself. The investigation that was carried out established the sequence of events. He'd filled the bathtub with hot water, poured paint thinner into it, undressed and entered the tub. Although the paint thinner must have irritated his skin, it wasn't unbearable. What was not harmful to him, however, was harmful to the painting. When he plunged the canvas into the water, the layers of paint on it started to dissolve. Some ten minutes were enough to remove the paint completely. After he'd destroyed the painting, he took a glass, squeezed some paint from each tube into it, and then added a bit of thinner. He waited briefly for the paint to dissolve, then drank the lethal mixture. The police did not report whether they'd discovered the identity of the painting. The unofficial word was that a celebrated and very expensive work was destroyed, and that the colors the poor man used to poison himself matched those on the painting."

"A very unusual death."

"Very. Nothing obliges you to stay here now that you know what happened. Changing rooms is quite an easy matter. I can do it for you."

"No, thank you. It doesn't bother me."

"As you wish," she said, hesitating once again. "In spite of everything, if you think that I might be of help, just press the button. Do you remember how many times?"

"Once."

"That's right. Well, then, goodbye. I won't take up any more of your time."

"Goodbye."

The hotel cemetery guide bowed, again forgetting to hold onto her conical cap. She quickly raised it from her eyes and left the room.

I turned the remote control over and over in my hand, but didn't use it. I got up, went to the player and took out the cassette. I put it back in the box on top of the television set, and then put the box in my jacket pocket. I turned towards the cabinet and stared at the baskets of fruit. I stayed there like that, stock-still, for several minutes. Then I went to the bathroom door and knocked on it.

Four people came out. They headed one after the other towards the opposite side of the room. As they passed, each one gave me a silent, fleeting smile. I joined them, at the end of the line. We each took a basket from the cabinet. The young man took the peaches, the elderly lady took the apricots, the girl took the strawberries, the elderly man took the plums, and I took the apples.

The procession then turned in the opposite direction, back towards the bathroom. Before I, as the last one, joined them, I looked briefly around the room. Nothing was left to keep me there anymore. I slowly closed the door behind me.

4. The Elevator

Someone knocked on the elevator door.

"Come in," I said, sitting at a small table covered with a brown tablecloth. The place before me was set for dinner. In the middle of the table was a slender vase resembling the neck of a giraffe, dotted with yellow and red flowers, and facing me was another chair, its back to the door.

The elevator door opened in the middle. The two halves slid aside, revealing a liftboy holding a tray. He was a lad of rather short stature with a trim mustache, wearing a brown uniform, and a round cap on his head. The neon lighting in the elevator did not make even a dent in the darkness behind him.

"Here is your appetizer," said the liftboy with a bow.

"Thank you," I replied.

He entered the elevator, approached me from the right side, lowered the tray and set on the table an oval plate containing slices of prosciutto and cheese with olives scattered around them. Then he took a bottle of mineral water from the tray, poured a small amount into the tall glass and took half a step back, waiting.

I raised the glass, took a sip of the water and nodded my head.

With a smile, the liftboy filled my glass, then placed the bottle on the table.

"Enjoy your meal," he said.

"Thank you."

The young man bowed again. No sooner had he left

the elevator, than the two parts of the door conjoined behind him.

I took the brown napkin from the table and tucked it into my shirt collar. First I tried the olives. They were fresh and not too salty. Then the cheese, which was spiced with herbs that brought out its flavor. Just as I was bringing a bite of prosciutto to my mouth, there was another knock on the door.

I lowered the fork to the table and wiped my mouth with the napkin.

"Come in," I said.

The two halves of the door separated and there stood a young man in a striped prison uniform carrying a bow and violin. A brightly colored bird was perched on his left shoulder.

"Hello," he said cordially.

"Hello," I replied in the same tone.

"Please excuse me for interrupting your meal."

"Think nothing of it. Please come in." I stood up and gestured with my hand to enter.

"You are very kind. I won't be long. Just to the first floor."

He stepped inside and the elevator door closed behind him.

"Please sit down," I said, indicating the empty chair.

"Thank you."

He sat down, placed the violin in his lap, then caressed the bird. It didn't move, as though it were stuffed. Only its eyes darted about vivaciously.

"I would ask you to join me," I said, "but the table, regrettably, is only set for one."

"Please don't give it a second thought. Even if there were another table setting, I would have to decline your offer." He turned his head briefly to the left. "I couldn't eat anything of animal origin in front of her."

The fork with its bite of prosciutto stopped once again on its way to my mouth. This time I lowered it with a feeling of discomfort, then quickly reached for another olive.

"Surely you've heard what they call the first floor?"

I shook my head. "No, I haven't."

"The killer floor."

"Is that so?"

"Yes, but I assure you the epithet is quite malicious and undeserved."

"Why do they call it that?"

"Because killers live there."

"Oh, that's why," I said after a brief pause.

"Technically, though, you can't object to the name. Everyone on the first floor has committed at least one murder. But is that the most important trait that characterizes the wonderful people who live there?"

"I wouldn't know. . . ."

"Of course it isn't. It would be, let's say, just like a vegetarian derisively calling someone who loves fine literature a carnivore. All right, most of them are, and thus strictly speaking they deserve the vegetarian's scorn, but should one vice be allowed to blight the many virtues they might possess? And one of them is immediately apparent—their refinement. Have you ever run across an admirer of fine literature who wasn't refined?"

"No, I haven't."

"There, you see. That's how it is with the residents of the first floor. They are indeed killers, but that shouldn't cast a shadow on their many good attributes. It would be quite unfair to neglect those. Don't you think so?"

"I do," I said, having to agree.

"Moreover, the crimes they committed aren't the usual sort you find in grim chronicles, inspired by dishonorable motives or base instincts. There are many extenuating circumstances; these might not exonerate them in the strictly legal sense, but one should take a broader view. The best way to reach your own conclusions about this would be to allow me to tell you one of the stories from our floor. I hope that this won't interfere with your meal?"

I looked at the full oval plate in front of me, then removed the napkin from my collar and placed it on the table.

"Not in the least."

"Let's take, for example, the case of the man from apartment number one. He's an extremely polished gentleman with exemplary manners, always well-dressed as befits the former literature professor that he is. In addition, he's slight of build and already well along in years, giving the impression that he couldn't harm a fly even if he wanted to. But looks can deceive. That man has no fewer than forty-four murders on his conscience."

"Forty-four?"

"Yes. And committed in only eleven days. Based on these two facts alone, wouldn't it be said that he must be a monstrous serial killer?"

I hesitated briefly. "Yes, it would."

"But that's not at all the case. Wait until you hear the whole story, then I'm sure you'll change your mind. First of all, the killer's gentle nature is best shown by the way he took his victims' lives. There wasn't a hint of the sadistic pleasure so characteristic of serial killers. Not a single drop of blood was spilled. Instead of cold steel or firearms, he used a poison whose effects were undetectable. The victims didn't feel the slightest pain or malaise. They just became drowsy and fell asleep. Unfortunately, they didn't wake up, but even so they should be envied. When you think of all the horrible ways there are to die, ending your life like that seems the best way to go, don't you agree?"

"I suppose so. But why did he kill them, anyway, and why so many?"

"Ah, yes, the motive. That's what redeems him most of all, if you look at things with an unbiased eye. By killing so many people he was actually punishing a terrible vice that has taken more and more of us in its grip in modern times. You certainly are aware of what it is."

I thought for a moment. "I'm afraid not."

The look he gave me was a mixture of reproof and disappointment. "The vice of not reading, of course."

"Of course," I agreed, this time without hesitation.

"While the gentleman from apartment number one was still teaching literature, he was confronted by the increasingly dramatic and lamentable fact that people were reading appallingly little. He did his level best to convince his students, if no one else, that if they didn't read enough they'd be left without the admirable qualities that fine literature instills in us—charity, magnanimity, compassion, kindness. Nothing, however, did any good. No one heeded his warning, not even those majoring in literature, who were supposedly making it their profession. Terrible, isn't it?"

"Terrible."

"He hoped that retirement would bring some relief, but this wasn't to be. He was in the grip of obsession, haunted by the feeling that his whole life's work had been in vain and that the world was plummeting madly to its ruin. His conscience wouldn't let him sit there twiddling his thumbs as he watched this freefall. He had to do something. He studied the state of affairs very carefully and concluded that only drastic measures would have any result. And so he devised a test."

"A test?"

"Yes. A very simple test. He made a list of forty-four great works of world literature. He felt that anyone who cared the least about himself had to have read at least these capital works, if nothing else. Those who hadn't read them didn't deserve to live. No harm would be done by removing such people. They would even serve some purpose. They'd be a warning to others about what awaited them if they didn't come to their senses and start reading."

"But that's being too strict. I mean, what about those who hadn't read just a few of the forty-four works, or maybe just one of them? Should they be punished too? For that matter, the professor's choice of books might be challenged. Someone else might have compiled a somewhat different list."

"You're right. The professor also realized that the criteria he'd set were too stringent. As an honorable man he abhorred the thought of wronging an innocent person. So he decided to lower the criteria. First he halved the number of works that had to be read to stay alive, but then he felt that this was still too much, and so he continued to reduce the number until in the end the only criterion was to have read one single work! Now, you tell me—was that asking too much?"

I shook my head. "No, it wasn't."

"Of course it wasn't. And to make matters easier for those who took the test, no proof was required that they'd actually read that one work from the list of forty-four. It was enough to say that they'd read it. The professor made no attempt to verify their claims. As an honorable man he took people at their word. Isn't that admirable?"

"Yes, it is."

"Unfortunately, although he'd been very accommodating, a great disappointment lay in store for him. Indeed, he'd expected there to be people among those he tested who hadn't read a single work on the list, but for them all to be like that went beyond his darkest fears. And that is exactly what happened. All the people he encountered were total literary ignoramuses. Can you believe that?"

"Unbelievable."

"This was not what upset him the most, however. In spite of everything, he might have spared the lives of these lost souls out of compassion, but they had one trait in common that finally turned him into a cold-blooded serial killer: they didn't feel the slightest remorse for not reading, and all of them without exception were proud of it, as though it were a virtue. Just imagine!"

"Horrible."

"You said it. Blinded by this horror, he started killing those he'd tested, one after the other. Four a day. Luckily, he kept his wits about him enough to do it painlessly, almost like euthanasia, although at times he was tempted to get rough. Some of the particularly arrogant nonreaders practically begged to be removed in the nastiest way possible. But if he'd succumbed to this temptation, he would have been no different from his victims and that, you will agree, would have served no purpose whatsoever."

I nodded my head in agreement.

"It is quite likely that his crimes would never have been discovered if he hadn't turned himself in."

"He turned himself in?"

"Yes. When the number of victims was the same as the number of books on his list, something snapped inside the professor. Perhaps he realized that he'd set out to do a job that had no end. Perhaps he came to doubt his intention to save the world. And perhaps the weight on his conscience became too heavy, because after all he was not a born killer. It's hard to say. He is reluctant to talk about it. In any case, after the forty-fourth murder he went straight to the police."

"And?"

"And nothing. What happened was inevitable. It didn't bother him that justice was deaf and blind to the noble reasons behind what he'd done. He became reconciled to the fact that there was no place for him in this hopelessly rotten human society. He did not appeal the sentence. All that was left was to atone for his sins somehow, to make amends so he could look himself in the eye. When he came here to the first floor, he finally got the chance. I don't suppose you'd ever guess what he chose for his penitence."

"No, I wouldn't."

"Cutting out letters."

"Excuse me?"

"He's cutting out the letters of the forty-four books on his list."

"All the letters?"

"All of them—from the first to the last. He bought two copies of each work for this purpose."

"Why, that's an enormous job."

"Yes, it is. And very tricky. Have you ever cut letters out of a book?"

"No, I haven't."

"I don't suggest you try it unless there's an urgent need. A great deal of patience is required. The letters are very tiny so you have to take extreme care to cut them right along the edge. And it destroys your eyesight in no time at all. The professor had proudly reached retirement without wearing glasses and now he has very thick lenses."

"It will take him a very long time to cut out all the letters."

"It will. But what kind of penitence would it be if it were of short duration? There's plenty of time here, so he will eventually finish the job."

"And then what? What will he do with all those letters?"

"No one knows. He bought forty-four large jars, stuck labels on them with the titles of the books, and the cut out letters go inside. Each work has its own jar."

"Literature like winter preserves."

"Yes, figuratively speaking. Since the professor refuses to tell us, various rumors are circulating about what will happen when he finally fills all the jars. Some feel that nothing will happen. His penitence will be over and his conscience will be clear again. Others, however, think things aren't that simple. Perhaps cutting out the letters is only preparation."

"For what?"

"He might, for example, take the letters out of a jar and try to put back together the work that he'd previously cut into its smallest component parts."

"But why would he do that?"

"Because he thinks that cutting alone is not enough. Don't forget he's a serial killer, not an ordinary killer, regardless of how justified he was. If you were in his shoes, would you be satisfied with a halfway penitence?"

"No, I wouldn't."

"Other possibilities are also mentioned. One of them is that he wants to use the letters from one great work of world literature to put together another great work."

"But that's impossible."

"It might be, but then again it might not. You can't tell in advance. As far as I know, no one's tried it yet. Have you heard of any attempt?"

"No, I haven't."

"Then the best thing is to wait and see what the professor achieves, if that's what he really intends to do. But maybe it's not. Some claim the whole thing was inspired by alchemy."

"What did alchemy inspire?"

"Apparently he's going to add various chemicals and other magic ingredients to the jars with the letters."

"And what will he get?"

"Most likely not the usual things that alchemists seek. There's not much use here for gold obtained by transforming other metals, or for the philosopher's stone."

"So what would it be?"

"Maybe a universal literary solvent. Or a novelistic

truth serum. Or maybe poison letter gas. If you ask me, though, I think that's all a lot of claptrap to make fun of the professor, although he certainly doesn't deserve it. You might find it a bit unseemly, but there are a lot of jokers among killers. Sometimes they go a bit too far."

"Well, I never."

"It's nothing unusual, if you think about it. If it weren't for a bit of humor here and there, who could make it through the long sojourn on the first floor? If you were to pay us a visit, you'd see for yourself how important it is. But I'm afraid that won't be possible unless you're a killer too. Anyone else is forbidden inside. Did you kill anyone by any chance?"

"No, I didn't."

"Not a single person? It's not at all necessary to have killed a lot of people. One murder is enough."

I shook my head.

"Even involuntary manslaughter."

I shook my head again.

"Too bad. I'm sure you'd like it where we are."

The door to the elevator opened unexpectedly onto an impenetrable darkness.

"Ah, we have arrived," said the visitor. He took the violin and bow from his lap and stood up. "Unfortunately I didn't have a chance to tell you some of the other stories from our floor, but such is life. Once again, please excuse me for disturbing your meal."

"You didn't in the slightest," I replied, glancing at the oval plate that was missing just one piece of cheese and two olives. I stood up and held out my hand. We shook hands firmly, smiling. As soon as he left the elevator, the door started to close. Just before the two halves joined, the bird on the man's shoulder turned my way. For a moment it seemed that her beak twisted a little, as though she too were smiling.

I sat down on my chair, picked up the napkin and

tucked it into my collar once again. The forkful of prosciutto, however, was not destined to end up in my mouth. It was already very close, but another knock prevented me from finishing the movement. I put it on the plate for a third time with a sigh.

"Come in!"

This time the liftboy was carrying a large porcelain tureen with handles that looked like ears. It had an oval lid that was not quite airtight because of the ladle sticking out of the tureen. Steam from whatever was inside seeped out of a thin opening along the edge of the lid.

"Here's the goose soup!" said the liftboy, smiling.

He put it on the table, and then his face darkened. He indicated the oval plate.

"Didn't you like the appetizer?"

"Yes, yes. It was excellent."

"But you barely touched it."

"Inadvertently . . ." I started, but couldn't find the right words to continue.

"I understand. It makes no difference. I hope you find the soup to your liking. It's first rate."

He moved the plate with the fork and two olive pits to a corner of the table. Then he took the lid off the tureen, releasing a cloud of steam, scooped a ladle full of soup, and poured it into the soup plate that was under the plate for the appetizer. Then he did it again. Soup filled the plate. He put the ladle back in the tureen and covered it.

"There! Enjoy your soup."

"Thank you."

The liftboy picked up first the oval plate and then the one with the olive pits, placing them along his left forearm. Then he bowed and went out, and the two sections of the door quickly joined together in the middle.

I picked up the spoon and stirred the soup for a few moments to cool it a bit. It was dark yellow and thick, with pieces of white meat. It looked very tasty. I took a spoonful, raised it to my lips and started to blow on it. I was just about to put it in my mouth when there came another knock. A feeling of defeat went through me. Inside me a brief battle was waged between my craving for food and good manners. The latter, of course, prevailed in the end, but I wasn't exactly proud of the fact.

"Come in!" I said, more stridently than courtesy demanded.

An elderly man appeared at the door wearing a brown bathrobe of the kind usually worn in hospitals. Beneath it were striped pajamas, and he had slippers on his feet. His hands were full. He was holding three goose quills, a brass inkpot, a blotter and a bundle of yellow paper resembling parchment.

"I hope I'm not disturbing you," he said as he entered. The door closed after him.

"Not at all," I replied, the spoon still at my lips.

"Please continue with your meal. I'm only going to the second floor."

I had to return his kindness. I indicated the chair across the table. "Please sit down."

"Thank you very much," he said, sitting down and placing the objects he was carrying on the table in front of him. "It's hard for me to stand."

His face suddenly darkened. He leaned forward a little towards the steaming plate and sniffed.

"Goose soup?"

I nodded.

The face he made articulated his disgust.

"You don't like goose soup?" I asked judiciously.

"It would be a veritable sacrilege if I took even one spoonful."

I hesitated a bit before asking, "Why?"

Instead of replying, the man picked up the three goose quills from the table.

"Ah," I said, with another nod. And then I did what

couldn't be avoided. I put the spoon back into the plate and took off the napkin once again. I was rewarded with a broad smile of gratitude.

"You surely know what they call the second floor?"

"No, I don't."

"The critically ill floor."

"Really?"

"Really. The name does indeed correspond to the truth, but what hurts us is the derisive tone that goes with it. As though we were a lower caste that doesn't even deserve to be here. And that is quite offensive, because we aren't your ordinary critically ill. Far from it. Each of us fell ill because of one of the arts. Did you know that the arts can be very detrimental to your health?"

"No, I didn't."

"They certainly can. Nothing triggers disease more insidiously, although medicine for some reason doesn't recognize this fact. It's enough to hear the experiences of those residing on the second floor to realize the true state of affairs. What do you think, which of the arts is the most lethal?"

"I wouldn't know," I replied after pondering for a moment.

"Music."

"Music?"

"Yes. There are more victims of music on the second floor than all the others combined."

"I never would have suspected. How can music have a harmful effect?"

"There are different ways. Each case is a story in itself. Take, for example, what happened to the spinster from apartment number two. She was a very prominent piano teacher. Some of her students became world renowned pianists. She had a unique pedagogical method and even though many disapproved of it, no one could deny its effectiveness. She regularly beat her students."

"Beat them?"

"Quite so. Don't be surprised. It turned out that nothing was better at removing piano students' inherent lethargy, slackness, inattention and disobedience than a nice little beating. Although small and slight of build, she was very skilled at handling a switch. No one was unresponsive to her blows. Have you ever been beaten with a switch?"

"No, I haven't."

"You've missed a lot. It awakens the best in you, particularly in the artistic sense. The students came to her classes terrified and went home tear-streaked, but in the end they were all grateful to her. And why wouldn't they be, when she turned the most untalented into real virtuosos? What are a few scars from a thin switch on a place where they normally aren't seen compared to a brilliant career in music? In any case it's a well-known fact that the road to the summit of the arts is strewn with thorns. You didn't expect it to be covered with rose petals, did you?"

"No, I didn't."

"Well, she was already thinking of taking her well-earned retirement when a young girl came to study with her who finally was her ruin. It was clear from the very first glance that she wouldn't have an easy time of it. The girl's fingers were short and fat, she was extremely clumsy, and she gave no sign of having any ear for music. These drawbacks, however, did not discourage the teacher. She'd come across worse cases, and she trusted the power of her switch. The most important thing in life is to have a reliable method, isn't that so?"

"Yes, it is."

"Unfortunately, that method, which had never let her down, failed for the first time. Not one of her former students had received as many beatings as this little girl, but to no avail. Under her fingers the piano produced nothing but offensive noise. What the teacher found even more exasperating, however, was the way the girl took her blows. She didn't let out even the tiniest whimper nor did a single tear roll down her cheek. She seemed to be defying her. You can imagine the effect this had on the teacher's pedagogical authority and particularly on her ego."

"I can."

"But even worse humiliation was to come. After letting loose a powerful and unbridled blow, the switch that had faithfully served her for years snapped in two. Owing to its great merits, it was to have ended up in the elegant display window of a museum of music, with the same status as a prized violin. Ghastly, don't you think?"

I nodded my head.

"The teacher was dazed, of course. And as she stared in helpless disbelief at the two halves of the broken switch, her student, affected not in the slightest by what had happened, calmly pulled up her lowered underpants, put on her skirt and sat at the piano. And that's when a miracle happened."

The gentleman with his writing supplies paused dramatically and gave me a knowing look.

"What miracle?" I asked, right on cue.

"When the little girl's fingers started flying over the keyboard, her astonished teacher let go of the now useless halves of the switch, turned all ears, and her mouth dropped open. In all her long years working in the world of music she had never heard a piano yield to someone so submissively. Sitting before her was not an unpromising beginner but a prodigy without equal. But that's not all."

There was another pause.

"Not all?" I repeated.

"No, it's not. Her performance was only part of the surprise. The composition that the little girl played was the very quintessence of perfection. The teacher, of course, was highly knowledgeable about the history of music, yet she simply could not identify the magical work. Enraptured, she closed her eyes and surrendered to the pure joy of listening. Would you have done otherwise if you'd been in her place, in spite of the exasperation of a moment before?"

"No, I wouldn't."

"She was so enthralled that she didn't open her eyes at the end of the music. When she finally did, there was no one sitting at the piano. She hadn't heard the girl get up and leave. The teacher lunged for the front door, but the stairwell was empty. She returned to the practice room in a woebegone state, longing with all her heart to talk with the girl. Her head was filled with so many questions and she had to find out the answers. She would have given anything for them. She would even have agreed to do what had seemed utterly impossible just ten minutes earlier—apologize for the furious beating she'd given the girl."

"Even that?"

"Yes. But the girl never reappeared, and the teacher didn't know where to look for her. As she waited in vain, her feelings grew worse and worse, and she fell prey to listlessness and depression. She started canceling her classes and withdrew into a shell. She hardly ever left her apartment anymore, lost her appetite and suffered from insomnia. Things didn't end with just these problems, however. I'm sure you've heard that mental exhaustion facilitates the onset of physical ailments?"

"So I've heard."

"This is exactly what happened to the teacher. Soon thereafter she had to be hospitalized. All the doctors could do was conclude with regret that nothing could save her. They, of course, couldn't have imagined that the real cause of her critical illness was music. Particularly since the teacher never confided in anyone to the very end. Sad, isn't it?"

"Very."

"Now the situation is much better. Ever since the teacher came to our floor she's been able to devote herself entirely to finding that perfect composition."

"But how can she when she knows nothing about it?"

"When you have time on your hands, many possibilities open up. She simply sits at the piano and tries every possible combination of notes. When she hits the right thing, she will have no trouble recognizing it."

"But such combinations are infinite!"

"That's right, but infinity isn't all that much here. There's another problem, though. After every unsuccessful composition the professor beats herself viciously. She acquired a new switch for this purpose. This one is guaranteed to be unbreakable."

"How cruel!"

"Yes, but as an honorable and punctilious individual, how could she spare herself such reproach? Would you be soft on yourself and fail to punish yourself properly for the sins you had committed?"

Before I had a chance to reply, the elevator door opened.

"Ah, here's the second floor. I hope I wasn't too much of a bother."

I looked at the plate of soup before me that was no longer steaming.

"You weren't in the slightest."

"Perhaps you'd care to visit us? The teacher would be very pleased, and there are plenty of other interesting people I didn't have time to tell you about. There's only one condition for coming to our floor. You have to have been terminally ill."

"Unfortunately I haven't."

"Well, maybe it doesn't have to be terminal. It would be enough to have been just critically ill."

"I was never critically ill either."

"How about something not so critical?"

I shook my head.

"At least measles or mumps? Everyone's had them."

"I haven't."

The elderly man in the hospital robe shrugged his shoulders. "More's the pity. Well, all right. I guess you can't harmonize everything in life. So it's farewell."

He stood up, collected his writing supplies and held out his hand.

"Farewell," I replied, rising to shake it.

We shook hands briefly, and then he went out into the darkness. The door to the elevator quickly closed behind him.

I sat down again, then picked up the soup spoon from the plate. I lifted it a little but didn't bring it to my mouth. As I looked at it in distaste, there was a knock at the door.

"Come in."

The liftboy was carrying a large plate with a dome-shaped cover. He frowned when he reached the table.

"The soup wasn't to your liking?"

"Yes, it was, but the circumstances, you know, . . ." I said, returning the spoon to the plate.

"I know, I know, you don't have to explain anything. I hope you have better luck with this."

He put the new plate on the table, removed the soup plate that was in front of me, then took off the cover. Underneath was a rather large breaded cutlet, puréed potatoes and steamed carrots. He put the plate in front of me. My mouth started to water.

Seeing my expression, the liftboy smiled.

"Don't let anything interfere this time."

"I won't," was my reply as I firmly took hold of the knife and fork. I didn't bother to tuck in the napkin again.

The liftboy took the cover and the plate full of soup.

"Enjoy your meal," he said with a bow and headed out.

"Thank you," I replied after him, as the door started to close.

I'd just cut a large piece of meat when the inevitable took place. Someone knocked on the elevator door again. I hesitated for a moment and then put the piece in my mouth. I started chewing happily, paying no attention to the repeated knock. It was not until the sound came a third time that I finally replied, my mouth still full.

"Come in!"

The door split open silently in the middle and a middle-aged man carrying a basketful of apples stepped in.

"I'm terribly sorry," he said. "I'm only going to the third floor. Pay no attention to me."

"Come now," I replied, struggling with the bite in my mouth. I stood up and indicated the chair across from me. "Please take a seat."

"Thank you, but I don't want to disturb you while you're eating."

"Don't worry, I'm used to it already."

The man hesitated a moment longer and then sat down, placing the basket on a corner of the table.

"Please continue. Enjoy your meal."

"Thank you." I pushed a bit of purée and a carrot onto the fork with my knife.

"It looks very tasty."

"Yes, it is. The cutlet is excellent." The potatoes and carrot were so soft that I swallowed them without chewing.

"I used to love cutlets too, but I stopped eating them after what happened to me in a hotel."

"What happened to you?" I asked, starting to cut a new piece of meat.

"There was a packing plant in the hotel."

I stopped cutting.

"A packing plant?"

"Yes. I didn't actually visit it, but what I learned

about it was enough to put me off meat for good, even though I'm not a vegetarian. Would you like me to tell you about it?"

I put down the knife and fork and pushed the plate away a bit.

"I'd rather you didn't."

"I understand you completely. I shouldn't even have mentioned it."

I looked with regret at the barely eaten meal. "It doesn't matter. I'm not hungry, anyway."

As I drank a little mineral water, the man looked at me apologetically.

"I hope you don't have any prejudice with regard to the third floor," he said after I'd set down the glass.

"Why would I?"

"Because that's the suicide floor."

"Really? I didn't know."

"But not your ordinary suicides, to be sure. There are none of the simple folk who kill themselves for such banalities as unrequited love, financial difficulties, or disappointment with life in general."

"Then why do they commit suicide?"

"Exclusively for artistic reasons."

"Artistic?"

"That's right. You might not be aware of it, but art offers a profusion of first-class reasons to do away with oneself. The residents of the third floor are the best confirmation of that. The stories there are extraordinary! Each one is more exciting than the last. They would make a wonderful anthology. Take, for example, what happened to the man from apartment number three. Would you be interested in hearing his case?"

I glanced at the cutlet once again, then nodded my head.

"Certainly."

The man's face broadened into a smile, erasing his apologetic expression.

"He's an excellent sculptor. His works are the pride and joy of the best museums in the world, and his monuments decorate the most beautiful parks. He was particularly noted for his busts. He not only depicted his models to perfection, but seemed to endow the marble with a soul. And even more than that. Has anyone ever carved your bust?"

"No, they haven't."

"If the man from apartment number three had done it, you might have suffered the same fate as many of his models. Each seemed to become hypnotized by their stone replica. They would sit there and stare at it, unable to tear their eyes away. The bust had to be covered in order for them to snap out of this enchantment. Some of them turned aggressive when they weren't allowed to look at their busts. Force had to be used, for their own good, to tear them away from the bewitched marble looking-glass. Not even that did the trick for some of the models and they ended up in an insane asylum."

"I never suspected that sculpture could be so dangerous."

"That's nothing. Wait until you hear the whole story. When he was just about to retire, the sculptor decided to make a bust of himself, something he'd never done before. It's not clear what led him to do it. Perhaps a guilty conscience for the fact that his art had brought misfortune to the people he'd immortalized in stone, even though he'd had only the best intentions. Did he want to punish himself, hoping that he would suffer the same fate as most of his models? All we can do is surmise."

"Why don't you ask him?"

"We did, but silence was his only answer. When he finished his bust, a punishment did indeed ensue, but not the one he expected. For the first time he was not satisfied with his work. He'd made the spitting image of himself, yet something was missing."

"The soul?"

"In all likelihood. So he broke the first bust and immediately set to making another one, sparing no effort. But the outcome was the same. Although physically true to life, once again the marble face had no life inside it. The sculptor's chisel destroyed this bust too and he began to make a third one."

"And that one didn't turn out right, either?"

"No, it didn't. Nor the one after it. The outside world ceased to exist for the sculptor. He was consumed by his frenzied work on his own busts. He destroyed them one after another, sinking ever deeper into despair. Finally, after the eleventh bust, his atelier was filled with ominous silence. When the authorities broke inside, a terrible sight awaited them. He was lying on the floor with the chisel stabbed into his heart, and the hammer was in his hand."

"Gruesome. I've never heard of someone killing themselves like that."

"Gruesome, yes, but if you think about it, what suicide could be more fitting for a sculptor?"

I thought it over. "No other."

"No other, of course. It didn't bring him deliverance, however."

"It didn't?"

"No. He's continued his penitence here in this place."

"Does he still make busts in his likeness?"

"Yes, but not in stone. There isn't a lot of marble on the third floor."

"Then what does he use?"

"Flesh."

"Excuse me?"

"His own flesh. He stands in front of the mirror and changes his face with a hammer and chisel. Every day all over again from the beginning."

"That must be very painful."

"It is indeed painful. Yet who has ever heard of penitence that is painless?"

"No one."

"But the pain is not his primary worry. He would endure it gladly if he knew that one day he would finally look in the mirror and see his ensouled likeness. That hasn't happened yet, and no one guarantees that it ever will, even though there is no dearth of time here. All that's left for him is to hope."

The elevator door opened at that very moment onto pitch black space. The man stood up and took his basket of apples.

"Here we are on the third floor, and I only managed to tell you one story. If you were to come and visit us you'd hear many more of them, some even more amazing than this one. But for that to happen you need to be a suicide. Did you take your own life?"

"No, I didn't."

"It doesn't have to be something spectacular, like with the sculptor. Even a completely unimaginative suicide would be enough. Hanging yourself, for example, taking poison or cutting your veins."

"I didn't kill myself."

"Even an unsuccessful suicide attempt would do."

I shook my head.

"Well, never mind. The time has come to say goodbye. I wish you all the best."

"I wish you the same."

After shaking hands, the man with the basket went out into the darkness.

I kept my eyes fixed on the door after it closed behind him, but my intuition let me down. There wasn't any knock. With no advance warning, the two halves were once again pulled aside and the liftboy entered the elevator, carrying a tray with a dessert plate of raisin cake.

I was almost certain that he would chide me for barely touching the main course, at least by the expression on his face, but there was no reproach.

"And here is your dessert for the end," he said, as he picked up the large plate in front of me and replaced it with the small one he'd just brought.

"I love raisin cake."

The liftboy smiled but did not leave as he'd done before. He stood next to me and the door quickly closed.

"I hope you don't mind if I stay with you until the fourth floor."

"I will be happy to have the company. Please take a seat."

"I really shouldn't. It's against regulations."

"But I insist."

The liftboy sat reluctantly on the edge of the chair and put the plate with the barely touched cutlet on the table.

"Thank you. I envy you for finding pleasure in cake."

"Would you like to try it? I'd be happy to share it with you." I took the knife and fork to cut it.

"No, no, you didn't understand me. I don't eat sweets at all."

"Do you have a problem with sugar?"

"No, I don't, and I don't want to have any either. It's a well-known fact that sweets are harmful to your health, but people still gobble them up, even though their lives are at stake. Of course, if you eat sweets in moderation nothing should happen to you, although medical books do mention cases of an onset of diabetes from just one piece of cake, even smaller than this one here. But it's highly unlikely that you of all people would have such bad luck. Please, go ahead and help yourself. Particularly since you haven't eaten much else."

I wavered a moment, then laid the knife and fork on the plate.

"I think I'll hold back."

"Wise decision. Many people consider themselves immune to bad luck, that it only happens to others.

But that is a big mistake. Bad luck is lurking all around us. We on the fourth floor are the best evidence of that. Bad luck is what brought us together there."

"Really?"

"Yes. And not just your ordinary bad luck. A man slips on a banana peel, falls, hits his head on the pavement. Or passes unsuspectingly by a building and a flowerpot lands on his head. Our cases are far more discriminating, and what they have in common is the fact that one of the arts is involved."

"I didn't know that art had anything to do with bad luck."

"It certainly does. I could tell you a whole host of unbelievable stories. I don't have the time, of course, but perhaps you'd like to hear just one. From the lady in apartment number four. It is truly exceptional."

"I'm all ears," I said with a sigh.

"The woman is a brilliant painter. Her landscapes are without equal. When you stand before her paintings of the countryside it's like looking out of a window into a perfect reality. Everything is presented so convincingly that you think you can hear the gurgling stream, the chirping birds, the sound of the wind in the treetops. A feeling of contentment fills you. It's no wonder that clusters of viewers often formed around her paintings in the galleries. People would stand there patiently, at length, absorbing the bliss that radiated from them. Did you know about this calming effect that works of art can have?"

"Yes, I did."

"In the end even doctors started to recommend the viewing of her pictures. It was scientifically proven that they had a beneficial effect on many mental problems. Not only simple neuroses and psychoses but depression, paranoid obsessions and different manias. Even mild forms of schizophrenia. Do you have any experience of one of these illnesses, perhaps?"

"No, I don't."

"Too bad. You could have cured yourself in an instant. Well, let me continue the story about the painter. Everything in her life was above reproach until the moment she recklessly listened to the advice of her greedy gallery owner about charging a fee to view her paintings for medicinal purposes."

"Why, that's inhumane."

"Inhumane, of course. That's the reason for the punishment she received, even though as a very caring woman she had reduced the fee to less than one-tenth of the price that the gallery owner first proposed."

"What punishment?"

"Bad luck started to plague her, one incident stranger than the next. The first happened at the seashore, where she had gone to paint a tropical seascape with a long sandy beach, palms swaying over the turquoise water and the sun sinking over a bay. Only a tiny bit of work remained to complete the canvas, when something terrible shattered the tranquility that surrounded her. Can you imagine what it was?"

"Was she attacked by a shark?"

The liftboy shook his head. "Something much worse than a shark. A tsunami."

"Tsunami?"

"Yes. A veritable tidal wave. It was more than twenty-seven and a half meters high. An enormous wall of water, such as had never been seen before in that region known for its mild climate, suddenly sped towards her from the open sea. Its cause was never discovered. The painter lost several precious moments staring in panic at the monstrous mass hurtling towards her. She finally came to her senses, grabbed the painting off the easel and ran from the beach, but it was too late."

"Did she perish?"

"No, she didn't, although at first everyone thought she had. It seemed impossible that anyone near the beach could survive the tremendous crash of the wave's front, scattering the palm trees like toothpicks. When the giant wave withdrew, the painter was found alive, although terribly bruised and with several broken bones. Unfortunately, there was no trace of the unfinished painting."

"That was the least thing that mattered."

The liftboy sighed. "If that were only true. But wait until you hear the whole story. After she recovered, the painter decided to paint her next canvas as far as possible from the sea. The chances of her being the victim of another tidal wave were practically nil, but after what she'd experienced, can we blame her for not wanting to be by water?"

"No, we can't."

"She went to the top of a mountain deep in the hinterland. There wasn't even a creek nearby to remind her of the trauma of the seashore. She took great pleasure in painting the idyllic mountain landscape. She was surrounded by tall firs, pure blue sky, a deep covering of grass, broad vistas. She was just about to finish the canvas when bad luck struck once again. Surely you can guess what it was."

"Was she attacked by a grizzly bear?"

"A grizzly would have been a real godsend compared to what happened. Although the region wasn't at all volcanic, the top of the mountain suddenly opened with a horrific roar, glowing hot rocks streamed into the air, and lava started to flow all around her. Disbelief froze the painter to the spot once again. She didn't get over the shock until the molten innards of the earth reached her feet. As she raced headlong down the hill, fiery rain pelted down all around her. She barely made it out alive. Indeed, she spent more than two and a half months in the hospital recovering from the burns she'd received all over her body. Although they were very painful, the fact that she'd been unable to save the almost finished painting gave her even greater pain. It had ended up somewhere on the mountain slope, set on fire by lava. Is there any worse fate for an artist than to be left without their work of art?"

"But at least she was alive."

"That is little consolation, as you will see. When she'd recuperated enough to be able to work again, the painter decided not to take any risks. She wouldn't go near the mountains or the sea. Her next canvas would be a desert landscape. The setting only seemed unchanging at first glance. The artist's experienced eye discerned a unique beauty in the curves of the waving dunes, the incomparable blush of the sky, the hint of distant oases, and the quivering, unearthly mirages. She set to work in earnest, but once more was not allowed to finish the painting, although several strokes of the brush were all that remained."

"What could happen to her there? Was she attacked by a wild animal? A lion or a snake? I'm not very well acquainted with desert zoology."

"Nothing of the sort. The bad luck was yet again of much greater proportions. The desert has always been considered a very stable tectonic region, but when lady luck has turned her back, you can't depend on anything. The earthquake that suddenly rocked the area was so strong that an enormous crack opened up in the earth right where the painter was standing. At the last moment she somehow managed to grab hold of the edge of the fissure. But when she saw the easel and canvas plunge into the abyss, she almost dropped into it herself. As crazy as that might seem, it's understandable, isn't it?"

"I would have climbed up to safe ground instead."

"That's only because you've probably never seen one of your works of art disappear forever. All kinds of dark thoughts run through your mind. Finally, after hanging over the chasm for seven hours and thirteen minutes, the painter pulled herself out of the crack. Then she wandered about the desert for another four days and seven hours because she'd lost her jeep in the earthquake. She was found at the end of her strength, completely exhausted and dehydrated. They barely brought her back to life."

"So in the end everything turned out all right."

"It all depends. After this unbelievable turn of bad luck the painter almost decided to abandon her art. She became superstitious, which isn't at all strange. Would you see mere coincidence in everything that happened to her?"

"I wouldn't."

"Of course you wouldn't. One stroke of bad luck maybe, but three in a row is really too much. This is why she didn't pick up a paintbrush for a long time. When she finally did, inspired by a pastoral landscape she couldn't resist, she took every precautionary measure that crossed her mind. She had a large first aid kit next to her, almost a small field hospital. There was also a rubber boat on a powered paraglider. She was wearing firefighter overalls with a canister of oxygen. There was a parachute on her back and she had a commando survival kit. One would say she was prepared for just about any disaster that could possibly happen, right?"

"One would say."

"Well, that's not what happened. One hundred percent protection from bad luck doesn't exist, as you will soon see. The initial tension inside her slowly subsided when work on the painting progressed without any interference. There was no sign of gigantic waves, eruptions, temblors or any other natural disaster. Everything around her was serene and harmless, just like in her paintings. But this landscape was never finished either. What do you think was the reason?"

I shrugged my shoulders. "I wouldn't know. Was she attacked by an animal? There aren't any wild animals in pastoral regions, but even domesticated animals can be dangerous at times. A raging bull, for example, or a rabid dog. Maybe a piqued turkey?"

The liftboy gave me a dubious look. "There weren't any animals in the vicinity, either wild or domestic. When the painter was found lying next to the easel with its almost finished picture, she was surrounded by an untouched idyll. It was not at all clear what had happened to her. She had no visible scars. The first assumption was that she'd had a heart attack. It wasn't until later that they established the cause. I doubt you would ever guess what it was."

"I'm sure I wouldn't."

"A meteorite hit the back of her head. It was smaller than a pinhead. Her hair covered the tiny trace at the spot where it had pierced her skull. The chances of something like that are practically nonexistent. But when bad luck is at your heels, probability ceases to play a role."

"A truly unbelievable way to die."

"It wasn't until the painter came to the fourth floor that she realized what lay behind the succession of calamities that had befallen her. She accepted her punishment for greed without complaint, and even increased it. Do you know what she chose for her penitence?"

"No, I don't."

"She paints landscapes, but doesn't finish them."

"Is she still hounded by bad luck?"

"No, there is no bad luck here. She does it of her own free will. Her apartment is filled with paintings that need just their finishing touches."

"How hard she is on herself."

"Yes, but should she be well-disposed towards her transgression and finish her paintings as though nothing had happened?"

"No, she shouldn't," I agreed after a moment's hesitation.

Impenetrable darkness appeared once again behind the opening elevator door. The liftboy got up.

"We're here. It's too bad there wasn't time for you to hear more stories from our floor. Would you like to drop by? You'd meet many interesting people with amazing fates. For that, however, you would have to have had an unfortunate encounter with bad luck."

"I haven't."

"It doesn't have to be of cosmic proportions like with the painter. Smaller unbelievable turns of bad luck also count. For example, getting hit by a stray bullet in the crossfire of a gangster fight, falling into the only open sewer shaft in the whole town or getting overexcited by winning the lottery and your heart giving out."

"I've never played the lottery."

"In the extreme case a banana skin or flowerpot?"

I shook my head.

The liftboy looked at me for several moments without speaking. "That means that you keep going."

"I keep going."

There was another brief pause. "Up?" he pointed his thumb upwards.

"Up."

A smiled flickered briefly on his face. "I wish you lots of luck."

"Thank you."

"Allow me to take care of this." He indicated the table and chairs.

"Certainly." I stood up and moved into a corner.

The liftboy adroitly lifted the table with everything on it and took it out of the elevator.

"I'm sorry you didn't manage to eat anything," he said after coming back for the chairs.

"It couldn't be helped."

He looked as though he wanted to say something else, but just smiled briefly again, raised the chairs a little as though shrugging his shoulders to exonerate himself of something, then went out. He was swiftly swallowed up by darkness.

The door closed behind him. The elevator didn't seem to be moving, but I knew that was just an illusion.

Twelve Collections

Contents

1. Days

When I entered the pastry shop, a purple wave swept over me. Almost every surface was in some shade of this color: the wallpaper, curtains, rugs, tablecloths, chair covers. So were the shades on the lighted table lamps. The muted light gave even the air a purple tint.

I squinted and took a look around. Not a single one of the six small round tables with three chairs each was occupied. The pastry chef was standing behind the display counter, wiping a glass with a purple napkin. His apron was inevitably of the same tone as everything else. He seemed more stocky than stout, and a thick, cropped beard and mustache compensated for his shiny bald head.

He smiled and nodded, putting down the glass and napkin.

"Good evening," he said cordially. "Sit wherever you like."

"Good evening," I replied, returning his smile, and took off my hat.

I hesitated a moment, then headed for the table farthest from the door. I put my coat and hat on the coat rack in the corner and sat in the chair next to the wall. The pastry chef hastened to my table with the napkin draped over his arm, smiling all the while.

"What would you like?" he asked solicitously.

"I'd like to have something sweet."

"You're in the right place. We have a fine selection

of pastries." He indicated the menu in the purple cover before me on the table.

I picked it up and opened it. The pages were a somewhat lighter shade of purple, while the words were written in orange. The pastry chef had not overstated the selection. The list of different pastries filled an entire eight pages.

My eyes skimmed the pages, making their way down the list. The farther I went from the beginning, the less familiar were the names. What, for example, could be hiding behind "livid lightning rod", "shambling violin" or "absent-minded bumblebee"? The "enamored water lily" brought a smile to my lips. Items on the fifth page had names that seemed intended to repel those with a sweet tooth. Indeed, who would order a "stinky grater", "putrid acrobat" or "cheerful carcass" without being in the know?

I closed the menu and put it back on the table.

"It's hard to decide with such a selection," I said. "Might you have something to recommend? I would like something special."

The smile that had seemed glued to the pastry chef's face abruptly vanished. I couldn't properly read the look he gave me. It seemed inquisitive and reproving at the same time.

"Special?" he repeated in a voice that had lost its warmth.

"Yes, something out of the ordinary. I like to try new things."

"We have something special, but it's not on the menu."

"It isn't?"

"It isn't. Have you ever tried stuffed monkey?"

If I hadn't just read the menu, this name would certainly have been a surprise. As it was, compared to some of them it seemed rather unassuming.

"I'm afraid I haven't even heard of it."

"Would you like to try it?"

"Is it some kind of cake?" I questioned in return.

"Yes, it is. Cake with a unique flavor. It's made according to a remarkable secret recipe. This is the only place it can be ordered."

"Then why isn't it on the menu?"

"Because of the price."

Now I was the one to eye him inquisitively. "It's that expensive?"

"It depends on how you look at it. For some it is. For others it isn't."

"All right, tell me how much it costs and I'll decide whether it's for me."

The pastry chef sighed, then looked around the empty room as though checking for eavesdroppers on our conversation.

"May I?" He indicated the chair across from me.

"Of course. Please sit down," I said, rising politely in my seat.

The pastry chef sat down and rested his folded hands on the table. He stared at them for several moments, then raised his eyes towards me. When he spoke again, his voice was softer.

"The stuffed monkey is not on the menu because it's not paid for with money."

"What is it paid for with?"

"Days."

"With what?" I asked, even though I'd heard him quite well.

"Days from the past of whoever orders it."

Silence followed.

"Oh, I see," I said at last. "But how can you pay with days from the past?"

"It's possible. The day you use to pay disappears from your memory. It's as though you never lived it. It becomes part of my collection."

"You collect days?"

"Yes. You shouldn't be surprised. Stranger things than the days of other people's lives are collected."

"I'm not surprised, I just didn't know anything about it."

"My collection is already quite large." He turned around and pointed above the display counter. "It's over there."

I had to strain my eyes. If the lighting hadn't been so soft, I might have already noticed the four long rows of vials, one above the other, resembling some sort of frieze extending the whole length of the display counter. There were lots of them, certainly hundreds: deep purple and spherical, with glass stoppers, like fancy perfume bottles.

"That's where you keep the days?"

"Yes. They must be kept tightly closed, in a dark and dry place."

"You don't say."

"Days evaporate instantly if you expose them to the sun. Humidity is also harmful to them. I have to maintain a stable temperature in the pastry shop the whole year round."

"Who would have thought?"

"Quite so. Regrettably, since I don't know anyone else who collects days, there was no one to show me how to maintain such a collection. I had to learn by experience. Many days were lost until I got the hang of it."

"Do you collect any days in particular?"

"No. I'm not choosy. I let the customers decide which day to give me. Some see a good chance to get rid of an unpleasant past and taste an exceptional dessert in return. Everyone has bad days in their lives that they would happily forget. You undoubtedly have such days as well?"

I gave it some thought. "I do."

"Would you give up one of them to try the stuffed monkey?"

Once again several moments passed before I replied. "I would."

The smile returned to the pastry chef's face. "Very well. I'll bring it at once."

He got up and hastened towards the display counter. He went behind it, bent down and briefly disappeared from sight. When he stood up he was holding a purple tray. Carrying it with one hand, he came back to my table.

He put a small purple plate in front of me along with a knife, fork and napkin. The cylindrical cake also looked purple, but that might have been because of the light. The pastry chef sat down, placed the tray at the end of the table, then took from it the last thing he'd brought: an empty vial. He had a bit of trouble removing the glass stopper.

"Think of the day you will pay with before you put the cake in your mouth. As soon as you taste it, the day will disappear. If you don't think of a particular day, one will be removed at random, and it might be one you'd really hate to lose."

I nodded my head, then slowly picked up the knife and fork. I cut a small piece. The inside of the pastry was a different shade of purple. I brought the bite carefully to my mouth.

The pastry chef swiftly closed the vial as soon as I took the fork out of my mouth. He lifted it up towards the table lamp. What he saw inside made his smile broaden.

"Well?" he asked after I had swallowed the first bite.

I took another, larger piece.

"Divine," I mumbled, my mouth full.

Soon there wasn't a crumb on the plate. I picked up the napkin and wiped my mouth.

"I knew you would be delighted. So far not a single person has been anything but pleased."

"I had no idea something that delicious ever existed. Could I have another stuffed monkey?"

"No."

I looked at him in bewilderment. "Why not?"

"It's for your own good. I'm an avid collector, it's true, but I'm not a dishonorable man."

"I don't understand you."

"In order to understand, you need to know something more about the stuffed monkey. It's not an ordinary cake."

I licked my lips. "I agree with you completely."

"Not only in that sense. It creates an addiction."

"Addiction?"

"Yes. The more you eat, the more you want."

"Doesn't everyone with a sweet tooth dream of finding a pastry like that? If you think I'll overdo it, there's no need to worry. I've had a sweet tooth my whole life, even to the point of overindulging, and I'm as fit as a fiddle."

"The stuffed monkey won't harm your health."

"Then how can it be bad for me?"

Before he answered, the pastry chef put the vial in the wide pocket of his apron.

"You would have fewer and fewer days from your past."

"So what? What do I need those days for, anyway?" I laughed. "This way at least they'll be good for something. I will thoroughly enjoy eating my past."

The pastry chef didn't find my witticism amusing. "That wouldn't be very wise," he said in a stern voice.

"It wouldn't?"

"It's not a good idea to be without a past."

"Why not?"

The pastry chef looked at me for a few moments without speaking.

"I told you I didn't have any experience when I began to collect days. I thought, just like you right now, that there was nothing to lose by paying with the past. I let my first customers eat the stuffed monkey to their heart's content, happy to enlarge my collection. Until they started to disappear."

"Disappear?"

"Yes. Gradually. Every new pastry increased the empty space inside them, like they'd become invisible in that spot. The spaces were quite small in the beginning. They went unnoticed. Now you too have one somewhere."

I looked at my hands, then felt my face. "Where?"

"I don't know. It's no use looking for it. You wouldn't even find it under a magnifying glass. That's why there's no harm in trying the stuffed monkey. It hardly leaves a trace. But after just a few pieces the empty space becomes visible and quickly spreads with each new day from the past that is consumed. The first customers hid this from me, fearing that I would refuse to give them the stuffed monkey. And they simply couldn't live without it anymore."

"So what happened?"

"In the end I found out what was happening. The empty spaces became so big that they could no longer be hidden."

"Did you stop giving them the cake?"

"No. It was impossible. They'd become completely addicted. I had to do the exact opposite to keep the whole thing from surfacing. I kept on giving them the stuffed monkey until there was nothing left of them."

"So, that's how you got rid of them?"

"Only partially. They became invisible, but they're still here."

"Here where?"

"In the pastry shop. Even though they're disembodied they are still drawn irresistibly to the stuffed monkey. So they hang around here all the time. It's because of them that everything is purple. For some reason that color does them the most good. That was the least I could do for them."

I looked around the empty room.

"You can't see them, of course. But it's not hard to guess where they are right now. They have all flocked around us. Poor things. Their invisible mouths are certainly watering. You can't imagine how much they envy you."

I pushed the empty plate to the middle of the table.

"Why don't you remove the stuffed monkey from your selection?"

"But it isn't part of the selection."

"You offered it to me."

"You asked for something special."

"I didn't mean something that special."

"You have no reason to be dissatisfied. Both of us, actually, fared well. You tasted an exceptional pastry without any evil consequences, and I added another day to my collection." He patted the pocket of his apron.

I made a vague circular motion with my finger. "What about the empty space?"

"You won't ever notice it. In any case, it will only do you good. It will remind you of the past and how precious it is. You'd been willing to give it up so easily."

I didn't know what to say in response. We sank into silence.

"Would you like to try something less special, from the menu?" said the pastry chef at last. "Even though they can't be compared to the stuffed monkey, they are excellent pastries nonetheless."

"No, thank you," I hastened to reply as I got up. "Perhaps another time. Until then, good-bye."

"Until the next time," said the pastry chef, getting up as well.

As I headed for the door with large strides, putting on my coat as I went, I was struck by the duplicity of this farewell.

2. Fingernails

Mr. Prohaska collected his fingernail clippings. He'd been doing it since the age of eight, when he cut them by himself for the first time. He was so proud of the fact that he'd managed to cut them without his mother's help and without doing himself any harm that he decided to save the ten little sickles as proof of this feat. He'd had to do it in secrecy because his mother certainly wouldn't have let him keep them. He put them in a little plastic bag and stuck a label on it with the date. Letters were still giving him trouble, but at that early age he was already skilled with numbers. He then put the bag in a hidden place.

Approximately two weeks later, when the time came to cut his nails again, he hesitated but a moment before putting the new little sickles in a bag with the date on it. There was no long-term decision behind this; that would only be formed later. He simply felt it was a shame to throw the nails away. It suddenly seemed that doing so would be throwing away part of his body. True, he was no longer physically connected to the nails, but this did nothing to lessen his attachment to them. They might have separated from him, but he could still keep them close by. Sadness filled him at the thought of the many nails his mother had cut off before he turned eight and which were now lost forever.

He continued to collect his nails in an orderly fashion, but the passage of time brought the problem of where to put the little bags. Every year there were twenty-five to thirty more of them. The shoebox where he kept them was not easy to hide; his mother almost found it two or three times. He felt no relief until his early twenties, when he left his parents' home. His fingernail collection at that time contained more than four hundred little bags that filled all of three shoeboxes. That's when he was finally able to put it in order and go through it without the constant fear of being caught doing something unseemly, although he wasn't the slightest bit ashamed of his secret.

He did feel ashamed, however, of keeping something he cared about so much in such an unsuitable place as a shoebox. It seemed like sacrilege to him; he had to find a more dignified repository for his unique collection. Although he still wasn't earning very much money, he nonetheless managed to set aside enough to order five hundred specially fitted cigarette cases. Had he been richer, they certainly would have been made of solid silver, but under the circumstances he had to be satisfied with silver plating. Every cigarette case had a date engraved on the lid and the inside was lined in purple plush with two curved rows, each containing five sickle-shaped indentations.

It took several months to transfer the nails from the little bags to the cigarette cases. It was a tedious and exacting job. He did it with great patience, meticulously, consumed by the constant fear of getting it wrong. It was extremely difficult to ascertain the finger from which each nail had been cut. He finally got the hang of it and then all he needed was a quick touch to place a given sickle accurately in the proper indentation. He proudly considered himself a genuine expert in this type of identification.

The collection was finally lodged in a suitable repository, but one day as he gazed at it with pride an uneasy thought spoiled his pleasure. What if a burglar broke into his apartment? He would certainly head straight for the cigarette cases, particularly since there was nothing else of any value. Perhaps, in his haste, he wouldn't even check what was inside them. Later he would certainly throw away the nails because for him they had no value. This possibility horrified Mr. Prohaska; he had to prevent it at any cost. He rushed to the bank, rented a safe-deposit box and without a moment's notice started transferring the cigarette cases. He felt no relief until the last one was secure.

He went to the bank once a month to deposit two new cigarette cases. He always spent a considerable amount of time in the safe-deposit vault, enjoying the sight of the neatly stacked little cases. It was on one such occasion that an unexpected thought yet again shattered his moment of pleasure. It all started with an innocuous reflection as to whether the safe-deposit box he had rented was large enough to accommodate all his future nails.

Naturally, he could not know how many more nails there would be, but as a good mathematician it was not difficult to calculate that if he lived to the age of eighty-seven and a half years, the safe-deposit box would be filled to the top with cigarette cases. If he were to live longer than that he would have to rent either a larger box or an additional one if there were no larger boxes. This particular problem had a solution. But not the ultimate problem, one that hadn't crossed his mind before and suddenly struck with all its might. What would happen to the collection after his death?

He needed to prepare for this eventuality as soon as possible. True, there was no reason to worry, he was in excellent shape for his age, but disease is not the only cause of death. Various calamities are lying in wait, beyond our control. The worst thing possible would be for him to die a sudden death, before he was able to arrange for the permanent care of his collection. The safe-deposit box would be opened as part of his estate, necessarily divulging his secret.

This had to be prevented by all means. Yes, but how? Perhaps he could rent another safe-deposit box, not under his own name this time, but anonymously, so that his death would not result in its being opened? The box would still be opened at the end of the rental period. All right, then he would rent a box for a very long period. He wasn't quite sure how long that really long period should be—various durations crossed his mind, from one century to an entire millennium—but they told him at the bank that safe-deposit boxes were rented for a maximum of twenty-five years.

This certainly did not seem sufficient to him. He left the bank depressed, and this dismal mood never left him. The situation only worsened when he remembered another undesirable fact that had slipped by unnoticed. The nails on a corpse continue to grow for some time. He couldn't do anything about retrieving the lost fingernails of his childhood, so he simply had to make sure he got these. Should his collection be missing what might be its most important specimens? So, what should he do? He'd be dead and unable to cut his nails in the grave. Whom could he count on to cut them in his place?

Although this problem never left his mind, he couldn't find a solution—until one rainy afternoon when he least expected it. The solution struck him in a moment of profound enlightenment. It was magnificently elegant in its simplicity, like a mathematical formula. He felt like dancing with joy. He refrained, of course, as a man accustomed to well-mannered behavior, although no one would have seen him vent his exultation.

If death was the main obstacle standing in his way, then there was only one way to overcome it, once and for all. Mr. Prohaska firmly decided that he would never die.

3. Autographs

"Good afternoon. Is this seat free?"

I raised my eyes from the newspaper I was reading on the park bench. The diminutive old man who had stopped in front of me took off his hat, revealing a shock of white hair. His thin mustache was also white, and under it stretched a wide smile.

"Yes. You're welcome to take it." I stood up slightly and indicated the empty part of the bench.

"Thank you." The old man sat down on the opposite end and placed his hat in his lap. He was wearing a double-breasted dark blue suit of an old-fashioned cut. The large, purple, slightly askew bow tie around his thin neck seemed ready to flutter off at any moment.

I went back to reading my paper, but not for long.

"Wonderful day," said the old man.

"Wonderful," I concurred, keeping my eyes on the paper to let him know I didn't feel like talking.

But the old man ignored this signal. "It's a real shame to die on such a day as this."

I closed the newspaper and looked at him inquisitively. "Die?"

"Yes. More than eighty people are supposed to die today in this large city."

"How do you know how many people are supposed to die?"

"That's what the statistics say. Around thirty thousand die every year. That's about eighty a day, or one person every eighteen minutes."

"Interesting," I replied and opened the paper again. But I didn't have a chance to continue reading, because the old man spoke again.

"Those are only averages, of course. On some days quite a few more people die than on other days. Can you guess the largest number of people to die on the same day in the last quarter century?"

"No, I can't." I looked at the paper, but didn't read.

"Two hundred and sixteen!"

"That many?" I said in an even voice, turning the page.

"Yes," affirmed the old man brightly. "It was a true pandemic. The day was as beautiful as this one, but that was just an illusion. Weather is able to generate very nasty surprises. Most of those who died were heart patients. Just imagine—not even seven minutes would pass and someone new would die."

"How awful."

"But then there are other days, of course. The sky descends almost to the earth, it rains without letup, the cheeriest people turn sullen and listless, those with a melancholic side fall into deep depression and are on the verge of committing suicide. Even so, almost no one dies. On one such day the number of people who died was a record low—only twenty-six. Just think."

"Unbelievable." I opened the newspaper up very wide and lowered my head a bit so I couldn't see the old man anymore and he couldn't see me.

"People die for a wide variety of reasons," soon came the old man's voice from the other side of my flimsy shelter. "When you read that someone's died of natural causes, that can mean any of a number of diseases. With some of them you'd never think they could be fatal. For example, just last year there were two cases of death from water on the knee. Didn't you hear of them?"

"No, I didn't," I replied crossly.

"And what do you say to death from hair-loss, from bunions or from tennis elbow?"

"Tennis elbow?" I asked in disbelief, peeking at the old man with one eye around the side of the newspaper.

"Yes, believe it or not. A very unusual case. I can tell you the story if you like."

"No, thank you," I hastened to reply, plunging into the newspaper again.

"Lots of deaths aren't natural," continued the old man unrelentingly. "Do you know, for example, the annual average number of people who die in this town just from being struck by lightning?"

I shook my head, although he couldn't see it.

"Five and a half, in spite of the fact that the area is well protected by lightning rods. But that isn't the only affliction that comes from the sky. Infrequently, people die from objects that fall to earth. Most come from the upper floors of buildings or from various aircraft, but there are actual heavenly bodies as well. Almost every year someone dies from a meteorite impact. Did you ever wonder what the chances are of being hit by a cosmic pebble no larger than a pea?"

I didn't reply or make any movement. My nose was pressed against the newspaper, so I couldn't even read.

The old man paid no attention to my silence. "Almost non-existent. The probability of winning the lottery is far greater. Even so, such misfortune does happen."

Silence reigned. My hopes that the old man had abandoned this one-sided conversation were nonetheless in vain.

"Something much larger might fall on your head too. One poor man met his maker under a piano that crashed down from the ninth floor."

I should have pretended I wasn't listening, but curiosity got the better of me. "Piano from the ninth floor?" I asked behind the newspaper.

"Yes, the ninth floor. They were moving it through

the window down to the seventh floor when the cable snapped. This accident at least makes some sense. The man who died was a retired piano tuner. What can you say, though, about a barber who was squashed by an elephant in the middle of the town square?"

I lowered the newspaper and stared at the old man.

"You didn't hear about that one?"

I shook my head.

"A circus was passing through. In order to drum up interest, they decorated the animals with banners and balloons, fitted them with parachutes and dropped them on the town. The rope on the elephant's parachute got tangled and an innocent barber paid the price. The elephant died too, of course."

I couldn't resist saying, "Really?"

The old man disregarded my scorn. "Yes. But there are happier outcomes too. Recently a reckless suicide jumped off an overpass right onto the head of an off-duty fireman who happened to be passing by. The fireman was killed on the spot and the suicide got off with minor injuries."

I closed the newspaper and folded it twice.

"All of that is interesting, but don't you think that on such a lovely day as this there are nicer things to talk about than dying?"

"Yes, there are, but as I said, people die on such days as this too."

That's when it dawned on me.

"Do you . . . feel all right?" It was an awkward way to phrase the question, but I couldn't think of anything else in my alarm.

"I feel great," replied the old man cheerfully. "And I'll feel even better if you give me your autograph."

He reached into the inside pocket of his jacket and took out a purple notebook and a metal pen. He opened it, leafed through it a bit, and then handed it to me along with the pen.

I took them both. The pages of the notebook were purple, too, and the pen appeared heavy.

"My autograph?"

"Yes," said the old man, as though this explained everything.

"Why on earth do you want my autograph? I'm not any kind of celebrity."

"Not yet. But if you were to become one then your autograph, dating from the time before you became famous, would be quite valuable."

I had thought I was more resistant to flattery. As I wrote my name expansively, however, my conscience wasn't pricked the least bit. I gave the notebook and pen back to the old man.

"I just don't see what could make me famous," I said diffidently, wanting to make amends for my lack of modesty. "I'm quite an ordinary man, I don't stand out in any way."

"Don't be like that. Even ordinary men can become famous. Here, take for example the retired piano tuner, the barber and the fireman I just mentioned. They received an unbelievable amount of publicity. They became authentic celebrities."

I looked at him warily. "I wouldn't exactly enjoy becoming famous for having a piano, an elephant or a failed suicide land on my head."

"Naturally, but we are not in a position to choose. These things happen against our will."

"I hope nothing like that happens to me." I smiled. "You won't get much use out of my autograph."

"That's what the others said. But they were wrong."

"What others?"

"The piano tuner, the barber, the fireman and many others. Just see how many autographs I have."

He took the notebook and thumbed through the pages. Dozens of signatures flashed by.

"Whose autographs are those?" I asked in a soft voice.

"People who died when something fell on them. I collected their very last signatures. My collection includes many more fine stories, some even more unusual than these three." He looked at his watch. "Unfortunately, I won't be able to tell you any of them because your time has run out. You have about forty-five seconds."

"Before what?" My voice had gone down almost to a whisper.

The old man stood up and put on his hat. He pointed upwards.

"Something is going to fall on you from up there."

"What?"

"Well, I can't tell you that. All I can say is that you will become very well known. The media will talk for days about the unbelievable accident that befell you. Your signature will be a real jewel in my collection. And now I hope you will forgive me. I must withdraw as soon as possible. It's not advisable to stay in your vicinity. Goodbye."

I looked at him for a moment as he hurried away and then I raised my eyes toward the heavens. The sky was filled with the blueness of a sparkling clear day, without even the trail of a passing airplane. As the seconds dragged slowly by, the impulse flashed through me to rush somewhere out of the way of the unidentified danger. I didn't, though, because it would have been in vain. I'd given my autograph, so there was no avoiding the fame that awaited me.

4. Photographs

MR. PALIVEC COLLECTED PHOTOGRAPHS of himself. He'd been doing it since he was thirty-three. That's when he'd bought himself a camera as a birthday present. It was one of the less pretentious cameras in a fancy photography shop, but even so he'd had to save up for it a long time. For this reason, he'd given himself very modest gifts for his previous two birthdays. When he turned thirty-one he'd had to be satisfied with a second-hand book, which he read with pleasure all the same, and one year later he'd given himself a framed watercolor which, after a bit of fixing-up, gave no indication that he'd picked it up at a sale.

He spent a full three and a half months studying the camera's instructions. He'd never been very good with mechanical things, so a great amount of effort was needed. But his innate persistence and diligence helped him master the art of photography. At least in theory. When he finally put the first roll of film in the camera, he already considered himself an experienced photographer. And then an unexpected problem cropped up.

Whose picture should he take? He couldn't just go out into the street, point his camera at a stranger and start snapping away. There was no way of knowing what the reaction might be. He for one wouldn't like to be accosted like that. There might even be a law that prohibited taking pictures without the subject's approval. What about taking pictures without any people in them? He could, for example, take pictures of buildings, empty landscapes or clouds. No, that didn't seem fitting. Photos should show real life and not still life like a watercolor.

Just when he thought he was up against a brick wall, a simple solution came to mind. He would take pictures of himself! Of course! What could be more appropriate? He was undeniably alive, and it was hard to think there was a law prohibiting a person from taking his own picture. After all, if it weren't allowed, why would the instructions have an entire section on how to take your own picture?

He went straight to work. First he chose the prettiest area in his apartment, prettied it up a bit more, and then read the instructions again just in case, even though he already knew them by heart. It took a bit of thought to find a way for the camera to be at the right elevation in the absence of a tripod. He put one chair on top of another, and then added a few books. The assembly wasn't very stable, but if he were careful nothing would go wrong.

He spent a few moments in front of the mirror sprucing himself up, and then finally sat in front of the camera, holding the thin silver wire used to take pictures from a distance. He didn't snap it right away, however. He suddenly realized that the pose he chose would make a big difference. True, he did not intend to show the pictures to anyone, but they would certainly outlive him. Should people get the wrong impression of him some far-off day just because he hadn't positioned himself properly? He went back to the mirror and spent some time trying different facial expressions. In the end he chose something that might be described as dignified and cordial gravity.

As soon as he'd taken the picture a new difficulty arose. He was dying to see it without delay, but that unfortunately wasn't possible. If he were to take the film to be developed it would be a total waste of money. The remaining thirty-five pictures would be wasted. No, all of the roll had to be used before he turned it in to have prints made. He was tempted briefly to sit in front of the camera again and quickly snap the remaining thirty-five shots. What held him back was the sober realization that he did not need so many copies of the same picture. What would they think of him at the photography shop, anyway? They would have to conclude he was an egomaniac.

He pondered at length about what to do. The decision he finally reached wasn't perfect, but nothing better came to mind. He would continue taking pictures of himself, but at one-month intervals. Every fifth of the month he would take a new picture at the exact same time that he'd taken the first one. This plan had an obvious drawback. Three years would have to pass before he finally saw the pictures. An onerous amount of patience would be required.

With regard to the possible criticism that he was egotistical, there were two recourses. Although the photographs would be similar, they wouldn't be the same as if they'd been taken all on the same day. Minor differences were inevitable. People change over time, and three years was not exactly a short period. In addition, he could do something to help make the pictures different. He didn't always have to be in a pose of dignified and cordial gravity. He could be grave and cordially dignified or dignified and gravely cordial.

He didn't sit twiddling his thumbs while the film in the camera steadily filled with his pictures, taken each time in the same place, wearing the same clothes. He had to make due preparations for the photographs before they arrived. They, of course, deserved the best possible album that money could buy. When he saw how much it cost, with leather covers, pages of highly refined cardboard and a gilded spine, he knew at once that his next two birthday presents would have to be quite unpretentious.

For his thirty-fourth he bought himself a phonograph record in a suburban secondhand store. True, he didn't have a record player, but the record had been quite inexpensive, and he was a great admirer of the symphonic orchestra's conductor. His thirty-fifth birthday present came from an even more unassuming place: the flea market. Only a glance was needed to see that the chipped statuette wasn't made of real marble, but one doesn't look a gift horse in the mouth.

He lit up with joy when he finally received the magnificent photo album for his thirty-sixth birthday. He went to the further expense of buying a pair of thin yellow rubber gloves so he wouldn't touch the album with his bare hands. He was quite fastidious about personal hygiene, but regardless of how thoroughly he washed his hands, they could still leave oily traces, something that most certainly had to be avoided.

Soon the need for a new acquisition appeared. He couldn't use just any old thing to write in the album. It had to be a special pen that slid across the cardboard, leaving a thin but distinct line. He bought it for his thirty-seventh birthday, received considerably in advance.

He set about meticulously writing dates above each photograph's place. He had nice handwriting, a bit slanted, but very legible. The album had sixty-nine pages, each one holding four photographs. He spent two full afternoons at work, concentrating solely on not making any mistakes. That would have been a genuine catastrophe.

After he'd brought the work to a successful close, he realized that the album would hold photographs all the way to his fifty-sixth birthday. That was really good. He would have no large expenditures on his hobby for all of two decades. He could save up for a new album and not have to tighten his belt very much. No longer would he have to make do with highly unassuming birthday presents.

Filled with anxiety, at long last he went to the photography shop to pick up the pictures, thirty-six months after he'd taken the first one. The night before, brow knitted with worry, he'd barely slept a wink. What if the pictures didn't turn out? That was possible, the film was already past its expiration date, and he might have done something wrong. He was horrified at the thought that all trace of three years of his life could disappear just like that. As though he'd never lived them.

When he received the envelope full of photographs, he breathed a sigh of relief. Great restraint was needed not to look at them right there in the shop or on the way home. Before he took out the pictures he put on the rubber gloves. Pride filled him as he looked at his dignified, cordial and grave face on the oldest picture, resembling a real self-portrait and not just a photograph.

His excitement rose higher and higher as he made his way through the bunch of pictures, easily recognizing which of the three traits prevailed in his expression. He couldn't decide what gave him greater satisfaction: how he'd turned out on the pictures or his mastery of photography. Not even a small technical imperfection was able to spoil his happiness. For some reason all the pictures had a slightly purple tinge—most likely because the film had been in the camera too long. Well, all right, he consoled himself, there was no need to split hairs.

He put the photographs in the album with care, making sure that each one was in the proper place. The negative helped him in this regard since it presented them in unerring chronological order. Then he took another look at them and even used a magnifying glass. He came to the conclusion that the pictures looked even better in the album, for that was where his dignity, cordiality and gravity were fully manifested.

Looking at the photographs became a well-established ritual—every Saturday afternoon. Periodically he got the urge to open the album more often, but he resisted the temptation. One shouldn't overdo one's pleasures. Then they lose their charm. Once a week was the right measure.

The Saturday rituals became longer and longer because a new set of thirty-six pictures arrived every three years. Although already an experienced photographer, apprehension still filled Mr. Palivec every time he went to pick up the new pictures, and delight took its place as he returned home from the shop. The only shortcoming was the ever-present purple tinge, but he'd become so used to it that its absence would have disconcerted him.

Just when he turned fifty-six, the album was finally filled. Although he'd saved quite enough money in the previous two decades, he didn't have to rush out and buy another album. Three years would pass before the new pictures arrived. He would spend that time enjoying what now seemed like a finally completed work. He imagined a writer felt the same way after finishing his long work on a novel. And not just any novel, but one in which he was the one and only character.

When he opened the album with gloved hands the first Saturday after inserting the last thirty-six pictures, an unpleasant surprise awaited him. The photographs on the first page had partially faded. His face seemed to be disappearing, while the background remained sharp. He flipped through the pages feverishly and discovered that the same thing had happened to the other pictures.

He closed the album, got up from the table and started pacing about the room. He'd already passed by the mirror when something forced him to go back. What he saw in it was the same as on the photographs. Only the contours of his face were discernible, while everything behind him was in sharp focus. He went all the way up to the glass, but his face was still blurry.

He went back to the table and opened the album in the middle. He was not very surprised at the further change. His chest was still on the pictures, but his head now seemed transparent. It had disappeared completely; in its place was the wall behind him. He drew yellow fingers across the photographs as though he could touch this invisibility. He didn't have to go back to the mirror, knowing without looking that if he tried to touch his face, his gloves would plunge into the emptiness above his neck.

He stared blankly ahead for a while, trying to collect his thoughts. A sober look at his new situation was needed. It clearly had many negative aspects. Not everything was black, however. Now he wouldn't have to buy a new photo album. He could spend his savings on something else.

5. Dreams

First I thought I heard the tinkling of the bells I wore as a child on Willow Day. But I was no longer a child. Then it sounded like the bell around the neck of the sheep leading the flock, the bellwether. But I wasn't in a village. Finally, I concluded from the intensity of the ringing that it must be coming from the belfry of a distant church. But in my dream there was no church.

The realization that I was dreaming inevitably woke me up. I couldn't even see the nose on my face in the pitch black, but there was no longer any doubt. The ringing was from the telephone on the bedside table, cutting the soft silence of the night with its persistent, jarring sound.

I stretched out my hand and felt for the switch to the wall lamp above the bedstead, then squinted in the bright light shining down on me. Turning towards the bedside table, I first looked at the clock. Three twenty-seven. Even though the ringing reverberated without letup, I stared at the clock hands for a moment in disbelief. At long last I lifted the receiver.

"Hello," I said hoarsely.

"Good evening." The voice was deep and mature. I had never heard it before. "Please excuse me for calling at this hour, but we must talk without delay."

"Who are you?"

"I am a dream collector."

I should have disconnected the phone before I'd gone to bed. But who would ever suspect that something like this might happen? I had yet to be the victim of twisted minds with nothing better to do than disturb people in the dead of night.

"Such tomfoolery does not befit your age," I said in annoyance and was just about to hang up when his words stopped me.

"Pygmy firefighters."

I was suddenly wide awake. "Excuse me?"

"You were dreaming about pygmy firefighters with purple helmets who were trying to put out a fire that was devouring a huge spider, and what came out of their hoses wasn't water but . . ."

"I know what came out of their hoses," I said, interrupting him curtly. "But how do you know what I was dreaming?"

"What kind of dream collector would I be if I didn't know what people dream? Not only do I know, I also remember them better than the dreamers. That's why I hastened to call before it was too late. In the morning you most likely won't have any memory of what you dreamed."

I was silent for several moments, gathering my thoughts. Before I said another word, I pinched my cheek with my left hand. The pain was real.

"What do you want from me?" I finally asked in a soft voice.

"Your dream."

"My dream?"

"Yes."

"Why do you want my dream?"

"I want to put it in my collection, of course. I collect dreams with purple details. If the pygmies hadn't been wearing helmets that color I wouldn't have bothered you at all."

"What stopped you from taking it without my knowledge, without waking me up? After all, as you said, I would have forgotten it by morning."

"That would be against the rules. You can't put a dream in your collection without the permission of the dreamer."

I did a bit more thinking. "Does that mean I could refuse to give you my permission?"

"Of course. But that wouldn't be in your interest."

"Really? Why not?"

"Because then you wouldn't get the reward."

"Reward?"

"That's right. Dreams aren't given for free. Everything has a price, dreams included."

"I didn't know."

"Not all dreams have the same price, of course. Most of them are actually worthless. No one collects them. You, however, are in luck. Dreams with purple details are among the very rarest, thus they are the most expensive. You could live a life of luxury for years on what I'm going to offer you for your dream about purple firefighters."

The dream collector waited for me to say something in return, but in my confusion I remained silent.

"Perhaps it would be easier for you to accept this," he continued after several moments, "if you imagine it's not about a dream but rather a work of art. The comparison is not at all incongruous. Many people try to create works of art, but only the exceptional few succeed. It's the same thing with dreams. Many people dream, but the number of successful dreams is very small. That's the nature of things. Talent is needed for dreams as well as art, and talented dreamers are a rarity. You are certainly one of them."

"I had no idea," I mumbled.

"That's what usually happens. Talented dreamers don't know they are talented until collectors tell them. I'm proud of the fact that I have discovered some of the most talented. If only you could see my collection. There's not a single dream collector who doesn't envy me. I have a complete gallery of purple dream masterpieces. Your dream will be in excellent company."

"How nice," I said, not very eloquently, but nothing more coherent came to mind at that late hour. "So all I need to do to get the reward is give my permission?"

"Yes. And answer some questions."

"What questions?"

"About yourself. I have to ascertain some facts. Sometimes there is an impediment that prevents a dream from entering a collection."

"Impediment?"

"Yes. We are not like art buyers in this respect. Such verification would be unnecessary if you were, let's say, a painter and I owned a gallery. Your private life wouldn't interest me in the slightest. But dream collectors have to stick to strict rules. Only the dreams of untarnished dreamers can enter a collection. This requirement has caused me to lose several unique specimens. Don't be concerned, I'm almost certain that everything will be fine with you. Shall we begin?"

"Go ahead," I said after a short pause.

"Have you ever killed anyone?"

"Whatever gave you such an idea?" I replied angrily.

"Please don't be offended. The question is by no means directed at you personally. Murderers dream too. Sometimes their dreams are of a much higher quality than those of ordinary people. One of the prettiest dreams I ever saw slipped away just because the elderly dreamer, when he was a young man, had inadvertently caused a traffic accident in which an old woman died, even though she would have died just the same a few years later. But what could I do? Rules are rules. Let's continue. Are you allergic to pollen or goose feathers?"

"No, I'm not."

"Fine. Has any member of your family in the past three generations been treated for a serious mental disorder?"

I bristled once again but all I did was say through clenched teeth, "Of course not."

"Very good. Have you ever had a contagious disease?"

I thought for a moment. "Scarlet fever and mumps."

"That's all? You haven't had typhoid fever, malaria, cholera, smallpox or the plague?"

I shook my head vigorously, although it was pointless. "No, I haven't."

"Wonderful. Do you take pleasure in torturing household pets?"

"I don't have any pets in my house."

"So, you don't take any pleasure. All right. Are you color blind?"

"How could I dream of pygmy firefighters with purple helmets if I were color blind?"

"That wouldn't stand in your way. You might not know it, but the dreams of the color blind are a real explosion of color. It's a shame that the rules won't let us include them in our collections. Are you afraid of heights?"

"A little," I said reluctantly.

"When you are on the edge of a cliff, do you become totally paralyzed, overcome by dizziness, and covered in cold sweat?"

"I stay away from the edges of cliffs."

"Smart thinking. That means we can conclude that you do not suffer from acute fear of heights. Do you collect stamps?"

"No."

"That's really good. Up until now I've lost the most dreams because the dreamers turned out to be philatelists."

"What's wrong with being a philatelist?"

"There's nothing wrong, of course. I personally have nothing against philatelists; I actually like them, even though they've caused me losses. But those are the rules and I wasn't the one who made them. In any case, you're making great progress. We only have three questions left. Did you ever go through an earthquake stronger than six and a half on the Richter scale?"

"I've never gone through an earthquake."

"Not even a tiny one?"

"Not even a tiny one."

"You're lucky. Even little earthquakes are quite unpleasant. Do you count the steps when climbing upstairs?"

"No. And I usually take the elevator to go up."

"That's not very healthy. It's been shown that people who prefer to take the stairs instead of the elevator live an average of three years, four months and seven days longer. On the other hand, it's hard to say no to comfort. And finally, here is the last question. Did you drink an alcoholic beverage before you went to bed last night?"

I hesitated briefly. "Yes, I did. Half a glass of wine, just like I do every evening."

"Red or white?"

"Red."

Silence reigned on the other end of the line.

I waited a bit and then asked, "That's not good?"

The dream collector sighed noisily before he answered. "No, it isn't. The rules are explicit. Not a drop of red wine is allowed. It counts as strong doping, unlike white wine, which is allowed in moderate amounts. Dreams under the influence of red wine are considered to be artificial, not natural."

"If I'd known, I wouldn't have touched it."

"If you hadn't, it's questionable whether you would have dreamed about pygmy firefighters with purple helmets."

"What now?" I said after a brief silence.

"Nothing, I'm afraid. We're both losing out. You won't get your lavish reward and I've forfeited an excellent dream. But don't lose hope. As I said before, you are a talented dreamer. Just avoid red wine before you go to bed. I'll keep a sharp eye on your dreams. I'll call you again as soon as a purple one appears, although quite some time might pass until the next one. But at least we won't have to go through the questions again. Now, go back to sleep. Good night."

"Good night," I said, after the line was already dead.

I hung up the receiver and turned off the wall lamp. I lay there staring into the impenetrable darkness surrounding me until the sound of ringing came from the distance. The thunderous church bell came first, followed a bit later by the muffled sound of the bellwether, which quickly segued into the soft tinkling of the bells from my childhood. Finally there was nothing around me but silence.

6. Words

Mr. Plushal collected words. He'd been doing this since the age of fifty-six, after reading his first anthology of love poems. It had been a small paperback with a beautiful purple flower on the cover, although the smell emanating from the book was wholly incompatible with this image. The copy had the stale, musty odor that inevitably permeates books after they spend a long time in a basement secondhand bookstore.

Mr. Plushal might not have bought the anthology. Although he periodically made the rounds of the bookstores, he rarely bought any books, and when he did they were of a quite different sort. He had a small library in his house consisting primarily of handbooks. On raising houseplants, for example. He himself didn't have any plants, but he considered himself very knowledgeable on the subject. Or on cats. He didn't have a cat because he was allergic to their fur, but if anyone were to ask him, he had plenty of useful advice to offer. There was also a handbook on freezer maintenance and repair. True, he had no need for a freezer, but useful knowledge is nothing to be sneezed at.

He had decided to buy the anthology because of the flower on the cover. As a plant expert he knew that such a flower did not exist, but that was the very reason it had appealed to him. He took the book to the cashier in a somewhat uneasy state. It seemed somehow unfitting for a man his age to show an interest in romantic verse. It was almost like buying a pornographic magazine. Luckily the salesgirl didn't take note of the title. All she did was look at the price and take the exact change he handed her.

He knew a thing or two about love, of course. Not from personal experience in this case, either, but was that necessary? Most likely people are born with such awareness. How else could it be? Nonetheless, when he set to reading the book, the unease from the store returned, despite the fact that he was alone. He even blushed. He only found relief with the thought that the anthology should be considered a handbook on love. Then everything became easier and quite pleasant.

He was surprised to find that the words in the book charmed him even more than the tender and exalted feelings. He suddenly became aware of something that had escaped his notice. Beautiful words exist. They weren't necessarily special or rare, rather ordinary words that were to be found in other books too. But for some reason or other they had never looked beautiful in the handbooks. Or rather, their beauty hadn't caught his eye.

The more he read, the more he was filled with the fear of losing something. When he turned a page, the words that stayed behind seemed to pale and evaporate. New ones came to take their place, but this was insufficient consolation. He had to save the earlier ones somehow. It made no sense to allow them to disappear. He could have gone back to them, of course, but then he would never finish reading the book. No, he had to find a better solution. And then he had a flash of inspiration.

He bought a large lined notebook with a leather cover. Nothing less magnificent would suffice as a repository for beautiful words. How could he write them in an ordinary notebook? That would have been almost sacrilegious. He returned to the beginning of the anthology, holding the open notebook in front of him.

Whenever he came across a beautiful word, he wrote it down promptly with his fountain pen. It was not made of gold, in actual fact, but it's hard to arrange everything to perfection.

His handwriting was neat. Not ornate but measured, even a little austere. Beautiful in its own way. Just what was needed to write down beautiful words, not overshadowing them yet consonant with them. He normally wrote with large letters, but for this occasion he made the letters smaller. Just in case. He didn't know how many beautiful words he would find. The notebook was quite thick, but he had to proceed with care.

It was not until he had written down all the beautiful words in the anthology that he mustered the courage to check the results. Would they remain beautiful in his notebook or would their beauty be lost, as in the handbooks? Holding the notebook a short distance away, he breathed a sigh of relief as he took in the four densely filled pages. Not only was their beauty intact, it seemed somehow enhanced. This was probably due to the fact that only beautiful words were present, not those other ones that were not exactly ugly, but did not stand out in any way. The notebook was concentrated beauty.

After he had finished the anthology, he wondered what to do next. The notebook was nowhere near to being filled, it had barely been touched. Could he leave it like that? It would be as if he'd merely chipped off a bit of beauty. No, he had to continue. There had to be many more beautiful words. They all deserved to be in one place. But where should he look for them?

What first crossed his mind, naturally, was another anthology of love poems. He couldn't go wrong there. He'd seen for himself that beautiful words find great expression in love poems. But if he kept buying just this type of book he would soon become conspicuous. Two or three more could pass unnoticed, but three hundred and thirty-five, the number he'd seen in the Main Library catalogue, would certainly give rise to derision. No, he would have to think of something else. And then he had a second inspirational flash.

Who said beautiful words could only be found in anthologies of love poems? They certainly had to be in other books too. Why not even in handbooks? He was already expert enough to grasp a great truth. Beautiful words are everywhere. The skill lay not in the choice of books but in detecting the words. You had to have an eye for them. And he suspected he already had one. There was a simple way to verify this. He grabbed the first handbook within his reach and opened it. The same moment he was blinded by a blaze of beautiful words, as though someone had highlighted them with a bright marker.

He was barely able to resist the temptation to open his notebook and start writing them down. What stopped him was his prudence, something that made him rightfully proud. One couldn't be so impulsive. Where would that lead one? Confusion would reign in an instant. He had to be steadfast and systematic. After thoroughly considering the circumstances, the solution presented itself at last, once again in the form of an inspiration.

He struggled briefly with the thought of tearing up the first four pages in the notebook so he could start over again. But he dropped the idea. Such an important undertaking could not begin in a disfigured notebook. He would have to buy a new one. That alone would be fitting. He chose the largest one he could find. It had a feature that he found particularly expedient: a gilded ribbon to mark the place where you had stopped reading or writing.

The enormous dictionary had sixteen heavy tomes. When he opened the first one, a bevy of sparkling, beautiful words met his eye. The magnitude of what lay ahead did not frighten him, however. He was perfectly prepared for it. Nor could he expect to find any shortcuts. Whatever time was needed to write them all down would be taken, neither more nor less. After all, what lay before him was joy and not suffering. Indeed, what can be more joyful than writing down beauty?

When he finally brought his work to a close, Mr. Plushal was considerably older than fifty-six. But this did nothing to lessen his feeling of satisfaction and fulfillment. On the contrary. How many people that old can say their lives have not been in vain, for they have collected beauty? Only one thing was left for him to do. There was room for just two more words at the bottom of the last page of the completely filled notebook. For the first time since he'd started his collection, he softened his handwriting a little. It was still austere, but also gentle, benevolent. Just the way a signature should be. Entering the notebook, he slowly pulled the back cover after him, as though lowering a heavy lid.

7. Stories

I TYPED THE LAST sentence of the story. But there was no time to sink into the unique feeling of relief brought by the completion of writing. Before I had managed to press two keys on the keyboard to save the file, the screen suddenly turned purple.

How awful! The monitor was indeed old, but I had nonetheless expected it to hold up for some time to come. Why did it have to go on the blink right then and spoil my moment of pleasure? What's more, the last thing I needed was an unforeseen expenditure.

Filled with frustration, I did something that actually made no sense. I turned off the monitor, waited a bit and then turned it on again. That's what people do who don't know anything about hardware, and I wasn't one of them. When things start going wrong, those not in the know first turn off everything they can. Whatever for? It might be their confusion, it might be to let off steam, or it might be the irrational hope that when they turn things back on, everything will be put magically back in place.

When the screen lit up again nothing, of course, was back in place. The purple shade was still there and at the bottom of the story, after a space of one line, something was written that hadn't been there a moment before. I bent down and looked at the short addendum:

Wonderful story! Congratulations!

Staring close up at the three words, I tried to figure out what was going on. The only thing that crossed my mind was that someone had linked up to my computer over the Internet and had been spying on me as I wrote. There is all manner of abuse over the Internet, but I had yet to hear of something similar. It would be truly terrible if such spying were possible. But that wasn't my main problem at the moment. Without even checking the lower right-hand corner of the screen I knew that the intruder hadn't come via the Internet because I wasn't online. Why should I be, anyway, when I was writing?

Bewilderment led me to repeat my senseless reaction. Even though I was aware that it wouldn't solve anything, I reached for the monitor button again. My hand remained in midair, however, because the cursor jumped down to the next line and started writing new text right before my eyes.

Turning the monitor off and on again won't get you anywhere.

I jumped back from the screen spontaneously, as though physically threatened. I felt the hair on the back of my neck stand on end. What was going on? How could he know what I intended to do? I started looking feverishly around my study, but a new message stopped me.

There isn't any camera, if that's what you're looking for.

Great restraint was needed to stop me from turning off the computer. If I did, though, I would lose the story, which hadn't been saved, and that had to be avoided at any cost. I brought my hands cautiously to the keyboard, as though it might bite me. I pressed two keys lightly, then quickly raised my fingers, but the normal confirmation that I'd saved the text was missing. In its place came a rapid series of letters in italics.

Everything is all right. The story is saved. Don't worry. We certainly couldn't let such a good story go to waste, could we?

I stared for some time at the four lines under the

last paragraph of the story. When I finally returned my hands to the keyboard, hesitating as before, I knew I was getting involved in something dodgy. But what choice did I have?

Who are you?

A collector of last stories.

There were much more important questions, of course, but all I did was type one word.

Last?

Yes. This is your last story. And probably your best. That is quite rare, by the way.

I paused briefly before my fingers touched the keyboard again.

Why would it be my last?

Isn't it obvious? Because you won't be writing any more.

This was completely crazy, but since I was already ambushed, I had to continue.

Why wouldn't I write any more? Who's going to prevent me?

You'll prevent yourself. At least I hope you will.

And why on earth would I do such a thing?

Because otherwise you'll die.

Irritation replaced my confusion. Nimble fingers typed angrily.

Listen here! I don't know how you're pulling this off and I really don't care. I've had enough. You've gone too far. I won't let anyone taunt me like that.

You haven't been to the doctor in a while, have you? It might be a good idea to find the time. How long are you going to pretend that the stitch at the base of your chest isn't getting worse?

I didn't answer right away. I brought a hand unconsciously to my chest.

How do you know? I haven't told anyone about it.

Is that important? You just confirmed it yourself.

I hoped it wasn't anything serious. I guess I'll have to go to the doctor.

The doctor won't be able to help you very much unless you help yourself.

By not writing?

That's right. Your very next story would be fatal. You would die of a heart attack just as you started to write it.

I thought of asking once again how he knew, but gave up. It really wasn't important.

And if I don't write anymore?

Then you will live to a rather ripe old age. The pains in your chest will disappear all by themselves. The doctor will give you a clean bill of health.

I thought it over a bit.

The choice, then, is between life without writing and writing that leads to death?

Yes. The choice is yours.

I hesitated briefly once again.

That's not much of a choice.

It isn't, but it's better than not having any choice at all.

Why do I deserve preferential treatment?

As I wrote the last word I knew what the answer would be.

Is that important?

What would happen if later on, when the doctor says I'm healthy, I started writing again?

You wouldn't get very far. Even the healthiest people can die a sudden death. There's no cheating with this. You have written your last story.

I sighed and pinched the bridge of my nose with thumb and index finger because a dull throb had started there.

Do you have a lot of last stories in your collection?

Yes. A lot.

Were their authors faced with this choice too?

They were.

What did they choose?

Most of them chose life. And longevity. Particularly since there is actually no alternative. There are some, how-

ever, who can't live without writing. They continue, even when they know what awaits them.

I can understand that.

Does that mean you'll join them?

I don't know. I have to think it over. It's not an easy decision to make.

It isn't, I agree. In any case, whatever you decide, I think you'll be happy to know that your last story is one of the nicest in my collection. I hope this brings you some consolation.

I laughed bitterly.

I feel better already.

Good. That's about all. I am honored to have had the chance to talk to a wonderful writer.

I'd already touched the keys, but there was no time to send an appropriate farewell. The text of our dialogue and the story that preceded it were suddenly highlighted in black, as when a block is marked, and then disappeared. The purple film went with it. The whiteness of the empty screen stared at me with blank eloquence.

I stared back at it, stock-still for a time. And then my fingers, already resting on the keyboard, seemed to start typing by themselves:

I typed the last sentence of the story. But there was no time to sink into the unique feeling of relief brought by the completion of writing. Before I had managed to press two keys on the keyboard to save the file, the screen suddenly turned purple.

I didn't have time to lower the cursor to a new paragraph. A sharp pain forced me to grab desperately at my chest.

8. Clippings

Mr. Pospihal collected newspaper clippings. He'd been doing this since the age of sixty-two, when he retired. He'd spent his entire adult life working for the post office, rising from postman to manager. Working in the post office had taught him to respect order above all things. He was an innately orderly man, but the work at the post office had fully impressed on him the importance of averting *any* kind of disorder. Even deviating quite innocently from the rules or yielding however slightly to confusion could have unforeseeable consequences.

Maintaining order took time. Even before he'd become manager, Mr. Pospihal stayed at work longer than regulations required. Thorough preparations were needed before the workday began, and when it was over many things were left that needed attention. If he hadn't proceeded in such a way he would never have become manager. And promotion to that position didn't soften him a bit. Quite the contrary. He spent almost every waking hour at the post office, arriving considerably before the other employees and leaving long after them. It couldn't have been any other way. Before, he'd been responsible solely for himself, while as manager he was responsible for many other people.

Such commitment to his work didn't leave much time for a private life. Mr. Pospihal had never started a family, although he might have wanted one in his younger days. Later this desire diminished, and he even saw the merits of not being married and having children. He'd sacrificed himself for the greater good. It would have been hard to be a successful postal employee, let alone manager, if he'd been hampered by family obligations. The example of many of his colleagues confirmed this. Chiefly because they were family oriented, they did not do their jobs anywhere near as reliably and conscientiously as he did his.

When he retired, Mr. Pospihal had to face a double blow. First of all, he wasn't at all certain he'd left the post office in good hands. His opinion of the manager who succeeded him was far from good. No sooner had he taken up his position than he dropped the strict rules on employee behavior that Mr. Pospihal had unofficially introduced that dealt, for example, with how long the employees' hair and mustaches could be, and prohibited them from wearing short-sleeved shirts regardless of the temperature. He'd written the new manager a detailed letter, polite but severe, expressing his reasonable grounds for concern with regard to such indulgence, indicating the far-reaching consequences it might have. The lack of a reply even after a reasonable time had passed gave him great cause for concern and vexation.

The second blow fell even more heavily on Mr. Pospihal. Now retired, he had an abundance of the free time he'd consistently avoided while he was working. Since he didn't know how to fill his days, they were unbearably long in the beginning. And then he hit upon the best way to kill time. He would read the newspaper.

Mr. Pospihal used to read the newspaper before he retired, when he got home from work, but in a cursory fashion. He'd been reading the same serious daily newspaper from the capital ever since he was a young man, opening it after dinner before he went to bed. Fatigue, however, didn't allow him to get very engrossed. He'd leaf through the first section just enough to see the main headlines and might read an article from the front page if it seemed particularly important. Then sleep would steal over him. After all, he had to get up early in the morning.

Now he was finally able to read the newspaper at his leisure and when he wasn't sleepy. Right after breakfast he would settle into the only armchair in his small living room and stay there all the way till lunchtime, reading the paper from cover to cover. He didn't omit a thing, since he'd realized the meaning of being systematic long ago. Furthermore, the classified ads and obituaries were sometimes more interesting than front-page news.

Under such circumstances, it was inevitable that Mr. Pospihal would come across the section devoted to science published every Friday in the same place in the second half of the newspaper, after the section on culture and before the sports page. But the science section most likely would not have especially caught his eye if the very first article he read there hadn't been so exceptional. It was all about the fact that man is made of cosmic matter.

He didn't understand very much about science, although he certainly held it in great esteem. He'd been turned off science by complicated words he didn't know and even more complicated ideas he couldn't grasp. The author of this article, however, had taken great pains to write in simple language, and the idea itself, although unusual in every respect, could be understood with a certain amount of effort. In brief, it said just one place in the cosmos is the origin of almost all the atoms that make up living beings. That place is the core of very large suns. Humans, therefore, come from the stars.

Mr. Pospihal's previous opinion of himself, which was already good, was further reinforced by the knowledge of his cosmic origin. He cut the article out of the newspaper to keep it as a sort of genealogy and briefly toyed with the idea of framing it, then thought this would be going too far. He was content to put it in a transparent purple folder like those used in the post office to hold especially important documents. That way he could reread it whenever he wanted without damaging it by his touch or in any other way.

He waited impatiently for the following Friday to see whether the science section would repeat the same topic and was a bit disappointed when it was about something else. The new text attracted his attention nonetheless. After the very first reading he felt that he'd penetrated deep into the heart of the mysterious black holes. Everything was explained coherently, there was no confusion or ambiguity. He found a transparent purple folder for the second article too.

When Mr. Pospihal's collection had grown a bit, he finally realized what he liked so much about science. Order reigned. Unlike mankind's activities, where the inclination towards chaos was so evident, the world of science was perfectly ordered. Had he known this before he would have surely become a scientist and not a postal employee. Given his propensity for order, he would have gone quite far.

Who knows how long Mr. Pospihal would have enjoyed his collection and new focus in life, if it hadn't been for the one hundred and thirty-seventh article. What he read gave him such a shock that it shook the very foundations of his world. His heart started to pound and for a moment he was short of breath. Before mustering the courage to reread this text about the end of the universe he had to take a sedative.

The very author of the articles he'd been collecting so diligently and placing in transparent purple folders, the scientific commentator whose expertise and competence he trusted so much, had now put forward something altogether shocking and impossible. The universe, he claimed, would meet a terrible end. In one hundred twenty-five and a half billion years there would be no more galaxies or stars or planets. Or even people. There would be nothing but elementary particles wandering aimlessly and even they would finally disappear.

Once he'd calmed down a little, Mr. Pospihal wrote an angry letter to the newspaper's editor-in-chief, directly accusing him of irresponsibly publishing positively incorrect and highly disturbing information. Was that a way for the universe to end? How could such magnificent order end in supreme disorder? This was betraying the very essence of science!

Was the author of the article conscious of what he'd said? If what he said were true, what would be the point of making any effort, since everything was doomed from the outset? This, of course, could not and must not happen. Had he made a supreme effort his whole life through to keep the post office in impeccable shape just to have it finally turn into scattered atoms, and maybe not even that, regardless of how far in the future?

He expected an immediate reply from the editor-in-chief with the apology he was due. The immediate dismissal of the science commentator was taken for granted. Partial amends might be possible if they proposed that Mr. Pospihal write for the science section in the future. He already had the expertise and an oversight such as this would never afflict him. He knew all too well the meaning of order.

In the following days, the first thing Mr. Pospihal did was to check the newspaper's editorial page. Since the editor-in-chief's reply and apology were not forthcoming, he concluded that the editorial board was trying to hush up the scandal. Instead of making the whole affair public, they would send him a discreet letter and try to keep him quiet. First they would try persuasion, and if that didn't work they'd use bribery or even threats. But he wouldn't give in. Had it been something less important he might have turned a blind eye, but this was of the broadest cosmic proportions. He didn't have the right to retreat.

After several weeks had passed with still no letter, Mr. Pospihal concluded dejectedly that a great conspiracy was at work and, alas, he alone could do nothing against it. Disorder had triumphed over order, and all he could do was stand by helplessly and watch.

Overcome by frustration, the first thing he did was destroy his collection. As with everything else in his life, he did it systematically. He took a large pair of scissors, sharpened them a bit and then cut all the articles together with their purple folders into small pieces of the same size. And then, for the first time in his life, he did something unreasonable. He ate this plastic-coated confetti slowly and determinedly, even though the taste was quite abominable.

Then he sat in the armchair, prepared for what would follow. He was not surprised when he began soon to disintegrate. With perverse curiosity, as though this were happening to someone else and not himself, he watched himself dissolve. The connections that kept the atoms of his body together, what used to be cosmic matter, slowly started to break, and particles scattered chaotically about the living room. Soon, in one hundred billion years or so, they too would disappear forever.

9. Deaths

I WAS JUST ABOUT to fall asleep when a knock roused me. I opened my eyes and looked angrily towards the hospital room door. Who could that be now? Hadn't we agreed they wouldn't come until morning? A man has the right to die in peace, doesn't he? They were well aware of the fact that nothing more could be done, and as an experienced doctor, so was I. I had taken a strong sedative to fall asleep as soon as possible. Dying in my sleep was the very last favor I could do myself. Why were they taking it away from me now?

"Come in!" I said, as sharply as my general condition allowed.

The man who came in was tall and slender. He was wearing a long purple coat, its cheerfulness somewhat incongruous with his late middle age. A gray or olive-green shade would have been more suited to his thinning, salt-and-pepper hair and softly wrinkled face. But that, of course, was hardly important now.

"Good evening," he said and, without waiting for a reply, headed for the chair next to my pillow. He sat down, folded his hands in his lap and stared at me in silence. We stayed like that for a few moments, looking at each other.

I was the first to break the silence. "Don't you think it's rather late to visit a sick man?"

"It would indeed be late in just a few minutes. As it is, until you fall asleep, there's still time."

"Time for what? Who are you? How did you get into the hospital at this hour?"

"In what order would you like the answers? Let's start from the last question. It's the easiest. I was able to enter the hospital because no one stopped me."

"Wasn't the security officer on duty?"

"He was, but he didn't see me."

"How's that? Were you invisible or something?"

"You might say so."

I sighed. "Well, you don't look that way to me. What do you want?"

The visitor did not answer immediately. He again threw me a brief and silent look.

"Your death," he said at last in an even tone.

Now it was my turn to stare at him.

"Listen, I don't know who you are or how you got here. It makes no difference anyway. But unless you leave here at once, I'll call and have them throw you out."

"I suggest you do exactly that."

I hesitated a minute, then stretched out my hand and felt for the buzzer on the night table. I pushed it longer than was necessary. The nurse's rapid footsteps were heard coming down the hall.

I didn't say a word when she came in. It was enough to look at the chair next to the bed to understand why I'd called. But she came up to me as though we were alone in the room.

"How are you?" she asked gently.

I stared at her in confusion, not knowing what to say.

"I can't sleep," were the words that finally came out.

She patted the back of my hand.

"You'll fall asleep soon enough. Don't worry. You were given a strong dose."

Quite an effort was needed for me to give a fleeting smile.

"Thank you."

"I'm here if you need anything. All you have to do is ring."

"Thank you."

She returned my smile, straightened my covers a bit and then headed for the door. She stopped at it as though about to turn around, but didn't.

I waited for the nurse's footsteps to fade down the hall before I looked at the visitor again.

"Who are you?" I asked in a low voice.

"A death collector." His voice was still detached, as though saying something quite commonplace.

"Death collector?" I repeated rather foolishly.

"Yes. I collect deaths. It's not as unusual a hobby as it might seem. There are stranger ones. If you give me your death you will get something truly priceless in return."

"How can I give you my death?"

"It's easy. All you have to do is give your consent."

"That's all?"

"Yes."

"And then I won't die anymore?"

"You won't die."

"And I'll get something in return too?"

"By all means."

I paused for a moment.

"What?"

He too waited a bit before replying.

"If you had to choose the most beautiful day of your life, which one would it be?"

"That's a difficult question. I'd have to think it over."

"You don't have much time for that. There must be one day you remember as being exceptional. A day when you were especially happy."

"There were days like that, of course. But why are they important now? They're gone forever."

"One could come back."

"How?"

"I could give you an explanation but it would take some time and the sedative will knock you out any moment. We have to be quick."

"In what way would it come back? I don't understand."

"In such a way that you would be in that day again. You would live through it exactly the same way you did the first time. You wouldn't know anything about your life to come. As though it never happened."

I thought it over briefly.

"And at the end of that day? Is that when I would die?"

"No. You would never die. Your death would be in my collection."

"Would I continue to live out the rest of my life?"

"No, you wouldn't. You would go back to your most beautiful day. You would relive it over and over, every day. Forever. So, do you agree to exchange your death for such an eternity?"

The sedative was starting to take effect. Considerable effort was needed to keep my eyes open.

"Why wouldn't I agree? Anyone in my place would say yes."

The visitor smiled broadly.

"Wonderful!" he said in a voice that was no longer indifferent. "That means we have a deal."

"It's a deal," I confirmed in a soft voice, eyes half-closed.

The smile stayed on his face a short while longer, but when he spoke again his voice had become detached like before.

"Not everyone accepts my offer, you know."

"Who would choose death when he's offered eternity, especially one filled with a beautiful day?" I asked almost in a whisper, finally closing my eyes.

His answer seemed to come from a distance. "Eternity lasts a very long time, even when it's ideal. I hope you'll enjoy it nonetheless."

A wave of fear suddenly coursed through my fading consciousness. I vaguely suspected that something wasn't right, but couldn't figure out what it was. And then it didn't matter anymore. I started to wake up, filled with unexpected joy. Something very nice awaited me in the coming day.

10. Emails

Mr. Pavek collected emails. He'd been doing this since he retired at age sixty-five. He hadn't been able to do it before because he hadn't had a computer at home. When he finally left the State Archive after four decades of dedicated service, he was given the computer he'd used for the last thirteen and a half years as a token of recognition. The satisfaction he received from this gift was not marred by the knowledge that it was to be written off as obsolete since new computers were on the way.

Had they given him a new computer, it would have brought him nothing but trouble, since he was unable to cope with any but his old one. He was used to it, although that had taken some doing. He'd needed considerably more time than the other employees to master a mischievous and unpredictable machine that seemed determined never to do what he wanted it to.

He'd gone through countless traumatic experiences during training. All his efforts were ruined by clumsiness and blunders: once he'd caused a fire and another time an ambulance was called because he'd had a nervous breakdown. But finally, after a little more than two years and two months, he could proudly say that he'd subjugated the computer at long last, at least as far as the basic archive program was concerned.

His colleagues used many other programs that often had nothing to do with work, but it never crossed his mind to do something similar. If anyone had asked why, he would have answered that he definitely did not approve of such an abuse of working hours and state-owned equipment, but since no one ever did ask, there was no need for self-delusion. He avoided other programs because they frightened him.

When he brought the computer home, fear came along with it. Since he now had nothing to do with the only program he was skilled at, he would have to learn new programs, i.e. go through the trauma all over again. He could, indeed, have avoided this by not using the computer at all. That's what he did at first. He put the housing and monitor in a corner and covered them with a purple flannel cloth. This soon seemed like an unnecessary waste, so he finally reconciled himself to the inevitable.

His first dilemma was which program to choose. Different computer games favored by his former colleagues were out of the question. He couldn't imagine wasting time so irresponsibly, even in retirement. The best thing would be to do something useful. But what? Lots of people use a computer like a typewriter, but what would he write?

Who knows how long he would have spent pondering what to do with his computer if he hadn't seen an advertisement in the newspaper lauding the benefits of the Internet, particularly if you were looking for a job. Mr. Pavek knew that the Internet was quite widespread and that people enthused over it, but he'd avoided it out of the same fear that prevented him from trying new programs. Now, however, he had no way out. He would have to overcome that fear.

A pleasant surprise awaited him: it turned out that using the Internet was not as difficult as he'd feared. There was no nervous breakdown and not even any lasting trauma. Twice he thought he'd backed himself into a corner, but he quickly got out of it by carefully following the clear instructions. Everything was set for simple and easy use.

Hooking up to the Internet was just like opening a big window onto a vast world that included many different possibilities. It soon became apparent that Mr. Pavek wouldn't have to look for something to occupy his time. Work came looking for him.

The very same day he hooked up to the Internet he started to receive emails. Even though he didn't know the senders and had no idea how they'd found his address, he was pleased nonetheless. Hardly anyone ever wrote to Mr. Pavek, and now whenever he looked at his virtual mailbox there were always a few letters waiting.

His mail consisted of various offers that didn't interest him very much. Those that made him blush were the most numerous. Indeed, how could anyone think that he, at his age, might need to lengthen certain organs or use products that brought fierce and long-lasting ecstasy? But he didn't get mad at those who sent the offers because their intentions were undoubtedly noble. How could you blame people who were trying to fill your life with pleasure, regardless of the fact that it was impossible?

As soon as Mr. Pavek read his first message, his archivist's instincts went to work. He knew quite well what happened to documents that were not quickly logged as prescribed. This was the basic principle of his profession. Things get lost in an instant and disappear without a trace unless they are filed properly. And one never knows how valuable they might be. Didn't it often happen that papers everyone considered inconsequential had turned out to be of great importance? Many people failed to realize that a proper archive was the foundation of every ordered society.

He adjusted his archive program slightly so he could store emails. Every message was first given a file number and classification. The abbreviation system he used at work came in quite handy. Instead of writing "erotic offer", which would make him feel awkward whenever he saw it, it was enough to put "er.ofr." This had a respectable and professional look to it.

Once the message was logged, he had to answer it. Good manners so required. What would the people who wrote think about him if he didn't reply? Remarks might be made about Mr. Pavek—that he was excessively fastidious, rather unsociable, too much a creature of habit—but certainly not that he was impolite.

His replies were short and official, as befitted correspondence with people he didn't know personally. He didn't go into a lengthy explanation as to why he wasn't interested in what had been offered. He thanked them for the offer, allowed for the possibility that he might change his mind in the future should his circumstances alter, and ended with a formal greeting. Everything in proper measure.

Although Mr. Pavek didn't see the connection, with every reply he sent he received more and more new offers. Barely two weeks after he'd hooked up to the Internet he was overwhelmed with work. His virtual mailbox never seemed to be empty and he spent an increasing amount of time logging his emails and answering them.

His replies sped up considerably when he remembered that he didn't have to compose a new email every time. While still at work he'd learned one of the facilities that computers provide. He'd had no use for it before, but now it proved quite convenient. Once a text was written it could easily be copied to another place, and his answers were always more or less the same anyway. He didn't do this mechanically, however. He would always introduce a small change, just enough to keep his conscience clear. He didn't want it to seem that he was merely skimming through his work. Something small would set each message apart: the word order, an added or missing adjective, the location of the signature.

His speedy replies only brought momentary relief because the influx of emails soon turned into an avalanche. While still employed, Mr. Pavek would occasionally encounter a large workload where great effort was required and he had to stay over-time. But that couldn't be compared with what was now pouring down on him. Hundreds of new mails gushed out of his virtual mailbox whenever he opened it.

This correspondence was no great hardship, however, because otherwise Mr. Pavek wouldn't have known how to pass the time. He didn't know how to be idle. He now spent almost all his waking time at the computer and had even reduced his sleep to only four and a half hours, but if that was the price he had to pay to fill his life with something, then he had no choice. The question as to whether the work had any meaning didn't bother him, just as it hadn't when he worked at the State Archive. Only uneducated and ignorant people needed to have the meaning of archiving explained to them; it was clear and obvious to those with any intelligence.

Although he could be unrelenting with regard to himself, forcing himself to work beyond all customary measure, the computer required due consideration. Unlike him, this device had physical limits. Three months and seventeen days after he'd started to log emails his hard disk was finally filled up. If he'd been given a new computer when he retired this problem would not have appeared quite so quickly, but the old hard disk had a very modest capacity.

Mr. Pavek was in a bind with no easy way out. Had his pension been larger, he could have bought a new hard disk, but he could barely make ends meet as it was. Unplanned expenditures were out of the question. And the virtual mailbox was getting fuller all the time.

He stared helplessly at the screen with its flickering warning in large letters: HARD DISK FULL! Something had to be done urgently, but he didn't know what. But just when panic was getting the upper hand, something happened. The warning suddenly disappeared and was replaced with his image, as though the screen were a mirror. But the reflection was not faithful, for Mr. Pavek's virtual face was deformed by a scream. It was soundless, because the old computer didn't have speakers. This made no difference anyway, as there was no one to hear it. The chair in front of the screen was empty.

11. Hopes

I HEARD THE DOOR open and then footsteps headed my way. Even though I couldn't see anything, my head turned in reflex towards whomever was approaching, giving my neck a bit of a crick. The kidnapper stopped next to me. Nothing happened for several tense moments, and then he took off my hood.

I squinted after spending so much time in the dark, even though the light wasn't very strong. I looked around, taking in my surroundings. I'd had no idea where I was, but for some reason I'd thought I was in some sort of windowless, sparsely furnished cellar. I could tell that I was sitting in an armchair, tied with handcuffs to the wooden armrests, and this had confused me. Such comfort was incongruous with a bare, subterranean cell.

One look was enough to realize that my suspicions were wrong. The armchair stood in the middle of a spacious and high-ceilinged study. All four walls were lined with shelves containing heavy volumes. There were only two interruptions to this uniform background. A padded door broke the wall of books to my left, while the opposite wall was divided in two by a window that reached almost to the ceiling. It was covered with heavy purple drapes.

Right above my head was a chandelier, but it was not switched on. The only source of light was a shaded lamp on the solid wood desk in front of me. Along with it were a pitcher of water, a glass and a small hourglass.

On the other side of the table rose the arched back of a deeply engraved black chair.

I'd been wrong in one other respect too. I'd been convinced that my kidnapper was a young, thickset male. True, he'd never spoken, so his voice had never confirmed this assumption, but it had somehow seemed natural. The person now standing before me was much more reminiscent of a retired literature professor than of a hardened kidnapper.

He had to be in his sixties, with thinning gray hair, and was slight of build. He was wearing a long bathrobe of the same purple color as the drapes. Small round reading glasses dangled on a chain around his neck.

"Hello," he said, smiling.

"Hello," I replied, after hesitating briefly, feeling this was a ridiculous way to start a conversation between kidnapper and kidnapped.

He indicated the handcuffs. "I'm sorry for the inconvenience. I believe you understand they are necessary for the moment. I hope they don't bother you too much. How do you feel? Is there anything you want?"

I hesitated again, keeping my eyes on him. "I'd like a sip of water. I'm thirsty."

He nodded. "Of course."

He went to the desk and poured some water into the glass. He brought it up to my mouth and tipped it. As I drank, water dribbled down my chin.

"Excuse me." He quickly took a matching handkerchief out of the bathrobe pocket and wiped my face. Then he went back to the desk, put the glass down, walked around to the other side and sat in the chair. His head dipped below the top of the chair back. He inverted the hourglass. The sand in the upper chamber started to seep into the lower chamber.

We looked at each other for several moments in silence.

"What do you want from me?" I said, breaking the stalemate. "If it's money you want, a real bundle, then you've kidnapped the wrong person. No one will pay to get me back."

"I'm not looking for a bundle of money."

"Then what are you looking for?"

"Some things are more valuable than money."

"Sure they are, but kidnappers couldn't care less."

"There are kidnappers and kidnappers. Let me ask you a question in return. What price would you be willing to pay to be free once again?"

I'd never been kidnapped before, but even so I hadn't expected negotiations with a kidnapper could be anything like this.

"I wouldn't know. If it's not about money, what else do I have that could possibly interest you?"

"There certainly is something, otherwise you wouldn't be here. But let's turn the question around. What would you be unwilling to give in exchange for freedom?"

I fixed my eyes on the old man. Had I not been bound to an armchair, I might have found this strange conversation in an even stranger place interesting, in a rather twisted way.

"I don't know," I said in all sincerity. "I'd have to think it over. It's not an easy question."

"It's not, I agree. But I'm afraid we don't have much time." He indicated the hourglass in front of me, its gray stream flowing steadily, as though this explained everything. "I'd like to help, if you consent. Would you abandon all hope if that would bring you freedom?"

"Hope?" I repeated, bewildered. "What hope?"

"Hope in general. The right to hope for anything in life."

"I don't understand. How could I abandon hope?"

"Easily. Just by saying so."

Then it hit me. This wasn't an ordinary kidnapper.

I'd been kidnapped by one of those demented types who are in the grip of deranged ideas. Looks can be quite deceptive. The polished elderly man sitting in front of me was the last person in the world I would have thought had lost his mind. I had to be very careful. He might be crazy, but he certainly wasn't stupid.

"So, it's enough to say that I abandon all hope," I said in a low voice, "and you will release me?" I raised my hands a little, making the handcuffs rattle.

"That's right," he replied with a smile.

"There aren't any other conditions?"

"No."

I sighed. "All right, then I abandon all hope," I said formally.

The old man's smile broadened. "Very good! I am very happy things went so smoothly with you."

He stood up, took the hourglass and placed it horizontally.

"Sometimes it can be quite unpleasant," he continued after going around the table and stopping in front of me. "Some people prefer hope to freedom. They feel they can live without freedom, but not without hope."

I was briefly tempted to ask him what had happened to them, but concluded that it was actually none of my concern. Everyone has the right to their preferences. But there was one thing I had to know.

"If it's not a secret, would you mind telling me what you get out of the fact that people abandon all hope?"

"It's no secret. I am a hope collector."

He was as laconic as when he'd mentioned the hourglass. Indeed, why explain something when it's as clear as day?

"Oh, that's it," I said, as though grasping a simple truth.

The old man picked up the hood from the back of the chair.

"I'm afraid I'll have to put it on you again. Discretion is very important in this business. You do understand, don't you?"

"Of course," I agreed from underneath the hood.

"You can take it off in about fifteen minutes. And you won't be handcuffed anymore. You will be completely free once again. Please don't reproach me too much for anything unpleasant you may have experienced. Unfortunately it could not be helped."

"Reproach you for what? It wasn't the least bit unpleasant. Quite the contrary."

When I took off the hood fifteen minutes later, squinting wasn't enough. I had to close my eyes, blinded by the bright sunlight. As soon as I opened them again, however, I knew at once that something wasn't right. I should have been overjoyed at getting my freedom back without paying anything. But all I felt was a deep sense of hopelessness.

12. Collections

Mr. Pokorni collected collections. He'd been doing this his whole life. He had neither the time nor the patience to put them together himself, so he got them ready-made. He was rich enough to pay however much it took if he found a collection to his liking. In spite of this, suspicions were raised periodically regarding how he'd come by some of his collections. Rumors were spread that he stole them, that he used blackmail, and that he would not shrink from murder just to get what he wanted. Once an investigation was conducted into the origin of one of the collections, but nothing illegal was ever proven.

He was very secretive about his collections. He did not deny that he had a rich collection of collections, but he refused to give out any details. In the normal course of things they would have remained outside the public eye, if it weren't for yours truly, the omniscient storyteller, from whom nothing can be hidden. Or almost nothing, as it turns out.

Given my privileged position as omniscient storyteller, the first thing to disclose is where Mr. Pokorni kept his collections. In view of his wealth and the value of the collections, one might expect him to have kept them in a special room, perhaps an armor-plated underground chamber protected by all-powerful electronic devices and guards who were armed to the teeth.

Nothing, however, could be farther from the truth. Mr. Pokorni kept his collections in a small side room.

It had previously been storage space for things that were rarely used. Then these things were thrown out and two gray metal shelves were installed on the walls, facing each other to the left and right of the door. The shelves stretched the whole length of the walls, from floor to ceiling, and each one had twelve partitions.

The small room would have had normal illumination if one of the collections hadn't needed purple lighting, as a result of which the bare light bulb hanging from a long wire was purple. The uninitiated will probably be most surprised by the fact that the collection storage room was not locked. All those with access to Mr. Pokorni's house could enter it without a second thought. This rarely happened, though, and even the owner went there infrequently. The most habitual visitors were the servants who went in to dust the collections every Wednesday morning, although there was hardly anything to dust.

At first glance it might seem that Mr. Pokorni had put his collections on the shelves at random. They did indeed look disorganized, as though put there only temporarily until a better place was found for them. This, however, was a mere illusion. Their owner knew exactly where each of the collections was located, although he might have had trouble explaining the criteria he'd used to place them there. Luckily, he didn't have to answer to anyone for his actions.

At the risk of an oversimplified explanation of this division, offered by your omniscient storyteller, and one that Mr. Pokorni might not agree with, it might be said that the left-hand shelves contained tangible collections while the right-hand shelves held collections with less substance.

A complete list of the collections naturally cannot be given here, because otherwise this story would turn into a catalogue, which would not be advisable. It is useful nevertheless to mention the most important ones, in order to add charm to the story. For example, one whole section on the left side was covered with cardboard boxes containing silver-plated cigarette cases filled with someone's nail clippings. There was also a notebook with the autographs of people who'd had the misfortune to die not long after they had signed it. Then there was an album to which an ardent collector had been adding pictures of himself for decades. Another interesting specimen was a notebook with words written in it that someone had found particularly beautiful. There was a remarkable collection of plastic folders containing newspaper clippings on scientific topics, and there was a computer hard disk filled with neatly filed emails.

While the left side featured a confusion of sizes and forms, the opposite side possessed a sort of uniformity, although here as well, had anyone been so inclined, quite a lot could have been done to improve the order, particularly the disposition of colors. The right side resembled a pharmacy, since it contained nothing but vials. They were all round with glass stoppers, and the only thing that differentiated them was their hue, resulting in a multicolored dissonance.

There was no way of telling what each little bottle contained. Mr. Pokorni had not put labels on them or denoted their contents in any other way, because this was unnecessary. He knew exactly what was in the bottles he'd collected. If it weren't for your omniscient storyteller, all this would have remained an absolute secret, but here is a chance to shed at least a bit of light on it.

The purple vials that required lighting of the same color and were the most numerous contained days of the pasts of people with a sweet tooth. The dark green ones were filled to the brim with a special type of dream. The bright yellow ones were the repository of the airy material that last stories are made of. The black ones, quite appropriately, received deaths, while the colorless ones, seemingly quite ordinary, were the home of hopes.

Who knows how long this collection of collections would have languished in the storeroom had the shelves been able to receive an infinite number of new collections. But even though they were large, they were not without limit and so one Thursday morning the inevitable happened. Mr. Pokorni came with a new collection and he had no place to put it. He tried to make room by shifting around the older collections, but to no avail.

This, of course, was not a serious problem, particularly not for someone as wealthy as Mr. Pokorni. He had several solutions at his disposal. The simplest would have been to put a new shelf on the third wall facing the door, currently unused. If this had not been to his liking for some reason, he could have moved the collections to a larger room. He certainly had plenty of them. He could even have set aside one whole house for his collections.

But he did not resort to any of these possibilities. When it became clear that there was no room for the new collection on either of the shelves, Mr. Pokorni put it on the floor and left the room. He soon returned with a large wicker basket. What follows is not recommended reading for overly sensitive or highly strung individuals.

As though these were worthless old things and not priceless objects, Mr. Pokorni started on the left-hand shelves and put the collections into the basket. He threw them in without the slightest concern that they might be damaged. Periodic sounds of breakage did nothing to slow him down or deter him. When he had filled the basket, he took it to the lighted fireplace in the large drawing room. He emptied its contents onto the floor then went back to the storeroom. After bringing four more baskets full, he drew a large leather armchair up to the fireplace, sat in it and got down to work.

It took hours to burn the tangible collections. Mr. Pokorni would wait patiently for one collection to burn completely before he threw a new one into the flames. Whatever wouldn't burn was returned to the basket to be thrown into the garbage. As he watched the flames engulf objects that others had lovingly collected for years, his face showed not the slightest emotion. It was as expressionless as if he were doing a daily chore.

When the time came for the right-hand shelves, he had to be more careful. He didn't throw the vials into the basket but placed them in an orderly fashion, making sure they didn't break. Instead of taking the basket to the fireplace, he took it to a large terrace overlooking lush gardens of evergreens. He brought five full baskets of bottles and placed them around a deckchair covered in purple canvas.

Dusk had already settled when he sat in the deckchair and started to open the vials. He paid no attention to the order in which he did this and was soon swathed in a mixture of floral fragrances. Days, as one might suspect, smelled of violets, dreams smelled of lilacs, stories of roses, death, contrary to all expectations, smelled of gardenias, and hopes of hyacinths. There was a multitude of other fragrances as well, heavy and light, penetrating and barely perceptible. They swirled around Mr. Pokorni invisibly for some time and then scattered about the gardens, making them briefly more fragrant than usual.

After the insubstantial contents had been released from the last bottle and the multitude of glass containers like so many empty shells had been taken to the garbage dump, one might pause to wonder why Mr. Pokorni had acted this way. This question, unfortunately, must remain unanswered. Even your omniscient storyteller is not powerful enough to peer into the head of this rich collector. Perhaps this is for the best. What would be the point in finding out why he destroyed the collections? It certainly would not bring them back.

The Bridge

Contents

1. The Raincoat

I MET MYSELF AT the entrance to the building where I live. I was just about to go inside after my afternoon walk, when someone pulled the door open from the inside. I stepped back to make room for the person coming out—and stared at my own self.

I recognized myself at once. Not so much by my physical appearance. It's possible to have a double or a twin brother you don't know exists. They might even look more like you than you do yourself. Here, however, the clothes removed all doubt. A double or twin brother would not be wearing my dark green raincoat. It was a recent purchase that I had yet to wear because the days were warm, even though it was already autumn.

The raincoat was singular owing to the fact that its lapels were inconsistent: one was narrow, the other wide. This insignificant flaw was why it had been on sale. No one wanted it, even though it was first class in every other respect. The defect didn't bother me. It was only noticeable if you stared really hard, and I had no reason to expect anyone to give me the once-over.

The recognition had to be mutual, because I looked at me intently for a moment. True, it might not have been quite like standing in front of a mirror, but it would be odd not to recognize yourself on a recently taken photograph, wouldn't it? And that's how I acted—as though a stranger was standing in front of the door. I didn't even nod to myself as a sign of gratitude for standing aside to let me leave, which would have been polite even under these unusual circumstances. I just walked past me and headed down the street.

Bewildered, I stood there for a few moments watching myself walk away and then headed after me. What else could I do? Certainly not go home calmly and pretend that this was nothing out of the ordinary. If for no other reason, I was dying to know where I was going.

I strode along determinedly, like a man on a mission. I was not just out for a stroll. I kept a certain distance from myself, not wanting me to notice I was following, although I didn't look back. I picked up my pace when I turned right at an intersection onto a side street. Reaching the corner, I peered around it. I was still making steady progress. I waited several moments for me to put some distance between us and then turned the corner myself.

We went along like that for around 150 meters and then I stopped and went in somewhere. Since I was about thirty paces behind me, it wasn't immediately clear which shop it was, but I didn't need to get right up close to find out. I am well acquainted with the neighborhood where I live, and I also know myself. I certainly would have no reason to go into shops selling ladies' hats, lawnmowers or pet food. The only place that would interest me in this part of the street was the barbershop. The one I regularly visit.

But what would I be doing at the barbershop? Less than two weeks had passed since I'd had my hair cut, and I always shave at home. What would my barber think when he saw me much earlier than expected? It might lead to a misunderstanding. Spurred by the desire to prevent this, I rushed towards the shop, but stopped dead in my tracks just before I reached the glass door.

I couldn't go in there now. I was already inside. What kind of chaos would ensue if another one of me appeared! It would require an explanation, and what kind of explanation was there to give? The barber might even resort to calling the police to straighten things out, and then there really would be trouble.

I wondered for a moment what to do. I wanted to see what was happening in the barbershop, but couldn't from my position in front of the hat shop. I couldn't just stick out my head from time to time and look through the glass door. Someone inside would notice my peculiar behavior and come out to see what was going on. The best thing would be to go across the street and watch from there.

I found a place next to the trunk of a bushy linden tree whose leaves were already yellow, but soon concluded that I couldn't just stand there and stare at the barbershop. Passers-by would become curious. One might even join me as I watched, convinced that something was about to happen on the other side of the street. People tend to imitate one another. A crowd might form.

I had to be less conspicuous. I went to a nearby newsstand and bought a newspaper in the largest format available. I folded it in two, then tore out part of the inside edge. When I opened it there was a small hole in the middle. I went back to the linden. Now passers-by would find nothing unusual in seeing a shortsighted man with his head stuck in a newspaper, and I had a good view of the barbershop through the hole.

There were no other customers. I saw myself sitting there, and next to me was the barber who'd been cutting my hair for years. He had yet to reach for his comb and scissors. We were talking, and the barber was gesticulating vigorously, which he was not in the habit of doing. He was always reserved. Normally we would merely exchange a word or two about the weather, and here he was waving expansively. I was curious to discover what we were talking about, but even if I'd been a lip reader the distance made it impossible.

The barber finally opened his arms wide, as though abandoning any further discussion, and then moved away for a moment. He came back with a washbasin. He placed it at the back of my neck and I leaned my head backwards. So, that was it. He was going to wash my hair. Well, he'd never washed my hair before, but why get so upset about it? It was nothing unusual. On the other hand, there was really no need to wash my hair. I closed the newspaper for a moment and ran my fingers through my hair. It was still quite clean. I'd washed it the day before yesterday.

When I looked through the hole again, the barber was already at work. He was standing with his back to me, blocking my view of his customer. Judging by the brisk movements, he was scrubbing vigorously. I didn't know how long it took to wash hair in a barbershop. At home I do it in a few minutes. Here, however, it was taking some time.

Some ten minutes later I got tired of looking at the barber's back, so I shifted my focus from the hole to the newspaper itself. On the left-hand side was the city's tabloid news. I started to read the articles, peering every now and then at the barbershop.

What first caught my eye was the story of a woman who had gone into a jewelry store and asked to be shown some diamonds. When they were placed before her, she grabbed a handful, stuffed them into her mouth and patiently swallowed every one in front of the dumbfounded salesmen. She made no attempt to escape. The police took her to the hospital where her stomach was pumped, but this did not return all the precious stones. Three failed to turn up for some inexplicable reason, and not even an x-ray of her innards could locate them.

Then there was an article about a thief who lurked around parks and stole white poodles. He'd already laid his hands on fifty-six dogs, whose fate remained unknown. The police had still found no trace of the man. Even though all the poodles were stolen in broad daylight, no one had noticed the thief, who seemed to be invisible.

The Museum of Modern Art had been targeted once again. Nothing was stolen, but during the night another two paintings had mysteriously changed places. As on the previous occasions, the switch had been announced in a letter to the curator. He'd done everything he could to stop the crank: he'd doubled the guard, set up infrared cameras, and even spent the night in the museum, but nothing helped. In the morning the two paintings were found in each other's places.

One of the headlines reported an unusual suicide on a bridge, but I was unable to read more about it because the rest of the article had been torn out to make the hole. My eyes shifted focus in frustration and I looked through the hole in the newspaper towards the barbershop—and what I saw almost made me faint. I was just coming out of the shop and my hair hadn't been washed but dyed!

No wonder it had taken so long and upset the barber. He clearly had made an heroic effort to dissuade me from this crazy idea. Indeed, how could something like that have crossed my mind? Well, some people dye their hair at my age to hide the gray, but gray doesn't bother me at all and besides there isn't much of it. And what normal person would choose such a bright red color?

I folded the newspaper and dropped it into a nearby trashcan, and then started to follow myself again, this time on the opposite side of the street. There was no danger of losing sight of me: this garish red made me distinctly visible. A multitude of questions swarmed through my head. Above all, why had I dyed my hair? And then, why had I chosen that color? Finally, how had I dared do it on my own whim? Didn't I have a say in the matter?

How was I going to face the barber when the time came for my next haircut? I couldn't appear in the barbershop with my normal hair. Would I have to dye my hair too beforehand at some other place? Furthermore, what if I ran into one of my friends or acquaintances with this red hair? They would be astounded when they saw me, and this would inevitably lead to gossip.

I didn't know where I was heading now, but I hoped I wouldn't stay outside very long. The sooner I went inside, the smaller the chance of an unwanted encounter. I stopped some fifty paces later in front of a wine shop. I took a look at the display window and went in.

This didn't bode well either. I have never drunk wine or strong alcohol. I have a glass of beer only on rare occasions. So what was I looking for in a wine shop? Was I intending to do something irresponsible again? After what had happened in the barbershop, I could expect the unthinkable from me.

I was both relieved and worried when I came out soon after. I was carrying three bottles of red wine in a transparent plastic bag. I hadn't done anything unseemly, but what was I going to do with so much wine? I wasn't going to drink it all by myself, was I? One bottle was enough to put me in the hospital. Had I bought it for someone, perhaps? After some hard thought I couldn't come up with anyone I would give three bottles of wine.

We continued along both sides of the street. Now I was even more fearful that someone would recognize me. I would leave a truly wonderful impression with this horrible dyed hair, obviously set for a binge. Such toying with my reputation was intolerable.

I stopped at the next intersection, waited for the green "walk" sign and then crossed the street. I scurried behind the nearest linden tree and peeked around it. After crossing the street I continued straight ahead. I waited a moment and then went after myself.

Once again I went into a shop I didn't frequent. I'd never liked sports, so I'd never needed sports equipment. I went up to the edge of the large display window and looked inside. There were lots of customers. I caught sight of red hair at the other end of the store, but couldn't see which section I was in because of the crowd.

As I waited impatiently for me to come out, I tried to figure out what might interest me there. My eyes went over the objects in the window. Boxing gloves? No, I shuddered at violence. Hockey stick? I couldn't even stand up on ice skates. Basketball? That didn't go at all with my height. Tennis racquet? Once I'd tried to grasp the rules of tennis, to no avail.

When I finally appeared at the door of the shop, what I was carrying was as foreign to me as everything else I'd seen in the window, although I had a little experience with it. I'd tried to bowl once, but given up after the first throw. I'd thrown the ball with such skill that it rolled diagonally, ending up in the fourth lane to the left.

My hair was no longer the most conspicuous thing about me. Now the bowling ball attracted attention. If they'd wrapped it in the store this might not have happened, but as it was the iridescent red color was painful to the eye. In addition, I was swinging it back and forth by my side, as though just about ready to throw it. People moved out of the way, then turned back to look at me. They either shook their heads reprovingly or snickered.

As I thought feverishly about how to prevent this disgrace, I suddenly halted at a tram stop. Passers-by were still staring at me, but not as much anymore because I'd stopped swinging the bowling ball so crazily. I had no idea where I wanted to take the tram, but it made no difference to me. Just so long as it came as soon as possible and took me away from this crowded street where I'd become a public spectacle.

Luckily, the tram had a second car, so we didn't have to be in the same one. There weren't a lot of passengers and we would have been easy to spot. They would certainly conclude that we were twins, and when you have a twin brother who is clearly crazy, what would be more natural than for them to question your sanity too?

I waited for me to enter the first car then rushed into the second. Overcome with dark forebodings, I went to the front of the second car to keep an eye on myself through the two windows. My fears were unfounded, however. I was no longer acting immoderately. I was sitting on an empty seat and had put the bag with the wine and the bowling ball on the seat in front of me. If you didn't count the hair, I no longer stood out. No one even looked at me.

The stops passed by one after the other, and I sat there calmly in the front car, looking out the window. Finally I could take a little breather in the rear car. I even sat down, although I didn't have a good view of myself that way. I hoped I had come to my senses. We were already quite far from the neighborhood where I live, and this helped put me at ease. If any more foolishness crossed my mind, at least we wouldn't be around anyone I knew.

As soon as I stood up in the front car, I did the same in the rear car. Then another problem arose. No one apart from the two of us intended to get off at the next stop. If I headed back after getting off, we would meet for sure. And then what? I had no answer to that question nor any choice. I couldn't stay on the tram. How would I find myself if I got off at the next stop, without any idea which direction I'd taken?

These quandaries were resolved as soon as we got off the tram. I left the front car and headed forward towards a nearby church. Bewildered, I stayed behind at the stop. I don't go to church at all, let alone equipped with wine and a bowling ball. What was this all about? When I reached the arched door, I shifted the bowling ball to the hand carrying the bag and then pulled down on the enormous handle. I had to push the door with my shoulder to get it open.

I hesitated but a moment, then headed after myself. Even though I didn't feel like going into the church, how could I stay there and wait for me to come out? Who could abide that suspense? I paused before the door, holding onto the handle, and then finally I too pushed with my shoulder to open it. I slipped inside and the door closed behind me.

It was quite dark inside. The only light was produced by two rows of candles on the floor that seemed to outline a long lane from the door to the altar. I walked along that lane towards two people standing at the opposite end. I had to wait a little for my eyes to adjust to the darkness in order to make out the priest and nun. He was short and stout and she was slender and at least a head taller than he.

When I reached them, not a single word was spoken. I shook hands with the priest and bowed to the nun, who returned the bow with a curt movement of the chin, like the top of a pole snapping. I handed her the bag of bottles. She removed one, raised it to the nearest candle and nodded her head.

I gave the bowling ball to the priest, and then both of us headed towards the door. I had to get out of the way quickly because they were coming straight towards me. I looked around and spied some pillars to the left and right. I disappeared behind the one to the right and peeked out cautiously. I was standing with the priest at the beginning of the lane and the nun was at the other end, placing the three bottles between the last two candles. Then she moved aside.

The priest tested the ball in his hand for a moment. Then he bent over and threw it. The church was suddenly filled with thunder. Echoes of the metal ball rolling on the stone floor came out of the darkness from all directions, forcing me to flinch in reflex. All eyes, including mine, were fixed on the glass pins full of wine as the ball bore down on them.

A strike was inevitable. The distance between the bottles seemed too small to let the ball through. But that's just what happened. The priest's feat was much harder than hitting the pins. The ball slipped between the left and center bottle as though guided with the greatest care.

The thud that sounded when the ball hit the base of the altar merged with two piercing sounds. The priest's rumbling shout sounded like wrath tumbling down from the firmament, but what stayed the longest in my ears was the nun's shriek, as though the bowling ball had hit her in a sore spot.

The silence that reigned after the shouts died away did not last long. It was shattered by the sound of the bowling ball once again. The nun had thrown it back towards the door, but gently, so the thunder was more subdued. The ball stopped right at my feet.

I was gripped by fear as I stood behind the pillar and watched myself pick up the ball. Knowing full well the extent of my skill, I feared the damage I could cause somewhere in the dark, far from the altar. The only safe things in the church were the three bottles. I could hit just about anything but what I aimed at.

Sometimes a man can misjudge himself. I was flabbergasted to see the ball head down the center of the lane as though guided by a groove. Sensing the inevitable, the nun raised her hands to her face and covered her eyes.

Broken glass from the three bottles and spilled wine splattered the nun's robe all the way up to her waist. This time there were no accompanying shouts. It seemed to me that she was sobbing quietly, but I might have been mistaken. Nothing happened for a time, as though everything in the church had turned to stone. She was the first to snap out of it. She shook the glass off her robe, then started down the lane towards the bowlers.

I shifted to the other side of the pillar to get a better look. No one had yet said a word. She stopped in front of me and stared down into my eyes. Her gaze didn't budge even when she removed her headdress. Long red hair, the same shade as mine, cascaded from under the black cloth.

She shook her head, loosening her locks slightly, then slid her fingers into the hair at the back of her neck. She rummaged around a while and took out something that had been hidden back there, holding whatever it was hidden tightly in her fist.

I wanted to draw a little nearer, but this, of course, was impossible. I was already standing there, watching up close. When she opened her fist, I didn't look surprised, as though I knew what would be there. Flames from the nearby candles danced in reflection on three jewels.

I didn't take them right away. First I turned towards the priest and extended my hand. He shook it after a brief hesitation. Then I bowed deeply to the nun. The pole now bent almost imperceptibly at the top. Finally, I stuck out the cupped palm of my hand and she poured the brilliant little stones into it.

As I was putting them in my coat pocket, the nun turned swiftly on her heel and headed towards the altar. The priest waited a moment and then followed her, although not as briskly. He stopped at every candle, bent down and extinguished it with his fingers.

I had to pull hard on the door to open it. I went out, leaving me inside to stare at the trail of darkness the priest was leaving behind him. It wasn't until he reached the last pair of candles that I snapped out of it. The nun had disappeared from sight long ago. Unconcerned as to whether someone would hear me, I covered the distance to the door in two steps, gave it a forceful tug, and left the church, too.

I ran after me. I was already on the other side of the street, rushing off somewhere, the raincoat fluttering behind me. From the way I was moving it seemed that I was very familiar with this neighborhood, although I had never been there before. I'd known where the church was, although I had never heard of it. It seemed I knew more than I knew that I knew.

It started to get dark. The streetlights hadn't been turned on yet. There weren't many stores in this part of town and the lighting in the display windows was subdued. There weren't many pedestrians, either. If I were to turn around, I could not fail to see me following me, but I was obviously not interested in what was going on behind my back. We went by a closed tailor's shop, then a shop full of knick-knacks and a shop with old-fashioned chandeliers and table lamps.

When I turned right, disappearing from view, I thought that I had gone into a shop. When I got closer I saw that it was an alley, barely thirty meters long and ending in a brick wall. I got there just in time to see me at the end of the alley as I opened a door on the left and went inside.

I'd made another wrong assumption. It wasn't the entrance to a house but to a shop selling secondhand books. I didn't go right up to it, but I took a sideways glance at the small display window. The glass hadn't been washed in a long time and the books behind it were stacked in disorder. I couldn't get a look at the inside without being seen.

Staying there in the alley was out of the question. When I came out of the bookstore I would run smack into myself. I went back to the street, a short distance away from the turn into the alley, and withdrew into a dark doorway. There was no danger of arousing suspicion since the street was almost empty. All that disturbed the silence was the sound of cars and the rattling tram passing in one direction or the other every few minutes.

Time dragged. What was I doing so long in the secondhand bookstore? I never stayed very long even in tastefully appointed bookstores. Was this some kind of ruse? Maybe I'd noticed that I was following myself and decided to shake me off the trail. Had I exited by some other door? I froze at the thought. I had to find out immediately.

I went back to the secondhand bookstore and stood in front of the window. The dirty glass and poor lighting made it hard to see inside. I had no choice. I reached for the handle, then jumped when a cluster of bells jingled above the door. I stopped in confusion, but no one paid any attention to me.

Although it hadn't seemed so from the outside, the room was rather long. Two elderly ladies were sitting at the counter on the right. They were dressed in identical bright yellow suits that clashed with the dreariness surrounding them, and both of them wore their gray hair in a bun. Staring at the chessboard between them, they didn't even raise their eyes towards me. I went in and closed the door to the sound of more bells.

At first I thought there was no one in the bookshop, but then I detected some movement in the gloom at the other end. I was crouched down next to a pile of books on the floor. Filled with relief, I went up to the long wall on the left. Shelves covered it from floor to ceiling, crammed with old books. As I browsed through them, I made my way towards the end of the room.

Now my back was turned towards me, so I glanced over my right shoulder from time to time to see what I was doing. I had opened a small book and was reading it in spite of the poor light. I stopped about halfway down the wall and I too took out a thick book and started leafing through it. My fingers felt dusty instantaneously.

The next time I glanced over my shoulder, I wasn't crouching anymore. I had stood up and was heading for the front of the store with long strides. I quickly turned towards the shelves so as not to be recognized, and after I slipped by me, I glanced over my left shoulder. I was convinced that I would go up to the counter and pay for the little book in my hand, but this didn't happen. I just passed by the two old ladies who were still engrossed in their game of chess and went outside with a sharp jingling of bells.

I couldn't believe my eyes. I had never stolen anything in all my life, and the last thing I'd steal would be a book. This was a sacrilege! Shame on me! Stealing from these two poor, trusting grannies. I might at least have stolen something with a little value. The slim volume couldn't have cost more than a few bucks. If I'd asked nicely, I might even have gotten it for free.

I could not let me get away with the theft, of course. I returned the dusty book to the shelf in haste, brushed my hands, then went up to the counter, mulling over what would be the best thing to say. It wasn't easy. I'd never had to justify a wrongdoing before. It turned out, however, that no explanation was necessary. Even though I cleared my throat to get their attention, the old ladies kept their eyes riveted to the board.

I stood there before them for a moment, feeling doubly stupid, and then took out my wallet, found a bill that I felt was more than enough compensation for a little used book, and put it on the counter. I stopped briefly in the open door, my ears filled with jingling, and looked towards the counter. The money was still where I'd left it. As far as I was concerned, it could stay there forever, I thought bitterly. No one could consider me a thief anymore, that was what was important.

As I suspected, the alley was empty. I rushed to the end and looked right. I was walking down the street a little ways off, whistling. Matters were going from bad to worse; the thief was rejoicing after pulling off a job successfully. But setting aside the reasons for his satisfaction, who but a vagrant would act like that in a public place? Luckily there were no passers-by. I would surely have caused a scandal.

Whistling all the while, several minutes later I went into a flower shop. It was brightly lit, the only one in the whole neighborhood I supposed, and flowers in large brass containers covered the sidewalk in front of the shop. I quickened my pace. If I intended to repeat my exploit in the secondhand bookstore, this had to be prevented at all costs, even if it meant openly confronting myself.

Standing in front of the display window pretending to look over the flowers on the street, I kept an eye on what was happening inside, although I couldn't hear the conversation. The plump young florist nodded her head, smiling, then asked me something with a look of disbelief, came out from behind the counter and bent down, disappearing from view. When she stood up some time later, she was holding an enormous bouquet of white roses. It must have contained at least fifty flowers.

She trimmed some of the stems with a pair of clippers, wrapped the roses in transparent cellophane and tied a narrow red ribbon around the bottom. The critical moment arrived when she gave me the bouquet. I drew closer to the door. If I took it and tried to run out of the shop without paying, I would prevent this, by force if need be. Even though I had no experience of this kind of confrontation, I imagined I would be able to cope with myself.

Luckily, this wasn't necessary. I took out my wallet and paid for the roses. I even waved my hand dismissively at the change the florist offered me. Her broad smile and bow indicated that I was being generous. I moved quickly away from the entrance, once again pretending to look over the flowers. Who could figure me out now? First I had stolen something almost worthless and right afterwards I turned out to be gallantly open-handed.

I left the flower shop but didn't continue down the street. I went up to the curb and looked left. Not long afterward I raised my hand up high, the one holding the book. A green taxi stopped at the curb. I opened the back door and got in. The taxi driver turned to me, I gave him the address, and he drove on.

I had to act quickly. If I didn't find a taxi soon, everything was lost. I had no idea where I was heading with so many flowers. I looked down the street anxiously but the first taxi that appeared was taken. I felt the cold fingers of panic start to tighten.

Then I saw a lighted sign on one of the other cars. Throwing caution to the wind, I ran almost in front of it, waving both arms. The blue car stopped with a screech. I jumped into the back, pointed straight ahead and blurted out the detective movie cliché:

"Follow that green taxi."

Asking no unnecessary questions, the driver floored the accelerator. The sudden departure pressed me into the seat. We caught up with the green taxi at the third intersection. When we stopped at a red light, there was only one car between us.

The taxi driver clearly had experience in tailing. He avoided the spot right behind the green taxi so we wouldn't be noticed, but he kept the distance between us small so we wouldn't lose it in the traffic that was worsening the further we went. He didn't try to strike up a conversation either. He must have understood I wasn't in the mood.

The trip took a quarter of an hour. When the green

taxi stopped, I was filled with bewilderment and discomfort. What was I doing here? I'd never been in the red light district. As I paid, my eyes avoided the taxi driver's. I could only hope he understood that I would never go to a place like this unless I was following someone. I sighed with relief when he drove off without a word.

The flashy hair color, swinging bowling ball and whistling probably would not have singled me out here, but what I was carrying now certainly did. Indeed, who would come to this area with an enormous bouquet of roses? Once again people turned to look as I went by. They even chuckled openly and pointed at my back.

I paid no attention, apparently not bothered in the least. The bouquet soon proved to have a good side too. The flowers seemed to discourage the garishly painted ladies and occasional, equally ostentatious males from approaching me. But I, having no such protection, was besieged.

It was hard to get rid of the vermin. At first I thanked them politely for the services they offered, saying that wasn't the reason I was there. This didn't put them off, however. They started to tug at my sleeve and stick their faces into mine, assailing me with the heavy odor of cheap perfume. In the end I had to use my hands to fight them off, bringing a flood of insults and even threats.

I stopped in front of the only house with no one standing in front of it. It was a low, narrow two-story building that seemed to be trapped between its stocky neighbors. The two windows were covered with pleated burgundy-colored drapes. I smoothed my hair a bit, put the book into my coat pocket and then rang the bell. The door opened right away, but no one was behind it. As soon as I went inside, the door closed behind me.

More trouble. I could stay outside, but curiosity gnawed at me. How could I miss such a chance? I was vaguely aware that the voyeuristic desire to watch myself in a brothel was rather odd, but strangely enough, this didn't bother me very much.

Just a few moments before, I'd felt a great resistance to going in myself. It's always hardest the first time. But since I had just broken the ice, it was easier for me. I went up to the entrance and rang the bell again.

The door opened as before. I hesitated briefly and then went in. After the door closed behind me, seemingly on its own, I was left in reddish gloom. Everything around me was covered with the same drapes I'd seen on the windows: the walls, floor, ceiling. It was as if I'd been enclosed in a box lined with velvet.

Before me was a small vestibule that ended in a steep staircase. As I stood there uncertainly, a very tiny figure appeared at the top of the stairs. At first I thought she was a child, and then I realized that the woman was a midget. She was wearing a long terrycloth robe, also burgundy, and was barefoot. She bowed and crooked her finger, indicating I was to go up.

I started up the stairs against my better judgment. She waited for me to reach her, and then, with a smile, motioned down the hall to her left. I peered in that direction cautiously. The hall was empty, short and dark-red throughout. There was a door in the middle on the right, and beyond it something resembling a small window with the curtain drawn.

She went first, her head turned towards me, a smile glued to her face. When we reached the door, she stretched out her hand, palm up. I stared at it briefly before I understood and quickly reached for my wallet, but didn't know how much to take out. I thought of asking, but that seemed gauche, so I took out a bill and put it in her hand.

Her hand didn't budge and her smile tightened. I

promptly took out another bill, which broadened her smile, and received a new bow. Both notes disappeared down her cleavage under the terrycloth robe. She pulled down the handle and drew the door towards her, stepping aside.

A multitude of tiny eyes turned my way, looking at me from all sides except the large empty bed in the middle of the room. I had never seen so many poodles in one place, or for that matter so many dogs of any kind. Their white fur seemed to take on a bloody hue in the subdued dark-red light.

I backed away instinctively, as though confronted by great danger, although not a single poodle made any threatening sound. On the contrary, most of them were wagging their tails. I started to shake my head, horror-stricken. Still smiling, the midget calmly closed the door.

As I leaned against the wall in alarm, my eyes as big as saucers, she took my hand, patted the back of it, and then led the way further down the hall. I went docilely, like an obedient child. At the end of the hall was another steep staircase that we took up to the second floor.

There we were greeted by the same empty hall with the covered window and door. When she pulled me towards it, I refused to go, shaking my head wordlessly. She patted the back of my hand again, and this time stroked my cheek as well. Even so, when we continued she pulled me more than I went of my own free will.

We stopped in front of the small window. Her hand stretched out again. Several long moments passed before I took out my wallet. I chose the smallest bill I had and placed it in her palm, then swiftly put the wallet back in my pocket without giving her a chance to ask for more. When this bill disappeared under her robe, the pint-sized woman opened the curtain on the window.

I didn't look up right away. She had to nudge me in the back before I finally looked through the square glass. In the middle of the otherwise empty room was an ordinary wooden table without any covering. On the right side, sitting on a stool, was a girl dressed in an orange firefighter's suit. Bright red curls flowed from under her high-crowned metal helmet.

She was holding the little book I had stolen in the secondhand bookstore. Although I couldn't hear anything, I could see that she was reading out loud. On the table in front of her was a small pile of torn paper. Soon she finished reading the latest page. She tore it out with a brisk movement and added a new handful of confetti to the pile.

I was sitting across from her, in the raincoat, eating. I would take the crown of a white rose from the bouquet on the table, put it on a plate, cut it in half with a knife, stick it on a fork, dip it into something that looked like sauce or dressing and put it in my mouth. This clearly gave me great pleasure, although it made my stomach turn.

The curtain was suddenly pulled across the window. I looked at the midget questioningly, and she stretched out her hand in reply. I shook my head angrily. She shrugged her shoulders, dropped the smile and motioned towards the stairs. I toyed briefly with the idea of defying her, then gave it up. I had already seen everything there was to see. It would only make me nauseous again. Really, eating roses! I turned and left.

At the bottom of the first staircase I looked behind me. For some reason I thought that the midget would see me out, but there was no one there. As I passed by the door on the first floor, I heard growling and then an angry bark. I quickened my steps and almost ran down the second staircase. As the door opened in front of me, I breathed a sigh of relief.

I was in for a wait. I wasn't going to stay up there

until I ate the whole bouquet, was I? In that case they might take me out on an ambulance stretcher. I moved a little away from the entrance and stood by a wall. This soon turned out to be a bad idea. Passers-by started to give me the eye. I didn't understand why I attracted their attention until one came up and openly asked me how much.

I don't know what stunned me the most: the question or the eruption of curses that I poured on the would-be customer. I never dreamed that something like that could come out of my mouth. This was where I was plainly mistaken. Vocabulary of that nature was quite suited to the person currently giving vent to such eccentricities on the second floor.

I felt like going back inside the narrow building and confronting the midget lady once again. I'd pay her as much as she asked, go into that room and sharply order myself to hurry up, regardless of how much I enjoyed what I was doing. Was any pleasure worth the humiliation I was going through?

That's when the door opened again. Not only did I come out, but I was in a terrible rush. Once outside, I didn't stop. I ran in the direction we'd come from, as though being chased, although no one else appeared at the door to the house, which closed immediately.

There was no time to hesitate. I ran after me. The sight of two men on the threshold of old age chasing each other must have looked odd even in this part of town, and the sound of whistles, expletives and even shouts soon started to echo behind us. I wanted the earth to open up and swallow me for the shame.

The chase did have a good side, though. In a twinkling we were out of the red light district and onto a busy street. The catcalls stopped, but people parted before us, sending us reproachful looks. Luckily there were no policemen in the vicinity to stop us and see what was going on, which was the last thing I needed.

Even though, owing to my regular walks, I was in good shape for a man of fifty-six, this demented running was too much for me. Covered with sweat, I soon started to grow short of breath. I would have had an easier time had I known where and why we were running, and particularly how much longer it would take until we got there, but I had no way of knowing.

When we finally stopped, everything seemed clear. A pharmacy, of course! This was exactly what someone who had stuffed himself with white roses needed. We ran inside at close intervals. I almost ran into my own back. The older pharmacist and the young woman who was being served eyed us suspiciously.

Panting, I started to list the medicine I wanted to buy. I listened in bewilderment, standing behind myself in the line. As far as I could tell, none of it had anything to do with indigestion. The pharmacist took three vials of pills from the shelf, each a different color: blue, yellow and brown.

I stuffed them into the pockets of the raincoat, paid the bill and hurried out. The pharmacist was left with her hand stretched forth, holding the change. I felt the need to offer some explanation, but since nothing convincing came to mind, I followed my own lead. Turning around, I too rushed out of the pharmacy.

The pursuit continued, although it slowed down a little. Had I been following someone else, and not myself, I probably would not have been able to keep up the pace, but as it was there was no fear of being left behind.

When we turned off the boulevard onto a side street, the running turned into fast walking. It would have been difficult to run there, anyway, because of the many small restaurants whose tables covered a good part of the sidewalk. I hoped we might sit for a moment in one of them, just long enough to catch our breath, but there clearly was no time to rest.

We did stop in a little while, though. Since I was only a few steps behind me, my loud panting seemed to echo back to me. The window of the store we were standing in front of was full of used theatrical equipment: costumes, overcoats and tricots, boots and ballet slippers, eyeglasses and monocles, wigs, fake beards, mustaches and noses, a jewelry box, a snuff box and powder box, lances, swords and daggers, parts of set designs, framed posters, autographed pictures of actors, programs, opera glasses.

We went in one after the other without opening the door twice. The counter was at the opposite end of the store. I went there, while I stayed by the entrance, staring at an upright suit of armor. I pointed to something on the top of the shelf behind the slim, hunchbacked salesman. The man climbed up a small stepladder and took down two masks: comedy and tragedy—symbols of the theatrical arts. He held them out to me.

I chose the tragedy mask and then beckoned the salesman to draw near. I whispered something to him, and he nodded. I paid and headed for the door. I passed by me without looking at myself, and went out. I was just about to step out too, when the salesman called to me.

"Sir!"

I turned around.

"This is for you." He raised the comedy mask.

I looked at him in surprise, pointing my thumb at myself questioningly.

"Yes, for you." He came out from behind the counter and headed for me.

"Thank you," I said tersely after taking the mask. I doubt I would have known what else to say even if I hadn't been in a hurry. I gave a little nod and went out.

I had already gone pretty far. I had to run again to catch up with me. The mask was light, probably made of aluminum, with slits for the eyes and mouth. It was worn by holding onto a short handle that ended under the chin. The gold paint was scratched in places, as though someone had tried out steel fingernails on the smiling face.

The restaurants and stores thinned out as we continued down the street. They were replaced by low houses in which, judging by the unlighted windows, no one seemed to live. There weren't many streetlights here, and it had already grown dark, so it became harder and harder to see. Even though I was walking close behind me, had I not known that it was me I would soon not be able to recognize myself.

Owing to the poor lighting I couldn't tell where we were when we finally got there. The brick wall we'd followed for the last fifty meters had no distinguishing marks. It could have been a large warehouse or a tall fence. I heard a metallic sound when I knocked on it. I had to stare hard to make out the dark outline of a door in the wall.

A lighted rectangle appeared head-high. I put on the tragedy mask. Darkness reigned once again when the rectangle disappeared, but not for long. The door opened inward with creaking hinges and I was bathed in light. I entered quickly and the door closed noisily behind me. I was alone in the darkness.

I might have been uncertain as to what to do, but the unease I felt decided matters for me. I didn't feel like staying there. I went up to the door and knocked. The metal was rough and cold. A small window opened and a large male head, totally bald, appeared. He glared at me without a word.

As I brought the comedy mask to my face, I wondered whether it might be wiser to stay outside. But there was no time to change my mind. The door opened with another creak and a giant appeared.

He was naked to the waist, wearing only broad cotton pants and slippers. His skin was shining, as though rubbed with oil. He waved me inside. I couldn't refuse that invitation. After all, I couldn't turn my back on myself.

Closing the door behind me, the giant turned and indicated the long hallway extending before me. The floor was covered with a thick black carpet. Framed pictures lined both walls, lighted from the ceiling by the slanting beams of spotlights.

I gave a brief nod to the Goliath and then headed down the hallway. As I followed my distant figure, I glanced at the paintings I passed. They were not ordinary portraits. The faces of the men and women of varying ages were anything but cheerful. They expressed anxiety, worry, fear, even despair. It was as if they had just come face to face with something dreadful. I scurried after myself.

I caught up with me at the place where the hallway widened into an enormous room. It was illuminated by four chandeliers resembling huge Christmas trees. The floor and walls were lined with marble, so white that it sparkled in the bright light. On the right-hand side were six tall windows with black drapes pulled over them.

I headed towards the left-hand side and the massive roulette table in the center of the wall. The croupier at its head was a girl with short red hair and a round face sprinkled with freckles. She was wearing a white blouse and green vest, with a matching green bow tie.

An easel had been set up behind her and a painter was sitting on a tall round chair, holding a palette. He was young as well and sported a thick beard. He was wearing a formal evening suit, and his tie was so colorful that it looked as though he used it to wipe his brush.

On the opposite side was a rather stout middle-aged violinist in a gray evening gown. Her hair was the color of coal and it reached almost to her waist. She was looking at the floor, head bowed.

On the wall above the roulette table hung two large paintings in heavy engraved black frames. The left one depicted a gold mask with its crescent-shaped mouth turned upwards, while the right one had the crescent turned downwards.

When I sat on the only chair at the table, placing the mask in my lap, the painter stood up and set to work. He mixed the paint on the palette a little with his brush, then started to lay it on the canvas with short, brisk movements. At the same time, the violinist raised her instrument and bow and started to play, her head still bowed.

When I too went up to the table, no one paid any attention to me. I stood behind myself, holding the mask behind my back. Although there were no bets on the table, the croupier spun the roulette wheel, then threw the ivory ball in the opposite direction. When it stopped, the long rake used to clear the bets was pointing at number three.

I reached into the pocket of my raincoat and took out the three vials. Without a moment's hesitation I put all three on the space for black numbers. The ball once again went on its circular path. As though uninterested in the outcome of the throw, I looked at the central area with numbers in front of me, arms resting on the edge of the table. I, however, bent over slightly so I could see better.

This time the croupier pointed at number twelve, then reached out with the rake to clear the vials. She drew them in with a skilled movement, without knocking any of them over. They disappeared into a round opening next to the roulette wheel. The rake went up again, waiting for a new bet.

My hand plunged once more into my coat pocket. Again there was no hesitation. I put the three jewels on the space for even numbers. My eyes focused on the table top once more, but I drew closer to the head of the table.

I didn't understand how I could be so indifferent. These weren't pills of no consequence but authentic gems. Where did I acquire the audacity to take such a risk? I had never gambled before. What if an odd number came up?

I stared dully at the tiny ball that came to land in pocket number fifteen. There was a lump in my throat as I watched the shovel at the top of the rake pick up the three precious stones and carry them inexorably towards the opening in the table next to the croupier. They disappeared as though swallowed up by a dark, round maw.

The monster was clearly insatiable because the rake went up once again, inviting new bets. But what was left to bet? The answer appeared straightaway: the mask in my lap went into the space for the first eighteen numbers.

The croupier bowed. The painter placed his palette and brush on the chair and clapped. The violinist raised her head for the first time, and the flicker of a smile crossed her lips. When the ball was rolled for the fourth time, I went right up to the head of the table. My eyes began spinning too, unintentionally following its circular movement.

My eyes kept moving even after the ball stopped, as though wanting to move it from number twenty-six where it had callously landed. Not wanting to watch the rake pull in the new booty, I turned towards myself. I was sitting stock-still, staring blankly, as though this had nothing to do with me.

The croupier cleared her throat. I didn't see what she did with the mask. The opening was too small for it to go inside. The rake pointed to the ceiling again. The painter picked up his palette and brush, but did not go back to painting. The violinist was holding her instrument at the ready, but did not put the bow to the strings.

I got up from the chair. The game was over. I had nothing else to lose. What a dupe I'd made of myself! A man really doesn't know himself, at least not when he's patently losing his self-control.

In utmost disbelief, I watched as I took off the raincoat, rolled it up and put it on the number zero. Although the space was considerably larger than the other numbers, the coat covered it completely, even going a little outside the rectangle.

The painter started laying paint on the canvas in feverish, almost frenzied strokes, as though suddenly overcome by a burst of inspiration. The tempo of the violin, striking up the same moment, lagged not a bit. The croupier threw the ball again, more forcefully than the other times. It spun so fast I thought it would fly out of the wheel.

When it started to slow down a feeling of sadness came over me. I couldn't take this lunacy any longer. I couldn't watch the final circuits of the ball or my own self as I stared at the tabletop. I raised my eyes from the roulette table to the two paintings hanging above it.

And that's when it happened.

The ball hadn't landed yet. Although I noticed the change, at first it seemed a matter of course, like something I see every day. It was not until the large wheel turned silent that I finally figured out that paintings don't change places just like that. The comedy mask should have been on the left-hand side and the tragedy mask on the right. And not the other way around, as they were now.

I stared fixedly at the two large frames, although there was a stir around me. It took a loud noise to snap me out of my fascination. The croupier stood up and broke the rake. The painter angrily jabbed the sharp end of the brush into the canvas, making holes and tears. The violin was on the floor and the violinist was stamping on it in wrath.

The wheel was moving very slowly now, carrying the ball where it rested in the only green pocket—the zero. On top of the raincoat covering this number's space lay the mask with the mouth turned down.

I first took the mask, then the coat, paying no attention to the demonstrations of anger around me. I threw the raincoat over my arm and headed towards the hallway. I didn't linger a moment. I headed after myself.

We weren't walking one behind the other anymore, but side by side. The hallway seemed shorter, as though we were getting to the giant faster than we'd reached the room. He was looming in front of the door, arms crossed on his naked chest. I handed him the tragedy mask I'd just received as my winnings. He took it, but didn't move. I quickly gave him my comedy mask.

The darkness we entered wasn't the least bit forbidding anymore. We weren't in it very long, though. Still walking side by side, we continued down the street, which started to curve to the right. At the end of the bend we reached a new boulevard with a river running along the opposite side. I hadn't been in this part of town, but I knew approximately where we were located.

The boulevard was bathed in neon light and had more cars than pedestrians. We took the first pedestrian crossing to the other side and turned left, going along the river under a row of bushy chestnut trees. We didn't talk. A man only rarely has something to say to himself.

A stone bridge soon appeared before us. It had a low, wide parapet and ornate lighting. We stopped in the middle and stared at the water, where the lights were shimmering in reflection as though in a dark, trembling mirror. A brightly-lit boat full of cheerful music started to emerge festively from under the bridge.

When it had gone downriver, I looked around me. There weren't any vehicles or people on the bridge just then. I laid the raincoat across the parapet, then climbed onto it. For a moment it seemed that I would turn and say something. But I didn't.

I took a step over the edge and disappeared at once, as though sucked in by the darkness below. I didn't watch myself go. I knew I wouldn't see a thing. Just as I didn't hear any splashing sound that might have disturbed the calm evening waters. Leaving the raincoat on the parapet, I headed back to the riverbank. Tomorrow I will buy a new raincoat with lapels of equal width.

2. The Scarf

MADAM OLGA REALIZED SHE'D made a mistake as soon as she left the shop with a large "Sale" sign spread across its window. The scarf hadn't been expensive, but she didn't need one. She never wore scarves. And even if she did, she definitely wouldn't wear one this color. Yellow didn't suit her, particularly not a shade as bright as this. Moreover, the scarf she'd bought had a defect. One end had two round spots of a distinctly darker shade, resembling the large eyes of a sleeping snake. Owing to their regular shape and symmetrical position they might have appeared a result of design, but a closer look revealed that they were due to a slip-up in dyeing.

Madam Olga, in actual fact, did not like sales. The crowds in the shops and the customers' behavior got on her nerves. There seemed to be something of the scavenger in their desire to buy things they most often didn't need solely because of the low price. Nonetheless, she was rarely able to resist the call of the showy signs on the windows, although most of the time, once inside, she kept the impulse to buy for the sake of buying at bay. She would usually leave a sale empty-handed and angry at herself for not being of stronger character.

Now she was angrier than ever because she'd not only purchased a defective scarf but had put it on immediately. She was unable to explain this to herself. The frenetic atmosphere in the shop must have been to blame. No one acted normally there. Where had she got the idea she could walk through town wearing such a scarf? Who else dressed so gaudily at her mature stage of life?

The answer to her unspoken question appeared before she had time to remove the yellow snake. In front of the window stood an older woman; she would not have given her a second thought if it weren't for the fact that she was wearing the same scarf. Madam Olga stared at it, trying to see whether it had a defect too, but all at once that ceased to be important. A fleeting glance was all she needed to realize that she knew the woman. Or rather, she used to know her. When she was still among the living.

Madam Vera, Madam Olga's fourth-floor neighbor, had died three and a half months ago. She'd had a weak heart for a long time, and it had finally failed her. They had not been very intimate. They would stop and chat whenever they happened to meet, but did not visit each other. Madam Olga didn't know much about her. Madam Vera was the widow of a retired bank clerk, without children. She'd been devoted to her two cats, taken in by a distant relative after the funeral.

Madam Olga might easily have failed to recognize Madam Vera. She'd cut her hair and changed the color. Before she'd hidden the gray with a black rinse, which suited her quite well, but now she'd chosen red. This might have been flattering too if it weren't for its youthful, flamboyant shade, which did not suit her age. And neither did the scarf, for that matter. But the woman was certainly Madam Vera. The mole on her right cheek removed all doubt.

Madam Vera turned away from Madam Olga and headed down the street. She walked with the short, slow steps of those with a heart condition. She was wearing the dark-gray coat that she usually wore when she went out, even when it was warm. On her it seemed long because she was short.

After watching her walk away for a few moments, Madam Olga started after her, intending to catch up and exchange a few words. Then she thought better of it. She didn't know what to say. She could ask her questions, of course, but was unable to formulate them properly in her head. She might have had an easier time if they'd been closer friends; as it was, everything that crossed her mind seemed like prying. How do you talk to someone who is dead, anyway?

In that case, she would just follow her. She couldn't very well continue on her way as though she hadn't run into Madam Vera. But Madam Olga had no experience of shadowing. How was it done? The street was full of people at this time of the afternoon and she might lose her in the crowd if she lingered too far behind. If she got too close and Madam Vera turned around, she couldn't help but notice her. Then what? And anyway, it was most certainly unseemly to shadow people.

She would try to stay at a moderate distance. Luckily, Madam Vera didn't walk fast, so she would not have to overexert herself. An elderly woman was only really up to shadowing another elderly woman. It didn't even have to be conspicuous. How could the sight of two elderly women walking along at a short distance from each other be suspicious?

Madam Olga stopped dead in her tracks when it dawned on her what made them conspicuous. She took off the scarf, rolled it up and put it in her coat pocket. In fact, she should have done that in the shop, once she'd been unable to stop herself from buying it. It would have been best if Madam Vera had removed hers too, but how could she get this across to her?

Madam Olga stopped once again and pretended to look in a shoe store window when Madam Vera paused in front of a grocery store. There were baskets full of fruit on the sidewalk in front of it. Out of the corner of her eye, she watched as Madam Vera pointed at the bananas. The storekeeper took a large bag, filled it and put it on the scale.

Why does she need so many bananas? she wondered when Madam Vera continued on her way. She remembered the time Madam Vera had told her she didn't like fruit. In addition, considering her heart condition, carrying something that heavy wasn't a good idea. The bag must have weighed at least two kilos, making her lean heavily to her right. If circumstances had been otherwise, Madam Olga would have offered to help, but this was clearly impossible now.

At the next stoplight Madam Vera joined the others who were waiting to cross the street. Madam Olga stood next to a kiosk not far away, all set to cross as soon as Madam Vera put some distance between them.

Just as she was about to cross, a girl handing out leaflets to passers-by, dressed like a majorette in a tall hat and high boots, came up and smilingly offered her a colorful piece of paper. Disconcerted by the rush to make the green light, Madam Olga took it, although she was not in the habit of accepting such offers. She had an aversion to aggressive advertising. She would throw it in the first trashcan she saw.

Not far from the intersection, Madam Vera entered a shop. When Madam Olga reached the edge of the display window, she saw that it was full of tableware. Everything on display looked expensive. The dinner plates, soup plates, dessert plates, cups, saucers and serving bowls were of fine porcelain, decorated with pastoral scenes in pastel colors. Crystal glasses and carafes sparkled in the beams of little spotlights that illuminated the window, even though there was still plenty of daylight. Boxes lined in velvet displayed silver knives, forks and spoons of different shapes, sizes and uses.

What was Madam Vera doing in a place like that? She'd constantly complained about her small pension, saying she barely made ends meet and spent more on the cats than on herself. Had her situation changed? This would be clear soon enough, when she came out.

But this did not happen soon. Madam Vera simply did not emerge from the shop, although she was the only customer in there. This put Madam Olga in a predicament. She couldn't just stand there in the street. She needed something to do instead of staring blankly in front of her. People would start to give her suspicious looks.

That's when she remembered she was still holding the leaflet the majorette had given her. She was certain that whatever it was advertising wouldn't be of the slightest interest, but that didn't matter. She would pretend to be engrossed in something important. Who would know it was just an advertisement, anyway?

The leaflet turned out to be something other than an ordinary advertisement using the characteristic superlatives. It was instead a pitch for a play called "Food". The only odd thing about it was the missing name of the playwright. The theater was in the vicinity and a small map on the back showed how to get there.

When she finally raised her eyes from the leaflet, after reading it several times, Madam Olga stared in amazement at an older man who had just passed by her. He was swinging a red bowling ball as though about to throw it and knock down pedestrians like ninepins. She also noted that his hair was as red as Madam Vera's.

She needn't have worried about attracting attention standing next to a shop window doing nothing. Who would notice her next to an oddball like that? People turned as he went by, staring with bewilderment or derision. If he'd been a young man, such behavior might have been understandable, but it was certainly not to be expected from someone just a few years her junior.

But she had no more time to spend on the man with

the bowling ball. Madam Vera finally appeared at the shop door, loaded down. The bag full of bananas was still clutched in her right hand and her left arm was hugging a large box wrapped in shiny paper tied with a purple ribbon. She continued down the street.

Her pace, however, had changed. As though her load were lighter and not heavier, she strode cheerfully, skipping even, like someone expressing joy with their feet. This was not only bad for her heart, if she continued like that people would start to turn and look at her too. She'd known Madam Vera as a reserved, polite woman, but people seemed to change after death.

This time Madam Olga realized where she was following Madam Vera before they reached their destination. She appeared to be sticking to the path marked on the map on the back of the leaflet that was still in Madam Olga's hand. But who went to the theater in the afternoon, inappropriately dressed, loaded down with bags and boxes?

The old-fashioned two-story theater with its yellow brick wall seemed squeezed in between modern buildings with glass facades on either side. Nothing indicated that a show was playing there, but the door leading to the vestibule was open. Madam Olga hesitated several moments before deciding to go in after Madam Vera.

Perhaps the dead could take the liberty of acting indecorously, but she still had etiquette to consider. Although she wasn't dressed properly for the theater, either, it would be even more embarrassing to stand in front of it until Madam Vera came out. She didn't know how long the play lasted. Smoothing her clothes a little and patting her hair, she stepped into the vestibule.

It was full of mirrors and chandeliers, but otherwise empty. While she'd hesitated, Madam Vera must have entered the auditorium. Obviously she had a ticket already, because a curtain was pulled across the ticket window to the right. The only person present was a short, obese middle-aged woman with very short red hair, standing in front of the auditorium entrance. She was wearing a tight, clinging turquoise leotard, a short blue skirt that didn't reach even halfway down her enormous thighs, and military boots. The long thin cigarette holder she clenched tightly in her mouth, even though there wasn't a cigarette in it, only enhanced the grotesque impression she made.

Madam Olga went up to the woman to ask how she might buy a ticket for the show, but before she had managed to say anything, the woman took the leaflet from her hand without a word, pulled aside the dark blue curtain and gestured broadly for her to go in. As she entered, Madam Olga looked at the woman inquisitively, but her face remained expressionless.

As Madam Olga's eyes adjusted to the darkness, she noted that the auditorium was considerably larger than it appeared from the outside. In the middle of the distant, brightly-lit stage was a long table with a high-backed chair on its opposite side. Since there were no actors, she assumed the show had not yet begun.

It was not immediately clear to her why the moderately large audience suddenly started clapping. Then a spotlight hit the middle seat in the front row and she saw Madam Vera stand up and head towards the stage. The spotlight followed her, and the applause did not subside until she was sitting at the table with the box in shiny paper placed in front of her.

Just as Madam Olga was wondering what had happened to the bag of bananas, the spotlight glided back down to the front row and stopped at a small figure sitting there. She couldn't make it out properly standing at the back of the auditorium so she started down the aisle. When she had got more or less halfway, she realized she'd been mistaken.

She dropped into the nearest seat in surprise. That wasn't a child in the front row, as she'd first thought, but a monkey. He had just taken a banana out of the bag on the seat next to him and was starting to peel it. When he brought it to his mouth, a chime sounded on the stage. Madam Olga raised her eyes and saw a silver bell in Madam Vera's hand.

A liveried servant in a bushy gray wig approached the table from the left side of the stage. He untied the purple bow, unwrapped the shiny paper and raised the lid, then started taking tableware out of the box. He placed a porcelain plate, tall glass, silver knife and fork and a pink silk napkin in front of Madam Vera. Then he picked up the packaging and left.

The moment he disappeared, an aged butler appeared on the other side of the stage. He was wearing a dinner jacket with a white vest, white bow tie and white gloves and was carrying a bottle of some green beverage. Dragging his feet, he reached Madam Vera, showed her the label on the bottle and waited for her to nod her head.

He had a rather hard time removing the cork, and then poured a small amount of liquid into the crystal glass. The foam that formed could be seen even from the middle of the auditorium. He waited once again for Madam Vera's approval after tasting it, then poured the glass about three-quarters full. He placed the bottle on the table, bowed, and headed back the way he had come.

Before he disappeared, a double door opened at the bottom of the stage and two men emerged. One was red-skinned, naked to the waist, wearing only brown leather breeches and moccasins. A feather was stuck into his hair, which was pulled back into a topknot, and his face was streaked with war paint. The other was wearing polished armor that glistened in the bright light. His visor was lowered and a sheathed sword hung from his waist; he rattled when he moved.

They were carrying an oval tray between them at least a meter and a half long. It contained an enormous roast bird. Madam Olga first thought it was a swan, but it must have been something larger. An ostrich, perhaps? They stopped in front of the table and placed the tray in the middle. The Indian gave a warcry, hitting his mouth with his hand, while the knight stamped his left foot thunderously on the floor three times.

As they headed back to the door, a tall ballerina in a long, fluttering, orange dress as transparent as a veil passed between them. She started to jump and pirouette, zigzagging towards the table. When she finally landed next to Madam Vera, she bowed deeply. She took something resembling a sword from the tray, cut a huge chunk of meat off the leg and put it on the porcelain plate, covering it completely. Then she seemed to float away.

When the double doors closed behind her, a gong sounded and then faded into the reverberations of an aria. The soprano sang *a cappella*, as though musical accompaniment would have sullied the crystal clarity of her voice. At the same time, something quite boorish had started: gorging.

You couldn't tell who was faster: Madam Vera wolfing down the roast meat or the monkey gobbling the bananas. Her cheeks puffed up in an instant but this didn't stop her from cramming more meat into her mouth, stopping just a moment to sip a little of the green beverage. Her eyes grew as big as saucers whenever she swallowed the under-chewed bites. The monkey soon stopped peeling the bananas. He simply shoved them down his throat along with the peel.

As the feast proceeded, the tempo of the aria sped up and the audience started to clap to the beat, shouting encouragement to the competitors. Madam Olga was the only one unable to get into the spirit of the show. This would not end well. Madam Vera had often complained to her of indigestion. She had had to be very careful about what she ate and particularly how much she ate. Death certainly had not improved the situation. Bolting food in such a manner would soon result in nausea. She didn't know about the monkey, but its stomach would certainly have a hard time with so many bananas, particularly the unpeeled ones.

Just as she was feverishly searching for a way to put an end to this madness, the gong suddenly sounded and stopped the aria at its peak. The brief silence that ensued was interrupted by the monkey's screeching. He was jumping up and down on his front-row seat, tearing apart the empty bag in rage.

Madam Vera stood up. The plate in front of her was empty too. She walked around the table, stood before it and bowed deeply. The audience jumped to their feet and gave her an ovation sprinkled with shouts of "Bravo!" The monkey sank back into its seat dejectedly.

Turning towards the bottom of the stage, Madam Vera signaled with her hand. The door opened and those who'd been part of the show came out in pairs and took their place around the leading actress. First came the liveried waiter and the butler, then the Indian and the knight. The ballerina received the most applause as she graciously jumped over the table and settled at Madam Vera's feet like a sleeping swan.

The curtain started to fall. The applause sped up when it completely hid the stage, and shouts of "Encore!" rose throughout the auditorium. But the curtain did not rise. When the lights came on, the audience sat down. A heavy-set young man in a firefighter's uniform entered through the side door next to the stage. He went up to the monkey, grabbed it around the waist and lifted it with one hand. It offered no resistance and hung there limply. As the young man took it out, whistles sounded from several parts of the audience.

When Madam Vera soon appeared at the same side

door, the audience said not a word, as if they didn't recognize the leading actress of a moment before. Now empty-handed, she went along the aisle towards the exit.

As soon as she passed by, Madam Olga turned and started after her. She didn't know why the rest of the audience didn't leave too. Were they waiting for a second act, perhaps? As far as she was concerned, she'd had enough. She'd seen more than she wanted. In any case, she couldn't lose sight of Madam Vera.

When Madam Olga reached the vestibule, the fat woman at the entrance to the auditorium stuck a leaflet in her hand, once again without a word. If there had been time she would have handed it back and explained that she no longer intended to frequent a theater with such a repertory. But since Madam Vera had already gone out into the street, she simply took the leaflet and rushed after her.

How can she even move, let alone so quickly? wondered Madam Olga, doing her best to keep up with Madam Vera who was walking as though her stomach wasn't the least bit bothered by all the meat she'd crammed into it. It must have been at least a kilo and a half. And why had she competed with a monkey? That wasn't at all like her.

They crossed three intersections before Madam Vera finally stopped. Madam Olga felt relieved. She didn't have a heart condition, but she hadn't walked so briskly in a long time. She was quite short of breath and had started to sweat. She was just too old to be shadowing anyone. Hopefully it would soon come to an end.

This time Madam Vera entered a large department store. Madam Olga went in after her without a second thought. Waiting outside was out of the question. She might leave by one of the other entrances. Luckily, the department store was full of people so her shadowing would not be conspicuous.

They took the escalator up to the third floor, where Madam Vera headed to a big section selling musical instruments. Madam Olga stopped at the toy department not far from it. She pretended to look over the little cars, plush bears, toy guns, dolls, puzzles, tricycles, lighted plastic swords and wooden building blocks. The awkwardness of feigning was mitigated by a sudden feeling of tenderness. She hadn't been in a toy store in decades.

Assisted by a saleswoman, Madam Vera was trying out the instruments. How strange, thought Madam Olga. She'd never mentioned an affinity for music, let alone that she played an instrument. She first sat at a drum set and drummed a little. After that she took a violin and drew the bow over the strings several times, then set it down. She raised the cover on the piano keys and played a few notes, but this didn't satisfy her either. She gave up on the double bass before making any sound, realizing it was too big as soon as she took hold of it.

She finally chose an oboe. She held the reed in her mouth for a while, her cheeks puffed out. She seemed to be playing, but there was no sound. She nodded her head in satisfaction and gave it to the saleswoman, then they headed towards the cash register. Madam Olga felt a pang of sadness as she left the toy department.

Taking the bag with the oboe, Madam Vera went up the escalator again. The entire fifth floor was filled with summer and winter sports equipment. It was no accident that Madam Olga went up to the long table with the skis. Until late middle age she'd gone skiing regularly. Glancing over the new models that had become too extravagant for her taste, she kept her eye on Madam Vera.

Of all the departments on this floor Madam Vera chose the last one Madam Olga would have expected. Why did she need a swimsuit? Who else her age still went to the beach or swimming pool? Well, maybe points of reference changed after death. One shouldn't be a slave to one's opinions.

She seemed to have a hard time choosing once again. Madam Vera took a dozen swimsuits in various shapes and colors into the fitting room. When she'd pulled the curtain behind her, two saleswomen exchanged amused looks, shaking their heads. She spent a good fifteen minutes inside. When she finally appeared and indicated the swimsuit she'd chosen, Madam Olga was astounded.

Did she really intend to appear in public wearing that? Why, Madam Olga wouldn't have been seen dead in it. The bikini was not only skimpy but a vulgar shade of red, suitable solely to a young vixen. The fact that Madam Vera was no longer alive was no excuse. It was not a matter of personal opinion. There is simply a line beyond which one does not go, living or dead.

Shopping was over. Carrying two bags, Madam Vera took the escalator down five floors. When they reached the ground floor Madam Olga got disoriented. She'd always had a bad sense of direction. She was convinced that they'd left the store on the same side they'd entered, but they emerged on the opposite side and ended up on a busy boulevard.

As Madam Olga was fearing another forced march, Madam Vera went up to a nearby bus stop. Madam Olga stayed by the department store entrance until the bus arrived. She let two other passengers go in after Madam Vera and then got on too, sitting several seats behind her.

When the bus set off, she suddenly realized she was still holding the leaflet that she'd been given when she left the theater. Just as she was about to put it in her coat pocket until she had a chance to throw it away, she noticed that it was not the same one she'd received from the majorette.

This one also recommended a play, again without the name of the author. Madam Olga shook her head in disbelief when she read the title: “Water”. “Food” had seemed harmless too, but that’s not how it had turned out. Never trust an advertisement, even when formulated in unassuming terms.

The back of the leaflet had a drawing of the bus route they had just taken, with circles representing stops. One was twice the size of the others, colored blue. Madam Olga raised her eyes dubiously to Madam Vera’s back. Was that where they were headed?

Was she intending to take part in the show again? What would be her role this time? Have a water-drinking contest with someone? That would really be insane. But then why would she need a swimsuit, and why the oboe of all things? Madam Olga hadn’t the faintest clue, but would soon find out. The stop marked with the large circle was not far away.

They were the only two to get off the bus, which put Madam Olga in a tight spot. If Madam Vera turned around and saw her, the situation would be awkward. She wouldn’t know what to say. But Madam Vera took the pedestrian crossing to the other side of the street without looking back.

She went up to the large entrance of a long, gray four-story building, the aperture wide enough for a truck to pass through. On the right side there was a smaller door for people. A tall policewoman was standing in front of the door with a white nightstick under her arm. Red curls poked out from under her small cap. They exchanged a few words and then the policewoman opened the small door and let Madam Vera enter.

What kind of a theater has a police guard in front of it? wondered Madam Olga. Then she noticed something that she’d missed at first glance. All the small windows of the gray building had bars on them. She knew that performances were held outside of theaters, but she'd never heard of one taking place in a prison. Who would want to watch in there? In spite of her rabid curiosity, she definitely would not follow Madam Vera inside the jail. She would wait outside. There couldn't be another exit.

The policewoman gestured with her white nightstick. Madam Olga didn't realize right away that this was directed at her. It wasn't until she repeated the movement more energetically that she turned around and, seeing there was no one else nearby, pointed her thumb at herself questioningly. The tall woman nodded her head and motioned with the nightstick for her to approach.

Madam Olga headed across the street reluctantly. What did this mean? She had never had anything to do with the police. Why was the woman summoning her? Had she committed an offense? Perhaps it was against the law to loiter near a prison. What should she say if asked what she was doing there? She couldn't say she'd come to visit someone because she didn't know anyone who was in prison. And if she said she was shadowing Madam Vera they would probably arrest her on the spot.

But there were no questions. The policewoman took the leaflet in her hand without any comment, then knocked on the small door with her nightstick. It opened at once and the policewoman motioned with her head to go in. The sullen expression on her face tolerated no objections, and the nightstick had started to swing. Knees shaking, Madam Olga entered a prison for the first time in her life and the door closed behind her with a loud click.

The walls and floor of the hallway she entered were covered with ceramic tiles the same gray color as the façade, and the dim lighting only increased the gloomy impression. A large mustachioed prison guard in a dark-blue uniform was waiting for her by the door. He was holding a yellow terrycloth robe for her. She put it on obediently, even though it was at least two sizes too large, then headed down the hallway with the guard. She couldn't muster the courage to turn up the sleeves, which covered her hands completely.

At the end of the hallway they stopped in front of a metal door. The guard took the bundle of keys that he carried on his belt, picked through them, chose the right one and unlocked the door. When he opened it, Madam Olga was struck by warm, humid air, and her ears were filled with cries.

As she was reluctant to enter, the guard pushed her in the back, then went in after her and locked the door. He indicated a brown leather armchair nearby. This time Madam Olga didn't wait for the guard to give her an encouraging push. She hastened to sit down, and he stood behind her, arms crossed on his chest.

An enormous swimming pool stretched before Madam Olga. Along its long left- and right-hand sides rose four levels of metal corridors. These were lined with cells and fronted with wire. Prisoners in striped suits were standing there, banging on the wire, shouting, whistling.

Madam Olga sank deeper into the armchair under the invisible pressure of this noise, covering her ears with her hands. The very same moment she felt a strong pinch on her shoulder. She turned and looked at the guard, who shook his head with a frown. She quickly lowered her hands to her lap and the unbearable sound poured over her once again.

When the double glass doors on the other side of the swimming pool opened, there was deafening applause sprinkled with obscene shouts and screams. A short woman wearing the same yellow terrycloth robe appeared between two stocky policewomen. Owing to the distance and because her hair was covered by a plastic yellow bathing cap, Madam Olga didn't recognize her at once. She only realized who it was when she saw the oboe by her side.

It's not possible, thought Madam Olga in shock, watching as one of the policewomen reached for the robe. The shouts had grown into frenzied bellowing by the time the old body in the bright red bikini appeared from beneath. Several of the prisoners started to shake the wire wildly while others climbed up it.

Head bowed, Madam Vera approached the edge of the pool. She set up the oboe next to her body. The spectators started to chant something unintelligible, accompanying the rhythm by stamping on the iron floor. When it reached a peak, Madam Vera simply stepped forward as though she had solid ground before her. A hush fell the same moment.

She barely disturbed the water. There was just a brief ripple at the spot where she went under, and then the surface turned calm again. Seconds passed but nothing happened. Madam Olga turned towards the guard anxiously, but he stared impassively ahead. The faces of the prisoners were also turned silently towards the swimming pool.

Sighs of relief came from all around when something started to appear in the middle. Madam Olga had to lean forward in her armchair to get a better look. She didn't recognize the oboe until it was halfway out. But the movement stopped before the whole instrument appeared. The reed stayed underwater, and so did Madam Vera.

Even if Madam Olga had wanted to turn and ask the guard something, in spite of his threatening behavior, it slipped her mind as soon as the music started. She gazed fixedly at the thin silver staff and the wet tones pouring out of it. She didn't need extensive knowledge of music to be enchanted by what she heard. The raging prisoners of a moment before were now listening intently.

The fragile notes of the oboe broke off into the large acoustical space above the swimming pool. As though they were becoming visible, the air started to shimmer with colorful sparkles. The beaming faces behind the wire stared open-mouthed at the quivering interplay. And then the water came to life. Drops from the surface rushed into the air, like rain falling upwards. When they hit the high ceiling, they dispersed silently and turned into watery powder that intensified the tiny sparks of lightning.

The instrument heralded the end of the music when it started to turn in circles. Moving slowly at first, barely noticeably, it turned faster and faster, forcing the water around it to follow suit. When a whirlpool had formed around the oboe, drops ceased pouring upwards and the sparks went out. Soon a funnel formed that became deeper and wider, drawing the silver staff into it. When the tip disappeared into the circular opening, the music stopped.

But the whirlpool continued to spin and the water level in the pool started to fall, baring the rectangular tiles that lined it. The rapture on the spectators' faces eroded into dismay. Alarmed, Madam Olga looked over her shoulder at the guard, but his face was all that remained unchanged.

When all the water had drained out of the pool, a small round opening covered with a metal grate became visible in the middle of the floor. Across it lay the oboe, the two parts of the swimsuit and the bathing cap, but there was no trace of Madam Vera.

Madam Olga stared several moments at the empty hole in front of her and then made a decision. She would stand up and ask the guard for an explanation. People couldn't just disappear like that in a prison, even if they were dead. They must have some human rights too.

But before she had a chance to turn around, commotion in the corridors caught her attention. She raised her eyes and saw the prisoners come off the wire and head for their cells. Their bowed heads and sluggish movements betokened defeat. It was the exact opposite of the sight that had first greeted her.

The cell doors closed one after another with a sharp clang. When the last prisoner had disappeared behind bars, a heavy hand landed on Madam Olga's shoulder once again. She turned around angrily, but before she had managed to say anything, the guard nodded sharply towards the door.

She got up meekly and started after him. He locked the door to the pool behind them and led her down the hallway. They reached the opposite end before she had a chance to formulate what she wanted to ask him.

At first she misinterpreted his extended hand. Did he really expect her to shake hands cordially after all she'd been through? Then she realized what he wanted. She quickly removed the bathrobe, having a bit of trouble with the long sleeves. She handed it to him disdainfully and waited for him to open the small door within the large one. She went out, head held high, into the falling dusk.

Once out in the street she was overcome by a twofold sense of relief. Everyone is happy to get out of prison, and all the more so if there is someone there they didn't expect to see. The tall policewoman was just saying a friendly goodbye to Madam Vera, several steps away from the prison entrance.

As Madam Olga set out after Madam Vera, who was heading down the street, she was suddenly stopped by a barrier in the shape of a nightstick. She looked at the policewoman in bewilderment. Once again no words were exchanged. The policewoman eyed her for several long moments, then reached for her breast pocket, slowly took out a leaflet, and handed it to her. The barrier only went down when Madam Olga took it.

As she quickened her pace to keep up with Madam Vera, she hastened to read the leaflet. She had already experienced enough to know that it was not the same as the one she'd used to enter the prison. She was curious to know what came after "Food" and "Water".

The new show was entitled "Life". Madam Olga smiled. It would be quite fitting for the late Madam Vera to play the starring role. This time there was no recommendatory hype. The front of the leaflet bore only that word and the back differed from the previous ones. When she turned the leaflet over, instead of a map there was just a large number eight.

Madam Vera turned right at the fourth street. When Madam Olga reached it, she saw that it was full of little shops, similar to a bazaar. It was a pedestrian zone and quite lively in the evening hours. There was a hubbub all around, and the lanterns that decorated the middle of the street had just been turned on.

Even if Madam Olga had walked with her eyes closed, she would have known which shops they passed. She was struck by the heavy odor of roast meat turning on a vertical spit, the moldy smell of wet books on a table in front of a secondhand bookstore, the exotic spices wafting out of a shop crammed with colorful little boxes, the sour smell of bird droppings from a multitude of chirping cages.

Madam Vera entered probably the only shop on the street with no smell emanating. Madam Olga looked at the shiny old-fashioned weapons and war trappings in the window. There were swords, spears, halberds, double-headed axes, sabers, spiked clubs, three-pronged spears, crossbows, shields with coats of arms, and banners in various shapes and colors.

The shop was barely wider than a hallway, but it was very long. She saw the lean salesman nodding as he listened to Madam Vera. He went to the back of the room, brought back a thin, rectangular, dark wooden box with a glass lid, and placed it in front of his customer. Madam Olga couldn't tell what was inside.

The customer briefly looked at it and then exchanged a few more words with the salesman as he wrapped the box in brown paper. He bowed to Madam Vera as she took it. Madam Olga did not wait for her to put a little distance between them once she came out. She headed after her straightaway.

They had covered barely fifty meters, one right behind the other, when Madam Vera stopped in front of a man leaning against a wall selling jewelry. Everything he had to offer was in a flat cardboard box at waist height, attached to a leather strap around his neck.

The seller was a short, totally bald man in early middle age. A white cane was attached to the pocket of his long, worn-out army overcoat, and he wore opaque glasses in a round frame. He raised his head a little when Madam Vera started to pick through the cheap pieces of jewelry on display, but didn't say anything.

He remained silent as she took a little paper bag from the pile on the edge of the box. Madam Olga was quite close now and could see what Madam Vera was buying. She chose a wide copper bracelet, a necklace of amber-colored uneven stones, and clunky plastic earrings.

She doesn't intend to wear those, does she? wondered Madam Olga. Regardless of the fact that it was costume jewelry, even if she weren't dead, these pieces certainly would not suit her. She would have to be at least four decades younger to wear them. At her age she would look vulgar.

Madam Vera took a large bill out of her coat pocket and placed it on the box without a word. Her purchase was certainly worth much less. The seller's lips curved suddenly into a smile. He did not reach for the money, however, nor did he return any change. He continued to stand there without moving, staring blindly ahead.

He didn't move until Madam Vera was several steps away and Madam Olga was before him, ready to follow her. He pushed himself away from the wall.

"Madam," he said.

She jumped, even though he said it softly, and looked at him in confusion.

"Just a moment," he continued, as he ran his fingers over the objects in the box. He quickly found what he was looking for. He handed her a small oval brooch in a mock gold frame, with the profile of a girl.

"This is for you."

She had never worn costume jewelry, or brooches. But she would offend him if she refused it. Suddenly she didn't know what to do with the leaflet she was still holding. It made it hard for her to take her wallet out of her coat pocket. But this turned out to be unnecessary.

"It doesn't cost a thing," he said with a new smile, as though seeing her predicament.

She took the brooch, but thought she should make herself clear. She couldn't accept a present from a stranger just like that. But Madam Vera had just disappeared around the next corner.

"Thank you," she replied hastily, returning his smile, then ran after her.

As she turned down the side street, she saw Madam Vera getting into the first of two horse-drawn carriages waiting for tourists. She said something briefly to the driver, who nodded his head and then signaled the horse.

Madam Olga had no choice. She rushed to the second carriage. It was obviously free, though good manners still required that she ask. . . . But there was no time for good manners. She climbed up and sank into the soft seat covered with a plaid blanket.

She leaned forward, uncomfortable at having to order the driver to follow the first carriage. Tourists certainly don't ask such things. What would the man think of her? But before she had a chance to open her mouth, he cracked the whip. The horse whinnied and broke into a trot.

She thought of asking for an explanation, but when she rose up a little in her seat, she saw that the first carriage was not far in front of them. This was for the best, she concluded. The less she had to explain, the less awkward she would feel. The important thing was to head in the right direction.

What she was unable to do, though, was decide what was the right direction. She rarely visited this part of town. In addition, when she sank back into her seat she couldn't see very much. All she could tell was that they had come out onto a boulevard.

They were hugging the right edge of a busy street lined with chestnut trees. Night had fallen in the meantime, and the streetlights created bright islands in the yellowing treetops. Madam Olga rose up from time to time to make sure they were still following the first carriage.

It was not until they rushed through an enormous wrought iron gate with gold-tipped spikes that she knew where they were headed. When they left the asphalt of the boulevard for the stone blocks that lined the paths and roads in the cemetery, the carriage wheels started to make a different sound.

She should have suspected as much. Indeed, where else can the dead end up but in this place? She, however, had no reason to be there. She didn't like cemeteries, particularly not this late in the day. She cleared her throat to attract the driver's attention, but he either didn't hear or was ignoring her.

The further they moved from the entrance the darker it got. When they turned left down a side alley they found themselves in pitch darkness relieved only slightly by the lanterns of the two carriages. Then, some distance in front of them, a place lit up.

She stared in that direction. Was that Madam Vera's burial place? She couldn't tell in the dark. Before they even got there, however, she realized that it wasn't. It was an enormous mausoleum resembling a small house, not an ordinary grave with a small tombstone. It was illuminated by spotlights placed about the ground. The black marble absorbed most of their radiance.

When the first carriage reached the mausoleum it was greeted with a fanfare. At the sound, the carriage with Madam Olga stopped too. Sticking her head out to the side, she saw two figures dressed in tuxedos and top hats approach the first vehicle. There was something unusual in their appearance, but she couldn't put her finger on it.

They stretched out their hands and helped Madam Vera descend. Then they led her to the mausoleum entrance. The door opened and she quickly disappeared inside. The first carriage went forward and the closer of the two figures signaled the second carriage to approach.

When hands were stretched out to help her too, Madam Olga realized what had seemed strange. The figures in tuxedos were girls. Their red hair was tucked up under the top hats. They smiled broadly, but this did not reassure the passenger. She would have preferred to order the driver to keep following the first carriage, but she suspected that he would not have obeyed.

She accepted the hands reluctantly. Before she descended, however, one of the girls took her leaflet and looked at the back of it, then nodded to the other girl. As soon as Madam Olga touched ground, the door in front of her started to open. She thought she would go in by herself like Madam Vera, but the girl with the leaflet went in before her.

Just beyond the entrance, steep steps of bare stone led downwards. Torches in iron sconces were placed at regular intervals on both sides. Since there was no railing, Madam Olga held onto the cold, wet wall.

There must have been at least thirty steps. Before reaching the bottom, Madam Olga heard a round of applause from down below. They finally reached a high, round room, lit by a ring of torches at head-height.

To the left of the entrance at the bottom of the stairs was a semicircular viewing stand with six rows of seats placed in steps one above the other, similar to an amphitheater. There was an aisle that cut through the middle, dividing the seats, with three on either side. All the places seemed to be taken. Madam Olga had never seen so many clowns together in one place.

Across from the entrance, a figure dressed in a long purple robe was sitting on a high-backed, throne-like chair. Its face could not be seen because its head was bowed and covered by a purple hood with no eye slits. Gloves of the same purple hid the hands placed on its knees. In front of the figure stood a square glass vessel like a fish tank, half-full of multicolored balls.

Madam Vera was standing on a mound in the middle of the room, her back to the audience. If it weren't for her black blindfold, she would be looking at a large wooden wheel with leather straps by the wall to the right of the entrance. The box she'd bought in the old-fashioned weapons store lay on a little table next to her. Its glass top was raised so Madam Olga could finally see the four long daggers.

The girl in the tuxedo who had brought her down the stairs motioned towards the stand. That's when Madam Olga noticed that it wasn't completely full. The middle place in the second row on the left was empty. She wasn't expected to join the clowns, was she? But there could be no doubt; the seat had a large number eight, the same that was written on the back of her leaflet.

She squeezed in between two clowns. The one on her left gave her a smile stretched literally ear to ear by makeup. The one on her right honked as he blew on a red paper snake that unwound towards her, forcing her to back away. But there was no more time for joking around because the show had just started.

The figure in purple raised its right hand. The crypt fell silent the same moment. The hand plunged among the balls in the aquarium, hunted around a bit, pulled one out, then raised it in the air. It had a sparkling number thirty-six.

The clowns burst into applause and one on the end of the top right-hand row jumped up and ran down the aisle. He handed his leaflet to the girl who gestured towards the wheel.

With her help he climbed up onto two small footrests, leaning his back against the wood, and spread out his arms. When he had taken position, arms and legs spread, the girl tied the wide straps firmly around his ankles and wrists.

Then she went up to Madam Vera and touched her on the shoulder. Madam Vera thrust her hand into her coat pocket. First came the sound of rustling paper, and then she pulled out the copper bracelet. The girl took it to the throne and laid it in the purple lap.

Then she went behind the wheel and it started to turn. It started off slowly, but picked up speed after the first cycle. Not long after, the clown's costume produced a series of dizzying concentric circles on the wood approximating a multicolored target.

When she realized what was about to happen, Madam Olga put her hands over her mouth to suppress a cry. Was Madam Vera really going to do that? she wondered in disbelief. She had always complained of being clumsy, always dropping, breaking or spilling something. And now this, with her eyes blindfolded to boot. Pure insanity. When they die people seem to forget what they used to be like. . . .

Bending over slightly, Madam Vera felt for the box on the table, then took out one of the four daggers.

She tested its weight in her hand and took hold of the tip of the blade. When she let it fly, the room fell silent once again.

The dagger flashed and plunged in, but where was not immediately clear. Following the clowns' lead, Madam Olga leaned forward a little as the turning wheel quickly slowed down. When it stopped, the entire audience jumped to their feet with a new round of applause. She was the only one who stayed in her seat, staring speechlessly at the forehead of the crucified clown, where only the handle of the dagger was visible.

The girl came out from behind the wheel and started to remove the straps. But the clown didn't crumple to the ground after she finished untying him. Just as though there were no dagger thrust into his forehead, he made a great arching leap off the footrests. First he bowed to the figure in purple, then to the other clowns who gave him another round of applause. Then, like a two-legged unicorn, he bounded back to his seat.

The silence that held sway was disturbed by new rustling. The girl went up to Madam Vera again and held out her hand. Now she was holding the amber-colored necklace. When it had joined the bracelet in the lap, the purple glove plunged into the aquarium once again. The new ball had a sparkling number thirteen.

Accompanied by applause, a clown from the end of the third row, behind Madam Olga, rushed towards the wheel. She watched in irritation as the girl tightened the straps. She was meant to assume, of course, that this was all just a circus number. What else could it be with so many clowns? While they were all having a great time, she was the only one to be genuinely perturbed.

She wouldn't let them deceive her anymore. She watched impassively as the wheel turned faster and faster, and then the second dagger hit home somewhere. She just waved her hand dismissively when she saw the handle poking out just above the heart. She did not join in the applause that ensued after the second clown jumped off the wheel and bowed to the audience.

After Madam Vera took the plastic earrings out of the bag in her pocket, a third number was drawn: eleven. The clown in the middle seat on the opposite side from Madam Olga ran joyfully towards the wheel. This is losing its originality, she thought. Thank heavens Madam Vera had no more costume jewelry to pay for the throws. One of the daggers would not be used.

This time the blade allegedly hit the middle of his stomach. Receiving a thunderous ovation, the clown returned to his seat, pointing to his dagger as he went like it was some sort of decoration. After the applause died down, nothing happened for several moments. All eyes were turned towards Madam Vera on the mound. Even the figure in purple lifted its covered head.

When Madam Vera started to raise her hands, Madam Olga thought for a moment that she intended to remove the blindfold. Instead of this, however, the blindfold was doubled. The narrow black band was completely covered by the wide yellow scarf. The clowns jumped off their seats and started to cheer. Even the girl in the top hat applauded.

The purple glove stayed in the aquarium longer than before, briskly stirring the balls. They spun all the way up to the brim of the glass vessel, threatening to spill over. But this didn't happen. When the hand finally came out it was holding a dark-red ball with a sparkling number eight.

At first Madam Olga didn't understand why all eyes had turned towards her. When it finally dawned on her that this was her seat number, she started to shake her head. The applause surrounding her was not the least bit encouraging. She raised her hands in front of her as an additional sign of refusal. There might not be any danger from the dagger, but she certainly wasn't going to let them spin her wildly on the wheel. There was no way she could endure that.

When it became clear that she did not intend to stand up, the two clowns on either side of her rose from their seats. They grabbed her under the arms without a word and carried her to the stage. Madam Olga tried to wrest herself free, but they held on firmly. She stopped flailing about when they left the stand, not wanting to give any more occasion for hilarious laughter.

The clowns didn't let go of her while the girl was tying the straps. When she was finally stretched out on the wheel, they returned to their seats. Still smiling, the girl grabbed the brooch from her, even though it was clasped tightly in her fist. She raised it into the air, causing an outburst of delight among the audience. The brooch joined the other pieces of jewelry in the purple lap, and the hood without eye slits slowly bowed.

Madam Olga closed her eyes as the wheel started to turn. She was unable to keep them open; this would make her feel lightheaded and she might even faint. Even without being able to see, the onrush of nausea told her precisely when her head was upside down. But at least the girl had pinned the hem of her skirt and coat to the wood. She didn't dare think what would happen otherwise while her legs were up in the air.

She just wanted to get it over with. The clowns cheered faster and faster, louder and louder. When the dagger finally flew, she didn't hear the whiz, just a dull thud somewhere around her head. The crypt fell silent. She kept her eyes tightly shut a few more moments, then opened them hesitantly.

The first thing she saw was the handle of the dagger above her like a ledge, still vibrating. She thought that it was sticking out of her forehead, like with the first clown, but when she bent her head back as far as the straps allowed, she discovered that the dagger had landed just above the top of her head. The part that had not entered the wood looked ominously sharp.

Then she turned towards the audience. The clowns were sitting with their heads bowed. In spite of their painted smiles, they seemed dejected, as though someone had just died. The girl came out from behind the wheel, her red hair in disarray. She was trying to bite a piece off the top hat's brim.

Madam Vera raised her hands and untied the scarf, then the black blindfold. Her eyes rested briefly on Madam Olga. Then she came down from the mound and went up to the figure in purple. She dropped the scarf and the blindfold into his lap, covering the four pieces of costume jewelry.

The sigh that coursed through the audience merged with a wheezing sound, like a death rattle, that came from under the hood. The purple glove rose tremulously towards the hood, waited briefly after taking hold of the pointed top, then pulled upwards.

When it was plain there was nothing underneath, the clowns broke into painful sobs, and the girl clutched the bitten top hat to her breast and screamed. The headless, empty robe remained upright for a long moment, as though defying the inevitable, then crumpled onto the high-backed chair like a discarded rag.

Madam Vera went up to the wheel and started to untie the straps that bound Madam Olga. She stretched out both hands to help her down. Without her support Madam Olga would certainly have stumbled or even fallen. Her head was still spinning from the turning wheel.

They stood there for a while, looking at each other silently. Finally, Madam Vera let go of her and headed for the exit. Madam Olga started after her without a moment's hesitation. As they climbed up between the torches a chant resembling a rhythmical dirge accompanied them from down below.

The girl who had stayed outside the crypt also held her top hat on her breast, with bite marks on its brim. When the two women appeared at the door, she turned away her tear-stained face, framed by luxuriant red hair. Madam Vera let Madam Olga climb into the carriage that was still there, then got in herself.

They didn't speak a word to each other during the short ride. The clattering of the carriage wheels subsided when they left the cemetery and hit an asphalt road. Lying back in her seat, Madam Olga gazed at the row of chestnut trees dotted with an archipelago of bright islands.

When they turned off the boulevard she wasn't sure where they were. She thought it was a side street, but when the carriage stopped and she got out after Madam Vera, she saw that they were in the middle of a bridge. As soon as she touched the pavement, the carriage moved on. It turned right on the other side and disappeared from view.

Madam Vera went up to the low, broad parapet between two ornate lampposts and stared into the river. Joining her, Madam Olga noted that a dark-green raincoat was lying on the parapet. She stood on the other side of it and looked down too.

The reflection of the lights rippled through the water, creating trembling, fleeting designs on the dark background. A boat festooned with countless colored lights, full of dance music, was coming upriver. They watched it slowly move under the bridge.

When the stern disappeared, Madam Vera held out her hand. Madam Olga needed a few moments to understand what was expected of her. Swiftly reaching into her pocket, she took out the scarf. Madam Vera held it before her briefly, as though inspecting it, then placed it on top of the raincoat.

With an agility not at all characteristic of the elderly, and particularly not of the dead, she climbed onto the parapet. Madam Olga looked left and right anxiously. Luckily, there was no one on the bridge to see this gymnastic feat.

So there was no one but Madam Olga to witness the jump that soon followed. Another eyewitness might have been amazed when there was no splash in the water, but she did not find this at all unusual. Indeed, any sound at all would have been cause for surprise.

She stayed on the bridge a while longer, looking at the scarf on the raincoat. In other circumstances, good manners would not have permitted her to leave one of her belongings lying around here. But the scarf, in actual fact, had not had time to become hers. She had only worn it once, very briefly.

As she walked away, she concluded once again that buying it had been a mistake. Not only because she never wore scarves and yellow didn't suit her. She would have looked quite grotesque with those two large snake eyes. The best thing would be to stay away from sales altogether.

3. The Sneakers

Miss Anita knew at once that the young man wearing unmatched sneakers, one white and one black, had to be her son. He was coming down the street from the opposite direction, pushing a fuchsia-colored bicycle. Even though he couldn't have failed to see her as he passed by, he kept going as though he hadn't noticed her.

She thought of calling out to him, but then remembered that she didn't know his name. She hadn't chosen one for him yet. Several names for boys appealed to her. She'd narrowed the choice down to three, but was still undecided. This didn't bother her. There was no reason to hurry.

It would be years before her son was born. She wasn't married and had yet to meet the boy's father. She knew nothing about him except what she'd just found out. Her future husband would be a redhead. Her son couldn't have inherited that fiery-colored hair from her.

If she'd had any inkling that this meeting would come about, she would have chosen a name for him. Now what was she to do? She couldn't catch up with her son and address him in some formal manner, with "Sir", for example. How would that sound? What mother addresses her son with "Sir"? He would certainly be offended, if he was anywhere near as sensitive as she was.

She had no choice. Since she was unable to approach

him, she would have to follow him. She couldn't let him wander about town without parental supervision. He might look grown up, one would say he was at least seventeen years old, a full three years older than she was, but he would always be a child to her. She would have to be discreet with her shadowing, however. Children hate to have their parents dogging their steps.

Watching him from a short distance as he walked along, she decided she was quite pleased he was wearing sneakers of different colors. This was a trait he'd inherited from her side. She liked to wear unusual clothes and shoes too.

She was also happy that he had a bicycle. She'd been riding one ever since she was little. As far as she was concerned, though, he didn't have to push it. She'd never thought twice about zigzagging her bicycle through pedestrians on the sidewalk, giving no heed to their disapproval. Even so, it was a good thing he wasn't riding it now because then she would have had a hard time following him.

He proceeded without stopping and didn't turn to look in the store windows. When he finally stopped about ten minutes after their first encounter, a smile crossed Miss Anita's lips. She liked to stop in front of stores selling baby things too. Every once in a while she would go in and browse, even though, of course, the day was nowhere near when she would have any reason to buy something.

She couldn't imagine what interested him there, but this was a chance to find out what he liked. Then she wouldn't have to worry about what to buy when her son was born. She would go into the store after him and see what he bought or at least what attracted his attention if he was just browsing.

Her son's negligence, however, forced her to stay at the entrance to the store. He had simply leaned his bike against the window instead of taking it in with him as she would have done, regardless of the store clerks' complaints. Children can be so irresponsible. He hadn't even tried to secure it; anyone passing by could simply mount it and ride away.

She placed her hand on the large wire basket over the back wheel. This would deter any thief. She looked through the display window, but it was so full she couldn't get a good look inside. She thought briefly of entering the store with the bicycle, but that might be asking for trouble.

She turned her back to the window and stared irately down the street crowded with people in the late afternoon. As always, whenever she was angry everyone in her vicinity was to blame. She started glaring at the strangers coming her way.

Her frowning face didn't soften until she saw a man in late middle age, his hair as fiery red as her son's, whose behavior brought looks of annoyance from the passers-by. Since she herself often received such looks, she felt an immediate affinity with him. What kind of cardinal sin was it, anyway, to swing a bright red bowling ball?

She felt like clapping in support, but didn't have time. Just as she raised her hand from the basket, her son came out of the store. Paying her not the slightest attention, he put a colorful bag in the basket, grabbed the handlebars and started to push the bike again.

This was careless, too, she thought as she headed after him. Why didn't it occur to him that all someone had to do was reach out and take the bag? He wouldn't notice what was happening behind his back. But luckily she was there, not far to the rear, to prevent any theft. What would he do without his mother's protection?

And then it dawned on her that she could take the bag herself! Not to steal it, of course. What mother steals from her son? She'd take it just long enough to peek inside. She was very curious to know what he'd bought. In any case, as his mother she had the right to know.

Just as she put out her hand, he stopped all of a sudden in front of another window. She almost ran into the back wheel. Fancy shoes were on parade in the brightly lit display behind the glass.

She looked at the back of her son's head in bewilderment. She would never buy anything in a store like that. But if he'd made up his mind to be a dandy, so be it. True, such an inclination was hard to imagine given the shoes he was wearing now, but perhaps he, much like herself, was full of contradictions.

This time he entered the store with his bicycle. She hurried in after him, ready to rush to his defense if the salespeople made a fuss. She knew from experience the best way to handle them. She would raise her voice to an hysterical pitch, at which point they would all become accommodating.

But there was no need to interfere. No one took any notice of the bicycle or of what her son had on his feet. It was as though a famous customer had entered the store and could do whatever he pleased. Three salesgirls flocked around him, smiling broadly, ostentatiously obliging. No one paid any attention to her.

The way he made his choice was the exact opposite of his mother. She would have exhausted the salespeople, leisurely trying on at least half the shoes in the store. In the end she most often didn't buy anything and took pleasure in the annoyance she left behind her. All he did was point at the shoes he wanted without even bothering to try them on.

As though the salesgirls already knew his size, they brought out the boxes straightaway. Miss Anita watched in delight as the pile on the counter got higher. She had always dreamed of shopping like this, hang the expense.

In the end there were eleven boxes on the counter.

Each was placed in a plastic bag and they were then hooked onto the bicycle handlebars: six on one side, five on the other. There was no payment. My son must have a charge account here, thought his mother proudly. There was a lot of bowing as he left. No one even looked down their nose at her.

They continued down the street. She didn't know where they were going but that made no difference. As far as she was concerned, he could keep walking for a long time to come. The confusion he aroused among the passers-by gave her pleasure, as though she was the one doing something unseemly.

Unlike the people in the street, the doorman at the entrance to the large city library saw nothing unusual in the young man passing by him, pushing a bicycle loaded with bags. He even stood up, raised two fingers to the brim of his beribboned cap, and bowed. She was tickled by the special treatment her son was receiving, but had he taken against it she would have been happy too. She took great pleasure in squabbling with functionaries.

Raising the loaded bicycle to his shoulder with ease, the young man mounted several steps to the elevator at the end of the entrance hall. She was hurt when he closed the door without waiting for her. She too often acted that way towards others, but they were strangers, not her own mother.

She rushed up the stairs, accompanying the metal cage of the elevator as it clattered upwards. Out of breath, she reached the third floor just as the back wheel of the bicycle disappeared behind a door at the end of a short corridor. On it was the inscription: "Old and rare books—no admittance".

This, of course, didn't stop her. The room she entered had a high ceiling but no windows. The walls were covered with bookshelves filled with thick, worn tomes. To the right of the door was a small desk. The woman sitting behind it, her hair graying red, couldn't have been more than forty-five years old. She was absorbed in writing something in a large registry and didn't even glance at Miss Anita when she entered.

In the middle of the room was an enormous white bathtub, its legs in the shape of human feet. Behind the bathtub was a screen with a yellow background painted with many different kinds of footwear, all brown: shoes, boots, army boots, sneakers, wooden-soled scuffs, slippers, clogs. The young man lowered the bicycle to the floor, took the bags off the handlebars and removed the boxes from the bags.

Then he took the shoes out of the boxes and placed them in the bathtub. When the eleventh pair was inside, he grabbed hold of the bicycle and went behind the screen, leaving a mess on the floor behind him.

Noises were heard briefly behind the screen. When he reappeared Miss Anita could not repress a silvery titter. She even applauded in delight. Her son had outdone her. This would never have crossed her mind.

He was wearing only a diaper and the sneakers. The diaper was too small and the tape barely held it up. He had a rubber duck in one hand and a large rattle in the other. He went up to the bathtub and got in among the shoes.

She was proud to notice that the young man was quite handsome half-naked like this. Girls would be wild about him. She would have been attracted too if it weren't for the fact that he was her son. He must have inherited his build from his father. She could barely wait to meet him.

He put the toy duck and rattle on the bottom of the bathtub, then started to scoop up the shoes. He tossed them into the air and watched them fall back into the tub with a gurgling laugh. This entertained him for a while; then he suddenly frowned, grabbed the rattle and shook it fiercely.

The graying woman raised her head for the first time and took the young man in with a glance. Then she picked up the silver bell with a wooden handle standing on a corner of her desk. The fading sound of the rattle was replaced by an equally sharp ringing.

When Miss Anita heard a thudding sound rapidly approaching from the other side of the door, she moved a little away from it. The door opened with a bang. A swarm of children burst in and flocked around the desk. They were barefoot but each of them was carrying a pair of little shoes.

The woman stood up and started handing out coupons with numbers on them from a little blue block. Each child who received a coupon ran up to the bathtub, threw in their shoes, then headed back toward the door, where a terrible jam was created. The surge from outside did not slacken, while the number attempting to leave got bigger and bigger.

The bathtub soon filled up. Before long only the young man's head was visible above the pile of colorful shoes. When a shoe finally slid to the floor, the bell rang out once again. The clamoring around the desk ceased the same moment. Children who had not received a coupon turned around and headed out. No one protested. The bottleneck at the door lasted a bit longer, until they had all left.

The graying woman went back to her notations, and Miss Anita to watching her son. Considerable effort was required for him to extricate the hand holding the toy duck. He placed the duck in front of him, then thrust his hand back into the pile.

The frown on his face indicated he was having trouble locating the rattle. His head slowly disappeared below the surface of the shoes, then went completely under. Miss Anita first thought this was fun, but as the minutes passed and the young man did not emerge, her face grew somber.

She flashed her eyes angrily at the woman at the desk. How could she sit there so calmly while a child was drowning before her very eyes? She wanted to sweep everything off the woman's desk. But there was no time to lose. She had to act quickly.

She reached the bathtub in two bounds and began feverishly throwing the pile of little shoes out of it. As she went deeper and deeper and her son still had not appeared, panic started to get the upper hand. Her nails were already scratching the bottom of the bathtub when the rattle started shaking. But not from where she expected it.

She raised her eyes towards the screen and saw her fully-dressed son as he emerged from behind it. He was pushing the bicycle with one hand and shaking the rattle with the other. She wanted to snap his head off. Was that any way to treat his mother? She might have died of fright, and here he was playing the illusionist. But she would forgive him this time. She liked magic shows. The trick had really been good. He would have to show her how he did it.

The young man placed the rattle on the desk as he went by. He departed without closing the door behind him. Before Miss Anita left the room, she too stopped for a moment next to the graying woman. She picked up the rattle, shook it and slammed it on the desktop. The plastic ball shattered and little silver spheres scattered everywhere. This, however, did not perturb the woman as she calmly made her entries.

At the exit to the library the doorman stood up once again to greet the young man, but his smile disappeared when Miss Anita passed by. He eyed her with a scowl. As though barely waiting for such a provocation, she gave him what she often did to guys she didn't like: she stuck her tongue out at him, all the way until it reached the tip of her chin.

At the first intersection the young man didn't wait

for the green light for pedestrians. He crossed the street, paying no attention to the sudden braking and angry honks. Miss Anita joined him without a moment's hesitation. She liked to cross the street like that too. Here was another thing they had in common, although when she gave it some thought, as his mother she should scold him. He was still a child, after all, he might come to harm.

When he entered the first perfume shop on the other side of the street, he left his bike by the window again. This annoyed Miss Anita. He seemed to be telling her he didn't want her to go inside.

As she stood with her hand resting on the bicycle basket, this time she managed a somewhat better look inside the shop. She saw a salesgirl put various boxes and tubes in front of the young man. Unlike in the shoe store, he seemed undecided here. The counter was soon covered with small objects.

If he'd been a woman she would have understood his quandary, but what need was there to pick and choose between men's cosmetics? They were a simple matter. A good quarter of an hour passed, however, before he finally made up his mind. He was already on the way out, carrying a blue bag, when he suddenly went back to the counter as though he'd forgotten something. He spoke to the salesgirl once again, pointing with his thumb behind his back, towards the window.

Miss Anita was puzzled. Was he pointing at her? She felt like hightailing it the same instant, but she couldn't leave the bike. It isn't easy with children, she concluded. They put you in impossible positions. As she was pondering what to do, the salesgirl went up to the window and took a long red wig off one of the gray plastic busts.

What does he need that for? wondered Miss Anita, caught in a dilemma. She brightened at the thought that he might be buying it for her. How nice! He wants his mother to have hair like his. She had never worn a wig, and up until then red had never been her favorite color, but she would certainly accept the gift. How could she refuse it?

But no gift was presented to her when the young man left the perfume shop. Once again he took absolutely no notice of her standing by the bicycle. He just put the blue bag in the basket and continued down the street. Offended, she stared at his back for several moments, then headed after him. If it had been anyone else, she would have made a scene. But her son, of course, was an exception.

The next time he stopped was in front of another luxury boutique. As she watched him enter, pushing the bicycle, she wondered in confusion what he was doing in a fancy shop selling women's lingerie.

Had she been on her own, she would never have set foot in there, but now it was clear she had to go in after him. She went quite unnoticed here too. Both salesgirls devoted their attention solely to the young man. There was no need to say anything. As though knowing what he'd come for, they hastened to a marble shelf and took down a thin box with a large gold crown embossed on it.

Miss Anita didn't wear such lingerie; moreover, she despised it. Even so, the pink silk camisole with thin straps and lace trim that was taken out of the box filled her with admiration. She tried to imagine herself in it. Suddenly there was nothing objectionable about it.

The young man just nodded briefly. The camisole was folded and returned to the box, which was wrapped in turquoise paper and tied with a dark blue ribbon. There was no payment this time either. With another nod, the customer took the box, put it under his arm and went out.

On a square not far from the shop, the young man halted at a trolleybus stop. Miss Anita smiled. Bicycles were not allowed in trolleybuses, but she still took hers in from time to time. Once she'd caused a traffic jam because the driver refused to continue until she got off. She did in the end, but only after someone had called the police.

When they entered the trolleybus, there was none of the usual grumbling from the other passengers. On the contrary, they were kind enough to make room for the bike at the back of the bus. This exasperated Miss Anita to no end. How unfair! Had she been the one, she would have already received a torrent of disapproval and even insults, while here they were all looking kindly on her son. Although she was aware that this should actually please her, she felt a pang of jealousy.

After they had passed several stops, a much stronger wave of jealousy washed over her. Why hadn't she thought of it before? Of course! Everything he'd bought in the perfumery and lingerie shop had been not for her, as she'd naively thought, but for some other woman. She barely suppressed the impulse to go up and give him a resounding slap in front of everyone.

Oh well, she must reconcile herself to the fact that one day he would leave her for someone else, he couldn't stay with his mother forever. But it wasn't time for that yet, why, she'd only just met him. Perhaps she was berating him unjustly. He couldn't be the one to blame, of course, he was too young and inexperienced.

Someone must have turned his head. The type wasn't hard to imagine. Certainly an older and unattractive woman. They liked to pounce on young men. But rich too. Of course! That's why he had charge accounts in fancy shops.

Wonderful. Since he was clearly heading for a rendezvous with her, this was a chance to tell the old bag what she thought about this seduction of her son. Buying him, actually. When she got her hands on the woman feathers would fly.

But when they got off the trolleybus she saw they were not in the part of town with villas surrounded by tall hedges, as she'd supposed. The neighborhood was rather gloomy. Gray four-story buildings lined both sides of the street and there were no shops.

They went some fifty meters and then he stopped in front of a house without a single window. The only thing interrupting the uniform olive-green façade was a small black door. Next to it was a dusty brass plate with the inscription: "City Mental Institution".

She did not enter immediately after her son. A rare feeling of guilt oppressed her. Accepting any woman he was attached to, old floozy or not, would be hard. But if he'd set his heart on someone from this place, that was another matter altogether. She felt kindly towards the poor souls locked up in there. People often said that she too was crazy just because she was unconventional.

She thought she'd find a guard behind the door, but no one was there when she entered. At the end of a long corridor she saw her son lean the bike against a wall, take the blue bag out of the basket and disappear off somewhere to the right. When she got there, she found stairs winding downwards.

Having descended after him, she found herself at the beginning of a new corridor, considerably shorter than the one above. There was a metal door to the left of the stairs and another with a reinforced glass window at the end of the corridor, which the young man had just closed behind him. When she got up close enough she managed to read the tiny inscription on the plate under the window: "Kitchen".

She pressed down on the handle, but the door didn't open. She tried once again, pushing with her shoulder, again with no result. Angered, she put her face against the window and looked inside.

A large table filled the middle of the room, while the walls were lined with shelves, cabinets, refrigerators and ovens. To either side of the table were three men wearing light-green pants, sleeveless undershirts and toques. They were rolling out dough with wide rolling pins and it covered almost the whole surface of the table.

Miss Anita put her face right up against the window so she could see the perimeter of the room, but her son was nowhere to be seen. He must have gone through the door on the right that probably led to the pantry. But why was he in there? Or rather, what on earth was he doing in the kitchen? Was he intending to treat his chosen one with something sweet? That would be nice. She liked to receive sweets, too.

Minutes passed and nothing happened. The cooks rolled their pins over the dough with harmonious movements, as though to a rhythm of music that couldn't be heard in the corridor. Miss Anita couldn't imagine what enormous thing they were preparing.

Finally they raised their rolling pins and looked towards the side door. Again she pressed her cheek against the metal edge of the window. A girl with long red hair stepped out of the pantry into the kitchen. She was wearing nothing but the pink camisole and was garishly made up in matching shades.

So that's it, thought Miss Anita. This is where they have their secret rendezvous. Clever. She couldn't see very well at such an angle through the reinforced glass, but the girl seemed attractive. She was almost as tall as her son, with regular facial features that seemed somehow familiar.

Head bowed, clearly feeling awkward, the girl headed around the table. When she was standing next to the cook in the middle, she started to go down and quickly disappeared from Miss Anita's sight. Her first thought was that the girl had gone down through an opening in the floor, which must certainly be the beginning of a secret passage taking her back to her cell without being seen.

But then the three cooks from that side of the table disappeared as well. What did this mean? And where was her son? Why hadn't he come out of the pantry? Nothing happened for a few moments, and then four figures came up from behind the table.

The three cooks had raised the girl horizontally, holding her under the shoulders, hips and calves. Even before Miss Anita caught sight of the black and white sneakers, she understood her initial misconception. Her eyes grew as round as saucers.

There had been no older woman or girl. What he'd bought in the last two stores was for him: the cosmetics, wig and camisole. She'd never imagined in her wildest dreams that her son would have such inclinations. How horrible! What was she to do? What position should she take? She couldn't forsake him, could she? She would have to accept him as he was. She was his mother, after all. How could she turn her back on him?

But that wasn't the most important thing at the moment. What did these strapping men want from him? Why, he was still a child, so to speak. She watched in bewilderment as they carried her son's rigid body to the middle of the table. Putting aside their rolling pins, three new pairs of hands stretched out from the other side and held him under the back and feet.

He lay there briefly without moving, as though in a living net, and then the hands started to descend. They slipped out deftly right above the tabletop, lowering the young man into the middle of the dough. What did these perverts have in mind? Although still willing to accept the fact that her son wasn't normal, she wasn't about to watch any debauchery.

But what she vaguely anticipated did not happen. The cooks started to slip their fingers under the dough along the edge of the table. When their hands reached the young man's body, they wrapped first one side of the sheet-like shroud over him and then the other.

Now he was lying in the middle of the table rolled up like an enormous sausage roll, his unmatched sneakers sticking out of one end and his tuft of red hair from the other. He'll suffocate inside, thought his mother frantically. Are these monsters at all aware of the fact?

And then she discovered there are worse fates than suffocation. One of the cooks approached the left-hand wall. She noted with alarm that the rectangular door belonged to a large oven and not a white cabinet. The cook opened it, then stepped back from the intense heat.

Fused to the small window, Miss Anita watched in disbelief as the six cooks picked up what she'd thought was the tabletop, but was actually a large tin surface. The end with the red wig sticking out soon started to enter the glowing hot compartment.

Miss Anita banged her fists on the window hysterically and started to scream. But no one in the kitchen paid any attention. The baking tin with her son wrapped in dough was steadily disappearing into the oven. When the sneakers were inside too, they closed the door.

Their job finished, the six cooks headed for the other side of the kitchen. One by one they entered the room which the young man disguised as a girl had left just a few minutes before.

Completely beside herself, Miss Anita started to kick the door and tug at the handle. The small corridor was now echoing with noise. If there was no one here in the basement, she reasoned, finally managing a coherent thought, there must be someone upstairs. This was indeed a madhouse, but not all of them had to be crazy.

Just as she turned to go up, the door next to the stairs opened. She stopped in mid-step and stared at her son standing in the doorway. He looked quite normal, as though the transvestism of a moment before, wrapping him in sticky dough and putting him in the oven, had been inflicted on someone else entirely. He ran up the steps.

Miss Anita saw red. Her helplessness and despair were instantly transformed into the quintessence of rage. Now he was in for it. Once she was through with him, he would never think of practicing his stupid circus tricks on her again. She could have died of panic. She hastened after him.

When she reached the top of the stairs, he was just going out of the black door into the street. As soon as she emerged into the falling dusk, she realized it wouldn't be easy to get her hands on him. He was pedaling fast and furiously on the bike, disappearing down the street. She stamped her feet on the pavement in frustration, then headed off in hot pursuit.

She paid no attention to the occasional passers-by who scrambled out of her way. She only growled at one of them who made a remark. It wasn't until they'd traveled three blocks that she realized her son wasn't trying to get away from her. Had he wanted to, he could have easily gone beyond her reach. His cycling speed was just enough to maintain the distance between them. When she started to pant and slow down, he did the same.

Exhaustion eased the rage that had consumed her. She was still mad at him for playing with her so cold-heartedly in the basement of the insane asylum, but now what annoyed her was the fact that she had no way of knowing when this dashing about would end. It wasn't fair for him to be on a bicycle while she jogged along.

She quickened her pace when he turned a corner. What she found when she got there was a side street with an open-air flea market. Both sides of the street were lined with stalls, some covered, some not, and the pavement in between was filled with people. Her son was off the bike and had just joined the throng. She picked up her pace so as not to lose sight of him.

He wandered from stall to stall, browsing idly. Even if he'd wanted to walk faster, he couldn't because of the bicycle. A wide variety of used goods were on sale, arranged without rhyme or reason: vases, candlesticks, shabby hats, gilded buttons, cracked cigarette holders, garden gloves, inkpots, castanets, paper cutters, corkscrews, phonograph records without jackets, nail clippers, monocle frames, dolls' clothes, bundles of letters, wooden legs, porcelain chamber pots, old-fashioned radios, rusty hair clippers, harmonicas, monogrammed napkins, batteries, shoe inserts, dental forceps, salt shakers.

She couldn't resist the temptation for long. She didn't need any of those old things, but she never stole because she was in need. It was just for the thrill of it. She never kept the things she stole and always left them where their appearance would cause confusion, as she watched surreptitiously and laughed.

They worked like a well-drilled team. He would cause a disturbance as he maneuvered his bicycle to get close to a stall, and she would take advantage of this distraction to steal something. Her fingers were swift and skillful. Even if someone was watching they would have a hard time noticing anything. Because of the help he was inadvertently giving her, she had already forgiven her son what he'd done to her in the madhouse.

First she stole a rather large eight-branched medal with a blue and white ribbon. She almost cried out when she pricked herself on one of the sharp points. Then she took something wrapped in paper. She unwrapped it in her coat pocket, and when she touched the object her faced twisted in disgust. She removed the false teeth, holding them gingerly with two fingers, placed them on the ground next to her foot and crushed them in anger. She shot the seller a piercing look.

She was almost caught in the act when she picked a white pipe off an overcrowded stall. When she pulled it out, the small pile of objects resting on it collapsed. But this didn't attract the seller's attention and he didn't interrupt his conversation with a customer at the other end of the stall. The pipe soon joined the medal in Miss Anita's pocket.

Another item ended up on the ground. She thought that the pink dice with white spots denoting numbers one to six was made of marble, but when she found out it was plastic, she threw it away in disgust. This seller received a dark look too. How did they have the nerve to sell such junk?

The last little thing she stole was the least valuable, but she liked it the most. As a little girl she'd had something similar, but hadn't seen one for sale in a long time. Inside the tiny glass snow globe was a house surrounded by a garden in some kind of liquid.

She knew what would happen if she shook the globe. Snow would start to fall on the house. As a little girl she would stare at length at the particles falling slowly on Santa's sleigh. She wanted to see that again, but would have to move at least a short distance away from the stall. She put her hand in her pocket but didn't let go of the snow globe for fear that the medal's spikes would damage it.

She decided to keep it. She would drop the other two items on the next stall, but not the snow globe. This would be her first real theft, although for some reason her conscience wasn't bothered. The seller probably didn't even know he had it in his pile of trinkets.

Nonetheless, as they continued on their way, he spoke to her. "There will be lots of snow this winter, young lady." She turned around and looked apprehensively at the short, heavy-set man behind the stall, who was smiling. He was wearing a tasseled orange knit cap. Before she had a chance to reply, he turned to another customer.

The crowd thinned briefly. They were at an intersection that interrupted the two rows of stalls. The flea market continued straight ahead, and a narrow little street went off left and right, its poor lighting emphasized by the deepening night. The young man pushed his bike to the left. As she followed him, she thought for a moment of simply dumping the medal and pipe, but then felt this would be out of place.

The hubbub subsided the farther they got from the flea market. There had been a few people at the beginning of the backstreet, but now they hadn't encountered anyone for some time. In addition, fewer and fewer of the store and house windows were lit. The low, dilapidated houses of sooty brick that now surrounded them seemed abandoned.

She finally decided to ask him where they were headed. As a mother she had a right to know. But then he stopped before a door that looked just the same as the others. He leaned the bicycle against the wall and knocked three times. No one responded, or at least not that she heard. He, however, concluded after a short wait that he could enter. He left the door ajar.

She hesitated just a moment before entering. If he thought his bicycle was safe there outside, so be it. She had no intention of standing guard anymore. He was gravely mistaken if he expected her to do such things without letup. She was his mother, not his nursemaid.

She found herself in a long and narrow corridor. Somewhere in the distance a bulb with a round metal shade was swinging on a cord, even though there was no draft. The young man was outlined in the dim light. She rushed to catch up with him.

At the end of the corridor were steps leading down. They descended into a small room, also dimly lit. Another shaded light bulb was swinging back and forth.

The place smelled of wet coal, although there was nothing but shelves full of empty, dusty bottles and jars along the left-hand wall.

Another door on the opposite wall opened onto a staircase leading up. They ascended cautiously because of the dark. The only light came from somewhere way up high. The wooden steps creaked under their feet as they climbed, holding onto the wobbly handrail.

If she remembered correctly, none of the buildings on the street was more than two floors high. Here, however, they climbed up all of five floors before they reached a small round room at the top bathed in light. Three tin mushroom-lights with short shiny stalks swung in harmony from the ceiling, forming a moving equilateral triangle.

The round table in the middle of the room had a single fat leg firmly fixed to the floor. Two domes of the same wood, resembling humps, rose from the tabletop.

Behind the table was a large barrel. The man standing in it was naked from the waist up, his shoulders, arms and head shiny as though rubbed with oil. The feminine features of his round face were emphasized by the thick braid of bushy red hair that sprouted at the back of his head and disappeared into the barrel.

When the visitors appeared at the door to the little room he gave a resounding clap. The three bright lights suddenly started swinging faster. He pointed at the humps with his right hand as his lips curved into a seductive smile.

The young man went up to the table, then turned towards Miss Anita who had stayed at the entrance. They looked at each other briefly, without a word, and then she headed towards him with slow steps.

When she was standing next to him, he raised his hand in front of her, palm up. She stared at it with a frown, and several long moments passed before she began rummaging through her coat pocket.

She took out the sharp-pointed medal with care and placed it in her son's hand. But the hand didn't move. She gave him a long, piercing look, her lips pursed in an angry grimace, before she reached into her pocket once again. The pipe was placed next to the medal in his hand.

The hand, however, was still waiting. Miss Anita started to shake her head. The anger on her face dissolved into a contorted plea. But he was unrelenting. The tips of his fingers even curled several times impatiently, hurrying her up. With glistening eyes she lowered the snow globe into the insatiable hand, but there were no tears.

The three objects quickly passed from one hand into another. The braided head bowed and his smile broadened. His hand disappeared into the barrel for a moment and laid the medal, pipe and snow globe down there.

When his hand re-emerged, he grabbed hold of the round table and gave it a sharp spin. The speed of its rotation transformed the two domes into the illusion of a single peak in the middle of the tabletop. The effect was soon destroyed as it began to slow down. Finally, the table was stationary once again.

Two plump hands with short fingers, palms up, motioned towards the two domes as though they had something to offer. The young man didn't hesitate a moment. He indicated the one on his right.

With a new bow, the man in the barrel took hold of the brass handle on the top of the dome and picked it up. Protracted giggling filled the little room when there was nothing underneath it. That same moment one of the three lights flickered and went out.

The young man looked at Miss Anita. There was no regret in his eyes. Just as hers had a moment before, his lips pursed in anger. The look she returned was a mixture of reproof and compassion.

He dropped down on his left knee and started to untie the lace on his right, white sneaker. His movements were nervous. He pulled the shoe off his foot half unlaced, stood up and offered it to the bare torso.

He was rewarded with another smile and bow as this wager also disappeared into the barrel. The Bactrian camel briefly became a dromedary and then returned to its initial shape.

The choice this time was preceded by hesitation. The young man's hand hovered between the two domes, and then he finally pointed his index finger at the right hand one again. This time the giggle seemed to echo from the emptiness underneath it. There was even soft feminine applause as the second light went out. The lighting in the little room was now as dim as in the basement.

The young man started to turn towards Miss Anita, but then changed his mind. He suddenly raised his left foot and yanked off the black sneaker without undoing the laces. The barrel's maw swallowed the third wager.

The table seemed to spin forever. When it finally stopped, no one moved for a moment. This standstill was shattered by the young man, but not in order to choose a dome. Moving swiftly, he grabbed both handles and pulled them up.

That same moment, the bare-chested man closed his eyes and started to sing as he sank into the barrel. The soprano carved a crystal dirge in the air that changed its timbre when the head sank out of sight. Once it was gone, the two extinguished lights turned back on, illuminating the little room once again. None of the three lights was swinging anymore.

Miss Anita watched wordlessly as the young man placed the wooden domes on the floor and took the black and white sneakers from the table. He patiently loosened the laces and then put them on. When he was finished tying the bows, the voice in the barrel fell silent.

There was a groan from inside, then the cut-off braid flew out and landed on the empty table. Miss Anita reflected that many years were needed to grow hair long enough for a braid like that.

When the young man grabbed her hand she tried to pull it free, but his grip was firm. He led her out of the little room. Although the stairs were shaky, they ran down all five flights, not bothering to hold onto the rail.

They sped through the basement room with several strides. She had just enough time to notice that the light had stopped swinging there too. The other change, however, was considerably more pronounced. Not a single one of the bottles and jars seemed to be intact. Slivers of broken glass covered the floor under the shelves now fronting the right-hand wall.

The light in the long corridor was barely flickering. If the young man hadn't been leading her, she would have had to advance with caution. They did not go out of the door as soon as they reached it. He knocked three times as before, and then waited. Once again she didn't hear anything before he finally opened the door and led her outside.

She breathed a sigh of relief when she saw the bicycle waiting for them. The thought that her son had a lucky streak brought a smile to her lips. But her smile disappeared when she saw him jump on the bike. He was gravely mistaken if he thought she was about to rush after him again.

He didn't leave without her, however. He nodded his head at the fuchsia-colored bar that joined the seat to the handlebars. She looked at him quizzically for a moment, then sat down and grabbed hold of the inner sides of the handlebars. It was a little uncomfortable, but certainly better than running.

They reached the flea market in no time at all. Night had already fallen so there weren't many people and they could continue without stopping. They did have to ring the bell, though.

Miss Anita's initial anxiety was replaced by delight. She greatly enjoyed watching people jump aside to let the bicycle pass. This was often accompanied by scolding and curses. Several times she turned around and made faces at them.

They picked up speed dangerously when they left the flea market. There was more honking and screeching of brakes as they coasted down the middle of the street. Miss Anita screamed in reply and thrashed her legs dangling down the sides.

She didn't know where they were headed, but that made no difference. She was safe in the hands of her son and nothing bad could happen to her. She hadn't had such a good time in ages.

They soon came out onto a boulevard lined with chestnut trees. The embanked side of a river stretched along one side. The young man turned off the pavement onto the sidewalk, under bushy treetops. Too bad there are so few people on the promenade, thought Miss Anita. It would look much more cheerful.

When they reached a stone bridge, the young man stopped the bicycle. He waited for her to get down and then got off too. He climbed up onto a wide parapet with a row of ornate lampposts on the outer side. First he lifted the bicycle up next to him, then put out his hand to help Miss Anita climb up.

She joined him without hesitation, although she had no idea what he intended to do. She watched him get on the bicycle, but didn't respond immediately when he gestured for her to sit back on the bar. She leaned over a little and looked into the murky mass of the river with the flickering reflection of streetlights on its surface.

She raised her eyes to his smiling face, gazed at it for a while, smiled finally in return and got on the bar.

He was now cycling slowly, formally, as though on parade. The lampposts they passed resembled a lineup of grenadiers.

They stopped in the middle of the bridge because something was blocking their way. He got off the bike, onto the parapet, and she did the same. He picked up the bicycle, held it over his head several moments, swung it and then let it go. She clapped as it curved downwards, hit the water with a splash and disappeared into the gloomy depths.

He bent down to pick up what was lying on the parapet. First he took the raincoat and held it out for her. It was a man's, at least two sizes too big and with mismatched lapels, but this didn't bother her in the slightest.

Then he handed her the scarf. She readily placed it around her neck, even though she didn't like yellow. There were two large dark spots on one end that made it more attractive.

He dropped down on his left knee, right foot forward, slowly untied the laces of the white sneaker and took it off. Then he grabbed her right foot above the ankle, raised it a little, took off her shoe without unbuckling it and hurled it into the river.

When he had replaced her shoe with his sneaker and tied the lace, she discovered that it was neither too small nor too large. She did not find this strange. How natural, she thought, for a mother and son to have identical feet.

The shoe on her left foot ended up in the water too, but she received nothing in return. When he rose and stood next to her, they had one shoe each. The two shoes were side by side again, but the same person wasn't wearing them.

He held out his hand. She took it and he bowed his head. She did the same and saw a boat starting to appear from under the bridge. It was magnificently lit and decorated with pennants, full of cheerful music and people waving at them.

When it got about halfway out, it stopped. The young man turned towards Miss Anita and smiled once again. She returned his smile, as she had at the beginning of the bridge. There was no need to say anything.

Their bare feet stepped forward in unison. They plummeted, but there was no danger. When they reached the deck, their landing on the sneakers would be as soft as down.

Miss Tamara, the Reader

Contents

1. Apples

Miss Tamara always ate apples while she read. She called this healthy reading. She only liked tart apples, even though their acidity gave her stomach trouble. She would choose three large apples, always the same dark-green variety. She did not peel them. First she cut them into quarters and then removed the core and seeds. Each quarter was subsequently cut into three slices so that she would have one for each of the thirty-six pages that she read every day.

She would take a slice at the beginning of a page and slowly nibble at it, making sure it lasted until the final line. She would keep the nibbled bits in her mouth, chew them some more, then finally swallow the pulpy mouthful when she reached the bottom of the page. As her reading progressed, the sour taste in her mouth grew more and more pronounced. The first thing she did when she set the book aside was to brush her teeth thoroughly. This usually wasn't enough, however, and the sourness lingered, but it didn't bother her. Some things must be endured for the sake of one's health.

This healthy reading continued until one day something unexpected happened. Out of the blue, a thought struck Miss Tamara that forced her to swallow the chewed part of the slice, even though two paragraphs remained until the bottom of the first page of her new book. If she turned the page and continued reading—she would die.

There was no immediate stimulus for this thought.

Death was not mentioned anywhere on the first page, and it rarely appeared in the works Miss Tamara read. Her general circumstances did not give rise to thoughts of death either. She had just turned forty and was the picture of health, unaccustomed to anything worse than sporadic winter sniffles.

Although nothing like it had ever crossed her mind before, Miss Tamara had no doubt at all about the veracity of her premonition: death lay in wait for her if she continued reading. It seemed absolutely certain, although she was unable to explain why. Fortunately, she did not have to explain herself to anyone.

She closed the book at once in order to stop the first page from turning by accident, and put it in her lap. Then she concluded that this was not safe enough, so she got up from the armchair by the window where she always read, went up to the big bookshelf on the opposite wall, and deposited the large hardback there. She stepped back to the middle of the living room, looked at the bookshelf from that distance, and realized that she had made a mistake.

The deadly book did not belong there either. The bookshelf held only works she had read and liked, and decided to keep so she could go back to them from time to time. She might have liked this one—the title was promising—but she definitely would not be reading it. Even if she'd wanted to, how would it be possible? She would never get beyond the second page. The dearly departed do not read.

She took the book out gingerly with her thumb and index finger, as though removing an explosive device. She stepped back from the bookshelf again and reflected. What should she do with it? She knew what she'd do if it were a run-of-the-mill volume. Books she didn't like were taken to the secondhand bookstore and sold at a loss or given to a friend with different reading habits.

This was clearly out of the question. She couldn't have an innocent soul on her conscience, particularly that of a friend. Others might be totally oblivious to the impending danger. After finishing the first page they would turn it unsuspectingly and start to read the second, and that would be the last one they ever began. If she allowed this to happen, she would be as culpable as a callous terrorist.

She had no choice. She had to commit the ultimate sacrilege: throw the book in the garbage. She felt terrible about it, but this would at least prevent a much greater misfortune. She headed for the kitchen and had already raised the lid of the garbage can, when it occurred to her that she couldn't get rid of it that casually.

Someone might find it at the dump before it was destroyed. There are those who sift through the garbage looking for things that can still be used. They wouldn't necessarily start reading it. People who hang around dumps aren't inclined to do that in general. But they would be in mortal danger if they just leafed through it.

She lowered the lid. The book had to be destroyed before she threw it in the garbage. That way no one would come to any harm. This was even more unpleasant, but what else could she do? And then a new problem cropped up. How was she going to do it? She couldn't keep her eyes open as she tore up the pages. That would be the same as continuing to read after the first page. She would have to tear them up sight unseen.

She took a long woolen scarf out of the clothes closet and went back to the kitchen. Sitting down at the table, she placed the book in front of her and firmly bound her eyes. She made two knots at the back of her head just in case, then put her hands in front of her face to make sure she couldn't see anything.

The torment that filled her because of what she was

doing was short-lived. It was driven away by the realization that this had to be done. She tore up the book patiently and methodically, page by page. The task turned out to be easier than she imagined. When she felt for the pile of torn-up paper, she was satisfied to find it constantly growing.

When only the cover was left, she removed the blindfold. She took a large plastic bag, filled it with the torn paper, added the cover, then put everything into the garbage can. There. Now this terrible book could not hurt anyone. It had been a stroke of luck that she'd gotten hold of it first.

On her return to the living room, her eyes were immediately drawn to the table next to the armchair by the window. There upon it was the plate with thirty-five slices of apple. How could she eat them just like that, without reading? The problem was easy to fix, however. She would take a book she'd already read and read it again. That was why she kept them in her library, wasn't it?

She chose one of her favorite works and settled into the armchair. She took a slice of apple, nibbled it, then opened the book, but didn't get further than the title page.

The awareness that she would die on the spot if she merely glanced at the first page was even more pronounced than before. She closed the book at once. She hesitated a moment about what to do with the nibbled slice and finally put it in her mouth. It seemed inappropriate to put something with a bite taken out of it back on the plate.

The scarf was waiting for her on the back of the chair in the kitchen. Luckily she hadn't replaced it in the closet, as though suspecting she'd still need it. This time there was sorrow along with the torment as she tore up the pages. There'd been no reason to be sad about the first book, as it was not uncommon for her to be disappointed in spite of a promising title. But this book had been a real favorite. It was hard to accept the dismal certainty that she would never read it again.

After the second bag was in the garbage can, she headed for the bathroom. She'd realized what she had to do while she was tearing up the dear pages. She had to test every book in her library. She hoped that only the two she had destroyed were contaminated, but what if it was an epidemic? She couldn't take the risk. The infection was fatal, so it had to be taken very seriously.

She put on the rubber gloves she used to scrub the bathtub. She knew the fatal effect was transmitted by the eyes, but why take a chance? Even if the gloves didn't help her, they would do her no harm. In any case, she would feel safer.

She went into the living room and started taking books off the shelf. It turned out there was no need even to open them. The moment she put her hand on one, she was swept by the unmistakable feeling that it was infected. If she so much as lifted the cover she would be past recovery.

Her darkest foreboding proved true. The epidemic was rampant. Literally not a single healthy book was left. She placed one after the other on the floor, watching in despair as the bookshelf emptied. It might have been easier if they'd been works as yet unread, but she was bound to each one by fond memories. She felt as though she was losing her nearest and dearest.

Without taking off the gloves, she carried armloads of books into the kitchen. By the time she had finished, the table was covered with stacks of books. Had the library been any bigger, the legs might have buckled. She sat down and put on her blindfold, then started to tear. She dropped the torn pages onto the floor next to her chair.

At first she was tormented by sorrow, and the awareness that the task was inevitable could not assuage it. But the repetitive nature of the work soon numbed her, stifling any feelings. She worked mechanically, concentrating solely on making sure that no single page slipped past her. As time passed she became more efficient and the fact that she couldn't see no longer mattered.

Seven hours and eleven minutes after she'd set to work she couldn't feel any more books on the table in front of her. She took off the scarf and looked around. The torn paper surrounding her was knee-deep, and the pile of covers on the table resembled the carcasses of dead animals.

She took a bundle of large garbage bags out of the kitchen cupboard and started to fill them. She wouldn't take them to the dumpster by the curb yet because it was too late in the day. If she was seen in the act she might arouse curiosity. . . . The best thing would be to throw away one bag every day, instead of throwing them all away at once. That way not even the garbage men would suspect anything.

After filling the last bag, she returned to the bathroom, took off the rubber gloves and scrubbed her soapy hands at length under the hot water, like a surgeon before an operation. Just in case. Such dangers are not to be taken lightly.

Fatigue finally overwhelmed her when she returned to the living room. The sight of the bookshelf, its emptiness gaping eerily on the wall, only compounded it. She collapsed rather than sat down in the armchair next to the now darkened window. What she needed was something to refresh her.

The sliced apples on the plate were already brown from sitting there so long, but she didn't mind. The only thing that seemed odd was eating them without a book in her hands. But what could she do? This might not be healthy reading, but it was certainly healthy. And what is more important than one's health?

2. Lemons

THE ADVERTISEMENT AT THE bottom of the page was inconspicuous: "If you have a nice reading voice, we have a job for you." There was nothing else but a telephone number. If Miss Tamara's eyes hadn't been drawn to the tiny vignette of an open book at the end, she would have overlooked it entirely.

There was no doubt that she met the requirement: she had a nice reading voice. She often read aloud when she was by herself, delighting in the sound of her voice. When she found a passage in a book that she really liked, she read it out loud and liked it even more. At times she was tempted always to read out loud instead of to herself. A whole book. Indeed, we listen to music instead of reading the notes, and those dead letters on paper should be transformed into living sound. But a whole book would probably be too tiring.

She had never read in public, though. If anyone were to ask why, she would probably say it was because she'd never had the opportunity. How could she, since she'd never responded to any proposition such as this? Very well, then, this time she would respond. She had no right to deprive the world of her beautiful voice.

She didn't dial the number right away, however. There was something suspicious about it. If this was an opening for an announcer's job on some radio or television program, why didn't it say so? Why was the ad so spare and insubstantial? If they weren't looking for an announcer, what else might it be? Where else was there the need for a nice speaking voice?

She first called Information and found out that the telephone number belonged to a reputable law firm. Even she had heard of it, although she had nothing to do with lawyers. That assuaged her fear that something shady and dangerous was hiding behind it all. A firm like that certainly wouldn't get involved in something that could damage its reputation.

Miss Tamara had trouble getting in touch with them because the number was always busy. That was most likely because lots of people were calling them. Although the advertisement had been inconspicuous, it had clearly been noticed. The unrelenting busy signal in her ear was exasperating, but what irritated her even more was the conceit and arrogance of these people. Did all those who were calling really think they had a nice reading voice? As if it was a commonplace, omnipresent ability, and not a rare talent.

When she finally got through, an officious female voice informed her that an audition was scheduled for the very next day. The voice told her when and where to appear, but was unable to provide any other details. If she got the job, she would find out everything she needed to know.

At first Miss Tamara decided not to go to the audition. This secrecy was peculiar, and suggested something shady was going on. The firm was indeed reputable, but they were lawyers after all, people whose services were only in demand when something was in dispute. The best thing would be not to have anything to do with them.

But the next day curiosity prevailed over her caution. After all, what did she have to lose? The audition was to start at eleven o'clock at an address in the middle of town. If anything seemed untoward, she would simply leave. No one could make her stay against her will.

The crowd that greeted her at the large law firm was certainly not to her liking, but even so she stayed. Casting an eye over the other candidates, she concluded that she had to do so. To spite them. She would show them what a good recitation was all about.

Her turn came. A secretary took down her personal details, then she was led into a luxuriously appointed room full of leather and mahogany. There she was met by a tall, stiff man in a black suit, wearing a pencil-thin mustache and small glasses in a round frame. He indicated that she was to sit in a deep brown armchair opposite a desk. Seated at the desk was a middle-aged woman wearing a gray business suit, its dull uniformity disturbed only by a large brooch and a white scarf.

The man took a sheet of paper off the desk and handed it to her.

"Please read this."

She thought of asking whether she could first read it to herself to find out what the text was about, but decided they would have said so if such a possibility existed. She cleared her throat softly and then slowly started to read. It was a prose excerpt covering just half the page. It didn't look hard to read. She didn't stumble over her words even once.

When she was through, she raised her eyes towards the man, then looked at the woman. She didn't know what to expect, but felt she deserved at least a smile, if not a commendation. Their faces were impassive, however. The man took the piece of paper and put it back on the desk.

"Thank you," he said stiffly. "We will inform you of our decision."

She left disappointed. It had all been so humiliating. Why had she let lawyers be the judge of her skill, or rather her art of reading? They didn't understand a thing about it. Why had they been so dispassionate? One of the other candidates would probably meet their standards. One look at some of the faces in question was enough to know speech impediments lurked there.

She went home mad at herself and resolved to put this ugly episode out of her mind. She would read only for her own pleasure. Others didn't deserve to share her gift.

That same evening they called and told her she'd got the job. They gave her another address and told her she should be there at five o'clock the following afternoon. She would be told everything she needed to know there and then.

Again she first decided not to go. She wanted to punish them for the cold reception they'd given her. Let them be satisfied with one of those stuttering candidates. It would serve them right. They didn't deserve her talent.

She arrived at about ten minutes to five. The doorman at the entrance escorted her to the elevator and sent her to the top floor. On the way up, she thought it strange that the foyer didn't have a board bearing the names of the companies in the building, as though it were a residential building.

The elevator opened directly onto a large room. The entire opposite wall was made of glass, affording a sweeping view of the town. The room was almost empty. In the middle was a swivel chair with one thick leg fastened to the floor. Behind the chair was a lamp on a thin pole, curved at the top. Even though it was still broad daylight outside, the lamp was on. Its bright beam illuminated the chair and a small glass table next to it holding several sheets of paper and a large glass full of a yellowish-gray beverage.

A young man dressed in a light-colored suit, without a tie, moved away from the large window and came to greet her. A smile spread across his handsome face. He took her right hand in both of his and squeezed it cordially.

"Welcome! Welcome! Please have a seat." He gestured towards the chair.

She looked at him quizzically for a moment before heading towards the middle of the room.

"Is it comfortable?" he asked, still smiling, once she had sat down.

"Yes, it is," she replied after another brief hesitation.

"Wonderful!" he said, then reached for the inside pocket of his jacket. He took out a document and handed it to her.

"This is your contract. Please read it carefully."

He moved a polite two steps away from the chair so as not to breathe down her neck as she read.

The contract cleared up some, but not all, of her uncertainties. She was to come to this address every day of the week at the same time. She would spend approximately half an hour reading a text that would be prepared for her. She was expected to read it clearly and smoothly. At the end of the session she was to drink a glass of lemonade. The fee far surpassed all her expectations.

There was nothing, however, about the purpose of the reading. Nothing was mentioned about broadcasting or recording. Indeed, there was no microphone, unless it was hidden somewhere in the lamp. And if there wasn't any microphone, why, or rather for whom, was she to read? She raised her eyes from the contract and looked at the young man in bewilderment.

As though reading her mind, he shook his head.

"I'm afraid I can't tell you anything more than what's written there. It's up to you to decide whether the conditions are acceptable."

He reached for his inside pocket once again and took out a fountain pen. He took off the cap, put it on the opposite end of the pen and offered it to her.

She was bothered by such assurance that she would sign. Masculine self-confidence always irritated her.

But she couldn't let that stand in her way. She must act professionally. Her reading talent had been properly evaluated for the first time. Should she turn down a well-paid job just because of a few minor details? More than this should be required to stop her. When she thought about it, the listener was none of her concern. What difference did it make? Announcers on radio and television don't know who is listening either.

She took the fountain pen and signed both copies of the contract.

"Wonderful!" said the young man. He put one copy and the pen back into his pocket. "Now, let's get down to work. If you please."

He indicated the sheets on the table.

As she put the contract into her purse and then picked up the text, he returned to the window. He stood there staring outside, his back to the room. Before beginning to read, she threw him a scathing look for this insolence, but said nothing.

This was another excerpt, from a larger piece of fiction. The story took place in a summerhouse surrounded by a large lemon grove. It was very hot, everyone was sweating profusely and complaining about the sultry weather. The main character was a nine-year-old boy.

Idling away the long summer, without the company of anyone his own age, he'd taken to hanging around the groom in the stable, trying the man's patience with his never-ending questions, or else he wandered among the lemon trees, looking in fascination at the tiny world that lived there: ants, butterflies, worms, cicadas, crickets and other bugs he didn't recognize. Once he even saw a snake.

The tranquility of these carefree days was spoiled by the feeling that something peculiar was happening among the grownups, although he couldn't quite put his finger on it. Hushed fragments of angry conversations reached his ears. His mother had become openly rude to his father, who was overly kind to her friend who had recently come to visit; the young man she'd brought with her, whom she'd introduced as a distant relative, had caused a bitter argument between the boy's two older sisters.

Oppressive heat was the augur of bad weather. The sky was still clear, but dark clouds had gathered on the southern horizon. A storm might break as soon as early afternoon. The boy was afraid of thunder, and after the downpour he would find massive death among the tiny creatures on the ground. And now the danger loomed of two disasters striking at the same time—one inside, the other outside.

Miss Tamara did not get as far as the two-pronged tempest, however. The excerpt broke off as the boy was running into the house, followed by the first heavy drops of rain. Filled with frustration at this, she sent another nasty look toward the back by the window.

He turned around when she had finished and went up to her again.

"Wonderful!" It seemed as though the smile had never left his face. "You read superbly." He paused briefly, then added: "Now please drink the lemonade."

She would have protested, even though she'd accepted the obligation, but he'd redeemed himself with the compliment. She raised the glass, wondering if the contract required that she drink it all. She didn't like such beverages because of their acidity. But the lemonade was excellent. She drained her glass in one go.

As she was placing the glass back on the table, he took a check from the outside pocket of his jacket and handed it to her.

"Until tomorrow then, at the same time."

Without waiting for a reply, he went over to the window again, turning his back to her. She stayed by the chair for several moments, holding the check, feeling humiliated, as though she'd been paid for another type of service.

In the elevator on the way down, she was barely able to calm the anger inside herself. If it weren't for the very generous contract she'd signed, she would never have set foot there again. Why did handsome men think they could do whatever they wanted? Particularly if they were rich. And eccentric.

So that was what this was about, and not radio or television. This young oddball clearly was rich enough to satisfy his quirky desires. Why on earth was he willing to pay through the nose to have someone read him that story? Was there a secret hidden in it somewhere? Perhaps the next day's episode would clear things up.

But there was no continuation. The next day everything in the room on the top floor was the same except for Miss Tamara's outfit: the young man was standing by the window, the glass on the table was full, the text she'd read the day before was waiting for her. After the first sentence, when she realized it was the same excerpt, her eyes darted in question towards his back, but he kept on staring out the window.

Reading mechanically, since she was no longer following the meaning, she thought about how to beat him at his own game. This was certainly part of a novel. It was very well written, and even the style seemed vaguely familiar to her. Why hadn't he given her the book to read from instead of a text typed out on paper? Probably because for some reason she wasn't supposed to know which book it was. She could find out if she took the text away with her, but she knew that would not be allowed.

Then it dawned on her that she could take something out without being noticed. Even if they searched her, they could never discover what was in her head. She would memorize one part. Something quite short but striking would be enough.

While still in the elevator, she rushed to write down the memorized sentence while it was still fresh in her mind. It contained a metaphor she was almost certain she'd never seen before. She ran straight to the library, where an enormous selection of books in electronic form was available to the public.

The search took some ten minutes, but came up empty. Thinking she might have made a mistake somewhere, she tried to change the sentence a little and look for just the metaphor, but the result was always the same: the book containing this fragment was not to be found in the library's digital book repository.

She went home disappointed. If she had the whole excerpt, she would have an easier time tracing the mysterious book. Even if it didn't exist in electronic form, she could ask for help from a literary expert, who might recognize the episode in the summerhouse and the lemon grove. But how could she get hold of the text entire?

First she thought of memorizing and writing it down sentence by sentence. But that would be unreliable and take a very long time. She didn't have the necessary patience. Then a simpler solution occurred to her. It required courage, but was facilitated by the listener's arrogant attitude. This was a chance to get even. She spent the evening refreshing a skill she'd mastered in the past, never thinking she'd need it for something like this.

As soon as the young man turned his back the next day, standing in his usual place by the window, she took the paper and pen she'd brought out of her purse. The bit of additional rustling did not attract his attention. She placed the paper in her lap, concealing it with the one she was reading. He would notice what she was doing if he turned around, but she counted on the fact that he had no reason to act any differently from the previous two days.

She read more slowly than before in order to take down in shorthand what she was dictating to herself, and also to cover up the inevitable excitement in her voice. She had no talent for such covert work and was haunted by the fear that he might hear her write, although she'd chosen a special pen that moved across the paper almost soundlessly.

As she was preparing for this the night before, the matter of how to end it off had given her the biggest headache. There was no time to put the paper in her purse because he turned around the moment she finished the last sentence. The simplest solution finally occurred to her: she wouldn't write down the whole text. It wasn't necessary, anyway. She would stop taking notes after finishing the penultimate paragraph. As she read the last one, she would put away her stenographic notes.

The tension inside her mounted as this moment drew near. Her index finger and thumb had gone numb from holding the pen so tightly. As she returned the pen and paper to her purse, she was convinced he must have heard. Her voice trembled perceptibly in the middle of the paragraph.

But the young man did not turn around until she reached the end. She gave an audible sigh as she replaced the sheets on the table. Without waiting for him to offer, she took the glass and drank the lemonade in large gulps. As he handed her the check, he praised her reading once again, saying it had been particularly moving. She forced herself to smile and nodded her head in thanks, then rushed out faster than she had intended.

Miss Tamara was filled with pride as she typed up her stenographic notes. She'd done the job courageously and with skill. There were only a few places where she had trouble reading her notes, but since she'd been writing blind, such an outcome was quite a feat. Her good memory helped her decipher the problem spots.

The next day she called her friend Sara who worked at the Institute for Modern Literature. They met in a café during her lunch break. Madam Sara, a short, plump black woman in her late thirties with closely cropped hair, read the typed pages, then gave her a measured look.

"Where'd you get this?"

"I can't tell you. For now. Can you tell where it's from?"

"No, I can't, but I think I know who must be the author."

"Who?"

Sara paused briefly before saying the author's name.

"Him?" asked Miss Tamara in disbelief.

"Yes." She started going through the pages, pointing at different places. "See. This sentence structure is his trademark. You can bet your bottom dollar it's his. His style is too unique to have any imitators."

"So that's why it seemed so familiar. But I've read all his books. As far as I can remember, this episode isn't in any of them."

"You've got a good memory. It isn't. That's why I don't know where it comes from."

"What does that mean?"

"It can only mean it's an excerpt from a new book."

"But didn't he stop writing?"

"That's right, almost a year ago. He announced in an interview when his last book came out that he would not write another one. He'd lost faith in the meaning of writing. After that he withdrew completely from the public eye."

"It seems he changed his mind," said Miss Tamara, knocking her index finger on the sheets of paper on the round café table.

"Writers' promises don't mean much. In any case, I'm glad he's back." Madam Sara stopped, then repeated, "You really can't tell me where you got this?"

"Please be patient. Something strange is going on. I'll give you a call as soon as I get a better fix on things."

Sara looked at her inquisitively, but stopped insisting.

On her way to the reading session that afternoon, Miss Tamara decided to force the issue into the open. She had a right to know what she was involved in. The contract did not strictly specify otherwise. She would simply ask the young man to confirm her suspicions.

He had talked the old writer into picking up his pen again, wanting only the best, such as befits a wealthy man. He had probably paid a fabulous price, but everyone has a price, even writers. Now she understood why she wasn't reading from a book. There wasn't any, all that existed was one episode. What she couldn't understand, however, was its meaning for the young man. Was he the boy from the summerhouse? But the episode didn't end; it broke off before the dénouement. Why didn't it include what took place during the storm?

The young man would have to answer these questions if he wanted her to continue reading. That was her price, and she was the best, wasn't she?

But she didn't get the chance to ask them. When she entered the room on the top floor for the fourth time, a young girl was waiting instead of the young man. She was tall, with long curly brown hair, dressed in a mustard-colored suit. Her oversized glasses were in an amber-colored frame. She was smiling.

As though nothing was amiss, she welcomed her, offering no explanation for the young man's absence. Instead, she indicated the glass of lemonade.

"Help yourself."

Miss Tamara looked at her in bewilderment. "Now?"

"Yes."

"But I drank it at the end of the reading before."

"I know."

She hesitated briefly, then picked up the glass. As she brought it to her lips, it dawned on her in fear that the lemonade might contain something disagreeable. She took a wary sip. The taste was the same as before. Nonetheless, she drank it slowly, then stopped halfway.

"All of it, please," cautioned the girl before she had time to put the glass back on the table.

Their eyes locked in silence. The girl's face was all smiles, and Miss Tamara's was unyielding. Finally, she continued drinking.

"Please," said the girl, indicating the sheets of paper, once the empty glass had been placed next to them. She remained standing by the chair.

As Miss Tamara slowly read, she pondered this unexpected turn. What did this mean? Who was this girl? Where was the young man? If something had prevented him from being there, why hadn't the reading session been postponed? What was the use of this girl listening?

And she was listening with utmost attention. Miss Tamara raised her eyes briefly from the text on two occasions and noted that the girl was staring at her fixedly. Being examined at such close range made her ill at ease. The young man's turned back had been haughty and insulting, but now that seemed better than such scrutiny.

A sudden thought almost broke off her reading. Did the young man know what she'd done the day before, and had that caused this change? But how could he know? She was convinced he hadn't seen her. What if she was wrong? She hadn't kept her eye on him the whole time. He might have turned around when she wasn't looking. So, what was he planning to do about it? Was the girl there to punish her in some way?

Miss Tamara spent the rest of the reading session on pins and needles, waiting to see what was in store for her. But when she finished, nothing happened. The girl thanked her in two words, gave her the check and walked her to the elevator.

On the way home, puzzling questions swarmed through her head. She felt more and more like a puppet whose strings were being pulled by invisible fingers, in a performance the meaning of which completely escaped her. This was not at all to her liking. Before she reached home, she had made up her mind. Regardless of who was waiting for her the next day, she would ask for an explanation. If she didn't get one, she would refuse to keep it up. They couldn't force her to read. It was too bad about the money, but anything was better than taking part in some twisted puppet show.

The phone started to ring as she was unlocking the door. The male voice from the law firm had the flat sound of a lawyer. She didn't have to do any more reading. There was no longer any need for her services. The contract was terminated. Feigning surprise, she tried to find out the reason, but learned nothing from him. All he did was remind her of her obligation to keep everything a secret.

So, they must have found out she'd taken down the text in shorthand. Why else would they let her go? She couldn't see any other reason. But why hadn't they done it the day before, right after she'd copied it? If they'd known what she was up to, why hadn't they put a stop to it instead of letting her leave with the notes? Asking her to give them back later wouldn't make any sense because they would assume, correctly, that she'd typed them up and had a copy.

What next? They were wrong if they thought the matter would end there. She would go to the law firm the next day. If they weren't accommodating, she would inform them that she might just renege on her obligation to secrecy. The media would have a field day digging up dirt about the incident, particularly after she let them have a look at the excerpt from the great writer's unpublished manuscript.

It took her a long time to get to sleep that night. She tossed and turned, and when she finally drifted off, she was visited by strange dreams. She was sitting once again on the chair in the large room, but now the young man was reading, not her. He was standing somewhere behind her back, out of sight, words pouring out of his mouth, and she was swiftly jotting them down, fearing she might omit something.

His words, however, made her blush. They were indecent, vulgar, even obscene. She was worried about the end of the recitation. That's when he would come before her, and she knew somehow that he wasn't wearing much. But the strangest thing of all was the fact that she too was almost in her birthday suit. . . .

The telephone rang on and on before it woke her up. As she lifted the receiver, she looked sleepily at the alarm clock on the bedside table and realized that the morning was almost over.

"Did you hear the news?" asked Madam Sara, getting straight to the point.

"I just woke up."

"He killed himself."

She was speechless for a moment.

"Who killed himself?"

"The writer."

There was another pause. "When?"

"Five days ago. He lived alone in the family summerhouse. They found him yesterday."

Still not fully awake, Miss Tamara didn't know what to say. Neither one spoke for a moment.

"Could you drop by the café at the same time as before?" said Madam Sara, finding her voice at last. "I'll try to find out something more."

"I'll be there."

Even though it was warm, a shiver went through her as she hung up the receiver. What had she gotten mixed up in? Things had taken a very serious turn. She might even be in danger. Should she go to the police and tell them what she knew? Not yet. She would wait to see Sara first.

She reached the café fifteen minutes early. She had already started her second espresso when Madam Sara finally arrived.

"I had to pull some major strings to dig up the details about what happened. Officially, the investigation is still ongoing, and when it's over, little of it will be made public. They have to consider the late writer's reputation. There wasn't any wrongdoing, though. And a bit of artistic caprice isn't against the law, is it?"

"Caprice?"

Madam Sara smiled. "You know what I mean. You were part of it. You were one of the readers, weren't you, otherwise you wouldn't have that excerpt."

"One of . . . ?" queried Miss Tamara.

"That's right. Did you think you were the only one? There were almost fifty of you."

She stared at her friend in disbelief. "Almost fifty?"

Madam Sara sighed. "Let's take it from the beginning. About a year ago the writer withdrew from the public eye. He seemed to have writer's block, but the real reason was his diagnosis. He was told he had only several months to live."

"Oh," escaped from Miss Tamara.

"Although he'd sworn he would never write again, he was writing his last work in that summerhouse where he lived alone. It was an autobiography. He was the boy from your excerpt."

"Really? I thought he was someone else."

"The novel, however, was not intended for publication. He wrote it in an attempt to outwit death."

"How is it possible to outwit death?"

"It isn't, of course. But who could blame someone in his shoes from trying the impossible? The plan he devised was described in his farewell note. He would write a novel about himself. About what he felt was the happiest period of his life."

"If that's all it takes, everyone would write novelized autobiographies."

"That was only part of the plan. The novel itself wasn't enough. It was dead words on paper. But if he could bring it to life, then the hero would continue to live. That's what he thought, in any case."

"How can you bring a novel to life?"

"By reading it out loud."

"Oh, I see."

"It would have been a lot easier if silent reading were enough. He wouldn't have had to take any action to ensure that. He could rely on the fact that, as he was an excellent writer, people would read his works long after his death. But no one has any reason to read books out loud. He had to make arrangements for such readers himself. And so he did."

Miss Tamara nodded her head several times.

"He was wealthy enough for such an extravagance. He changed his will and signed over the bulk of his fortune to the law firm that was to take care of finding the best readers. Like you." Madam Sara smiled.

"Thank you."

"They selected forty-eight readers. Each read for about half an hour, thereby providing practically non-stop reading all day long. You replaced each other at short intervals, never meeting, so that everything remained completely discreet."

"You said he killed himself five days ago, didn't you?" asked Miss Tamara. "That was when they selected us."

"Yes. He waited for everything to be put in place, then ordered the law firm to start the reading, without telling them that he was going to commit suicide. They had no reason to suspect anything of the sort since they knew nothing of his illness. For them it was simply satisfying the whim of a rich and eccentric client."

"But why did he commit suicide when he was going to die soon anyway?"

"Why do the terminally ill kill themselves? From fear of the pain, the agony. But there was something else here as well. He had to synchronize his departure with the beginning of the reading. And the only way to do that was suicide because, of course, he had no way of knowing when his natural death would occur. It might have happened before he managed to give the signal to start, and for him that would have meant his final death."

Miss Tamara got to thinking. "Why was the reading stopped after less than five full days?"

"That was at the insistence of the writer's disinherited heirs as soon as his body was found. The judge agreed to their request. He annulled the new will since it had clearly been given in a state of mental incompetence, and returned the previous one into effect."

"But that was the same as giving the writer a death sentence."

Madam Sara gave her friend a dubious look. "How can you sentence to death a man who is already dead?"

They looked at each other in silence for several moments. Miss Tamara was the first to break it.

"What happened to the novel? Will it be published?"

"No, unfortunately. It's gone."

"Gone?"

"Yes. The law firm destroyed the sole copy of the manuscript, respecting the writer's wishes. His final work was not intended for the reading public. It had another purpose, and as soon as that ended, there was no longer any reason for the novel to exist. All that's left is the excerpt that you managed to note down. What will you do with it?"

"I don't know."

"I'd advise you to be careful. Don't let anyone publish it, no matter how much they offer. You would be asking for trouble."

"I won't give it to anyone."

Madam Sara looked at her watch and stood up. "I'm late already. We'll be in touch."

"We'll be in touch," repeated Miss Tamara, nodding her head with a smile. "Thanks."

She received a smile in return, but no words.

She finished her espresso, then headed home. On the way she stopped at the greengrocer's. She asked for a kilo of lemons, but that didn't seem enough so she took two.

When she got home she made a pitcher full of lemonade and put it next to a large glass on the small table next to the armchair by the window where she liked to read. Then she took the sheets from their hiding place and settled into the chair. She would have preferred a turned back somewhere before her, but what could she do? She would be the only one enjoying the sound of her own voice.

3. Blackberries

When the optometrist told Miss Tamara that she would have to wear reading glasses, her reaction was the same as if he'd said she had a grave illness. Although the symptoms of longsightedness had been with her for quite some time, she had hoped against all odds that she would not contract it, holding her book farther and farther away from her eyes in order to be able to read.

If her arms had been just a little bit longer she might not have had her eyes checked, but when the text became illegible even when she stretched them all the way out, she had no choice. As though reading the thoughts behind her dejected expression, the doctor immediately suggested contact lenses instead of glasses, but she shook her head vigorously. The very thought of poking around her eyes while she put them in and took them out gave her the shudders.

She spent many hours with different opticians trying on frames. Some she tore off as soon as she put them on, horrified at her altered image in the mirror. Others she tried for a longer period as she turned her head this way and that to see herself from all angles, but in the end she turned them down too. Finally, she lost interest and simply chose the frames that seemed the least conspicuous. They were almost rimless. The lenses were joined in the middle by a thin arch that rested on her nose and two slender silver-colored arms went behind her ears.

Miss Tamara realized at once that even with such discreet glasses she would no longer be able to read in public places. This was a heavy blow, for she loved to take a book with her to read in parks and cafés, on public transport, and even while walking down the street. The urban noise around her wasn't the slightest hindrance to her engrossment in a book. Silence was actually more of a distraction, so she avoided the city library.

Until she got used to her glasses, she would have to sit at home alone and read. Silence would not be a problem, because she could chase it away with music, but she would miss having people around her. It was like being thrown into solitary confinement. Sometimes she wondered if there were something strange in her penchant for reading in a crowd, but she always came to the conclusion that if it was a sin, it certainly wasn't a cardinal sin.

When Miss Tamara complained to a girlfriend that she would soon have to wear glasses, her friend suggested blackberries. Apparently they alleviated the effects of longsightedness. Not at once, however; you had to be persistent. But there would certainly be an improvement after several months. The good thing about it was the fact that blackberry juice was just as good; you didn't have to eat the seasonal fresh fruit that was not available most of the year.

Just in case, Miss Tamara asked the optometrist what he thought about the benefits of blackberries. He thought it over, then replied that they certainly could do no harm. Even if they weren't beneficial to one's eyesight, they were certainly good for blood pressure and digestion. Taking this to be a recommendation, she filled half her refrigerator with bottles of blackberry juice.

Since she hadn't been given any instructions as to when she should drink it, she decided to do so while she was reading. The best thing would be for the medicine to take effect when it was most needed. She also knew nothing about dosage, but here as well she could make no mistake: the more she drank the better the effect. She filled a tall glass to the brim and put it together with the bottle on the small table next to the armchair by the window.

She settled into the chair and put on her glasses, thankful that the living room didn't have a mirror in which she might see herself. If there had been one, she would have covered it up. She raised the glass and started to drink. The taste of blackberries wasn't to her liking, but she'd taken more revolting medicines in her time. If she wanted her sight to improve she would have to grin and bear it. She knit her brow as she drained the glass, wiped her mouth with a napkin and opened the book to where she had stopped reading.

One glance was enough to tell her that something was amiss. The first page of the new chapter was dotted with empty spaces. Inspecting it more closely, she realized that letters were missing in some of the words. What a shame, she thought in vexation. I've bought a bad copy. Now I'll have to go back to the bookstore and exchange it for a good one.

She didn't feel like going out, however, because it was raining heavily outside. The window next to her was crisscrossed with watery streaks that distorted the landscape beyond the glass. How about trying to read the text in spite of this defect? It would require some extra effort, but that was better than having to go out.

After three sentences she realized that the typographical omissions were not random. The letter "a" was missing. Well, at least she'd found the key. Although difficult, it was possible to read if she made the effort. She wondered how much of the book had this defect. Maybe it was just the one page, which wouldn't be too bad.

She turned the page. It took no more than a glance to realize that the problem was worse, not better. There were more empty spaces than on the previous page. Her first thought was that the letter "a" appeared more frequently on this page, but when she looked more closely at the unusually fragmented text, she discovered that one more vowel was missing: "e".

Now it was really hard to read. How strange, she thought. Only two letters are missing and the text is almost indecipherable. This would probably not be the case if they were consonants, particularly infrequent ones, but "a" and "e" appear in at least half of all words.

How could this have happened? It must have been a computer error. Miss Tamara didn't like computers at all. Everyone stressed their advantages, particularly in the publishing world, but something like this would never have happened if books were still printed in the classical way when they checked that every copy was as it should be. Just see what happened when you put too much faith in computers.

If it was like this to the end of the book, she would certainly not be able to continue reading. She turned another page—and saw at once that here it was even worse. This time it required several minutes' staring at the two pages in front of her before she discovered what was missing. The network of letters and blank spaces resembling a random design or very complex code contained not a single "a", "e" or "i".

Instead of increasing her anger, this realization filled her with pride. She had outwitted the computer. Those heartless machines were unable to deviate from a pattern even when they made a mistake. She was sure before she turned another page which vowel would be the next one to go missing. And indeed, the meaningless network of letters did not contain a single "o".

She quickly turned to the next two pages and set out almost feverishly to hunt for the letter "u". She felt like clapping when there weren't any. And then an unexpected thought compelled her to leaf through to the end of the book. Perhaps the computer hadn't stopped at the vowels. Did it start to throw out consonants too?

A cursory glance as she leafed through the book bore out this assumption. Each of the subsequent pairs of pages had fewer and fewer letters. She was briefly tempted to continue the game of one-upmanship with the computer by trying to grasp the pattern by which it removed the consonants, but she didn't have the patience.

She stopped leafing through when the pages became completely blank. Her brief feeling of satisfaction was displaced by her earlier irritation. What was she to do? This gloomy afternoon seemed made just for reading, and this was the only new book she had. Should she go to the bookstore and get a proper copy? Even if it turned out that all the copies had defects, which was quite possible in the computer age, she would exchange the book for another.

She looked out the window again. The world still seemed distorted, but then she realized that this was not just from the water pouring over the pane but also because of her reading glasses. When she took them off, things were more in focus. She looked at the rainy panorama for a few minutes, then lowered her eyes pensively to the open book in her lap.

She spent perhaps a full minute staring blankly at it before she realized what was wrong. Although indecipherable, the two pages before her were completely filled with text, whereas a moment before they had been totally empty.

She put her glasses back on and the textual emptiness returned. She stared at it briefly, then removed her glasses. She repeated this several times before she finally had to accept the obvious. No computer was to blame for the disappearing letters. Her glasses had done it.

She barely resisted the impulse to fling them off her

face. The only reason she kept them on was to check something that had suddenly crossed her mind. She picked up the book and started to leaf through it from back to front. Pages should start appearing with more and more letters, but all she saw was a uniform whiteness. The text had vanished from the entire book.

She slammed the book shut and almost threw it aside, but then remembered that it was not to blame, so she put it on the table next to the glass and the bottle. She took off her glasses and held them indecisively in her hand, but then a new idea forced her to put them back on. She got up and headed for the bookshelf.

She had an inkling of what she would find, but had to double-check it anyway. She took volume after volume off the shelf, leafed through them and put them back. From time to time she lowered her glasses to the tip of her nose and looked over them at the blurred text that suddenly appeared. She didn't stop until she'd checked every book in her library.

Miss Tamara stood for some time staring without her glasses at the wall of unusable books before her, then returned to the armchair. She looked at the volumes and could easily read the titles on their spines from the other side of the room. She wondered if she would be able to see the text inside that way too. Not from such a distance, but if the book were, say, in the middle of the room, if she could set it up there on some kind of a stand, and she sat in the armchair, then she wouldn't need the glasses at all.

But this wouldn't be practical. She would have to get up all the time to turn the pages and she would be condemned to read forevermore only in her apartment. She obviously couldn't take a reading stand to a park, café or onto public transport, let alone use it while walking down the street. And she certainly could not bear the thought of being condemned to a lifetime of reading in solitude. But what else could she do?

She thought briefly of visiting the optometrist once again. Perhaps there was a cure for the misfortune that had befallen her. But she doubted that. If the doctor had had the slightest suspicion that something like this might happen, he would have given her fair warning. He would certainly want to examine her case in more detail, and she didn't look forward to being his guinea pig. No, she wouldn't go to see him again; he had already done quite enough for her.

Her eyes dropped to the empty glass on the table. She filled it again. As she sipped the juice slowly, she decided to fill the refrigerator with bottles. She had to be single-minded and patient. There was no guarantee that blackberries really alleviated longsightedness, but she had to believe it if she hoped ever to be able to read again.

4. Bananas

Miss Tamara noticed the postcard the moment she left the City Library. As usual, impatience led her to leaf through the book she'd checked out before she got home. This gave her a first impression regarding what she would soon start to read. Although she was loath to admit it, she preferred books full of dialogue to those wherein dense paragraphs stretched over several pages.

When she raised the book a little to take a look, it opened by itself to the place where a postcard was inserted. Miss Tamara stopped in her tracks and stared at it in amazement. The person who had read the book before her had probably left it there. We all know how forgetful people are.

Of course, any number of methods are used to mark the place where one has stopped reading. This was one of the more innocuous. In fact, there had been no need to use the postcard at all, since the book had a ribbon bookmark. But this was better than folding the corner of the page, as many people did, which made her especially angry. Sometimes she found her book full of dog-eared pages.

She wondered what to do with the postcard. Should she go back and give it to the librarian? He would be able to tell whose it was from the files. But why should she waste time just because the owner of the postcard had been so careless? If he needed it, would he have forgotten it? She would return it in a few days along with the book.

She hesitated a moment before taking it out. Strictly speaking, she didn't have the right to inspect someone else's property. The picture showed three garishly yellow bananas against a blue background. That was all. Goodness, what kitsch, thought Miss Tamara. I'd only send this to my favorite enemy.

Just before she stuck it back in the book, she turned it over. She had even less of a right here than she had with the picture—what was written concerned no one but the owner—but she couldn't resist. I'll have to find a way to curb my curiosity, she thought with contrition.

Miss Tamara—began the note on the back of the postcard—*Please be at the Museum of Modern Art at four-fifteen today. Look for the statue "Girl Reading" in the third hall. There is a bench facing it. Sit on it and start reading the nineteenth chapter of this book.*

There was no signature or return address. The postcard clearly had not been sent through the mail.

What did this mean? The person who'd taken the book out before her had been named Tamara too, and of all the items she could have used as a bookmark she'd used a postcard with that inscription, and then to top it all had left it in the book? This, of course, was not impossible, but was certainly highly improbable. There had to be a better explanation.

It didn't take her long to find it. The postcard was intended for her, and the librarian was behind the whole thing. He was the only one who could have put it in the book after finding out which one she had selected. All she had to do was figure out why he'd done it. Once again Miss Tamara didn't have to think too hard.

She'd known for some time that he liked her. He always blushed and smiled when he saw her. When she returned his smile, he became all thumbs and overly accommodating. He was tall and lean, not particularly handsome, but with regular features. She might be interested in him too.

But why had he chosen this strange method of approaching her? There was a simpler way: he could ask her out for coffee, for example, instead of writing this mysterious message on such a horrid postcard.

Perhaps shy men had strange courting habits. True, a museum for a first date was certainly more romantic than a café. But she couldn't understand why she had to read a chapter from the book in front of some statue, although she didn't find anything wrong with that. If he wanted to see her reading in that very spot, so be it. Why deprive him of the pleasure?

She was at the museum by three-thirty. She pretended to be a casual visitor and made her way from hall to hall. She proceeded through the third hall and almost didn't stop. If "Girl Reading" hadn't been written underneath a small statue on a slender square pedestal she never would have recognized it. It was made of white marble and looked like a banana with a row of protuberances that presumably represented the head, arms and book.

The librarian was not among the handful of visitors. From time to time she surreptitiously glanced back to see if he was following her, but he was nowhere in sight. That's good, she thought. What would he think of her if he found her there way ahead of time?

She went as far from the third hall as she could and spent about twenty minutes in a small room without windows looking at pictures in triangular frames. There again she was only able to recognize what was depicted after reading the titles of the paintings. When she finally left she felt dizzy from the explosion of bright colors and psychedelic forms.

At exactly four-fifteen she sat on the bench across from "Girl Reading" and opened the book. As she read, she felt the curious eyes of the visitors on her. She hoped that the librarian was among them. She raised her head briefly several times, but did not see him. He must be watching covertly, she concluded. Well, he would have to overcome his shyness when she finished the nineteenth chapter.

When she closed the book, someone came up to her, but it wasn't the librarian. It was a girl in a museum guard's uniform, with short dark hair and a round face. She was barely twenty years old.

"This is for you." She handed her an object wrapped in bright paper, bowed, and walked away before Miss Tamara had managed to utter a word.

She sat there a little while, inspecting what she'd received. She looked all around before unwrapping it, but there was no trace of the person she was looking for. Inside the paper was a banana. At first she thought it was real, but as soon as she touched it she realized it was made of rubber. She turned it this way and that for a moment, examining it, and then checked the paper. In the end she put them both in her purse.

Instead of leaving the museum right away, she went through all the halls again. She didn't expect to find the librarian, but hoped she'd run across the girl who had given her the banana. There was no sign of her, however. In the room with the paintings in triangular frames another guard with a mustache addressed her.

"We close in fifteen minutes, Miss."

For a moment she thought of asking him about his young colleague, but then changed her mind. What could the girl tell her that she didn't already know? The librarian must have given her directions for handing over the banana after Miss Tamara had finished reading.

Miss Tamara went home filled with frustration. She understood what it meant to be shy, she often suffered attacks of that herself, but this was really too much. Making a date and then failing to muster the courage to appear—what kind of a man was he? She'd made a fool of herself, reading where you weren't supposed to read, and what did she get in return? A rubber banana!

She reached for her purse, intending to take it out and throw it in the nearest trashcan, but thought better of it at the last moment. No, it could still serve a purpose.

The next day when she entered the City Library right after it opened, she put the book she'd taken out the day before on the counter in front of the librarian, and laid the banana next to it. He raised his eyes and blushed, as usual. She couldn't tell whether this was because he'd seen her or seen the banana. Or perhaps both her and the banana.

"You've already read the book?" he asked with a smile.

"Just one chapter," she replied, frowning.

"You didn't like it?"

"Not at all."

He hesitated briefly. "Would you like something else?"

She showed him the title of another book.

"Wonderful choice. I read it not long ago. I'm sure you'll like it."

"That's what you said yesterday."

"I'm sorry, I thought . . ." He didn't finish the sentence. He got up hastily and headed for the rows of shelves behind the counter. Her face brightened when he turned his back. She always found his discomfiture amusing.

Although he was tall, he had to go on tiptoes to take down the thick volume from the top shelf. He returned to the counter, typed something into the computer, then handed her the book.

"Here you are," he said timidly.

She took the book, nodded, and headed for the door. She was just about to make her exit when he called to her.

"Miss Tamara!"

She turned around.

He was holding up the rubber banana.

"You forgot this."

She stared at him for a few moments, deliberating what to do. Finally she went up to him, took the banana wordlessly, put it in her purse, and left the library with brisk steps.

She was too full of anger to leaf through the book right away and had to wait until she got home. The sight of another postcard elicited a deep sigh. She should have suspected as much.

This time there were only two bananas in the picture. The one on the left was missing and in its place was a gaping hole in the blue background. Damaged like this, the picture was even more dreadful than before. Let's see what he has to say in his defense, she thought, turning over the postcard.

Miss Tamara, please be in the City Park today at two-thirty. If you take the right-hand path from the main entrance, after some fifty meters you will reach the statue "Woman with a Book". There is a bench next to it. Read the forty-second chapter of this book.

Again it was unsigned.

Did he really think she was that naive? That he could string her along? This wasn't timidity anymore but straightforward impudence. Of course she would refuse to take part in his perverse games like a puppet on a string. If he wanted someone to read in front of various statues, he could do it himself. The last place she would be at two-thirty was the City Park.

She went through the main gate at twenty past two. When she sat on the bench, she thought, Strange. She passed that way frequently but could not remember the statue, even though it was by no means small. In addition, it had a detail that caught the eye. The middle-aged woman reading was holding a book in one hand and a banana twice the book's size in the other. It was half-peeled with the top bitten off. The statue must have been put there recently. The whiteness of the marble hadn't been spoiled by atmospheric pollution.

She glanced about the park before starting to read. She knew she would not see the librarian among the many strollers. He was certainly hiding somewhere, probably behind a tree or bush. He might even be in disguise. Nothing was impossible when timidity joined forces with perversity.

She did not stand up when she had finished the forty-second chapter. She laid the book in her lap and looked around again, not knowing what to expect. She hoped he wouldn't let her down once more. Wasn't the fact that she'd done as he wanted a second time enough of a signal that he had no reason to hold back? What further encouragement did he need?

If the woman on roller blades heading towards her down the path from the entrance had been younger, she would not have attracted Miss Tamara's attention. Although the woman must have been in her forties, she was agile and moved with skillful ease, winding her way among the strollers. I would like to look as good when I reach that age, thought Miss Tamara.

When the woman on roller blades reached the bench where Miss Tamara was sitting, she slowed down a little, smiled at her broadly and threw what she was carrying.

"This is for you," she shouted as she went by, then sped up again.

Miss Tamara reflexively caught the long object wrapped in bright paper and stared in confusion at the woman, who rushed down the path without looking back. It was pointless to run after her. How would it look if she chased after someone in a park full of people? Besides, she would never catch up with her.

She didn't have to unwrap the paper to know there was another rubber banana inside. It was easy to feel the shape. Better to leave it wrapped: what a fine impression she'd make, holding something like that. It would only invite derision.

She got up from the bench and headed for the exit. She knew from the previous day's experience that there was no reason to stay. The librarian would not appear, although he must be somewhere in the vicinity. He'd waited for her to finish reading, then talked the woman on roller blades into doing him a favor. He wasn't embarrassed to do that, yet he didn't have the courage to approach her, even though she'd done everything she could to facilitate the matter. What more did he expect from her?

On her way home, she firmly resolved to end the whole thing. She felt hurt and betrayed. None of this made any sense. The best thing would be to change libraries. She would have quite a walk to the other one, but that didn't signify. Then she remembered she would have to go back to the old library once more. She had to return the book she was holding.

She didn't have to see him to do it. She could go there right away, while he was gone. She would return the book and leave him a little present. Going out into the street, she took the paper off the second banana. Then she took the one she'd received the day before and the two postcards out of her purse and wrapped them together with the second banana.

At the City Library she found the older, plump librarian with the dispassionate face on duty. The woman didn't say a word when she saw that Miss Tamara was again returning a book just one day later. That was fine because Miss Tamara didn't feel like having to explain herself.

"Would you please give this to your colleague from the morning shift?" she asked, handing her the package of bananas and postcards.

"Oh, so you are the one," replied the librarian, taking the package. "I have something for you here too."

She reached under the counter and took out a rectangular object wrapped in the same bright paper.

Miss Tamara hesitated briefly before accepting it. She wanted to ask who had left it for her, but that would also require an unwanted explanation. In any case, she already knew the answer, although not how the young librarian had figured out she would come here straight from the park.

When she thought it over, however, it wasn't hard to deduce. He had to assume there was an end to her patience. Even if she hadn't put a stop to everything the day before, he certainly couldn't expect her to disregard what he'd staged for her today. He was gravely mistaken if he thought she could be placated by a present.

She started to tear the paper angrily as soon as she left the library, concluding it must be a book before she even saw it. She also had an idea of what would be inside it. This time only the banana on the right-hand side stood against the blue background. She turned the postcard over.

Miss Tamara, only one reading remains. Please go immediately to the city cemetery. Look for the grave under number AN33/24. There is a bench next to it. Please sit on it and read the last, eighty-third chapter of this book.

He was crazy if he thought she would go there. What did he think she was? All he had to do was order her where to go and she would run there obediently like a puppy dog? Let him go ahead and wait for her, hiding behind some tombstone. She had absolutely no intention of reading next to any grave. In any case, she didn't like cemeteries.

Although it wasn't even four o'clock, the city cemetery was almost empty. As she searched for grave AN33/24, the only person she encountered was an old woman in black standing at the edge of the path. Her eyes were closed as she raised her face towards the sun. When Miss Tamara walked past her, the woman opened her eyes briefly, nodded her head and smiled.

The tombstone over grave AN33/24 was different from the others. Instead of a bust it had a large open book atop its vertical stone. The marble had lost its original whiteness long ago and had turned gray, even black. In the middle of the book was a ribbon bookmark resembling a banana peel. There was no name on the stone, only dates of birth and death. The person buried there had lived to a very old age.

Miss Tamara did not look around her before sitting on the bench nearby. She didn't expect to see him yet, but he would probably appear at the end, if this were truly the last reading. Without that prospect, she would never have come. She still had no idea why he needed all of this, but who was she to understand the male intellect? In any case, if he let her down this time she would despise him for good.

As with the previous excerpts she'd read, the eighty-third chapter was short. She stood up as soon as she had finished. If he finally intended to approach her, let him come after her. She had no intention of waiting for him. She took several steps from the bench, then stopped in mid-stride. Something was wrong, but it wasn't immediately apparent what.

She slowly went back to the grave and studied the tombstone for a good half-minute before she finally noted what was missing. If the change hadn't been so glaring, she probably would have noticed it right away. The date of birth was still there, but not the date of death. Now there was only the rough grayness of stone that had yet to feel the engraver's chisel.

She turned all around. Not a single movement disturbed the afternoon tranquility of the city cemetery. Part of her mind told her she should be upset, but she seemed wrapped in the embrace of the peace that surrounded her. Before heading off once again, she drew her fingers gently over the open pages of the marble book.

When, soon after, she came across the old woman, she was not surprised to find the lady had company. The girl in the museum guard's uniform was standing on her left and the woman on roller blades was on her right. All three were smiling at her. She stopped in front of them, returning their smile.

They stood there for some time, smiling and motionless, and then the old woman took a small package wrapped in bright paper out of her purse. Miss Tamara took it silently with a brief bow and placed it in her own purse. There was no need to open it; she knew that it contained the third banana and a postcard whose blue background was no longer blemished, just as nothing tainted the sky above the cypresses surrounding them.

When she left the cemetery she knew what she had to do. First she would buy bananas. They hadn't been her favorite fruit, but that would change. Then she would go home and settle in the armchair by the window. She would start to eat a banana before she opened the book. Never before had she read a last chapter first, but that made no difference here. It certainly would not detract from the pleasure of reading the previous eighty-two parts of this long book.

The next day she would go to the City Library. Not to take out a new book but as a subterfuge. She would ask the librarian to return what she had left him by mistake. It would only be a pretext, of course. She would use the opportunity to strike up a conversation with him, and then do what he didn't have the courage to do, but certainly wanted. Shy men need a bit of help. She would ask him out for coffee.

5. Apricots

MISS TAMARA REALIZED THERE was something wrong with her memory when she was unable to recollect which fruit she ate while reading. Whenever she sat in the armchair by the window with a book in her hand, she had a plate full of fruit waiting. Now she was in the kitchen staring at the empty plate on the table. She needed to put something on it, but didn't know what. How strange, she thought. She'd been eating the same fruit every day for years, and now she couldn't remember what it was.

She was so proud of her memory, remembering even trivial details, so how could she have forgotten something so important? This wasn't at all like her. What was she to do? She couldn't possibly read without fruit. She had to find a way to remember. And then a simple solution crossed her mind. Of course! All she had to do was look in the pantry. The fruit she ate while reading had to be in there.

But there wasn't any fruit in the pantry. How is this possible? wondered Miss Tamara. On giving it some thought, she concluded there could be only one explanation. She had used up all her supplies and forgotten to replenish them. Her memory had failed her there as well. She would have to go to the market right away and buy some fruit. Admittedly, she didn't know which fruit, but she was sure to recognize it as soon as she saw it. Sometimes one's memory just needs a small jog.

Having spent forty-five minutes at the market, she

was in real trouble. The stands were full of fruit, but she couldn't say with certainty that she ate any of them while reading. She fixed on two or three as possibilities, then immediately vacillated again. After standing there for a moment in doubt, she came to a decision. She would buy them all. If appearance was not enough, perhaps she would identify her reading fruit by taste.

But a new problem cropped up at the very first stand. The seller looked at her in bewilderment, waiting for her to say what she wanted, while she struggled to remember the names of the fruits. Her efforts were in vain, however. No fruit names were lodged in her memory.

She extricated herself from the predicament by asking the seller to give her a little of everything. At the next stand she pointed at the fruit she wanted, saying only the amount, as though she were in a foreign country using a language she could barely speak. She felt very ill at ease.

On reaching home she took her biggest plate and started to arrange her purchases upon it. She left the smaller fruit whole and cut the larger fruit into slices. Eventually the plate was completely covered and looked like a colorful circular painting.

Delicate fragrances rose from the painting, ruffling the surface of her memory, but nothing emerged from the depths. If they weren't so jumbled, thought Miss Tamara regretfully, something might stand out.

She entered the living room, sat down in the armchair and put the plate in her lap. Fork poised in midair, she was uncertain where to begin. Suddenly she was sorry to spoil the painting. But how then could she hope to remember which fruit she preferred while she read?

First she pierced two large berries, one dark blue and the other green. When she tasted them, the names of the fruits were on the tip of her tongue but she couldn't call them to mind. Frustration rose in Miss Tamara as the painting quickly lost its colors—yellow, orange, red, pink, brown, purple. Although she was familiar with all the tastes, the fruits still had no names.

She put the next-to-last piece in her mouth—and her memory stirred at the same moment. This was no longer a rustle but a flurry of recall. She realized at once that this was the fruit she ate while she read. There was no doubt about it. She made a small additional effort, eyes tightly shut, and the word that had eluded her finally burst out from the depths.

Apricot!

She jumped up from the chair in delight, almost dropping the plate. Of course! Why had she been unable to remember such a simple word? And then the joy of remembering was dampened by an onrush of fear. What if she forgot it again?

She hurried to her small desk, tore a page out of a notebook and wrote APRICOT on it in large letters. Then she returned to the armchair and put the page on the side table next to it. There. Now she was safe. If she forgot it, she would have this reminder.

She went back to the kitchen and poked among the bags of fruit until she found the one containing apricots. She washed them, cut them in half and removed the pits. Now the round painting was elegantly monochrome. This prompted the thought that she could make another arrangement using all the fruit. After her success with apricots, she might remember other names too. But that could wait. Now it was time to read.

She put the plate of apricots on the side table and settled into the armchair once more, then opened the book to the ribbon and started to read. But she didn't get very far. After just one paragraph she realized that something was wrong. She frowned, then began leafing through the first part of the book, stopping briefly here and there. When she reached the beginning, she had to face facts. She couldn't remember a thing from the first half of the book. It was as though she hadn't read it at all.

This is terrible, thought Miss Tamara in dismay. She'd spent so much time and energy reading, and now her memory was playing dirty tricks on her. Very well, there was nothing for it. She would have to start reading again from the beginning.

She sighed and put the ribbon at the end of the book. The first chapter was just getting her in its grip when another unpleasant thought yanked her from the page. What if she forgot what she had read a second time? This possibility could not be ruled out. She no longer dared trust her memory.

There was no simple solution to this, like the one for apricots. First of all, any aide-memoire for what she'd read could not consist of just one word. She would have to take extensive notes. But she wondered if they would be of any use. If her memory had been permanently erased, nothing could bring it back.

Miss Tamara closed the book and stared into space, drowning in despair. She could seek the help of a doctor, but what if it was too late? Her memory might improve in the future, but the past was at risk.

She wondered how much she had forgotten. At first it seemed there was no way to find out. How could she determine what she no longer remembered when it wasn't in her memory anymore?

Her eyes came to rest on the bookshelf across from the window. She stared at the books dully, and then it suddenly dawned on her that there was a way to check whether she remembered anything.

She rushed to the bookshelf and started to read the titles. These were the books she had liked and decided to keep. After just a few titles it was clear that she didn't remember a thing about them, but even so she checked them all with relentless desperation.

When she started to take down book after book and leaf through each one, she realized she was waiting in vain for a miracle. But she didn't stop there either until she'd checked the last book. She stood in front of the bookshelf for some time, dark thoughts crowding her mind.

Life seemed to implode inside her. Reading had been her greatest passion. What she'd read was a treasure surpassing all else. And now she'd suddenly lost it, just as people lose everything it's taken years to acquire in an earthquake or similar disaster. This was actually worse than that. They still had the life they'd lived, while she had lost hers. Without her memory, it was as if she had never existed.

She returned to the armchair and absentmindedly picked up half an apricot. The pleasant flavor had a calming effect. She had no way out of this misfortune, but life must go on. Even though it was no consolation, she knew such a loss was inevitable in the end. The inconsequential value of what she'd read would disappear along with her one day. It had just happened sooner than expected.

She put another half an apricot in her mouth and with it came new reassuring thoughts. Things weren't so bleak after all. Oblivion had benefits of its own. When she finished a book that she'd especially liked she was often sorry it had ended, envying those who had yet to read it. She could have reread such books, of course, but it was impossible to repeat the experience of a first reading.

Now every reading would be the first one. She smiled. Before her was a library full of books that she had liked. She would be able to enjoy them again just as she had the first time. Actually, when she gave it some thought, she really didn't need so many books. One would be enough. If she could remember which she'd liked the best, she would keep only that one. Is there anything better than reading your favorite book for the first time over and over again?

She concentrated very hard, but no title rose to the surface of her memory. Well, fair enough, that was no difficulty. She would come across it when she read the books one after the other. Then she would do the same as she had with the apricots. There would be two notes on the side table to remind her of everything she needed for the rest of her life.

6. Gooseberries

Miss Tamara had just filled her mouth with gooseberries when the telephone rang. She was sitting in the armchair by the window, getting ready to read. Before she started, she would fill a saucer with berries. She didn't chew them, rather pressed them against her palate with her tongue, enjoying the juice that squeezed out. When she was finished reading she would spit the remains into a napkin.

I wonder who that could be, she thought angrily. Her friends didn't call at this time of day because they knew she was reading. Could there be some sort of emergency? As the unrelenting sound shattered the silence in the living room, Miss Tamara wondered in agitation about what to do with the gooseberries. She certainly couldn't talk with a full mouth.

Finally, after the fifth ring, the handful of berries still swollen with juice ended up in the napkin. As she picked up the receiver, looking sorrowfully at the wasted gooseberries, she thought there'd better be a really good reason for this call. If not, whoever had disturbed her without cause would have it coming.

"Hello," she said almost in a bark.

"Miss Tamara?"

It wasn't any of her friends. She didn't recognize the young male voice.

"Yes," she said in a softer tone.

"Please forgive me for calling at what might be an inopportune moment, but I need to talk to you."

"Who is this?"

"My name won't mean anything to you."

"All the same, I'd like to know who I'm talking to."

"Of course. My name is Marko."

"What do you want from me?"

"I have a business proposition for you."

"Business proposition?"

"Yes. I'd like you to read something to me. I'll pay you handsomely for this service."

Her dampened anger flared up again. Someone was trying to pull her leg. She should simply hang up the phone and then unplug it. Instead of that, however, she placed the napkin full of gooseberries on the little table.

"Where did you get the idea that I read for money?"

"Don't you do it twice a week on the radio's Third Program? Listening to you is a real pleasure."

Her angered was allayed once again. "Thank you. But that is something else entirely. I don't do private readings. There's no need to throw your money away. Why don't you read what interests you yourself?"

"I can't."

"Don't you know how to read?" She realized this was impolite, but she couldn't resist. She might not have let it slip out if he hadn't been a young man.

"I'm blind."

Painful silence filled the living room.

"I hope this isn't a practical joke," Miss Tamara said at last in a soft voice.

"Unfortunately, it isn't."

"Please forgive me. I didn't know. . . ."

"Of course you didn't. How could you? So, would you do me this favor?"

She hesitated slightly. Under other circumstances she would have turned him down without a second thought, but now she had no choice.

"All right," she said. "How much is there to read?"

"Not much. It's the first chapter of a novel. It won't take more than twenty minutes or so. I hope that you can spare that much time for me."

"I can. But please don't expect me to continue reading the novel. I'm very busy."

"Of course. I won't inconvenience you any further."

"Fine, where do you want me to read?"

Now I'll see if this is some sort of joke, she thought. If the place he invites me to is even the slightest bit suspicious, I'll turn him down at once and hang up the phone.

"Would you agree to meet me in the City Park in one hour?"

She couldn't see any trap there. They certainly would not be alone. As far as she could tell, she was not in any danger.

"Where exactly?" she asked.

"To the left of the main entrance is a bench under a cypress tree. You can't miss it. I'll be waiting there."

She was just about to ask how she would recognize him, but stopped in the nick of time. There would certainly not be two blind young men on the bench.

"I'll see you there," she said and hung up the receiver, only realizing afterwards that she'd used the wrong word.

Miss Tamara spent most of the time until she left for the park deciding what to wear and getting ready. She was aware that this was foolish; she could appear in a housecoat and without any makeup since he, of course, would not see her, but it still mattered to her. Women in contact with blind men certainly did not let themselves go because of this defect. In any case, the park would be full of sighted people, so she certainly had to look her best. But most important of all, she felt much better when she was fixed up nicely.

When she entered the park fifteen minutes before the appointed time, he was already sitting on the bench. She could not go up to him right away. What would he think of her if he realized she had arrived so early? She would stay by the entrance and use this opportunity to get a good look at him. A man's blindness, she thought with a prick of conscience, had its good side. It let you look at him intently without feeling awkward.

He was wearing a light blue sports suit with a navy blue t-shirt instead of a shirt and lightweight shoes. The glass in the round metal frames of his spectacles was so dark that he wouldn't have been able to see through it even if he could see. A large book lay in his lap.

When her eyes caught his face, she could not tear them away for a long time. Her conscience no longer bothered her for using this advantage. If she had had to describe him to someone, she would probably have resorted to a euphemism. She would say he was sweet, for example. But she could be open with herself. She hadn't seen such a handsome man in a long time, and she hadn't crossed paths with someone like him for even longer.

When she finally headed along the gravel path towards the bench, he stood up before she reached him. He was taller than she'd imagined. She stopped in mid-step, eyeing him suspiciously.

"Miss Tamara," he said half-questioningly. As happens with the blind, his head was not turned directly towards her.

"How did you recognize me?"

He smiled broadly and stretched out his hand. "By your step."

"My step?" she repeated, crossing the short distance that separated them. His large hand seemed to swallow up her tiny one.

"Yes. That's just how I imagined it. When you don't see, you have to rely on your imagination. Please sit down."

He indicated the bench, waited for the sound to tell him that she was settled, then sat down himself.

He turned towards her. If he can see, she thought, he'll look a bit to the side. If he's pretending to be blind, he's very convincing. But there was a way to expose him. On her way to the park she'd figured out a test. The lack of passers-by at that moment made it all the easier. All of a sudden she swung her hand as though about to hit him straight in the face, then arrested it right by his cheek. Anyone who could see would have jerked back in reflex, but he didn't budge and the smile stayed on his face. She was embarrassed by her distrust.

"Thank you for coming."

"I'm glad to be of assistance. That, I suppose, is the novel you want me to read from?"

She nodded towards the book, although this was unnecessary. If I continue seeing him, she thought, I'll have to get rid of some of my gestures. But, then, why would she continue seeing him? Hadn't she told him not to expect any more readings after the first chapter?

"Yes, it is."

He handed her the large volume. It was a luxury edition with a leather binding. Although she prided herself on her knowledge of literature, the title of the book and its author were unknown to her. As she leafed through the book, she decided to drop by the City Library on her way home. She would take out the book and make inquiries into the author.

As she read in a low voice, she realized the eyes of those strolling through the park were on them. Their conversations would go softer or stop as they passed by the bench where a girl was reading to a blind young man. One couple even paused a little to one side, but when Miss Tamara raised her eyes towards them, they walked on in embarrassment. She was unaccustomed to drawing attention, but it couldn't be avoided. If he asked her to read him the second chapter, she would propose a less crowded place.

From time to time she glanced at him briefly between two paragraphs. He was sitting motionless, his head slightly raised as though gazing somewhere into the distance, intently absorbed in listening. His dedication pleased her. When she was finished, it seemed to her that much less than twenty minutes had passed.

After she had closed the book, they sat there for some time in silence. Finally he lowered his head and turned towards her.

"Thank you for doing me this great favor."

"It was my pleasure, think nothing of it."

She held out the book. Several moments passed before she realized why he didn't take it. She placed it in his lap with a feeling of discomfort.

He put one hand over the book and reached for the inside pocket of his jacket with the other. He took out a white envelope.

"This is for you."

She shook her head briskly even though she knew he couldn't see it.

"No, please put that away."

"But we made an arrangement . . ."

"We didn't arrange anything. I told you I don't read for money."

Silence surrounded them once again, and he finally put the envelope back in his pocket.

"I have to find a way to repay you," he said softly.

She'd hoped for this chance. "Perhaps you would lend me the book? I would like to read it."

His hesitation confused her. Did he doubt she would return it?

"Don't worry, I won't steal it," she added with pointed irony.

"I know you won't steal it. That's not the issue."

"Then what is?"

"The book isn't . . . harmless," he replied after another pause.

"Oh, don't worry, I love dangerous books."

"This one is more dangerous than you might imagine."

Her voice took an ironic tone once again. "Maybe so. But that might just be an excuse for not letting me borrow it."

He raised the book towards her slowly and she rushed to take it.

"Thank you. I'm a fast reader. I'll return it to you very soon." She stopped a moment. "How can I reach you?"

"It will be simpler if I contact you," he said after giving it some thought.

"All right," she replied as she got up. "Give me three days. I think that will be enough."

Again she made the wrong move, her hand outstretched. And then she did something she probably wouldn't have if she hadn't been so flustered. She grabbed his hand and it quickly wrapped around hers.

"I'll call you before then," he said, standing up. He was still holding her hand.

"As you wish. See you soon."

He finally let go of her hand. "See you soon."

She bit her lip as she turned and walked away. Another wrong word. It would take her some time to get used to the situation. But now she might be able to count on having that chance.

She stopped at the entrance to the park and turned around. He was sitting on the bench again, seeming to stare straight ahead. She briefly toyed with the idea of waiting there until he left and then following him. She was curious to know more about him. What if he didn't call her, even though she had this expensive book? She wouldn't know how to get in touch with him. But she gave up on the idea, concluding that it would be unseemly to follow someone who couldn't see. In addition, he might really have a heightened sense of hearing and would recognize her footsteps following him.

On the way home she bought gooseberries. She didn't need to, there was a supply at home, but felt that fresh fruit would be fitting for a new book. Settled in the armchair, she filled her mouth fuller than usual; there was a long read ahead.

But she barely got started. As soon as she lowered her eyes to the first paragraph of the second chapter, she found herself in the dark. She couldn't figure out what had happened. At first she thought it was a power cut. Then she remembered that the table lamp was not turned on. There was no need because abundant afternoon light was pouring through the large window.

So why couldn't she see? She raised her fingers to her eyes and rubbed them. This did not bring back her sight, although she did see stars for a moment. What was happening? The panic that started to fill her didn't have a chance to take over completely because the telephone rang that very moment. She stretched her hand desperately towards the phone on the table and felt for the receiver. Then she realized that she had to empty her mouth first. There was no time to find a napkin in the dark so she spat the gooseberries into her hand.

"Hello," she said, almost shouting.

"Marko," was all he said.

"I can't see a thing!"

"I know."

"You know?"

"I know, because I can see."

She was silent for a moment. "I don't understand you," she finally replied.

"My sight came back when you lost yours. That's how it goes. I told you the book was dangerous."

"The book?" She could feel its weight in her lap.

"Yes. I don't blame you for not taking me seriously. Even now it will be hard for you to accept, although you have become its latest victim."

"Victim of the book?"

"That's right. It's a book that won't let itself be read. It blinds all those who try."

"Why, that's crazy!" Her voice became hysterical. "Do you expect me to believe such nonsense?"

"Believe your own eyes."

"But I already read it out loud to you—and nothing happened to me."

"You read the first chapter. The book lures its victims with it. You lose your sight if you try to continue reading."

Silence reigned briefly once again.

"If that's really true, why didn't you warn me?"

"Because you wouldn't have believed me."

"But you could have refused to lend it to me under any sort of pretext. You knew what would happen to me."

"If I had refused to lend it to you," he said softly after a moment's hesitation, "I would not have regained my sight."

"How . . ." she didn't finish her sentence.

"The book returns your sight when you find it a new victim."

"So that's what it was about from the very beginning," she said under her breath. "Looking for a new victim?"

"I know it seems heartless to you now, but don't forget that you will have to do the same."

"Do you really think I could be as unfeeling as you? I would never cause an innocent person to go blind."

"That's the only way for you ever to see again."

"Not even at that price."

"The next victim's blindness won't be permanent, it will be like mine and yours. They will have to find someone to replace them too. In the end it all boils down to a small amount of discomfort without irreversible consequences for either your sight or your conscience."

"Only someone without a conscience can see it like that."

"You've got it all wrong. Listening to you as you read, I decided not to give you the book and to find someone else instead, although that would have extended my blindness."

"But you still gave it to me."

"Because I wanted to see you as soon as possible."

"Why?" She realized this was a stupid question as soon as the word came out.

"Because of your voice. I'd heard it before on the radio, but it wasn't until you were reading next to me that I realized how rare it is to meet someone with a voice like that. Maybe only once in a lifetime."

"But you don't know what I look like. You might be disappointed. A person's voice and looks don't necessarily go together."

"They do with you. They have to. In any case, now it will be easy to find out. When may I see you?"

It took great strength of will not to say "Right now!" But she couldn't let him see her blind. Blindness might not look as good on her as it did on him. And how could she get all fixed up if she couldn't see?

"As soon as I can see. Before long."

"I'll be seeing you soon, then, Tamara."

"See you, Marko."

7. Melons

Miss Tamara was in the kitchen cutting up a melon and arranging the slices in a circle on a plate when she suddenly wondered, what was the first book I ever read? She stopped preparing the fruit for a moment and stared blankly ahead. Under this unfocussed gaze, the thick veil covering her childhood became a little more transparent.

She remembered some early books, but was unable to pinpoint which had been the first. How embarrassing, she thought, heading for the living room. I certainly should know which book I read first. It matters, after all. It's like not knowing what day I was born.

She put the plate of melon slices on the small table next to the window and then settled into the armchair. She stabbed a slice, put it in her mouth and frowned. Of all the fruit she ate while reading, she liked melon the least. It was too sweet and its taste reminded her of flour. Luckily, melon season was of short duration. She preferred apricots and blackberries, but apples were her favorite, particularly the sour ones that were available all year round, so they ended up on her plate most often.

Unlike other fruit, she ate most of the melon slices before she started to read. She swallowed them quickly, half-chewed, as though wanting to rid herself of something unpleasant before surrendering to pleasure. Just as she was raising a fresh slice to her mouth, her eyes turned towards the bookshelf on the wall facing the window, another odd question crossed her mind. What will be the last book I read?

What thoughts are filling my head today! she reflected. This question was even harder to answer. She might finally, at long last, remember the first book she'd ever read, but she certainly had no way of knowing which one would be the last. No one knows that, just like no one knows the exact moment they will die. What a shame. Her reading biography would be missing both her date of birth and date of death. And without those two markers to keep what was in the middle from vanishing into thin air, it would be just as though she'd never lived as a reader.

Then it suddenly occurred to her that exceptions do exist. Suicides know when they will die. That was most likely their only privilege. If she decided to kill herself, then it would be easy. She would arrange it so that she had already read the book she'd chosen to be the last one and everything would be clear. Her biography would thus be bounded at least at one end, and this would give even suicide some sense of purpose.

Miss Tamara had no reason to think about suicide, of course, but couldn't help wondering which book she'd choose to be the last one she read, should she decide to kill herself. It certainly couldn't be just an ordinary book. One's last book had to be exceptional in all respects, perhaps the most important of all those read during a lifetime. This was the book by which the reader would be remembered.

The choice was limited to books she'd already read. There might be better books among those she hadn't read, but how was she to find them? There are so many books in the world and the time one has to read is so short, even for those who live a long time, to say nothing of those who shorten their life by committing suicide.

So, which of all the books she'd read did she prefer?

She had three favorites that she reread regularly. The first time she'd read the melodrama with a sad ending she was very young. How many tears had been shed then and every subsequent time she read it, even after her salad days were well over.

For a long time she'd been convinced it was the book of her life, until she came across a work that was the exact opposite. Instead of emotions, it was filled with wisdom. She hadn't been very attuned to this type of book before, but in middle age they became more and more attractive. Each new reading of the book seemed to take her deeper into its essence.

The satisfaction this work brought was refined and mature, and for a long time she felt she could aim no higher as a reader. And then quite by accident she came across a book that had nothing to do with wisdom and even openly mocked it, deriding everything Miss Tamara held dear.

At first this ridicule offended her. Vexation almost led her to abandon the book, but she held back from this ultimate reader's heresy and continued. And didn't regret it. As she progressed, her initial frown gave way to a smile, and her smile to muffled laughter. In the end something happened that had previously seemed unimaginable for someone who had never laughed out loud before. The living room echoed with roaring laughter, and her eyes filled with tears once more, but this time for another reason.

It didn't take long to make up her mind. She might have decided otherwise had she been younger, but at this age she clearly recognized what she needed most and made no bones about admitting it to herself. Emotions and wisdom were still precious, of course, but laughter alone contained the healing magic of rapture and oblivion.

So, if she had the chance to choose her last book, it would be the book of laughter. She got up from the armchair, picked up the novel she was reading and headed for the bookshelf. She put the thick volume back with the books she'd read, even though she hadn't finished it, and then took the slender book of laughter, its edges worn from frequent use.

She returned to the armchair and continued eating the melon. Three more slices were left on the plate when she started to read. The room was soon filled with the sweet sound of laughter that delighted her as much as the book. That sound, *inter alia*, she thought, is the best defense against suicide. A human being has yet to take his own life while laughing.

Laughing with a full mouth, however, was imprudent, especially if you were swallowing under-chewed bites of even so soft a fruit as melon.

8. Fruit Salad

Miss Tamara looked at her watch. It was eight and a half minutes to five. She should not have appeared before the scheduled time. That was something ladies didn't do. Actually, she shouldn't have come at all. A lady with any self-respect would never have responded to a semi-anonymous invitation.

The letter she had received that morning was signed, to be sure. Actually, more than that: it had three signatures instead of one. But what difference did it make when they were all illegible, so she had no idea who had invited her to meet them at the "Fruit Salad" café. She also did not know the reason why she'd been invited. The brief letter made no mention of it.

At first she thought she wouldn't be able to make it to the "Fruit Salad" at five because that was the time she was home reading. She had never yet broken this daily routine, even for far more important reasons than this. Furthermore, it was clearly someone's idea of a practical joke. She was not about to give them the pleasure of laughing as they hid somewhere and watched her wait in vain.

At ten minutes past four when she started getting ready, she repeated to herself that there was no reason to go. At twenty-five minutes to five, when she left for the "Fruit Salad," she tried to find plausible excuses. She would not be giving up her afternoon reading. She could feel the heavy book in her purse. The only difference was that she would not be sitting in the armchair by the window. But was that so important? She could read in the café. In fact, the change of scene would do her good.

If anyone there was determined to make fun of her, she would simply ignore them. What could be amusing about a girl sitting in a café engrossed in a book? The would-be jokesters would be the ones to look ridiculous. It would serve them right. Maybe the joke was that no one would appear at five. That would be the least damaging scenario. She would pretend that she'd gone there of her own free will.

The "Fruit Salad" had been almost empty when she'd entered at fifteen minutes to five. There was just a young man reading at a table to the left of the entrance by the large picture window. She breathed a sigh of relief when she saw him. Now she would be even less conspicuous with a book in hand. She went to the opposite side and sat at a table with three chairs in the corner.

The waiter came up to her right away. She opened the blue menu—blue seemed to be the trademark of the café—and vacillated briefly over what to choose from the selection that was customary in such places. Instead of a cappuccino, which first came to mind, she decided to take the fruit salad. This seemed fitting, given the name of the café, and in any case she always ate fruit while she read.

When the waiter had gone, she took out her book and opened it, but didn't start to read right away, although she kept it in front of her. She peeped over the upper edge at the young man on the other side of the café. She liked men who wore their hair long, particularly if they were blond. Then even glasses looked good on them.

She was surprised at the size of the dish of fruit the waiter brought. She would never be able to finish it, particularly when she saw it had a thick coating of chocolate syrup. One taste, however, and she was hooked. Perhaps she could make a salad like that at home, even without the syrup, instead of just washing and cutting up the fruit. Why not spice life up a bit?

The salad was a real explosion of flavors. Strong chocolate prevailed, but she could clearly detect apples, lemons, blackberries, bananas, apricots, gooseberries and melon. There were other, exotic flavors that she couldn't make out, both sweet and acidic, sour and pungent. She was glad that there were no other customers around because this let her eat faster than good manners allowed.

At eight and a half minutes to five Miss Tamara started to fidget and to doubt the wisdom of having come here. She tried reading to calm her nerves, but to no avail. Whenever she reached the end of the first paragraph of the new chapter she had to go back to the beginning because she couldn't remember a thing. She didn't put the book down, though. She could still use it as a screen.

Just as she looked at her watch at four minutes to five, the door to the café opened. Three ladies came in, chattering and smiling. They could easily have been grandmother, mother and daughter. The grandmother, though perky and spirited, must have been in her late seventies. The slender figure of the middle-aged woman made her look at least half a decade younger than her age. The girl with short dark hair and a round face had not yet turned twenty.

Without looking towards Miss Tamara, they headed for the side where the young man was sitting. They too sat at a table by the window, talking without letup. When the waiter reached their table they made him wait a little while and then ordered through their laughter without looking at the menu. Bowls full of fruit salad soon appeared before them.

Did they send the letter? wondered Miss Tamara.

The number of signatures matched the number of people, but that might be just a coincidence. She was sure she had never seen them before, although they did seem somewhat familiar, as though she'd heard something about them somewhere. Or maybe read about them. She gave it concerted thought, but was unable to remember. Well, it didn't make any difference; if they were the ones behind the letter, she would soon find out.

She glanced at her watch under the table once again. Five on the dot. She raised her eyes and started when she realized that someone was coming toward her, although she hadn't heard the café door open. She must have been lost in thought. He was a tall, older man in a long coat wearing a wide-brimmed hat that covered his abundant silver hair. Miss Tamara started once again when she recognized him.

He smiled when he reached her table.

"Hello."

"Hello," said Miss Tamara in reply after hesitating briefly.

"You know who I am." It was more of a statement than a question.

She paused briefly again before saying, "I know, but . . ."

His smile broadened.

"May I?" He gestured towards one of the two free chairs.

Miss Tamara quickly put the book out of the way on the table, then rose slightly. She was aware that good manners did not require this of her, but she felt the need to show her respect in some way.

"Of course, please sit down."

"You thought I was dead," said the gray-haired gentleman after he'd taken a seat, removed his hat and placed it on the free chair. Again this was not a question.

"Yes . . . well, no . . ." said Miss Tamara in embarrassment. "I mean . . . that's what it said in the newspaper."

"Never believe that a writer is dead. Particularly if you read that he committed suicide."

She didn't know how to answer that, so she continued to stare at him as her discomfort intensified.

He also was silent, his smile still broad. Then he pointed with his index finger at the book.

"Would you like me to read you something?"

She looked at the book in confusion, then nodded her head and handed it to him.

He opened it and started to read the first chapter. He read louder than was necessary, so the whole café could hear, but the customers in the other half paid no attention. She eyed him suspiciously after the first sentence. What she was hearing certainly did not come from her book.

A short passage was enough to remove all doubt. She was well acquainted with his style, but couldn't recall which work this came from. It didn't really matter, though. She abandoned herself completely to the pleasure of the moment. His velvety voice had captivated her as soon as he spoke, but now it received full expression. She listened to him spellbound, ignoring the fact that she was staring at him rudely.

When he reached the end of the page he stopped, closed the book and laid it on the table. His eyes locked with hers. They stayed that way for several long moments before she finally lowered her eyes in embarrassment.

"I hope you enjoyed it?" This time it sounded like a question.

"Very much," she hastened to reply. She wanted to say more, but couldn't come up with anything.

The smile returned to his face. "I'm pleased to hear that."

He rose, picked up his hat and bowed before placing it on his head.

"Goodbye."

She bobbed slightly again. "Goodbye."

She stayed in that position, watching him head for the door where he met a new customer. The young man gestured for him to go out first, then entered the café and headed for her table. She quickly sat down in her chair.

She didn't have time to wonder at the appearance of the tall, lean librarian, dressed in casual clothes as usual. Seeing him was actually no less unusual than seeing the writer. He smiled at her too, but with more restraint.

"Hello," he said when he reached her, stumbling a little over his words. "How are you?"

"Fine, and you?"

"Oh, very well, thank you. May I?" He gestured towards the chair.

"Of course." This time she did not rise.

"I'd like to read you something, if you will allow me," he said, taking the book.

She nodded her head.

He leafed through the book a bit and then stopped when he reached a postcard. He took it out and quickly put it in the inside pocket of his jeans jacket.

"Excuse me," he said, blushing as though caught doing something improper.

"Think nothing of it."

He started to read in an uncertain and muffled voice, so that she had to strain her ears to follow him. Why are shy men always so awkward and quiet, she wondered. She thought of asking him to read louder—it certainly would not bother the other customers—but didn't do so. She would probably just embarrass him even more.

What she was now listening to was not part of her book either. It seemed vaguely familiar, but again she was unable to recognize the source. As the librarian progressed, he read louder and louder, although still not very smoothly. If he'd continued much longer, his voice might have reached the pitch of the writer's, but he too stopped at the end of the page.

"Did you like it?" he asked, eyes lowered, placing the book back on the table.

"I liked it," she said.

"Thank you. Thank you very much," he said, standing up.

She didn't understand why he was thanking her, but even so replied, "You're welcome."

She saw by the fact that he didn't know what to do with his hands that he was uncertain about the manner of his leaving. He finally mustered the courage to stick out his right hand with a bow.

"Goodbye, then. It was nice to see you."

"Goodbye." His hand felt damp in hers.

As he turned to leave, he almost ran into the adjacent table. She could barely repress a giggle. At the door there was another encounter. The librarian helped a blind man enter the café and then left. As soon as the new customer headed towards her, Miss Tamara remembered where she'd seen him before. He sat on a bench in the park from time to time, a book in his lap. He was always elegantly dressed, most often in a light blue suit, a dark blue t-shirt instead of a shirt and lightweight shoes, as he was now. The white cane didn't spoil this harmonious image.

She stood up before he reached her.

"May I help you?"

He turned his head a little to the side. "Thank you. Would you be so kind as to let me sit at your table?"

"Of course."

She went up to him, took him by the arm, pulled out a chair and sat him in it. Then she returned to her own chair and looked at her reflection in his glasses.

"We met before," he said. "In the park."

"How do you know? I mean . . ."

"By your fragrance. It's as reliable as eyesight. You passed by my bench several times."

"I had no idea . . ."

"It's not all black when you can't see. There are certain advantages."

"Really?" She bit her tongue. This might have seemed sarcastic. She might offend him accidentally if she wasn't careful of what she said.

"Yes. You shouldn't underestimate the abilities of the blind. They can do a variety of things. Read, for example. Would you like me to read you something?"

"I'm afraid I don't have any books for the blind."

"It doesn't matter. I'll use this one on the table."

He felt around in front of him, found the book and opened it to the place where Miss Tamara had put the thin canvas ribbon.

"May I?" he asked.

"Yes, please."

As he read, his head was raised and turned towards her. This soon began to bother her. She was haunted by the feeling that the blind eyes were observing her from behind the opaque glass. She lowered her head, concentrating solely on his voice.

Now that she wasn't looking at him, it was easy to imagine that she was listening to an actor's long monologue. Everything was just right: the emphasis, cadence, pauses, drama. She closed her eyes a moment so sight didn't stop her from focusing completely on listening.

When he stopped speaking she didn't move right away, but only opened her eyes and looked at him when she heard the sound of the book closing.

"Well?" he asked, placing the large volume on the table.

"Exquisite."

He bowed. "Thank you."

He stood up and took his white cane. She got up quickly after him.

"Shall I take you to the door?" she asked.

"I'll do fine by myself, thank you. I'm glad we met again. I'll be seeing you."

"See you." The greeting did not seem at all out of place.

She watched him leave. He moved with greater assurance than the librarian, lightly using his cane. She sat down when the door closed behind him, pulled the book over from the opposite side of the table, but did not open it. She stared at the cover for a while.

A commotion roused her from her reverie. The waiter was holding the chairs of the ladies who had stood up. They were still bright and cheerful. They headed for the door but did not go out right away. All three turned towards her and waved, smiling broadly. She waved back, returning their smiles.

She looked briefly at the book cover once again after they had gone. Then she drew out her wallet and put a bill on the table. She picked up the book, took her purse and headed for the opposite side of the café. She stopped in front of the table where the young man was sitting. He raised his eyes from the book he was reading and looked at her.

"Would you like it if we read together?" she asked.

He stood up and stared intently into her eyes.

"Yes."

Her face lit up. "Let's go. There's room for another armchair by the window. And I'll make you some fruit salad."

Amarcord

Contents

1. Crime and Punishment

When I opened my eyes, it was like I'd been submerged in milk. An undefined, amorphous whiteness surrounded me on all sides. I stared at it emptily for a while until my eyes focused enough to make out where I was: lying in a bed without a frame, like a sort of catafalque, in the middle of a small square room. There was nothing else in it. The walls and high ceiling were covered with immaculate white padding. A bright light from an invisible source increased the glare of the whiteness. I squinted to protect my eyes from snow blindness.

The sheet that covered me up to my chin was also white. Wanting to see something that wasn't white, I tried to take my right hand out from under the sheet. But the wide belt strapped over my lower arm prevented me. My left arm was strapped down too. A belt bound me across the chest and another one bound my ankles. I could squirm but not get up.

"How are you?"

I was unable to determine the origin of the deep male voice. It seemed to be coming from all around me.

"Restrained," I replied, not knowing where to look.

"That is unavoidable. But except for that, how do you feel?"

I ruminated briefly. "Fine."

"There isn't any nausea? You don't feel like vomiting?"

"No."

"Please shake your head several times, keeping your eyes open."

"Why?"

"To check whether there is any dizziness."

"How can I feel dizzy if I'm lying down?"

"It's possible. Please move your head quickly from side to side."

I hesitated slightly, then did it. Everything began to rock as though I was suddenly on a ship caught in a storm. I closed my eyes to regain my balance.

"Wonderful," pronounced the voice.

"Wonderful that I'm dizzy?" I asked, opening my eyes again. The rocking sensation had not quite passed.

"That's right. Dizziness is a good sign. Nausea would be bad."

"Sign of what?"

"That everything is all right."

"Nothing looks all right to me. What kind of place is this? What am I doing here? Why am I restrained? And who in the world are you?"

Several moments passed before the voice spoke again, but it was not to give me any answers.

"What is your name?"

I opened my mouth to say my name, but nothing came out. All I did was stare blankly straight ahead.

"What do you know about yourself?"

My answer was silence once again.

"When and where were you born?" continued the voice relentlessly. "Who are your parents? Are you married? Do you have any children? Where do you live? What do you do for a living?"

The questions washed over me like a huge confusing wave. I had to know the answers to them, of course, but all there was in my memory was a hollow whiteness resembling the one that surrounded me.

"I can't remember anything," I said at last in a soft voice. "What happened to me?"

"You have complete loss of memory about yourself."

"Did I have an accident?"

"No. Your memory has been artificially removed."

The voice said it as though telling me that my nails had been trimmed. Dead silence filled the room.

"Why?" I finally asked.

"Because that is the sentence you've been given."

Once more I needed a little time before I spoke.

"What have I been sentenced for?"

"You committed a crime."

"What crime?"

"That's no longer important. Don't let it weigh you down. The crime was erased along with your past."

I shook my head in disbelief. This made everything start to rock again.

"Was whatever I did so bad that I had to give up my past?"

"Yes. Actually, it could have been worse. If it weren't for the mitigating circumstances, you would have been executed."

"What's the difference? This is like being executed too. Without any memory of my past I'm no longer myself."

"You have no reason to complain. It's true that you are no longer your former self, but it's unlikely you would want to be if you knew what you'd done. It wouldn't be at all easy to live with such a burden on your conscience. And you are not by nature a psychopath who would be unperturbed by your crimes. The remorse you showed at the trial tipped the scale in your favor and the judge handed down a lighter sentence. The expert's opinion also helped. He said the chances of you repeating the crime under other circumstances were negligible."

"But how is it possible to live without a memory?"

"You won't live without a memory. You'll get a new one without any stains. You will leave here as a completely rehabilitated man. Think of it as being part of a special witness protection program. The only difference is that protected witnesses are aware of their first identity, while you won't be. For you, the new memory will be all you have."

"What new memory?"

"One tailored just for you. Everything that could be was kept from your former life. You will have the same education, for example. You will remember—and even better than before—the things you learned, the books you read, the films you saw, the music you listened to. And everything else, except for actual people you were in touch with. Particularly friends and relatives. Your memories of them will be replaced by new ones."

"I'll get new friends and relatives?"

"No. That's impossible. You won't have any relatives. But there's nothing unusual about that. Is the number of people without kin so small? You will be able to found a family, though, and get relatives that way. The same thing with new friends. When a person moves to a new town, which is what you will do, they quickly forget old friends and make new ones, isn't that right?"

I didn't say anything for several moments, mulling this over.

"But old friends and relatives will remember me. Their memory hasn't been erased. What if one of them runs into me by accident and recognizes me?"

"They won't recognize you. A new face goes with your new memory. Actually, you already have it."

My hand moved automatically towards my head but was stopped by the belt.

"What do I look like?" I asked hesitantly.

There was a brief pause before the voice replied.

"Different."

"Will I like myself?"

"Everyone likes themselves. More or less. In any case, you won't know about any other face."

Once again I thought this over.

"There's something I don't understand. Why are you telling me all this? Won't my memory of this conversation jeopardize my new life?"

"No, it won't. This conversation will also be erased before we implant a new memory."

"So why did we have to have it?"

"We didn't. We could have left your questions unanswered or made up something less drastic. But basically it's all the same. We found out what we wanted to know. There wouldn't be any conversation at all if the procedure of removing an old memory and implanting a new one could be done in one fell swoop. But we have to make sure that the old memory has been erased before we put in the new one. This doesn't always happen. Some memories are really stubborn, and then there is nausea and vomiting. Luckily, everything went smoothly with yours. Dizziness is a guarantee that everything is all right."

"I won't remember a single thing about my former self?" I asked in a soft voice again.

"Nothing. You will soon wake up in your bed a new man. With a new memory." The voice stopped suddenly. "Although the old one won't be destroyed."

"How's that?"

"We keep memories that have been removed so we can study them. Your old self will come alive whenever an expert activates it from the data bank. It will stay that way even after your new self is gone. In a way, you will outlive yourself. The opposite would be fairer, of course, but it can't be helped. You are only of interest to researchers as a murderer and not as a normal man. Well, then. We must get on with things. Please close your eyes and relax. Soon it will seem that you are falling asleep."

I thought of asking one more thing, but didn't. What was the use of knowing something I would forget in just a few moments? When I lowered my eyelids I was not surrounded immediately by darkness. The lingering picture of milky whiteness evaporated slowly and unwillingly, like a stubborn memory.

2. Vanity Fair

I ENTERED THE "LITTLE Shop of Memories" antique store. Its interior and exterior were exactly in keeping with the neighborhood: dilapidated, poorly lit and full of stale smells. Respectable people don't go to places like that. I wouldn't have had any reason to be there either if I could have found what I was looking for elsewhere.

The antique dealer looked as though he had stepped out of one of the old novels on the dusty shelf to the left of the door. Tall and thin with tiny eyes behind round wire-framed glasses, a gaunt face that hadn't see the sun in ages, unkempt greasy hair, wearing a shabby plaid jacket with elbow patches and a dark-red shawl even though it wasn't cold.

I didn't go up to him right away. He was talking to a short elderly woman at the counter. He glanced at me briefly over her little black hat. I headed towards the open showcase on the right and pretended to be absorbed in looking at the objects in it stacked every which-way. There was a monocle without a lens, a snuff-box, a chipped medal, a marble ink blotter, a gilded tie pin, an ivory cigarette holder, a brass paper cutter, a jewelry box of inlaid wood, a graceful figurine of an egret made of jade, a gramophone record without a sleeve, a bundle of letters and postcards tied with a blue ribbon and several faded photographs. The dead past that no one needed anymore.

Even though I was wearing gloves, I used just my

thumb and index finger gingerly to pick up the creamer from a tea set on a tray in the upper part of the case. The silver must have gone unpolished for at least half a century. I took a small spoon with a coat of arms at the end and shook it in the creamer. It rang like a bell summoning a servant.

The antique dealer looked at me again over the little hat. Then he came out from behind the counter, took the elderly lady by the arm and guided her towards the door. She didn't feel quite like going yet, but he made relentless progress. He bowed several times before she went out.

He repeated the bow when he came up to me, adding a deferential smile.

"Good evening, sir. How may I help you?"

I went straight to the point and gave the password. "Do you have a live past by any chance?"

The smile disappeared from the antique dealer's face. His tiny eyes scrutinized me several moments in silence. Then his smile returned, broader than before, followed by another bow.

"Yes, indeed. We have a splendid selection of live pasts. You have come to the right place, sir. If you will allow me."

He went back to the door and turned over the rectangular sign hanging on the glass. Now it said "Open" on the inside.

"This way, please." He indicated a door behind the counter and took the lead, moving sideways so as not to turn his back on me.

He disappeared for a moment into the darkness of the side room. A click was heard and a dim light went on. A dirty bulb with a broad tin shade hanging from the ceiling cast a conical light on the uncovered table and two high wooden stools. The shelves that lined the walls were filled with objects but they were hidden in the gloom in that part of the little room.

Mumbling an apology, the antique dealer quickly collected the food remains on the table in a paper bag. He turned around briefly, clearly not knowing what to do with it, then finally put it on the floor.

He shrugged as though in apology before motioning to one of the stools. “Please sit down.”

I removed my gloves, brushed off the stool with them, then put them back on. The second-hand dealer waited for me to sit down, then sat on the other stool.

“Would you like something special, sir? As I said, we have . . .”

I motioned with my hand for him to stop. I took a photograph out of the inside pocket of my lightweight coat and showed it to him.

“Ah, I see. A great painter. What am I saying? She’s one of the greatest. The greatest, actually. And such a tragic end. Taking her own life and she wasn’t even thirty-five. Terrible. But who can understand an artist? In any case, now her works will be even more valuable. And more expensive, of course. Artists only receive the recognition they deserve after they die. That is indeed a great injustice, but it can’t be helped. Such is the world in which we live. . . .”

I raised my hand again. “Do you have it?”

“Yes, indeed. Didn’t I tell you that we have an excellent supply? Although it’s harder and harder to come by the goods. Things aren’t like they used to be. Surveillance is very tight, the police are always sniffing around, and the suppliers have become extremely greedy. You can’t imagine how unscrupulous they are. Nothing is sacred to them, not even art. Especially when they sense there might be a great demand for something. Like in this case.”

He pointed at the photograph I was still holding in front of him. I put it back in my pocket.

“Show me.”

“Right away, sir.”

He got up and went towards the shelf, then rummaged around there for some time, rustling the objects he moved. When he sat down again he was holding a shabby wooden chess box. He put it on the table, opened it and picked up the white queen. He turned it upside down and pulled off the round felt pad. It was hollow underneath. He stuck two fingers into it and took out a blue oval pill in cellophane. He put the pad back in place, laid the piece in the box, then raised the pill slightly.

"Do you have any experience with this, sir? It's taken before sleeping on an empty stomach. That way it has the best effect. When you wake up, the new memory will be with you, sharper than your own. And there are almost no bad side effects. You might feel stomach cramps briefly, but that's normal. Arrhythmia only appears in those with high blood pressure. Do you have such problems, sir?"

"No, I don't."

"Excellent! I'm sure you understand that this is not her entire memory. One pill would not be sufficient. But who knows, in a few years even that might be possible. Miniaturization is a true wonder. But the selection has been made to satisfy every predilection. I'm certain you will find what it is that attracts you."

"Perhaps. Let's hear the contents."

"Right away, sir."

This time he took the black queen. He squeezed his thumb and index finger around the top and started to unscrew it. A small roll of paper was in the hollow space. He unrolled it on the palm of his hand, took off his glasses and placed them on the table, then brought the paper up close to his eyes.

"This is the easiest way for me to read small print," he said, as though excusing himself. "Let's see. First, of course, the suicide itself. With lots of blood, although rather bungled. We were lucky, in fact, that she didn't do a more professional job. She was still alive when they took her to the hospital, so they were able to record her memory. In any case, if you are attracted to dramatic suicides, sir, you'll really enjoy this one."

"They don't attract me."

"Very well. And what do you say about her erotic life? I've heard it was not only tumultuous but very imaginative. But that's probably true of all painters. The most arousing events have been chosen. From her first sexual experience to wild orgies. Some are quite shocking even if you are completely open-minded. And she had an excellent memory for detail. . . ."

"Go on."

"Of course. Then there are the diseases that afflicted her. She didn't take very good care of her health. If she hadn't killed herself, it's unlikely she would have lived much longer. That's also a typical artistic trait, I presume. Some ailments really tormented her. She had a vivid memory of vomiting and diarrhea. . . ."

"Go on."

"To be sure. Perhaps you are interested in her remorse? There was lots of it, although she hid it behind a mask of arrogance. Her conscience pricked her the most because of the child. Almost no one knew she'd had one. She had her when she was quite young, and since she couldn't keep her, gave her up for adoption. The little girl died in a traffic accident. If you are fond of the suffering of others, sir . . ."

I raised my hand more abruptly than before.

"Forgive me." He stopped for a moment. "At the end is something especially spicy. Her memories of other painters. Not at all complimentary, to put it mildly. It seems that she was full of herself and very vain. But aren't all artists? They all think that they are the best. Even so, such disdain towards one's colleagues is rarely seen."

"She was the best," I said in a low voice.

The antique dealer glanced at me quickly from under the little piece of paper.

"Undeniably. I said so too. The greatest."

He wrapped up the piece of paper and set it on the table next to the pill, then put his glasses back on.

"Did you find something to your liking in this selection, sir?"

"No, I didn't."

"I see. And might I ask what would be to your liking, sir?"

I didn't answer immediately. We stared at each other in silence for several moments. When I finally spoke, my voice was soft again.

"Her memory of the act of painting. Of what comes right before it. Her creative exaltation. Her inspiration. Can you get that for me?"

He scrutinized me once again.

"We can get whatever you want. The only question is whether you are willing to pay the price, sir."

"How much?"

"It won't be easy, of course. As I said, the suppliers have become ruthless. But we have to understand them too. They expose themselves to great danger."

"How much?"

"If they were to get caught, they wouldn't be the only ones to spend a long time in prison. Everyone involved in this would too. I'm afraid not even you would be spared, sir."

"How much?"

Our eyes met silently again.

"It's free."

I stared at the antique dealer in confusion.

"What's that?"

"You wouldn't have to pay a cent, sir."

"Then how would I pay for it?"

Before he answered, he ran the tip of his middle finger twice across the cellophane wrapped around the pill.

"Your memory."

I almost jumped off the stool and hit my head on the tin shade. The bulb began to sway and the conical illumination along with it.

"Have you taken leave of your senses?" I shouted.

The antique dealer stood up as well and stopped the light-pendulum.

"Please don't get upset, sir. This is just an ordinary business proposal. I suggest you think it over. I certainly don't expect an immediate answer."

"There's nothing to think over! It's out of the question."

I walked briskly out of the little room and headed for the exit. Almost running, the antique dealer caught up with me so he could open the door. He bowed as I passed by him.

"You know where you can find me if you change your mind, sir," he said as I left.

I wanted to turn around and shout that I would never change my mind. How could I let some perverse stranger get his kicks out of my memory? Something that was so intimately mine? Never!

And then I remembered that up until a moment before I myself had been ready to delve into someone else's memory. Indeed, not to get any kicks, but was that any excuse? My motive was actually even more dishonorable.

Although I walked away quickly, I knew that I would return to the "Little Shop of Memories". And accept the offer. Regardless of the price. What other choice did a hopelessly minor painter have than to steal the secret of inspiration of a great one?

3. Great Expectations

The doorbell woke me from my doze.

Still groggy, I couldn't remember what time of day it was. I lowered my glasses to the tip of my nose and brought my watch up to my eyes. The large numbers showed 15:32. Who could it be? I wasn't expecting anyone. I hadn't been expecting anyone or anything for a long time. The mailman would drop by periodically, but only in the morning.

The bell rang a second time.

"Coming," I said in a raised voice. I struggled out of the armchair and shuffled towards the door.

The face of the short middle-aged man standing on the doorstep holding a briefcase was beaded with sweat. It was no wonder, considering everything he was wearing in such heat: a dark-blue suit, white shirt, tie and hat. But what kind of success could a traveling salesman hope to have unless he was perfectly dressed for all occasions?

"Hello," he said with a smile, taking off his hat.

"Hello."

"Forgive me for disturbing you when you might be resting. Could you spare me a moment of your time? I have something to offer that will certainly be of interest to you."

"There aren't many such offers at my age."

"I firmly believe this is one of them. It won't cost you a thing to listen. I won't take more than about ten minutes of your time. Is that very much?"

It wasn't very much. Actually, it was not enough, bearing in mind the fact that I hadn't spoken a word to anyone in days. I was certain that whatever he was trying to sell wouldn't be for me, but what did it matter? The conversation alone would do me good. And he could certainly do with a bit of refreshment. I didn't have the heart to deprive him of a short break.

"Please come in," I said, stepping back a little so he could enter.

His face lit up. "Thank you. You won't regret it."

It wasn't until we entered the living room that I realized how messy it was. When a man lives alone he stops noticing. I would have cleaned things up a bit had I known I would have a visitor. All I could do was quickly clear a space on the two-seater so my visitor had somewhere to sit.

"Sorry," I said apologetically.

"Think nothing of it," replied the traveling salesman politely.

"Would you like a cold drink?" I asked after he had sat down and placed his briefcase on the floor. And then I remembered that the choice was quite limited. I sighed.

"I'm afraid that all I can offer is a glass of water. But nice and cold."

"I would be most grateful."

I came back from the kitchen with a tray, put it on the end table between the two-seater and the armchair, then sat down. My visitor drained his glass at once.

"It's really hot today," I said.

"Unbearably so." He took out a handkerchief and wiped the sweat from his brow. New beads appeared immediately to replace the old ones.

"You'll be more comfortable if you take off your jacket."

He hesitated a moment. "No, thank you. I'm fine like this."

"Unfortunately, I don't have air conditioning. But I can turn on the fan. I don't use it very much because it's noisy."

"Thank you, there's no need. I'm used to the heat. Let me get straight to the point. I promised that I wouldn't keep you very long."

"I'm all ears."

"What expectations do you have out of life?"

I smiled sourly. "What could they be given my position? I've almost reached the end of my life's path."

"But your position is not at all bad. Quite the contrary. It's far better than the position of someone who is only twenty, for example."

"Really? I never would have thought as much. Better in what way?"

"A twenty-year-old has great expectations. He feels that his life has just begun. Such hopes do not necessarily have to come true, however. One never knows what the day or night will bring. Is the number so small of those who never reach middle age, let alone old age, like you?"

"There are such cases, I agree. But I don't understand what you're trying to say."

"I'm trying to say that the future, the object of everyone's obsession in the modern world, is like a high-risk speculation. It can bring great profit, but much more often completely fails. Unlike the future, however, the past is solid capital not exposed to any danger. It cannot be lost. In that sense you are a very rich man. Compared to you, a twenty-year-old is a wretched pauper. All he can do is envy you."

This time my smile was bitter. "Nevertheless, I'd willingly exchange my wealth for his poverty. What kind of wealth is it, anyway? Although my past is long, it's primarily filled with the tedious job I did that ate up most of my time. Sometimes I feel that I haven't really lived at all."

The traveling salesman drew his handkerchief across his brow again. "Well, you see, that's where we can help you."

I didn't even try to hide my sarcasm. "How? Can you change my past?"

"I'm afraid that's impossible."

"Then how can you help me?"

"Have you ever wondered what the past really is?"

I gave it some thought. "Memories of it?"

"That's right. Your past exists only in your memory. And that is subject to change."

I nodded my head. "I know that quite well. Mine has changed a lot. I've been rubbing shoulders with senility for a long time. There's so much I've already forgotten."

"I wasn't thinking of senility. We can offer you a completely new memory, but not your own."

I looked at him for several moments without speaking.

"Then whose?"

"No one's. It's artificial."

"Artificial?" I repeated in bewilderment.

"Yes. Fashioned to give you the greatest use. You receive a past that you remember vividly and with great joy. Never again will it seem that you haven't lived. Quite the contrary. You will have a very full life behind you. Enormous capital."

I briefly fell silent again.

"But it would be only an illusion. . . ."

"Isn't every memory only an illusion?"

"That's true. But mine is somehow less of an illusion than that artificial one. Regardless of all its defects, I wouldn't like to be without it."

"You won't. It will always return when the effect of the injection wears off after about twelve hours."

"What injection?"

"Memory is given intravenously. It's only a slight inconvenience. A nurse would come in the beginning, but soon you would learn how to give it to yourself whenever you want to feel good. And is there any better reason for a man to feel good than knowing he has a long and very prestigious life behind him?"

"That sounds to me like drug addiction," I said in a low voice.

"I don't deny that a certain addiction might appear. Once you've experienced a perfect memory, you won't care that much about your own. But unlike drugs, the elixir of memory isn't harmful to your health. Even if you were on it all the time, it wouldn't shorten your life. Many of our customers have been taking it without interruption for years without any bad side effects."

I stood up and took the glass off the tray.

"I'll bring you some more water." I went into the kitchen. I needed a little time by myself.

I came back with a full glass and put it in front of him. Although he was still sweating profusely, this time he only drank half of it.

"You know," I said, "even if I wanted an artificial memory, I wouldn't have the money for such a luxury. I have a small pension and barely make ends meet, and every drug addiction is expensive. Even such a harmless one is certainly no exception."

"Oh, don't worry about that. You wouldn't have to pay a thing for the memory elixir. At least not right away."

"Then when? I've never taken anything on credit in my life. And I won't start now. In any case, how would I repay it, regardless of when it's due?"

"You wouldn't repay it until after you die."

"How's that, after I die?"

"You own this house, don't you? And you don't have any heirs."

"I can see you came well prepared."

"No special preparations were needed. People buy

houses in this neighborhood primarily to spend their last days here. Most of them have no relatives. After they die, the municipality acquires ownership. They get something for nothing that way. And that's not fair, I'm sure you will agree. At least we give you an illusion. If you try the artificial memory just once, you'll see for yourself that's no small thing."

I got up from the armchair.

"I'll have to think it over."

My visitor got up too. "Certainly. Perhaps this will help you make up your mind."

He opened his briefcase, took out a colorful brochure on glossy paper and handed it to me.

"Our catalogue. We have a splendid selection of memories. If none of the existing memories suits you, we also do tailor-made memories. You can give free rein to your expectations about your past."

We shook hands at the door. "I'll drop by again in a few days to see what you've decided. And now it's out into the sun again. Goodbye."

"Goodbye."

I returned to the armchair and started to leaf through the catalogue. Its bright colors slowly supplanted the grayness of the disorder that surrounded me. Life does indeed become more cheerful when a man has some expectations.

4. Sentimental Education

I WENT OUT THE back door of the sanatorium. Before me stretched a flat lawn bordered by a tall hedge. The early autumn sun had turned the tops of the linden trees more golden than green. Dressed in identical light robes, the patients standing or sitting on benches resembled blue statues dotted about an open-air exhibit. Nothing moved, like in a movie-still.

Disrupting this tranquility, I headed across the lawn towards the farthest bench on the left. The patient I wanted to see was always sequestered there. But even if I didn't know where he was, I could easily spot him by his shock of pure white, yet still luxuriant hair.

He didn't look at me right away when I stopped in front of the bench. He kept his eyes on the hedge, seeming to see through it to something that brought a smile to his lips. His hands were resting on an old-fashioned book in his lap.

I stood there for some time in silence before addressing him.

"What a beautiful day."

His head turned towards me slowly. The smile didn't disappear, but it softened.

"Yes, beautiful."

"How are you?"

"Fine, thank you. How about you?"

"I'm fine, too, thank you."

"Have you come out to the park for a bit of sun too?"

"No. I've come to see you."

"Me? Do we know each other?"

"Yes." I indicated the space next to him on the bench. "May I?"

"Certainly, please sit down. How strange. I can't remember having met you before. How awkward to have to ask, but would you mind telling me where we met?"

"Six-and-a-half years ago, when you came to our sanatorium. I am your doctor."

"Have I been in the sanatorium that long? Why? Is there something wrong with my health?"

"You health is fine. But not your memory."

His smile evaporated. "Come again?"

"You haven't been able to remember anything for a long time. And even what you remembered before has been almost completely forgotten."

"Why, that's terrible. Is there a cure? A person can't live without memories."

"Yes they can. You've been doing it for years. And quite successfully, one might say. Actually, I know lots of people who'd give everything they have to be in your place. To be able to forget the past."

"But I have no reason to forget it." He paused a moment. "At least I hope not. Do you happen to know any details about my past?" he asked hesitantly. "Is there something dreadful in it?"

"Listen, we have this same conversation almost every day. For you it's new every time, while I am like an actor who's been playing in the same show for a very long time. When we get to this place, I shrug my shoulders helplessly and reply that I know even less about your past than you do. We haven't been able to find a single one of your friends or relatives, someone who knew you before you came to the sanatorium. But today the show will take a new turn."

"Did you find someone from my past?"

"No. But we found your past."

"Where?"

"Where it had been mislaid."

"How can a past be mislaid?"

"The human brain doesn't always act like we expect it to. In your case, there isn't anything where the memory is most often registered. To put it in computer terms, all the files there have been erased. But we accidentally found a backup copy in a totally unexpected place."

His face lit up again. "So that means I'll get my memory back?"

I didn't answer right away. We looked at each other in silence as his smile started to fade.

"It's not quite that simple. If we were dealing with a computer, it would be an easy matter. Unfortunately, the mechanisms of remembering are damaged in your brain. We could bring back your memory, but it wouldn't be permanent. The very next day you would have forgotten everything. It wouldn't be worth the effort to do it every day, either, because the procedure is complex and not completely without risk."

"Well, then it's like you didn't even find my past," he said dejectedly.

"Not exactly. You won't be able to have all of your memory any longer, but we think we can revive one part permanently. A very small part. Perhaps only one day."

We sank into silence again.

"Something's better than nothing, I suppose," he said at last.

Now I was the one who smiled. "I'm glad you think so. All that's left is to choose the day you most want to remember. And this is where we run into a new obstacle."

He looked at me in bewilderment, and then he got it. "How can I know which day I most want to remember when I can't remember any of them?"

"That's it. But that's where I might be able to help."

"You? How?"

"I saw your past all the way up to your arrival at the sanatorium. It's clearly registered on the backup copy. I know you, actually, as well as you once used to know yourself."

"That's . . ." he started, but seemed at a loss for words, ". . . very unusual. What kind of a man was I?"

Before I had time to answer, he spoke again.

"No, don't say a word. What's the use in finding out when I'll soon forget it anyway. Which day would you recommend?"

"That's not a simple question. There are many days in your past that are worth remembering. I might make a mistake."

"That's an unavoidable risk, I'm afraid."

"I suppose so. Well, all right. You know, there's something in your case that's intrigued me all these years. Something seemingly unimportant I haven't been able to explain."

"What's that?"

"The book," I said, pointing at it.

He raised it a little from his lap. "*Sentimental Education.*"

"Yes. That's the only personal item you brought with you to the sanatorium. I tried to work out why it was so important to you, but kept running into a wall of oblivion. The most logical explanation was that you brought it because it was your favorite book, but not once have I seen you read it."

He put the book back on his lap. "I don't remember having read it."

"You haven't. I know that now. Not only here, but even before you joined us. You bought it just before you came to the sanatorium, when you already knew that your memory was failing irreparably."

"Why?"

"I wondered the same thing. When we discovered

your memory, I hoped for a moment that it would be easy to find out. But it wasn't easy at all. Even after carefully examining the backup copy, there didn't seem to be a trace of the book. I had already lost hope, when I finally found it in your memory. This same edition."

"Where?"

"It's no wonder it was hard to find. You had seen it only once before. Briefly. Very long ago. Just after you turned nineteen. It was a beautiful day just like this one. A girl was sitting on a bench in the park reading *Sentimental Education*. You walked past her and then sat on another bench nearby even though you were in a hurry. When she got up and walked away not long thereafter, you wanted to follow her with all your heart, but you couldn't pluck up the courage."

His eyes glazed over.

"Was she pretty?"

"Very. There are many women in your memory, but you found none more beautiful than her. She was wearing a summer dress."

I stopped because he'd mumbled something. I hadn't caught it.

"Excuse me?"

His voice was softer than a whisper when he repeated, "Light blue."

He placed his hands on the book in his lap, then turned his head away from me towards the hedge. The smile returned to his lips and so did the look in his eyes that saw through the dense foliage. Through the sediments of time. Through his dead memory.

I stood up and headed back across the lawn to the sanatorium. I had nothing more to do there. He'd given me the answer I wanted.

5. Dead Souls

He was my best customer. A polished gentleman in late middle age, rather short, a bit stout, with red cheeks, a soft voice, discreetly dyed hair and manicured nails. Before I put the merchandise on the market, I took it to him first. It was a pleasure doing business with him. He asked for nothing but the best, thus the most expensive. He paid whatever the price, without bargaining. In cash, of course.

He received me in the drawing-room, as usual. The china cabinets were filled with little statues that could have been museum exhibits, the walls were almost completely covered with paintings that would have been the pride of any gallery, the carpet was as thick as a lush lawn, and the original owners of the furniture had certainly been bluebloods. He was wearing a long wine-colored smoking jacket with a matching bow tie and shoes that had been polished to a high luster. His eyes glistened with eagerness.

"What pleasure have you brought me this time?" he asked with a broad smile after we'd settled into the two armchairs in the corner. Between them was a small table with thin arched legs.

"You will be delighted, I'm sure."

"Wonderful!" he said, clapping his hands with glee. "Please show me. I can hardly wait to see."

I placed my crocodile briefcase on the table and opened it. The dark-blue plush lining was particularly suited to the merchandise I sold. Four indentations held little leather bags tied with ribbon at the top.

I showed him the first one.

"Early twentieth century. A great poet. He died in the maelstrom of the Great War. . . ."

"You aren't thinking of . . . ?" he said, interrupting me.

I just smiled without a word.

His face lit up. "I can't believe it. Tell me, tell me."

"While they sat in the trench for months, he passed the time by writing. He had just finished the epic poem when the order was given to attack. There wasn't time to put it away. He just stuck it under his army coat and headed out. A grenade blew him up only a few steps from the trench. Luckily, under the cover of night, the remains of the dead were picked up and buried in a large mass grave. Not a trace was left of the manuscript, of course, but a tiny bit of him was nonetheless preserved. Two tiny pieces of his femur."

A worried look crossed his face. "Both of them are there?"

"Both, of course."

He sighed with relief. "Oh, wonderful! Truly wonderful! And you say—he had finished the epic poem? Completely?"

"Completely."

"Divine! Let's see the next one."

I indicated the second little bag. "Mid-nineteenth century. A writer who was not understood in her time. She was mostly published under male pseudonyms."

"I know who you're talking about! Is it possible? You have something of hers too? What? What?"

"A novella. Perhaps the best one she ever wrote. It seems so modern. No wonder her contemporaries didn't understand. She destroyed it in a bout of deep despondency brought on by the ridicule she was subjected to."

"But didn't she end her life by jumping off the cliffs into the sea? Her body was never found. Or am I mistaken?"

"You're not mistaken. It wasn't."

"But how then?"

I smiled. "Right before she went to her death, she sent a farewell letter to her girlfriend and enclosed a lock of hair."

"Oh, what luck!" He pointed at the bag. "It's all there, I hope?"

"Do you have any doubts?"

"No, no, none at all. What's the third? I'm dying of curiosity."

"Late eighteenth century. A novelist. Very productive. Well known for his absentmindedness . . ."

"Him? Amazing! You're wonderful!"

I bowed. "Once he forgot to put out the candle before falling asleep. It fell off the candlestick next to the bed somehow and started a fire. He barely got out alive, but two finished manuscripts disappeared in the flames. This didn't bother him too much. He wrote one of them over again from memory. But for some reason, he didn't rewrite the other."

"Didn't he die in the turmoil at the end of the century? As far as I know, he has no grave."

"That's right, he doesn't. But he did have a barber."

"Another lock of hair? Or from his beard? He may have been balding, but he had quite a beard, if I remember well."

"None of that. In those days barbers were dentists too. He pulled out his wisdom tooth. But he didn't throw it away. He probably thought it was something noteworthy. He couldn't even imagine all that he saved along with that tooth."

"Magnificent!" Suddenly his face darkened. "You're sure he didn't pull out any others?"

"If he did, he didn't leave anything else behind. I checked it out thoroughly."

"Wonderful! And the fourth little bag? I suspect you've saved the most valuable item for last. You won't disappoint me, will you?"

"I hope I won't. Early seventeenth century. A playwright. Many consider him the greatest . . ."

Forgetting his manners, he jumped up from the armchair and brought his hands to his cheeks.

"Don't tell me. . . ."

I said nothing in return. All I did was smile.

He sank back into the chair slowly, staring at me in disbelief.

"But everything he wrote has been preserved. There's not even a hint of a missing work."

"There isn't. And yet it exists. His last play, written the same year he died. He was already feeble and it was stolen from him. That's probably what finished him off. The manuscript never turned up and seems to have been destroyed. Envy is as strong a driving force as greed in human affairs."

"What do you have of his?"

"A sliver of the frontal bone."

This time he put his hands over his mouth. When he lowered them and spoke, it was almost in a whisper.

"Where did you get it?"

"From his grave, of course," I said in an even tone.

"But how? You didn't have the nerve to desecrate it, did you?" He eyed me suspiciously, then continued before I managed to say anything. "You didn't, I'm sure. That would have hit all the headlines. So how did you do it?"

"I have my ways. If you, however, think you're running some sort of risk, I'll have no trouble finding a more daring customer. . . ."

"By no means!" he shouted with a squeak, then was immediately ashamed of his outburst. "Forgive me. I'm not the slightest bit afraid of any risk. It's something else that troubles me. What if someone gets the idea of following in your footsteps? There must be more bones in the grave."

"Not anymore."

His mouth opened, but nothing emerged for several moments.

"Ah," he said at last. "So this is all of it?"

"All of it."

I'd seen that expression before. Few human exaltations can be compared to the fierceness of the collector's. Especially one who considers that he alone can have something. I was sensitive to this passion, of course. If it didn't exist, would I be living so well?

"May I?"

He put his hands together unconsciously as though begging me. He knew I never unveiled anything on offer in advance. I only gave intimations. I also didn't allow trials before the conclusion of the deal. Nothing raises the price as much as uncertainty combined with impatience. But I could make an exception here. It was obvious that he wouldn't be able to resist, regardless of how much I asked.

I pretended to hesitate briefly, then said, "All right."

"Thank you!"

He quickly reached into the wide pocket of his smoking jacket and took out a pair of yellow rubber gloves. He pulled them on with feverish movements, then extended his right hand towards me. I untied the ribbon on the fourth little bag and slowly shook out the piece of frontal bone into his cupped hand.

Holding his hand rigid, he stood up, went across the drawing-room and opened the double doors of a cabinet in the opposite corner. Behind them was something that certainly didn't go with the rest of the drawing-room: high technology. Under an enormous screen was a device full of buttons, switches and colored lights. It had a very professional four-word name. I simply called it a player.

I was not a fan of high technology. Luckily, I didn't need it in my part of the job. It was required in the after-sale part, however, but that no longer concerned me. I had only a general idea of what the flashing device did.

Someone very clever had discovered that memory is not located solely in the brain but, like DNA, is stored in every cell. It stays there even after death. As long as you have the tiniest part of the deceased, you can reconstruct everything they ever heard, saw, felt, experienced or suffered. All of this might have disappeared from their memory while they were alive, but the cells forget nothing.

The polished customer cried out when the sight of a yellow sheet of paper appeared on the screen with a quill pen flying across it. He was looking at the same thing as the long-dead bard had done as he wrote his last play. Seemingly lost forever, it was now recovered but would still be registered as lost, since only one man would have it. It was clear why such a unique privilege could by no means be inexpensive.

I cleared my throat.

It was hard for him to tear his eyes from the screen. As he headed for the armchair, he carried the bone carefully in his cupped hand. While he took off his gloves, I put the little bag back in the briefcase and closed it.

We sat there briefly in silence. And then I surprised even myself at the figure I gave him.

The client was less surprised, it seemed. His face showed no expression as he left the drawing-room. He came back several minutes later with a briefcase identical to mine. There was no need to open it and count the money, of course. My business is based on reciprocated trust. We merely exchanged briefcases.

I had already risen to leave, when I remembered something.

"Soon I will have something new to offer. What do you say to one of the living writers? I could get you the memory of a contemporary giant. A very unusual individual. I'm already in contact with his pedicurist. The price, of course, would be considerably lower. . . ."

He didn't hesitate a moment. "No, thank you. I'm not interested in the living. But as soon as a dead soul appears, I expect you to come to see me first."

6. Lost Illusions

Even though the telephone hadn't rung, the secretary picked up the receiver. Without a word, she listened to what was briefly said to her, then hung up the phone.

"You may go in." She motioned towards the padded door.

I got up and went into the office of the memory agency owner. The prevailing color was green. Plants of varying shapes and sizes were placed everywhere. The owner's large desk was covered with vegetation. When he stood up to greet me, holding a plastic sprayer, he looked like he'd just stepped out of a botanical garden.

"Hello. Please sit down."

I settled into a ponderous dark-brown leather armchair facing his desk. Tall oleanders in brass pots were placed on either side. When the owner sat down, all I could see was his head above the plants.

"So, you'd like to cash in your memory. Fine, fine. This is the first time you've put it up for sale, right?"

Before entering his office I'd filled out a questionnaire that the secretary gave me. She'd entered my answers into the computer, so the owner could see them right away.

"Yes," I said.

"Many people find their first visit here quite a hardship. But please be assured that there is absolutely no reason to worry. First of all, the actual procedure of giving your memory is completely painless and not the least detrimental to your health. In addition, we don't remove your memory, we only make a copy of it. And finally, the buyer doesn't know whose memory he has purchased."

"It isn't easy, though. My memory is the most intimate part of me. It's like being without some part of my body."

"I agree it isn't easy if you look at it like an amputation or donating an organ for transplant. But it's not like that at all. Have you ever wondered what a memory actually is?"

He waited briefly, then continued since my reply was not forthcoming.

"Nothing real, tangible. Just an ordinary illusion whose loss is hardly felt. And why shouldn't a man lose some of his illusions if he can benefit by it, particularly when he's in trouble? Would you rather lose an organ?"

"No, I wouldn't," I had to admit.

"There, you see. And quite a profit can be made by selling illusions today. Some of our customers have really struck it rich. The market pays an excellent price, but is rather selective. I hope you have something interesting to offer us."

"I hope so, too."

"It would have been easy to find out if you'd let us scan your memory. Would you consider changing your mind?"

I shook my head briskly. "No, I wouldn't."

"I don't blame you. Few of our clients agree to it. People don't want to be an open book. That is something we understand and respect. Some things are kept even from the doctor. To tell you the truth, I myself wouldn't let anyone have unlimited access to my memory. A person has to keep some secrets to himself, right?"

"Indeed."

"The market, however, has the greatest demand for

the very things we would most like to hide. That's also understandable. The urge to peep behind the curtain exists in all of us, whether we admit it or not. We are all voyeurs to a greater or lesser extent, and some people are ready to really loosen the purse strings to find pleasure in that passion."

I sighed. "Voyeurs won't be very attracted by what I have to offer."

"Ah, you never know. You can't imagine what all attracts the aficionados of other people's memories. Not long ago we sold the memory of a difficult childhood. You'd think that no one would be interested in it, yet it fetched an excellent price. Or, for example, the memory of days spent as a prisoner of war. Quite an unpleasant experience, but we found a rich buyer for that too. And what's there to say about a man who would give his eyeteeth for the memory of a childbirth. The more difficult and painful the memory, the more he is prepared to pay for it."

"There's nothing like that in my past." I smiled. "Certainly no childbirths."

He raised the sprayer and started to spray the plants on the desk in front of him. Several drops made it all the way to me.

"Of course. Perhaps there is something bizarre? Episodes with animals are in great demand right now. One customer received a pretty penny for the memory of eating a live snake. If it had been poisonous, she would have been set for life. The guy who sold his memory of falling off a horse didn't fare badly either. Too bad he was only bruised and not seriously injured. He would have gotten at least three times more. But you can't have everything. The highest price we ever received was for the memory of a night spent in a cage with a gorilla suffering from a toothache. We had to hold an auction."

"I don't have anything to offer with animals either."

"Very well. Then what do you have to offer?"

"I've read a lot of books."

He shook his head. "There's not much demand for that. Even if we find a buyer, you won't get hardly a thing. People are less and less interested in books. It doesn't help that they don't have to waste time reading anymore, since they can buy books already read. All they have to do is remember them. Such are the times, unfortunately."

"Unfortunately," I agreed.

"We might be able to raise the price if you've read a book that can't be found anymore and is enmeshed in a dangerous secret. The best would be a conspiracy of mammoth proportions that includes secret services, secret societies and the church, to be sure. There will always be fans for that."

I gave it some thought.

"There aren't any books like that among those I've read."

"What else do you have to offer?"

"I've been to a lot of celebrated classical music concerts."

The owner frowned. "There's not much profit in that either. A very narrow circle of people is interested in classical music, and they aren't very wealthy. We might attract one of the wealthier buyers if you have the memory of a concert that was involved in a scandal. An assassination attempt on the conductor, for example, or something like that."

"There weren't any scandals surrounding the concerts I attended."

"That's the downside of classical music. It's so stuffy and sterile. The very opposite of popular music where everything is bubbling with life. Live concerts have it all: fights, drugs, rape, weapons are even drawn. If you were a fan of that kind of music, you'd certainly have salable memories in abundance."

"Unfortunately, I'm not."

"Yes, unfortunately. What else do you have?" I could tell by his voice that he was starting to lose patience.

"I've visited famous museums and galleries."

The look he gave me was a mixture of reproach and pity. He raised the sprayer again, but didn't use it. He held it pointed at me.

"We won't get very far this way. You clearly don't know what's in demand on the memory market. It would be better if I asked you questions."

"All right."

"Is there any trauma from your childhood? Preferably with lots of abuse. Violence is always popular, particularly against children."

I shook my head. "There was no violence in my family."

"Too bad. Have you ever been in a traffic accident? Those with lots of casualties are highly prized. An airplane accident would be perfect."

"How could I be here now if I'd been in a plane crash?"

"Sometimes there are survivors. Their memories fetch a fabulous price."

"The only fall I remember was off a bicycle when I was seven and a half. I was covered in blood."

He seemed to be hesitating over whether to activate the sprayer.

"Have you witnessed an unusual event?"

"Unusual event?"

"Yes. The stranger the better. We got an excellent price for a chance bystander's memory of a three-story building that collapsed. Unprompted, without an earthquake. Thirteen dead. The witness of a suicide by jumping into an enormous vat full of honey also did well. The man who watched a tornado funnel suck up a train like it was a feather turned a good profit too. If it had been transporting people instead of sheep, he could have gotten whatever price he asked."

"Once I watched a heavy safe being lifted up to a fifth-floor window. They'd almost reached it when one of the cables snapped."

"Did it fall? Were there any casualties?"

"No. They somehow managed to get it inside."

"Tough luck. What about your sexual experience?"

"Excuse me?" I asked in amazement.

"Don't be surprised. Other people's sex life arouses voyeurs the most. Not just any, of course. No one's interested in ordinary lovemaking anymore. Perversity of any kind is all the rage. From incest to sodomy. You can't imagine the price that was paid for the memory of doing it with a giraffe. How about you?"

"Did I ever do it with a giraffe?"

"Not necessarily. Insects are currently in fashion. If you have any memory of intimate contact with termites, for example, or hornets, you'd be able to write your own check."

"My sex life is quite ordinary. No incest, giraffes or insects. And it's not for sale."

"As you wish. There's only one field left—crime. Traditionally it's the most lucrative."

"What kind of crime?"

"All of them sell superbly, particularly the most serious. Murder is highly valued. If the memory comes from the murderer himself, the sky's the limit. Can you offer something like that?"

"I haven't killed anyone."

The owner stood up and so did I.

"Then I'm afraid we can't be of any help at the moment." His tone spoke volumes of the fact that he was sorry he'd wasted his time with me. "If anything happens to enrich your memory, however, we will be glad to reconsider you."

He finally shot the water pistol. This time more than just a few drops reached me. If that hadn't happened, I would have simply left, equally unhappy with the time

I'd lost. And for the humiliation I'd suffered. As it was, I had no choice.

I took out a real pistol and pulled the trigger without a second thought. The owner collapsed in silence onto the botanical garden.

I had to act quickly. Before the secretary collected her wits and the police came after me in hot pursuit, there was just enough time to go to another memory agency and leave a bit of first-class illusion there. If the sky was the limit, I'd get more than enough to spend a tranquil old age after I got out of prison. Filled with books, music and all kinds of art.

7. Les Miserables

"I CAN'T TAKE IT anymore," said the new patient in a barely audible voice.

He was lying on the leather couch, while I sat in an armchair behind the headrest, where the back of his balding head lay on a disposable cover. His short stature seemed even shorter from that perspective. One look at the middle-aged man's face was enough to know that he should have visited me long ago. In all my years of practice I'd never seen such pronounced anxiety.

"Is something troubling you?" I asked carefully.

"I want to forget."

"Are you burdened by memories?"

"Intolerably so."

"Would you like to talk about them?"

"You won't like them."

"It makes no difference whether I like them or not if you feel better after talking about them."

"It's not evident that I'll feel better."

"You certainly won't feel worse, so you have nothing to lose. Talking usually helps. Tell me about some of the memories that plague you."

He didn't start right away. He pinched the root of his nose with his thumb and index finger. I knew the pain that he felt there from my own experience. Dull and throbbing. When he spoke, I had to strain my ears to hear him.

"A six-year-old boy loses his parents in a train accident in which he is seriously injured. Since he has no close relatives, when he gets out of the hospital they put him in an orphanage. That's where his misery begins. Everyone mistreats him, from the older wards to the counselors. He puts up with the humiliation, beatings, sexual abuse. Day in, day out. Year in, year out."

He fell silent. Stillness surrounded us for a while. It's not advisable to interrupt a confession with superfluous questions or comments. Patients open up the most when they have the impression that they are talking to themselves. That's why I don't sit within their field of vision. When I don't speak, it's as though I'm not there.

"The young man joins the army. He goes through grueling training that completely breaks his character. He is sent into battle before he is sufficiently prepared. He watches his peers get wounded and killed. Shrapnel grazes his head. Thinking he's dead, his comrades-in-arms leave him in the tumult of battle, and when he regains consciousness, he is captured by the enemy. They subject him to various tortures. The worst for him are the electric shocks, having the dogs set upon him and being taken to simulated executions. The starvation and forced labor turn him into a bag of bones. He is not released until months after the war is over."

It was not unusual to hide behind a third person. Some patients ease the trauma by talking about it as though it concerns someone else. Such cases are always complex. Considerable time and effort must be invested to get them to accept that they themselves are the main characters of their stories. It was already clear that a difficult task lay before me.

"The first years of his marriage are idyllic. He's married a girl he loves and she returns his love. They have a little girl, but she contracts leukemia when she's three and a half years old. They do everything within their power to help her. They sell the house so she can go to the most expensive hospital. But there is no hope for the little girl. She melts away and finally dies. Unable to bear the pain of losing her child, the mother commits suicide by jumping out a high window. The father follows in her footsteps and takes a full bottle of sleeping pills, but they save him at the last moment."

My work has put me in contact with a variety of human fates, but never had I seen life be so cruel to a patient. No wonder his memories plagued him. Who could keep a sound mind with such a past? But this was not all. He continued after another short interruption.

"Driving a car with his nerves shattered, he runs into a group of boys. One dies. He doesn't even try to defend himself at the trial. He pleads guilty and asks for the harshest sentence. They give him several years in prison. Thoroughly depressed, behind bars he's an easy target for sadistic criminals and perverted guards. He spends more than half of his sentence as a patient in a penal mental institution."

Since we had clearly reached the end of the story, the time had come for me to get involved.

"What dreadful experiences you've gone through. It's entirely understandable that you don't want to remember the past."

He didn't reply right away. He pinched the root of his nose again.

"You don't understand. I haven't gone through any of that. Those are not my memories."

"Oh, I see. Then whose are they?"

"Other people's."

"Other people's?" I repeated in an even voice. A psychiatrist must not be surprised by his patients' statements, regardless of how unusual they are. "I thought they all referred to the same man."

"No man could endure that much."

"Indeed. But how do you know about those memories? Did these other people recount them to you?"

"I never talked to them."

"How, then?"

"I see other people's memories."

This time I couldn't suppress a certain note of amazement. "You see them?"

"Yes. Not only do I see them, but I can hold onto them as well."

"Why would you hold onto someone else's memories? Particularly if they're bad?"

"Isn't it obvious? To take the load off of miserable people in danger of collapsing under the burden of their memories. When I take them over, they forget them. Completely. Should I let them suffer when I can help?"

"But by taking them over, you burden yourself."

"I'm tougher than they are. Or at least I was until recently. Now it's become too difficult even for me. You can't imagine how many traumatic memories there are in the world."

"As a psychiatrist I have some insight into the matter."

"Perhaps. But the real magnitude would only become clear to you if you saw them like I do. Even though you don't believe that I see them."

"How do you know whether I believe you or not?"

"Because I can see it. Just as I can see what you'd most like to forget from your past."

The conversation had taken an undesired turn. I could feel myself losing control of it. As though we'd started to exchange roles.

"There's nothing in my past I'd like to forget," I said as firmly as I could.

"Nothing, except, let's say, still painful memories of your father's drunken bouts. It's like you can still feel every one of the blows he gave you and your mother in such a state."

"How do you know . . . ?" I blurted out, even though I knew the answer I'd get while I was still asking the question.

"I can see. Your past is before me like an open book.

And there are some recent pages that you'd rather not remember too. The one, for example, about the patient who committed suicide because you didn't take her seriously enough."

I stared at the bald head on the headrest.

"Nothing gave any indication of such an outcome," I said softly. "Officially I have been absolved of all responsibility. . . ."

"Officially, yes. But has your conscience absolved you of the guilt?"

I shook my head slowly, although he couldn't see it. At least not with his eyes.

"You wouldn't like the incident to be repeated, right? And have another one of your patients end up the same way because you didn't believe him?"

"I believe you," I hastened to reply.

"Good. Otherwise you won't be able to help me."

"How can I help you?"

"By making it possible for me to forget all those memories belonging to other people that have accumulated inside of me. In return, I will release you from the several memories that trouble you."

"But how can I remove what you've remembered? I don't have your gift to see and hold onto memories."

"Not yet. But you can acquire it. I'll pass it on to you. Just like the one who had it before passed it on to me. It will stay with you as long as you can bear the burden of dark memories. When you are no longer able, you'll pass it on to someone else."

I gave it some thought.

"Why me of all people?"

"Because as a psychiatrist, you are the perfect choice. You don't have to go in search of people who are tormented by memories. They come to you by themselves."

"I don't know whether I could endure other people's memories. I've barely been able to cope with the few that are my own."

"You'll bear up, don't worry. At least for a while. In any case, you will gain an enviable reputation. No other psychiatrist will be able to measure up to the number of patients you will have permanently assisted. In that regard, you have a great advantage over me. Not a single one of the miserable souls I released from their unwanted past has ever thanked me. Indeed, how could they when they weren't even aware that I had anything to do with it? You, however, will be showered with praise, and that will make it easier for you to cope with the accumulation of dark pasts. So, do you agree?"

I agreed with a nod of my head. And a smile. His eyes didn't see one or the other, but when he lowered his legs from the couch and turned towards me, he was smiling too. We shook hands. This was something that was to be repeated with increasing frequency in my office: a patient restored to health and a satisfied psychiatrist. The price to pay had not been small, but is any price too high for such an outcome?

8. The Magic Mountain

THE MAN ON THE phone didn't have to say his name, even though he did. His voice—deep and velvety, like distant thunder—was more of a giveaway. I recognized it immediately, of course, although I hadn't heard it in a long time.

It took me a moment to recollect myself.

"You?" I said at last. "I can't believe it!"

"It's me all right."

"This is quite a surprise. What've you been up to? Are you alive and well?"

The thunder seemed to draw closer when he laughed. "I'm not calling you from beyond the grave."

My laughter in return sounded more like a popping firecracker. "How long has it been since the last time we talked?"

"More than seven months," he replied without a second thought.

"That long? Where were you all that time? On a trip?"

"No. In *The Magic Mountain*."

"In *The Magic Mountain*?"

"Sanitarium. Haven't you heard of it?"

"No, I haven't."

"It's a mountain health resort for people with memory trouble."

"I can't ever remember you having that kind of trouble."

"I didn't. I went up there to visit my cousin, not as a patient."

"That was an awful long visit."

"I would've come back within a few days if one of the doctors hadn't proposed they examine the state of my memory, since I was already in the sanitarium. They said if I shared my cousin's tendency toward senility, timely measures could prevent a great deal of it."

"And?"

"It was supposed to be a routine checkup, but when they hooked me up to the machines, something went wrong."

"What?"

"That's what they tried to figure out in the following seven months."

"How dreadful. You're better off staying away from doctors. All they do is ruin your health. You should sue, you might get a bundle in damages."

"I'm not going to sue."

"Why not?"

"It wasn't their fault. The disorder could have appeared spontaneously. And then they did everything they could to help me."

"Is you memory back to normal again?"

"No."

"They discharged you with a damaged memory?"

"Damaged isn't the right word. I can still remember everything perfectly, just like before."

"Well, then, what's wrong?"

He sighed deeply before answering.

"What's wrong is that now I don't have a loss of memory, like in senility, but a surplus of memory."

"Surplus? How's it possible to have a surplus of memory?"

"It's possible. I remember things that didn't happen."

For a few moments I didn't know what to say.

"I don't get it. How can you remember what didn't happen?"

"It's not easy to explain. It took me a long time to

get used to it myself. In order to understand it properly, you have to forget the usual way you think about the past."

"In what respect?"

"In thinking that there is only one past behind us."

"If there's more than one past, how many are there?"

"Lots. Maybe countless."

I fell briefly silent again.

"You're pulling my leg, aren't you?"

"I wish it was a joke. But it isn't."

"That's impossible. There aren't even two pasts. There's only one."

"That's what it looks like to you because you only remember one. If you had my memory, you'd remember a multitude of pasts. Behind you there wouldn't be just one thread going back in time, but an infinite bunch of pasts that meet in one point, the present."

"What are those other threads? Other pasts? They couldn't be real. I mean . . ."

I knew what I meant, but for some reason I couldn't express it.

"They all seem real. And that's the crux of my problem."

"You don't know which past is real?"

"I don't. All the threads appear equally convincing to me. Countless pasts that differ from each other in some detail."

"That must be really . . . confusing."

"Yes. It was particularly so at first. Unbearable. I would have lost my mind if I hadn't been in *The Magic Mountain*. The doctors had a hard time too. There's no previous record of this kind of memory disorder. It was a completely new experience for them as well. That's why it took so long. It took seven months for me to get used to my new memory."

"But how do you cope with it if you still can't tell which past is real?"

"I manage. I run checks to see what happened and what didn't. That's why I called you. Do you remember what you asked me at the beginning of the conversation? If I'm alive and well? That's just what I wanted to make sure about you. Are you alive?"

"Am I alive? Why wouldn't I be? I'm in the pink of health. Everything's just fine with me."

"Healthy people can die too. In a traffic accident, for example. What happened three days ago a little after five o'clock when you jaywalked across Elm Street?"

This insignificant incident didn't come to mind right away.

"Oh, yes. Nothing happened. The lady hit her brakes harder than she should have. I don't know why she got so excited. I was fast enough. She wouldn't have hit me."

"She did hit you."

"No, she didn't."

"Yes, she did. I saw you lying on the pavement covered in blood. Dead."

We sank into painful silence.

"You mean, in one of the other threads?" I asked at last in a low voice.

"Yes. In another past."

I knew for some reason I shouldn't ask, but I couldn't resist.

"How did I look . . . dead?"

The question seemed to make him uncomfortable.

"It wasn't a pretty sight. Death is never pretty."

"I'm glad I'll never see myself dead."

"Unfortunately, I don't have that privilege. I saw you dead two other times."

"How?" I asked after hesitating briefly.

"First in the bathroom. The day before yesterday. You slipped getting out of the bathtub and hit your head on the edge. Unlike the traffic accident, there wasn't a drop of blood. But that didn't make death any the prettier."

Once again I had to strain to remember the incident in the bathroom.

"I did slip, that's true, but I hit my shoulder on the edge, not my head."

"I'm happy that was the real past for you."

"I'm even happier. And the third death?"

"Last night. At dinner. You had dinner alone at home, didn't you?"

I gave it some thought.

"Yes, I did. I was eating in front of the television."

"That's right. Some comedy was on, you were laughing out loud."

"It was really funny."

"You shouldn't laugh and eat at the same time. Particularly when there's no one nearby to help you. A bit of food got stuck in your throat."

"That's right, but a sip of wine helped it down."

"Not in every past. Death by suffocation is one of the ugliest. The face becomes completely distorted, the eyes bulge out. Good thing you didn't see yourself on the living room floor."

"Good thing, yes. But there's something I don't understand. Why did you wait for me to die three times before calling to see if it really happened? Why didn't you call right after the traffic accident?"

"Now that I have enough experience with multiple pasts, I know that one bad incident is still no cause for alarm. But three at short intervals is."

"Well, with me it was a false alarm."

"Maybe not quite. Such a frequency of detrimental threads usually indicates that you are currently more exposed to danger than usual. You should be on your guard."

"Thanks for the warning. I'll be on my guard. As much as I possibly can, of course."

"Yes. It isn't easy to be on your guard when you don't have any idea of what the danger is."

"You can call me in a few days to see if everything's all right. I guess the danger will have passed by then."

The voice on the other end went silent. When he spoke again, it sounded like very distant thunder.

"I'd rather not call anymore."

"Why?" I asked in bewilderment.

"I only called now with great reluctance."

"I don't understand."

"Not just one thread of the past is real. Any one of them could be. When I call you the next time, you might have a past behind you where you weren't lucky. I can't put you at risk."

It took me a little while to accept this.

"I'm sorry I won't be hearing from you again."

"That's the curse of surplus memory. You lose those you care about. To protect them."

"What kind of life is it without those you care about?"

"It's hard. Maybe I'll go back to *The Magic Mountain*. I'll be an unusual patient for another reason too. I'll ask them to speed up and not slow down the senility."

"Saved by oblivion."

"Yes. Enjoy what poor memory you have. You can't imagine what a blessing it is."

"Farewell, dear friend."

"I'd like to be able say the same thing, but I'll run into you in other threads of the past. At least for a while. So for me it's better to say—until we meet again."

9. The Book of Laughter and Forgetting

ALTHOUGH I WAS THE only person at the bar, the new customer sat down on the stool next to mine. I glanced at him briefly. He was short, solidly built. Early fifties. Sharp, even coarse features. His disheveled hair was already thin and receding. He didn't even unbutton his coat with the collar turned up, even though it was warm in the bar.

The barman came up to him.

"What'll you have?"

"The same as him," he said, gesturing towards me.

The barman nodded and went off.

The man apparently needed someone to talk to. But I didn't feel like talking, particularly not to a stranger. I'd come to this place, which I'm not in the habit of doing, because I wasn't in the mood for company.

The barman placed a round white napkin in front of the new customer and placed a mug on it capped by a frothy dome of white foam. Then he went to the other end of the bar.

The man must have been really thirsty since he drank almost half the mug in one go. When he placed it next to mine, they looked like twins.

"It's really windy tonight," he said, smoothing his hair. He stared straight ahead at the wall covered with bottles on the other side of the bar. The muted bar light coming from invisible sources twinkled off the multi-colored glass.

"Windy," I replied dryly, also staring ahead.

"It wasn't easy to find you," he added after a short silence.

I turned my head toward the irregular lines of his profile.

"Why would you be looking for me? Have we met before?"

"No. But I know a lot about you."

My eyes went back to the bottles.

"What do you know about me?"

"I know, for example, why you're alone here in this bar."

"Really? Why am I alone?"

"To forget."

"You don't have to know me to reach that conclusion. Why else would someone be alone in a bar unless it was to forget?"

"I know what you're trying to forget."

"Tell me."

"Her death."

"Who are you?"

"We'll get to that. No death makes any sense. Particularly not this one. If that old lady's dog hadn't pulled the leash free and dashed across the street, if the young man had been a more skillful driver, if the girl hadn't been standing on the curb next to the wet roadway, waiting for you—if none of that had happened, you wouldn't be in this bar trying to forget. But nonsensical coincidence shapes our lives."

"It's no coincidence that you're here."

"No, it isn't. You loved her a lot, didn't you? She wasn't one of your many fleeting adventures, but probably your last great love. Forbidden love, all the same, and all the fiercer for it. How many years separated the professor and his student? A quarter of a century?"

I didn't reply immediately, gazing at his broken reflection in the bottles.

"Twenty-three years," I said softly, as though exonerating myself.

"You should certainly have been at the funeral instead of hiding in the background. Your presence would have started tongues wagging, but they would soon have stopped. Your absence earned a scorn that will stay with you a long time."

"Who hired you? The University? What's the point in hiring a private detective now that it's all over? What do you want from me? To admit that there was something going on between us? That's not a secret anymore. If they want to fire me because of it, I'll turn in my resignation."

"I know you better than any private detective could. I know things about you that you'd like to block out of your memory."

"Really? For example?"

"This isn't the first time that coincidence played harshly with your life. On that November evening long ago, if you'd gone home at your usual time you would have found your wife still alive. Most likely the doctors would have been able to save her, even though she'd taken almost a full bottle of sleeping pills. But you'd been detained."

I lifted the mug and drank two fingers of foamless beer. He did the same. Identical twins were back on the counter.

"I'd just gotten my teaching job. I couldn't refuse the head of the department's invitation to have a drink after work. It was an honor for me. And why should I have refused him? I didn't suspect a thing."

"But you knew your wife was going through a crisis. She was a hypochondriac. She imagined that she was suffering from an incurable disease. She'd told you she was terribly afraid of the suffering she thought was in store for her."

"Nevertheless, I couldn't imagine that this unfounded fear would push her to take her own life."

"It wasn't fear that pushed her to commit suicide."

I turned toward him again. He stayed in the same position, without returning my look.

"So what was it?"

"What she said in her suicide note."

Neither of us talked for several moments.

"There wasn't any suicide note."

"Of course there was. You destroyed it physically, but not in your memory. If you make a little effort, you'll remember every word in it. She was a hypochondriac, but also a jealous woman. And that is a highly volatile combination. She found out you were flirting with the wife of one of your colleagues."

I reached for the mug again but didn't pick it up.

"You won't be able to blackmail me. You don't have solid proof. No one will believe that story. Too much time has passed since then anyway."

"I'm not going to blackmail you. But your memory will. It's the merciless blackmailer of your conscience. You won't find any bar that can offer the solace of forgetting. And as far as time is concerned, there's no statute of limitations in your memory. Not even for long-ago events. Like the one when you weren't even five years old."

I started to drink the rest of my beer slowly, as though this could postpone the inevitable. He waited for me to put the mug back on the counter before continuing. The mugs before us were no longer identical.

"She jumped into the river without a second thought when you got caught in the whirlpool. Although she was a girl and therefore weaker, she managed somehow to push you towards the shore. Then the whirlpool reached her. Petrified, you watched your twin sister disappear into it."

"What could I have done?" I asked, my voice barely audible. "If I'd tried to save her, both of us would have drowned."

"Perhaps. But that thought hadn't stopped her from rushing to your aid."

"She was braver."

"Remembering is the price of cowardice."

"But that's my memory. How do you know it? Who are you, anyway?"

The barman came up to us and took my mug.

"Another one?"

I stared at him blankly, as though not understanding the question.

"No, thank you," I finally replied.

After he'd moved away, the customer turned towards me for the first time and looked me in the eye.

"I'm someone who also has problems with his memories."

"I don't know what your problems are, but I wish they didn't include me. It's quite unpleasant to find that someone else shares your memories."

"I've only been sharing them recently. Since this morning."

"Since this morning?"

"Yes, since this morning. Yesterday I didn't know anything about you. Not even that you existed."

"Then how . . . ?"

He shrugged his shoulders. "No one knows. They don't even have a name for my disorder. Let alone a cure. Nothing like it has ever been recorded."

"Disorder?"

"Yes. It appeared without any apparent cause. I simply woke up one morning three months and eleven days ago with a double memory. Mine and someone else's."

"Whose?"

"Someone I didn't know. At first I thought it was just an illusion. But the memories were very vivid and convincing. Real. I followed the trail of the memories and found the man they belonged to. It wasn't difficult because I knew as much about him as he did himself. Some things I even remembered better."

"What did you do?"

"Nothing. At first I kept my distance. I was too confused. And then when I got used to it, I started going up to people whose memories seemed particularly gloomy. Like yours."

"Why?"

His lips twisted momentarily into a grotesque smile.

"For some sort of balance. If I have to put up with warped memories, then those who burden me with them should at least know about it."

"But that's not fair. We aren't to blame for your double memory. We're its victims too. That's not balance, that's sadistic abuse. You might come to harm because of it. Particularly since you know too many secrets."

"No, I don't."

"What do you mean, you don't?"

"When I wake up tomorrow morning, I won't know anything about you anymore. Just like I didn't yesterday. All that I will remember, and it will be vague, is that I had a superficial conversation with a stranger in a bar. The double memory only lasts from one night's sleep to the next."

We looked at each other in silence for several moments.

"If only I could forget that easily," I said, breaking the silence.

He picked up his mug and finished his beer. He took a bill out of his coat pocket, put it on the bar top, and got up.

"If only I had just one memory to deal with."

10. Fahrenheit 451

WHEN I OPENED MY eyes, it was like I'd been submerged in milk. An undefined, amorphous whiteness surrounded me on all sides. I stared at it emptily for a while until my eyes focused enough to make out where I was: lying in a bed without a frame, like a sort of catafalque, in the middle of a small square room. There was nothing else in it. The walls and high ceiling were covered with immaculate white padding. A bright light from an invisible source increased the glare of the whiteness. I squinted to protect my eyes from snow blindness.

Then something broke the monotony. Part of the wall to the left of the bed started moving as though giant scissors had cut three sides of a rectangle that was swinging towards the interior of the room. The man had already stepped inside when I finally realized it was a door, although nothing had indicated it was there.

He was short, stout and balding, with a bushy mustache and ruddy cheeks. He was wearing a white coat and gloves, and the file under his arm was white as well. He closed the door and came up to the head of the bed, smiling.

"How are you?" he asked in a deep voice that was better suited to a taller man.

"Confused," I replied after hesitating briefly.

"That's natural. Do you feel nauseous? Do you feel like vomiting?"

I gave it some thought.

"No."

"Wonderful. With your permission."

He placed the file on my stomach and slightly raised the white sheet that covered me up to my chin. It was not until he'd unfastened the strap around my right forearm that I realized I was restrained.

"Why am I strapped down?" I asked when he started to unfasten the straps around my ankles.

"For your own good," he replied tersely, as though this explained everything.

"And this one?" I said, indicating the broad belt that went across my chest.

"We'll leave that one a little longer. Also for your own good. Don't try to stand up. You're still weak. Your head might start to spin."

"Where am I?"

"In a hospital."

I looked at his smiling, robust face for several moments in silence.

"Why am I in a hospital?"

"You had trouble with your memory."

"I don't recall ever having trouble with my memory."

"I know. That's why you're here, because you don't remember. We have yet to establish what you do remember."

He picked up the file and opened it.

"I'd like to ask you a few questions. I hope you don't mind."

"I don't."

"Wonderful. So, let's begin. Do you remember committing a crime and being punished for it?"

I thought it over.

"No."

He looked at me inquisitively over the file.

"Did I commit a crime?" I asked softly.

"You didn't if you have no memory of it. That's one of the privileges of forgetting. It relieves even the nastiest conscience." He lowered his eyes to the file. "Let's go on. Does the 'Little Shop of Memories' antique store mean anything to you?"

I shook my head.

"You didn't go there once to buy something under the counter? Something you had to have so you could go on painting?"

"I don't remember that I ever painted."

"A person can forget that he was a painter, but not how to paint. If you'd been a painter, it would come back as soon as you stood in front of a canvas. Forgetfulness is powerless before art. Let's continue. Did an unusual traveling salesman ever knock on your door? He had colorful brochures that offered a variety of pasts."

"How can you sell pasts?"

"You can sell anything if there's a buyer for it. The past, the future, hope. The more surreal the merchandise, the greater the demand. So, do you remember such a salesman?"

"No."

"All right. Does a girl in a light blue summer dress mean anything to you?"

"Should it mean something to me?"

"You are the only one who can tell me. Imagine her sitting in a park reading a book, and you walk past her."

"I can imagine a girl dressed like that reading in a park, but not myself. I can't remember what I look like at all."

"That's to be expected in your state. It's easiest to forget what is most familiar. Your own face, for example. But don't worry about that. Usually looking in a mirror is enough to remember yourself. Here's another question. Did you ever sell rare works of literature? Sole copies of manuscripts?"

"I don't think I did," I replied after a moment's thought. "At least not that I remember."

"Did you ever search for the mortal remains of great writers?"

"Why would I do that? How utterly morbid."

"It is utterly morbid. But utterly lucrative too." He turned over the sheet of paper in the file. "Did you ever try to sell someone your memory?"

"Who would want to buy my memory?"

"It's the same as with the past. There's a buyer for everything. The gloomier the memory, the higher the price."

I smiled. "I doubt that anyone would give a plugged nickel for my current memory. It's so dark that you can't see anything inside it."

"Well, you never know. Be patient, maybe we'll find some light inside it. Let's try this. Did you ever meet a man who takes on other people's bad memories?"

"Does someone like that exist?"

"Yes, he does. The world isn't as dark as it seems. So you don't remember meeting such a person?"

"I'm afraid not."

"All right. Did you ever get a phone call from a friend of yours suffering from surplus memory?"

"Surplus memory?"

"Yes. I realize with your memory loss that might seem like bragging, but it's no bed of roses when you have more memory than you need. It usually goes hand in hand with losing your friends." He turned over another sheet of paper in the file. "This is the last question. Did a stranger ever come up to you in a bar and tell you that he was sharing your memory that day?"

"That day?"

"Yes. From the moment he woke up that morning until he went to bed that night."

"I don't remember ever going to bars."

"People usually go there to forget."

"I'd rather go some place where I could remember."

"You are in just such a place."

"It doesn't look like that to me. We've reached the last question, so you say, and there hasn't been any progress. I don't remember anything."

He closed the file and gazed at me fixedly for a moment.

"Oh, you do remember, perfectly well. That's the crux of the problem."

"What do I remember?"

"Books."

Now I stared at him.

"Which books?"

"Great works of literature. That's the only good thing about your case. It's a blessing in disguise. You could have remembered dime store novels."

"What great works of literature? I don't understand you."

He sighed and his smile faded for the first time.

"I have to prepare you for this. It comes as a shock. There is a tremendous flash."

"What comes as a shock?"

We looked at each other in silence for some time. Then he spoke. The words were almost a whisper.

"*Crime and Punishment.*"

The flash was truly terrific, forcing me to close my eyes tightly. Whiteness seemed to explode around me. If it weren't for the strap tied across my chest, I would have bucked on the bed as though from an electric shock.

And then the book appeared before my eyes. Every chapter, every page, every paragraph, every line. I saw it all crystal clear. Even better than that. I knew the position of every letter and every punctuation mark in the gigantic mosaic of the whole. Flawlessly. Far better than the writer himself. The gateway to absolute remembrance stood wide open before me.

The whisper of the man I could no longer see reached my ears again.

"*Vanity Fair, Great Expectations, Sentimental Education, Dead Souls, Lost Illusions, Les Miserables, The Magic Mountain, The Book of Laughter and Forgetting, Fahrenheit 451* . . ."

Orgasms of light burst all around me, followed by a boundless clarity of vision with total perception. I knew that I could repeat by heart effortlessly each of the ten works he'd mentioned. And I would never be able to forget them, even if I wanted.

"Please, that's enough," I muttered after the last flash had ebbed. "I can't take any more. . . ."

"That's all there is."

I opened my eyes and stared at the man who was smiling again.

"What happened?" I asked weakly.

"Virus 451."

"Come again . . . ?"

"That's what it's known as. The medical term has five long and difficult words. Even though it's not a virus, that's how it behaves. It erases everything from your memory and replaces it with what you've read. That's why I said you had a blessing in disguise. You've read great literature. It's much more frequent for the memory to be filled with trite or worthless copy. If they read at all, people today mostly read pulp novels."

"Is there a . . . cure?"

"For a perfect literary memory? No, there isn't, I'm afraid. What's been erased cannot be brought back. You paid for this ideal access to literature with your own memory. It might not be such a bad trade, though."

"How can I live without a past?"

"You'll get used to it. People with amnesia live more or less normally. But there's another setback."

"What's that?"

He didn't reply at once, but raised the bed sheet and started to unfasten the strap across my chest. He put the file under his arm and then stretched out his hand to help me up. My head swam a little when I sat up, so I stayed on the edge of the bed with my legs dangling.

"Virus 451 is still inside you. We can't remove it. You won't be allowed to read anymore. Anything you read will be to the detriment of your new memory. You would erase everything you remember from now on."

"But I can't live without reading. . . ."

He took me by the arm and helped me to my feet. My knees bowed briefly.

"That's what I thought. Most people would have no trouble giving up reading. They would consider it a reward and not a punishment. But as soon as I heard the works you remembered, I knew it would be different with you."

"What's in store for me?" I asked softly, like a terminally ill patient asking how much longer he has left.

His smile broadened.

"Reading, of course. But of a special kind."

"But you said . . ."

"That was for those who can live without reading. For those who can't, we have a special library."

"Library?"

"A living library. With people just like you. You won't learn anything about their past. They have no memory of it. But you will have the chance to hear the greatest works of literature from them. And they from you. And you will remember them. I told them that someone else might be joining them soon. They can hardly wait. Let's go."

We headed slowly for the invisible door in the wall.

Contributors

About the author

Zoran Živković was born in Belgrade, Serbia, on October 5, 1948. He is a full professor at the Faculty of Philology, the University of Belgrade, teaching creative writing.

Živković is one of the most translated contemporary Serbian writers. By the end of 2017 there were 93 foreign editions of his books of fiction, published in 23 countries, in 20 languages.

Živković has won several literary awards for his fiction. In 1994 his novel *The Fourth Circle* won the Miloš Crnjanski award. In 2003, Živković's mosaic novel *The Library* won a World Fantasy Award for Best Novella. In 2007 his novel *The Bridge* won the Isidora Sekulić award. In 2007 Živković received the Stefan Mitrov Ljubiša award for his life achievement in literature. In 2014 and 2015 Živković received three awards for his contribution to the literature of fantastika: Art-Anima, Stanislav Lem and The Golden Dragon.

Zoran Živković has been recognized with his selection as European Grand Master for 2017 by the European Science Fiction Society at the 39th Eurocon in Dortmund, Germany.

Živković is the author of the 22 books of fiction:

The Fourth Circle (1993)
Time Gifts (1997)
The Writer (1998)
The Book (1999)
Impossible Encounters (2000)
Seven Touches of Music (2001)
The Library (2002)
Steps through the Mist (2003)
Hidden Camera (2003)
Compartments (2004)
Four Stories till the End (2004)
Twelve Collections and the Teashop (2005)
The Bridge (2006)
Miss Tamara, The Reader (2006),
Amarcord (2007)
The Last Book (2007)
Escher's Loops (2008)
The Ghostwriter (2009)
The Five Wonders of the Danube (2011)
The Grand Manuscript (2012)
The Compendium of the Dead (2015)
The Image Interpreter (2016)

About the artist

Youchan Ito was born 1968 in Aichi prefecture, Japan. She launched her career as a graphic designer in 1988, becoming a freelancer illustrator in 1991 and founding Togoru Co., Ltd. with her husband in 2000. In 2017 the company was reborn as Togoru Art Works. She works with a wide range of genres including cover art and design for science fiction, mysteries and horror titles, as well as illustrations for children's books.

www.youchan.com